Through her marriage to Reggie Kray, Roberta Kray has a unique and authentic insight into London's East End. Roberta met Reggie in early 1996 and they married the following year; they were together until Reggie's death in 2000. Roberta is the author of many previous bestsellers including *No Mercy*, *Exposed*, *Survivor* and *Stolen*.

ROBERTA
KRAY
TRAITOR

SPHERE

SPHERE

First published in Great Britain in 2024 by Sphere

1 3 5 7 9 10 8 6 4 2

A CIP catalogue record for this book
is available from the British Library.

ISBN 978-1-4087-3003-4

Typeset in Garamond by M Rules
Printed and bound in Great Britain by
Clays Ltd, Elcograf S.p.A.

Papers used by Sphere are from well-managed forests
and other responsible sources.

MIX
Paper | Supporting
responsible forestry
FSC® C104740

Sphere
An imprint of
Little, Brown Book Group
Carmelite House
50 Victoria Embankment
London EC4Y 0DZ

An Hachette UK Company
www.hachette.co.uk

www.littlebrown.co.uk

TRAITOR

1

Jem Byrne was being followed. It wasn't all the time, not every day, but occasionally when she was going to work or coming back from it, she would get that odd sensation on the nape of her neck, the prickling that told her someone had their eyes fixed on her. When she turned, *he* wasn't there, but the feeling persisted. It left her on edge. It left her anxious and jumpy.

They say there are two places to hide: in the middle of no-where or in a crowded city. Not being a country girl, Jem had opted for the latter. It had been one of the worst moments of her life when, just over a year ago, the police had called to say that Aidan Hague was coming out of prison. Since then, she had moved four times, working her way down the country from Lytham to London, always looking over her shoulder, always waiting for him to catch up with her. He wasn't the type of man to let things go.

She had considered changing her name. From Byrne to ... what? Smith? Harris? Williams? And it wasn't as if she loved being called Jemima – people either thought of Beatrix Potter or assumed she was some rich girl from Chelsea – but it was the name her mother had chosen for her, and she didn't see why she should give it up. Anyway, even if she did take on a new identity, she knew that he'd find another way to trace her, to track her down. Still, she wasn't going to make it easy for him. She had dumped her mobile and bought a pay-as-you-go, cut off contact with as many people as she could, closed all her social media accounts, and was even lying to her family about where she was living now.

The Mansfield estate was big and sprawling, three tall concrete towers set in a landscape of unrelenting dreariness. Kellston, unlike neighbouring Shoreditch, wasn't a fashionable part of London's East End. It was run-down, poor and starved of resources. Many of the residents eked out a living on benefits or the minimum wage while others turned to drug dealing, thieving or prostitution to make ends meet.

The Mansfield wasn't a safe place. It was ill-lit and dirty, with a rat-run of tunnels and passageways criss-crossing the estate. Figures lurked in shadowy corners. Men stared. There was a general air of menace. As Jem hurried along the path that led to Haslow House, head down, shoulders hunched, she felt like a fugitive. And that, of course, was exactly what she was – a fugitive from Aidan Hague's vicious brand of justice.

A shiver ran through her. She knew that in this day and age it was hard to disappear. Unless you were on the streets, there was always some kind of electronic footprint from your bank account or the tax man or an energy company. And Aidan had a network of contacts, tentacles that reached into every corner. She might be making it hard for him, but she could never make it impossible.

She had almost reached the door to the lobby when she heard it, a thin male voice carrying on the evening air. 'Jem,

Jem.' Her head jerked back in alarm, and she stared up at the tower. It had come from above, she thought, although she couldn't be sure. Her gaze raked the windows but there were hundreds to search, half of them lit, the other half in darkness, and she couldn't make out anyone behind the panes of glass.

Jem held her breath and listened. Her heart was thumping. Had she imagined it? Not the voice, there had definitely been a voice, but perhaps the name. No one knew her name here. Had it been 'Jen' rather than 'Jem'? She waited. People passed by, going in and out of the building, some giving her quick sidelong glances, most just ignoring her. Still she remained, motionless as a statue, with only her eyes moving as they frantically scoured each floor in turn.

Nothing. Nobody.

Perhaps the voice had come from somewhere else.

She quickly turned her head to look back along the path. It was quarter past six and there was a small but steady stream of residents flowing on to the estate. Everybody walked at a swift pace as if to slow down was to invite trouble. Only a group of teenagers was standing still, loitering by the gate.

She couldn't stay here for ever. It was dark and cold, raining, and the chill was starting to creep into her bones.

But what if the enemy was inside the building? What if Aidan or one of his henchmen was waiting for her there? The rational part of her brain said that they'd hardly announce their presence by calling out her name, but the fearful, panicky part said that it was just the type of thing Aidan *would* do. He was a master tormentor. Like a cat with a mouse, he took pleasure in playing with his victims, toying with them, creating the maximum level of fear before crushing them to death.

When a few minutes had passed and nothing more had

happened, she made the decision to go inside. It was either that or freeze to death. And anyway, she had nowhere else to go. Well, she could go back to Blooms and ring the bell to the flat above the florist where her boss Stefan lived, but then she would have to explain why she was too scared to go home and that would open up a whole new can of worms.

Jem considered taking the external stairway so she could approach her flat from a different direction than the one that would be expected, but it was eight floors up and by the time she got there, if she *did* find someone waiting for her, she'd be too exhausted to do any effective running away. So she took a deep breath, stepped forward, and went through the door.

The lobby smelled of wet coats, stale cigarette smoke, dope and urine. The floor was littered with the usual garbage – mainly tin cans, fag ends and used vapes – and the tiled walls were covered in graffiti. It was a depressing space. One of the overhead lights, a long fluorescent tube, flickered on and off, creating a disturbing, slightly disorientating effect. Two of the lifts were out of order and the other four were already travelling up or down the tower. A small group of people – a youngish man in a beanie hat, an elderly lady with a walking stick, and a couple of kids – were waiting to ascend. The old woman had been talking to the kids, but everyone fell quiet when she approached.

Jem joined the loose queue, paying most attention to the man while pretending not to look at him at all. A threat? She guessed he was about the same age as she was, in his late-twenties, tall, and dressed in an army-green parka with fur around the collar. The sort of coat that had deep pockets. The sort of pockets that could easily hold a gun or a knife. She didn't have time to pursue this disturbing line of thought before a lift arrived, gave a ding as its doors opened, and then discharged its contents. The five of them shuffled inside, each of them stopping briefly to press the floor number they wanted.

Jem, the last one in, checked out those numbers as she prepared to press her own. But there was no need. Eight was already illuminated. A tremor passed through her. Which of her fellow passengers was heading for the same destination? She was tempted to step straight out of the lift again, to wait for the next one, but forced herself to stay put. If she let fear get the better of her, she'd never make it back to the flat.

Jem tried to position herself as far as possible from the man, not that that was very distant given the confines of the metal box. Nobody spoke. She stared at the door, blank-faced and silent, enduring the awkwardness of being forced into close proximity with strangers.

The old woman got off on the first floor, and then there were four of them. The next stop was the sixth. As the light above the door tracked their progress – two, three, four, five – Jem felt a new flicker of alarm. If the kids got off next, she'd be left alone with the man. Should she leave with them and take the stairs the rest of the way? Better to be safe than sorry. She was still feeling rattled by what had happened outside.

But it was the man who got off on the sixth floor. She gave an inner sigh of relief, suddenly aware of the tightness of her shoulders and the fact that her jaw had been clenched. For the first time since getting into the lift she relaxed. Now it was just her and the kids. The girl looked about ten. She was skinny with long light brown hair in need of a wash, a pale oval face, a small mouth and serious eyes. The boy was younger, five or six, with blonder hair but the same features They were both dressed shabbily, wearing jeans and thin denim jackets that were more suitable for July than December.

'That woman who got off was Mrs Floyd,' the girl said, catching Jem's eye. 'She's a right old gossip so be careful what you say to her.'

Jem, slightly startled by the unsolicited information, gave a nod in response. 'Oh, right. Okay.'

'I'm Kayleigh. And this is Kit. We live along the landing from you.'

'Do you?' Jem replied, deliberately not volunteering her own name.

'Yes, not next door but the next one along.'

'Right,' Jem said, raising a smile. 'Nice to meet you.'

'Kit doesn't talk,' Kayleigh said, as if Jem was about to attempt a conversation with him.

'Okay.' Jem wondered if she meant he didn't talk or he couldn't talk, but it seemed rude to ask. Anyway, it was none of her business and she had no desire to prolong the exchange. For the past three months, since moving here, she had made it her mission to *not* engage with other people, even people as apparently harmless as a ten-year-old girl.

The lift ground to a halt and the doors opened. Jem gestured for the kids to leave first, hoping they'd go on ahead of her and that would be that. But Kayleigh had other ideas. Once she had exited the lift she hung back, her right hand firmly holding Kit's left, and waited for Jem to join them.

'So what's *your* name?' Kayleigh said as the three of them walked along the corridor.

It was an innocent enough question – or at least it would have been for someone who had nothing to hide. Jem hesitated. Should she lie? Make something up? She was paranoid, that was the trouble, always reading things into questions that were perfectly normal. But she wouldn't put it past Aidan to use a kid to establish her identity, not if he'd heard a whisper that she was now in London and living on the Mansfield. Panic raised its ugly head again.

Flustered, Jem made a point of looking at her watch. 'God, is that the time? Sorry, but I've got to go.'

Even as she was hurrying away, Jem knew she'd made a big mistake. Refusing to give a name would only make her appear more suspicious. She was an idiot, a fool. As she put her key in the lock she glanced back along the corridor. Kayleigh had stopped outside her own front door and was watching her. Jem gave a quick wave and scuttled inside.

After switching on the light in the hall she smartly closed the door and pulled the two bolts across, top and bottom. Why in God's name had she just behaved like that? She could hardly have invited more curiosity if she'd tried. The girl was only being friendly, neighbourly, and she'd acted as if she couldn't wait to get away from her.

Jem rolled her eyes, hung up her coat and went into the living room, turning on the light for a moment to make sure she was alone and then switching it off again. She went over to the window and looked down on the estate. The teenagers were still by the gate. People came and went. Everything was as normal as it ever was on the Mansfield.

Jem almost missed the Covid days when it was harder for people to move around, and the wearing of a face mask gave her protection from more than the virus. She had always felt safer when half her face was obscured. With her long blonde hair cut to shoulder length and dyed brown, and the acquisition of some glasses that she didn't need, she had done all she could to disguise herself.

Opening the window, she leaned out, feeling a rush of winter air on her face. She peered up towards the top of the tower and then down again towards the ground. Her first instinct had been that the caller of her name – if it *had* been her name – had come from the building, and if that was the case . . .

Jem shivered and not just from the cold.

Would she ever be free of Aidan Hague? Not until he was dead, she thought – or she was.

2

Phillip didn't know exactly why he'd done it. It had been a spur-of-the-moment thing, more mischief than malice, or so he told himself. He had seen her walking along the path as she always did at this time of day, and before he'd barely had time to think, he'd opened the window, called out her name and then quickly withdrawn to the side where he could watch without being seen. Her reaction had been telling, more than just surprise. There had been a genuine sense of alarm, a jolt of the head, a sudden paralysis. She had stood there for a long while staring up at the windows.

If he'd needed any confirmation that the girl was afraid of someone, he'd seen it right there in how she'd responded. That could be useful. He'd already picked her out as one of his victims, mainly because she was always alone, and solitary women were women who wouldn't be missed.

Gem, short for Gemma he presumed, had been here for about three months now, living two floors above him in Haslow House. He knew her name because a few weeks ago, early one morning, he had followed her down the high street where she had taken a left at the junction, crossed the road, walked past the station and gone into the florist's next door to the café. He had followed her because he'd wanted to know what it felt like to do that. Curiously satisfying as it turned out.

Because the shop hadn't opened yet he'd adjourned to the Station Café and ordered a full English and a mug of tea. The place had been busy, mainly full of workmen, and he'd studied them all without staring, storing up the information, squirrelling it away for use at a later date. Detail was what he was after – the way they spoke, ate, dressed – so that no one could ever again accuse him of being inauthentic.

After breakfast, Phillip had randomly picked up a bowl of hyacinths from the display on the pavement outside the florist's and taken it inside. Disappointingly, his girl hadn't been serving, but as the man behind the counter had been ringing up the sale on the till, he had helpfully called out to her, 'Gem, love, could you put some of those wreaths outside?'

Gem had walked straight past him, smiling faintly, leaving in her wake a light trail of perfume. Or maybe it had been something else he was smelling, something that had come off the wreaths or the flowers that were artfully arranged around the shop in big tin buckets. Close up she'd been more attractive than he'd thought, with high cheekbones and a pretty mouth. Behind the black-framed glasses her eyes were wide and hazel.

Phillip had followed her a few times since then. It was interesting how she'd somehow sense his presence, glancing over her shoulder to search the faces behind her. But she'd never clocked him. He was always careful to keep his distance, to make sure there were plenty of other people around, to blend into the crowd. Anyway, he was one of those men who were invisible to pretty girls – middle-aged and running to fat with a receding hairline and a dwindling bank account. It hadn't always been like that.

Thirty years ago, the name Phillip Grosvenor had been on everyone's lips – well, everyone who mattered – and he had moved in what he liked to think of as exalted circles. He had been the new kid on the block, the writer to watch, a rising star. But it had all been downhill from there. Although he'd tried – God, how he'd tried – he'd never been able to reproduce that early success, and one book after another had met with the same lukewarm response from the critics. Over the years his reputation as an author had floundered and died. Pretty much like his marriages, now he came to think about it. His third had hit the rocks over two years ago and he'd been single ever since.

Back in the day, however, he had managed to secure the post as literary editor of a magazine, a position he'd held for over twenty-five years until they'd decided to 'let him go' eighteen months ago. They had thrown around phrases like 'a fresh approach', 'new blood' and 'a different perspective' before severing his contract with a pitiful payout.

In a last-ditch attempt to resuscitate his career as an author, he'd decided to immerse himself in the world of the poor, the working classes and the criminal. An advert in *Loot* had led him to the Mansfield and a twelve-month sublet of a small, rather shabby one-bedroom flat. His back story, should anyone be interested enough to ask, was that his name was Joe Chapel and that he worked from home as a bookkeeper.

Phillip had laboured over the choice of name, wanting something ordinary enough to not stand out, but with certain connotations. In the end he had gone down the religious route, the combination of Joseph and Chapel providing a satisfying mix of the mundane and the holy.

So now while a visiting professor from the USA was living

in his comfortable Primrose Hill flat until next summer, he was slumming it in Kellston. He had spent the last six months putting the Mansfield under the microscope, watching all the comings and goings, inveigling himself into the company of his neighbours, and building up profiles of the most useful residents – men and women who would people his new novel. He had learned who the drug dealers were, the fences, the thieves, the pimps and the tarts. He was forming a picture of their miserable lives.

So far, he had chosen three possible victims for his psychopathic killer. The first was a small West Indian girl called Charlene, who worked in a charity shop on the high street and lived alone. His second was Nola Dunn, a skinny blonde in her late twenties who touted her trade down Albert Road and had two kids who'd be better off without her. His third, and current favourite, was Gem. She was a girl with secrets, he thought, and secrets could be useful in a crime novel.

Phillip spent long hours slaving over his laptop trying to get inside Joe Chapel's head. What constituted a psychopath? Someone who lacked empathy, who had intelligence, an inflated ego, and superficial charm. Someone who felt no remorse and blamed everyone else for their problems. Chapel was a man who would kill not for the pleasure of murder but for the satisfaction of getting away with it.

'You think you know me, but you don't,' Chapel said smugly, lounging on the sofa with his legs stretched out. 'I'm a complicated person. You've barely scraped the surface.'

'I'm aware of that. You're a work in progress.'

'Well, don't take for ever over it. It's boring sitting here doing nothing.'

'You're not doing nothing. You're *planning*. You're a smart, meticulous man who doesn't intend to make any mistakes.'

Chapel inclined his head and frowned. 'Like leaning out of the window and calling out that girl's name? I'm not sure that was wise. Now she might guess that her stalker lives in the building.'

'I've not been stalking her. Not exactly. I've just followed her once or twice.'

'Four times.'

'All right, four times. I didn't realise you were counting. But her reaction was telling, don't you think? We gave her a scare.'

Chapel nodded, almost smiled. 'Yes, we gave her a scare. She'll be dwelling on that for the rest of the evening. But where do we go from here?'

'Have some patience. These things can't be rushed. Rome wasn't built in a day and all that.'

'I've been patient for the past six months.'

'So a little while longer won't do you any harm.'

'You're in charge,' Chapel said. 'I'm in your hands. But may I suggest you do something soon? I'm getting restless here. I'm losing interest. A little *momentum* might be in order before I lose the will to live.'

For Phillip, assuming a new identity was proving curiously liberating. He was a fraud, an imposter, and he was revelling in it. Phillip Grosvenor and all his disappointments had been – more or less – put aside since he'd started work on his evil creation. On the surface Chapel was friendly, polite and helpful, but underneath he was a monster moving freely among his would-be victims, planning his next step, waiting for the right moment. Nobody saw him for who he really was.

Phillip had left his smart clothes at home, stored in the wardrobe of the spare room, and replaced them with well-worn shirts, old sweaters and a beige anorak. In this disguise, and with some moderation to his accent, he was able to blend effortlessly into his surroundings. For the first few months he'd been worried that he might bump into someone he knew, but those fears had faded now. His friends and acquaintances would no sooner set foot in Kellston than they would shop at Aldi. So far as they were concerned, he'd absconded to a remote cottage in Wales where he was considering his future while he tramped the hills.

He had, however, noticed a distinct tailing off when it came to contact with these so-called friends: the odd phone call, the occasional email, was all he was getting these days. Now that he no longer moved in their circles, he had virtually slipped off the radar. Out of sight, out of mind. Phillip curled his lip, deciding they'd be sorry when his star was in the ascent again.

'How many pages is it now?' Chapel asked.

'Eighty-three.'

'Still a long way to go. You need to get a move on. You're not going to win any prizes with eighty-three pages.'

'Thank you for reminding me.'

Phillip paced the room, turning his mind back to murder. Of course, it had all been so much easier years ago, before CCTV and decent forensics and bloody mobile phones that tracked you wherever you went. But then that was the challenge: how to kill without being caught. Joe Chapel had to be smart enough to not leave any evidence behind him, clever enough to outwit the police, organised enough to always be one step ahead of the enemy.

There were occasions, he had to admit, when he could relate to Chapel and his desire to kill, especially when it came to two of his three ex-wives. Both of them had fleeced him, taking him for every penny they could when it had come to divorce. Should this sense of affinity be a worry? He pondered on it for a moment. No, he knew the difference between right and wrong, between reality and fiction. There was a line, and he knew not to cross it.

3

Kayleigh watched the girl until she'd gone into her flat before looking down at Kit and saying, 'What's her bleedin' problem?'

If Kit had an opinion on the subject, he didn't share it.

Kayleigh took out her key and unlocked the door. She could tell as soon as they stepped inside that the place was empty. She flicked the light switch, but nothing happened. The meter had run dry again. *Damn.* It was two days now since their mother had gone AWOL. Not the longest she'd been away but infuriating all the same. What were they supposed to do with no electricity, no heat and hardly any food?

After school she'd taken Kit to the library where it was warm, and he could read the books about planets and moons and distant galaxies. He felt at home there, content in a building where being silent was an obligation rather than a disability. It was over a year since he'd stopped talking, since he'd decided that he had nothing left to say. Not that Nola had noticed, not for weeks, and with all that Covid business no one else had done anything about it either until they were back at school.

Now Kit was being seen by a child behaviourist once a week and there were words like 'social anxiety' being bandied around. Kayleigh didn't know what this meant but she knew that grown-ups liked to put names to everything: none of them were happy until the problem was put in a box with a neat label attached to it. Personally, she thought his muteness was more down to Nola and her neglectful parenting.

'Not to worry,' Kayleigh said brightly. 'I'm sure she'll be back later.'

They made their way through the gloom of the living room – lit only by the streetlamps on the estate – to the kitchen. Neither of them took off their coats. Kayleigh dug out the stump of a candle from under the sink and put it on a plate, found the matches, lit it, and set about the business of making Kit a sand-wich. There was no spread left but there were still a few scrapes of peanut butter in the jar, and three slices of bread.

'She must have got held up,' Kayleigh said, trying to keep her voice as matter of fact as possible. She did this as much for her own benefit as for Kit's. Staying calm was the important thing, not panicking before you had to. She hated Nola, but she loved her too. Or at least loved the old version of her before she'd come apart at the seams. Inwardly referring to her mother as Nola was a way of distancing herself, of dealing with the constant let-downs and the persistent chaos of their lives.

Kayleigh stole from her whenever she got the opportunity. This was usually when Nola was smashed or stoned, lying flat out on the sofa with one arm hanging over the side and thin ugly breaths rasping from her mouth. Once she was sure that Nola wasn't going to wake up anytime soon, she would unzip the pocket in the black leather miniskirt and carefully reach inside to see what was left of her earnings. She never took it all – Nola wasn't stupid – just enough to buy some food and top up the leccy.

There had been slim pickings, however, a couple of nights ago. Most of what she'd made, Nola must have spent, or handed over to that lowlife pimp of hers. A fiver was all Kayleigh had been able to snaffle, which she'd folded up into a tiny square and put into one of her shoes. But all that was gone now apart from a few copper coins.

Kayleigh put the sandwich on a plate and pushed it across the table. 'Here.' She opened the fridge, which was dark inside, took out the plastic bottle of milk, unscrewed the cap and sniffed it. Deeming it drinkable, she poured what was left into a glass and gave it to Kit. She smeared the tiny amount of peanut butter that was left on to the last slice of bread and nibbled it slowly.

While she ate, she thought about walking down to Albert Road to see if they could find Nola, but it was probably too early for her to be working. She might be in the pub or at a mate's or with some bloke who'd eventually kick her out with a pair of black eyes and a cracked rib or two. The pattern of her life was predictable. Kayleigh could have called her if she'd had any money for a phone card, although past experience had taught her that Nola usually had her phone turned off and didn't respond to any messages she left.

Kayleigh wondered if Kit remembered the time when it hadn't been like this, when their dad had been around, and everything had been different. He was probably too young. In those days there had always been food in the fridge, money in the meter, clean clothes, shoes without holes and presents at Christmas. She didn't want to think about Christmas. The shops were full of fake snow and tinsel and big red Santas. Did Nola even know what time of year it was?

'Make sure you eat all your school dinner tomorrow,' Kayleigh said. 'You need one hot meal a day.'

Kit looked at her through sad eyes. His lips parted slightly but no words came out.

Kayleigh had seen a flyer in the library for a new food bank near the church. It said everyone was welcome so hopefully that meant there wasn't any need for an official note. She could say her mum had the flu and had sent them instead to pick up the food. What was the worst that could happen? Well, the worst was that someone might recognise them and contact social services who'd find out that Nola had gone missing again, and then she and Kit would be taken into care. Was it worth the risk? If it meant not starving to death, it probably was.

Avoiding the social was one of Kayleigh's primary objectives in life. They were always poking their noses in where they weren't wanted, asking questions, staring at her and Kit like they were exhibits in a zoo. Nola had already been warned about what would happen if the two of them were left alone again. That's why Kayleigh made sure that Kit was at school every day, as clean as she could get him, neat and tidy with his hair brushed. At least she didn't need to worry about him saying anything. The secrets of the Dunn household were safe with Kit.

Because sometimes the silence got too much for her, Kayleigh tended to talk just for the sake of it, a monologue about Nola or the weather or what they'd do next year when everything would be different. It was always better in the summer when it didn't matter so much if the power went off because the days were long and light and warm. She imagined a time when Nola would miraculously change and go back to being the kind of mother she'd been before Dad had disappeared. Not that she'd been perfect then, but she'd usually been sober.

'I'll be seeing Dion on Friday,' she said. 'He's always busy at the end of the week.'

Dion lived on the sixth floor and sold weed to people he trusted. He never let customers go to his flat but took their orders by phone and either delivered it himself or got someone else to do it. Kayleigh was happy to take the little packages and go up and down in the lift or walk over to Carlton House or Temple Tower, drop off the weed and pick up the money. Dion had taught her to be careful, to always check the corridors were empty and never to hand over the package until she'd been paid for it. At the end of the evening, he'd give her a tenner, and more if they'd been busy.

Dion had been in the lift this evening, but they hadn't talked to each other. They never did when other people were around. Old Mrs Floyd, with her beady eyes, was forever on the lookout for the next juicy piece of gossip. She knew everything that went on in Haslow House, or thought she did. Dion said you couldn't have a shit without her hearing about it.

The girl who lived along the landing had been in the lift too, the one who'd hurried away when Kayleigh had tried to talk to her. What had that been about? All she'd done was ask her name and she'd shot off like a rat up a drainpipe. That was a saying her father used to use.

'I wonder where Dad is now,' she said, glancing longingly towards the window as if he might fly past like Father Christmas on a sleigh, and give her a wave. She still clung on to the hope that he might come back, although that hope was dwindling as the years passed by.

They had come home on the day he disappeared to find her dad's boss, Carl Froome, waiting on the doorstep, all hot and bothered with a face like a tomato. Telling Nola that Ray hadn't come back to work after lunch, asking if she knew where he was. 'Have you tried the pub?' Nola had said, not that worried. It had only been quarter to four. Froome was all agitated, jigging around like he had ants in his pants, saying that Ray wasn't answering his phone. Nola had shrugged her shoulders.

It was only later, much later, when he still hadn't come home, that Nola had rung round the hospitals, but Dad hadn't been taken in. The next day she'd reported him as missing, but the law hadn't done much about it. Kayleigh could remember standing in Cowan Road police station beside her mother while the duty sergeant took down the details. He'd had a slightly impatient look on his face, as if it was perfectly normal for blokes who lived on the Mansfield to go to work in the morning and never come home. As if Nola was wasting police time by even reporting it.

'Ray Dunn. Raymond. It's not like him,' Nola had insisted. 'He's the reliable sort. He wouldn't just take off.'

The sergeant's eyebrows had shifted up a fraction.

'He wouldn't. Something must have happened.'

Eventually, grudgingly, the law had checked it out, gone round to where he worked – a second-hand car dealership in Hackney – and discovered that the last sighting of him was on the company's forecourt CCTV which showed him getting into his black Nissan at one o'clock on the day he'd disappeared and driving away. And that was that.

Nola had still refused to believe that he'd abandoned them. Even though she had no alternative explanation for his disappearance, even though it looked as though he'd just walked out on his family, she'd continued to press for answers. She had gone to see Carl Froome and raised merry hell, refusing to accept that he was as much in the dark as she was. She'd confronted all his mates too, but none of them would admit to knowing anything.

It had been another three weeks before the parcel came through the post by Special Delivery. Inside was a cardboard shoebox and inside the box was a wad of notes, more than five thousand pounds in all, and a printed note that said simply, 'Sorry'. Nola had stared at it for a long time before upending the box off the kitchen table and sending the notes fluttering down to the floor.

'Bastard!'

After that, Nola hadn't gone to Cowan Road again. She didn't tell the law she'd heard from him. She didn't tell them about the money, either.

4

Jem had woken twice in the night, sure that she'd heard someone in the flat – a movement, breathing, the *sense* of another
human being close by – and had frozen both times before forc-
ing herself to get up, grab the old piece of wooden curtain rail
that she kept under the bed, and creep into the living room. It
was only after checking that this room and the bathroom were
empty, and the front door still securely bolted, that she was able
to start breathing properly again.

Now, with dawn on the horizon, she stood at the window,
sipped her coffee, looked down on the estate and yawned.
Nothing seemed as bad in the morning. The terrors of the night
melted away to be replaced by the low-level fear that was always
there. It was the man calling out her name, or someone's name,
that had rattled her, sending her spiralling down into a pit of
panic. The thought of Aidan being nearby had infiltrated her
dreams and made her paranoid.

Jem could barely recall the last time she'd felt safe. Even after
they'd locked him up, she'd still been afraid. But when they'd

let him out, she'd known he'd be coming for her. Which was why she'd run, and kept on running, until she'd ended up here in Kellston. She glanced over her shoulder at the living room, irrationally frightened by the idea that the very thought of him would make him materialise like some evil spirit who could magically sniff out exactly where she was.

The flat belonged to her boss Stefan's partner, Al, who had chosen to sublet rather than give it up after the two of them moved in together. To Jem this hinted of a fallback position, of a certain lack of confidence in the relationship, but perhaps Al was just being practical. Council flats were hard to come by, even on estates as dire as the Mansfield, and love wasn't always as permanent as you wanted it to be.

Jem prepared herself for the day ahead. She liked her job, but business wasn't as brisk as it should have been at this time of year. The rail strikes had meant more people working from home, reducing the commuter footfall in Station Road, and takings weren't as healthy as Stefan had hoped for. Still, at least the buses were running, which was some consolation. Every morning Jem tried to make the outdoor display as tempting as possible: she didn't want to get laid off so soon after finding the job.

Her eyes fell on the spot under the table where all her artist's paraphernalia was packed into a couple of boxes. She hadn't painted since she'd arrived in London, hadn't even picked up a pencil to make a rough sketch. Her watercolours were too dark and sinister for everyone's taste, but occasionally she had sold one through a gallery or her website. The site was closed now: she'd been too worried that Aidan would use it to track her down.

Aidan. He was always with her, no matter how hard she tried to shake him off. From the moment they'd met – and she'd go over this time again and again – she'd been on the road to no-where. She could claim that she'd only been fifteen, too young to know better, but it was a lousy excuse. The truth was that she'd been a stupid teenager, wide-eyed and gullible, desperate for attention and blind to the kind of person he really was.

So many things were down to chance. What if he hadn't come into her grandad's shop that Saturday morning? What if she hadn't been behind the counter? What if she'd never set eyes on his sly, handsome face? He'd said he was nineteen, which was the first lie. He'd said he was looking for a gift for his mother, which was another. He'd said she was the prettiest girl he'd ever seen, which was the biggest lie of all. He'd said . . .

No, she wasn't going to think about him. That was what he wanted, to get inside her head, to settle in and make himself at home. She wouldn't allow it. There was a difference between being on your guard and spending twenty-four hours a day trapped in an agony of black anticipation. She had to get on with her life. She had to make the best of what she'd got.

Jem took her mug through to the kitchen, rinsed it under the tap and placed it on the draining board. She paused for a moment, gathering herself, and then pushed back her shoulders, strode across the living room, grabbed her bag, took her coat from the peg in the hall and put it on, briefly checked her reflection in the mirror, opened the door, stepped into the corridor and locked the door behind her. Even after she'd turned the key, she rattled the handle to make sure.

There was a short delay while she waited for a lift to come up from the ground floor. Jem glanced along the landing towards the flat that housed the two kids, but there was no sign of life yet. Too early for school. There was something about them that bothered her, something about those flimsy clothes and hungry eyes, and that weird thing Kayleigh had said about her brother

24

not speaking. But none of that was any of her business. Keeping herself to herself was all that mattered, keeping her head down and staying as anonymous as possible.

When she got outside, Jem wished she'd put on a scarf. The temperature had dropped a further few degrees since yesterday and she could feel the cold seeping into her. She pushed her hands deep into her pockets and walked briskly off the estate, along Mansfield Road and on to the high street. Here, because she couldn't help herself, she looked back over her shoulder. There was only a couple of young women behind, chatting and laughing. That was what she missed the most: having someone to talk to. But the girl she'd trusted most, the girl she'd known since infant school, was long gone and nobody had ever replaced her. When she thought about Georgia, she felt like someone had put a stone in her mouth and forced her to swallow it.

Jem walked even faster as if by sheer speed she could out-pace the past. Loss lay in her wake: Mum, Gramps and Gran, Georgia, everyone she'd ever cared about. Only her dad re-mained, but he was across the other side of the world playing happy families with his Australian wife and their four sun-tanned children.

After her mother's death, her father had married again within six months. Unseemly haste, her gran had called it. Well, she'd called it other things too when she thought Jem wasn't listening. Even Gramps, usually prepared to give anyone the benefit of the doubt, had muttered under his breath about common decency and their daughter being barely cold in the ground.

Jem's upper lip curled. She might only have been nine at the time, but she'd known there was something dubious, something wrong, about her dad falling in love again so soon. Or had the two of them been at it behind her mother's back? For years, per-haps. The thought of it still made her angry. She had never liked

Miriam with her sun-bleached hair and her overlarge breasts and her strident opinions. Given the choice between Australia and England she had decided to stay with her grandparents and that was the one thing she'd never regretted.

Jem didn't have much contact with him now. He had moved on, as they say, and left the past behind. The photos she received with his occasional emails – him standing by a barbie or lazing on a beach with a fat self-satisfied grin on his face – didn't seem to bear much relation to the man she'd known. And she didn't feel connected to her younger half-siblings, three boys and a girl, either.

The sun would be shining in Australia. Under a blue sky, people would be walking around in shorts and T-shirts feeling heat on their faces instead of the cold wind of London. Jem hunched her shoulders, pushing her chin down into the collar of her coat. There was nothing, other than her feelings towards her father and the pitiful state of her finances, to stop her from flying out to Sydney. If she asked, he would probably send her a ticket.

But she wouldn't ask. She didn't want to. Even if it meant being thousands of miles away from Aidan. Anyway, he was more than capable of following her there. And then what? She might dislike her father and his wife, but she didn't want to be responsible for whatever carnage Aidan might choose to bestow on them.

Miriam was one of those people who constantly posted on Facebook – everything they did, everywhere they went, everything they ate and drank – thus making it easy for anyone to track down the family should they be so inclined. She suspected Aidan kept an eye on the page just in case Jem's photo suddenly appeared. Would he be allowed to leave the country if he was on licence? Jesus, he wouldn't let little things like rules and regulations get in his way.

Jem frowned. Here she was thinking about him again. *Stop it.*

She reached the junction with Station Road where it was much busier, and she had to wait for the traffic lights to change before she could cross. As she stood there, pressed in on all sides, she suddenly felt a hand clamp tightly on to her wrist. The shock caused her heart to miss a beat, her pulse to race. She gasped, turning to see an old man with a grey bushy beard. He pushed his face into hers and said, 'Repent! God sees everything!'

Jem wrenched her arm away. 'What are you doing?'

'Repent!' he repeated, his oniony breath floating into her nostrils. His right forefinger jabbed at her shoulder. 'She is as bitter as poison, as dangerous as a double-edged sword.'

Jem was assailed by two distinct feelings: relief that it wasn't Aidan and mortification that the God-botherer had singled her out from this small crowd of people. Like she had a sign on her forehead or something. Everyone else was looking the other way, glad it wasn't them, pretending that nothing was happening.

'God sees everything,' he announced loudly. '*Everything.*'

Jem thought that if God did see everything, he should have the decency to intervene in this embarrassing harangue from one of his advocates. 'Please leave me alone.'

But the old man had other ideas. As if he had spotted a weakness in her, a vulnerability he could exploit, his gnarled fingers clamped round her wrist again and his eyes gleamed with fervour. 'If we confess our sins, he is faithful and righteous to forgive us the sins, and to cleanse us from all unrighteousness.'

Jem was considering taking her chances with the traffic, anything to get away from him, when suddenly another hand appeared – male, strong, insistent – and forcibly removed the old man's fingers.

'Give the lady a break, Moses. She doesn't need you harassing her at this time of the morning.'

'At any time,' Jem said, looking up at the man who had decided to rescue her. He was tall, in his forties, dark haired, with a handsome if slightly gaunt face, distinctive blue eyes and two short vertical lines engraved between his eyebrows.

The man grinned as he gently pushed Moses aside and then said to Jem, 'Are you all right?'

'Yes, I'm fine. Thank you.'

The lights changed and they crossed the road together. 'You don't want to mind old Moses. He's a little crazy but he's harmless enough.'

'Is his name really Moses?'

'I've no idea. It's what everyone calls him, though. He usually stakes out the girls on Albert Road, trying to save them from a life of sin.'

Jem suspected that the women who worked Kellston's redlight district would be as pleased about this as she had been. 'And is he having much luck with that?'

'Not so you'd notice. Still, it's good to have ambition. Are you sure you're okay?'

'He just startled me, that's all. Although I can't say it's entirely flattering to be mistaken for a prostitute.'

The man shook his head. 'Oh, don't take it to heart. Moses doesn't differentiate when it comes to women. As far as he's concerned, you're all equally sinful whether you're a call girl or a princess.'

'Well, that's reassuring.'

'I'm Harry by the way, Harry Lind.'

And instantly she was faced with that exchange of names thing again. And, as usual, she decided not to play along. 'Well, thank you, Harry,' she said as they reached the other side of the road. 'I appreciate the intervention.'

'Not hoping to get a bus, are you?' he said, gesturing towards the long, ragged queue that snaked along the pavement. It was another train strike day. 'You'll have a long wait.'

'No, I'm walking. Thanks again.' Jem smiled and hurried off before he could prolong the conversation.

When she reached the shop, Stefan was standing by the door holding a bucket of yellow chrysanthemums. 'Who's your good-looking friend?'

'Huh?'

'Don't give me all that "huh" business. You and the tall dark guy. I just saw the two of you together.'

'Oh, him,' she said. 'We weren't together. Some crazy God-botherer started giving me grief at the corner and he stepped in to save me from being damned for ever.'

'A white knight. How adorable! I hope you got his number.'

'Of course not. What would I want his number for?'

'You could do worse, sweetheart. I wouldn't kick him out of bed.'

Jem went past him and into the shop, slipping off her coat. 'Perhaps you should give him *your* number then.'

'I've seen him around. He works across the road.'

'I'm not interested. I've told you before, I'm sworn off men for the foreseeable. I'm perfectly happy on my own.'

Stefan, undeterred, put down the bucket, followed her into the back and watched as she hung up her coat and put on her tabard. 'The office over the newsagent. I think he's a private detective.'

Jem flinched, her eyes widening. Shock ran through her. 'He's what?' She suddenly wondered if their meeting today had been more than coincidental. Could Aidan have hired him to look for her? She went hot before she went icy, feeling the blood drain from her face. And then, to try and disguise her reaction, she quickly laughed and added, 'I mean, what kind of job is that, sneaking around after people? Pretty weird, don't you think?'

'At least he *has* a job. Are you all right, sweetheart? You've gone white as a sheet.'

'Have I?' Jem briefly raised her hands. 'It's just the cold. It's freezing out there. I can barely feel my fingers. Anyway, I'll get started on the displays. We're not going to do much business standing here.'

Stefan sighed and shook his head. 'You should give people a chance, Jem. They're not all the same.'

'I'll take your word for it.'

As Jem laid out the Christmas wreaths, the hyacinths and poinsettias, she kept glancing along the street but there was no sign of Harry Lind. She looked across to the newsagent's, her gaze rising to the floor above, but there was nothing to see there either. She couldn't shake the suspicion that the whole Moses thing had been some sort of set-up to give him the opportunity to speak to her. First the man calling out her name last night and now this. It had to mean something, and that something could only be bad news.

5

Harry Lind went into the café and joined the queue. While he waited for a takeaway coffee that would cost him ten times more than if he'd made it at home, he thought about the girl with the brown hair who had almost jumped out of her skin when Moses had approached her. He'd seen the fear on her face as she'd turned, the horror in her eyes. Not just embarrassment or irritation, but genuine alarm. As if she'd expected to see somebody else.

Not that it was any of his business. He was always up to his ears in other people's problems and didn't need to add to the list. So why had he deliberately watched to see where she went? It was to do with how she'd reacted and the way she'd avoided telling him her name. It was to do with his job: when you spent so much time dealing with secrets and lies, with distress and evasion, you started seeing them everywhere. And let's not kid himself, it was to do with the girl herself and her fragile prettiness. He was a sucker for a damsel in distress. And that was probably a sexist thought if ever he'd had one.

The woke police would have him in handcuffs if they could get inside his head.

Of course, there could have been another reason as to why she'd reacted the way she had. Maybe having already been alarmed by Moses she was even more shocked to find herself the object of some other random male's attention. Had she thought he was chatting her up? Had he been? No. Well, not exactly. Just being helpful. But it didn't do much for his ego to think she might have looked at him – a forty-something male past his prime – and recoiled from his perceived advances.

Harry wondered how old she was. Late twenties, he guessed. He shuffled forward in the queue. It wasn't easy coming to terms with the ageing process. One minute you were young and fit and strong, the next you were staring middle age squarely in the face. He raked his fingers through his hair and thought some more about the nameless girl. None of your business, he repeated to himself.

The clock above the café counter said eight thirty. He had an appointment in an hour with a woman called Celia Mortlake, a difficult and delicate case that was already causing him sleepless nights. He'd had to think twice about taking it on and was still not convinced that he'd done the right thing.

When he reached the front of the queue Harry changed his mind about his order and asked instead for two lattes and a couple of warm croissants. He paid and left the café with his hands full. Grabbing the opportunity to dodge between the cars and buses while the traffic was at a standstill, he crossed back over the road. His left leg was aching from the cold, or perhaps it was the metal rods that were making it ache. Being part bionic wasn't all it was cracked up to be.

Harry had been a cop before he'd had the misfortune to walk into a booby-trapped crack house. He knew he was lucky – the

32

two guys who'd gone in before him hadn't made it out again – but it had still meant the end of his career. He could have accepted a post pushing paper all day long, only that wasn't his style. Being confined within four walls would have sent him mad. Not that this job didn't have its drawbacks, but at least he was his own boss.

As Harry let himself in, juggling the coffees, the croissants and his keys, he took a moment to admire the brass plaque on the door: Mackenzie, Lind. Private Investigators. It still gave him a sense of achievement to see it there, and if he'd had a free hand, he'd have been tempted to give it a quick polish.

Upstairs the office was unlocked and the lights on. Lorna Green, their PA, was already at work in the reception area, tapping away at the computer. She was Mac's better half although they didn't live together, and mother to two teenage daughters. Lorna was the kindest woman Harry knew, a sucker for waifs and strays, but she also had a backbone of steel. The office was run like a well-oiled machine, with appointments, surveillance and billing all accomplished with military-style efficiency.

'Morning,' he said, placing a coffee and croissant on the corner of her desk. 'These are for you.'

Lorna raised her eyes from her screen and looked at him. 'What are you after?'

'Nothing. Just showing my appreciation for everything you do. Can't I buy you breakfast without my motives being brought into question?'

'I suspect the answer to that is no. But thank you anyway.'

In truth, Harry's motives weren't exactly selfless. He had started to worry recently that Mac might decide to retire completely – he was only working three days a week now – leave London and take Lorna with him. The thought of having to find a new PA and train them up to a standard that came anywhere near hers filled him with gloom. It was time to stop taking her for granted. 'You're welcome.'

'You've got Celia Mortlake at nine thirty,' Lorna said.

'Yeah, has Mac had any joy in tracking down the cops who worked on the original case?'

'Not yet. He's got a few leads, though. He might have something for you later.'

Harry went into his office, put down his breakfast, hung his overcoat on the peg behind the door and sat down behind his desk. Almost immediately he turned his head to look across the street at the florist's, but most of the shop front was obscured by the bus-stop queues. You're making something out of nothing, he told himself. Drop it. If he wasn't careful, he'd end up like one of those creepy old men who stalked pretty women for a pastime.

The croissant had been demolished, the crumbs disposed of, and he was halfway through his coffee when Harry reached into the top right-hand drawer of his desk and pulled out a file. For the next ten minutes he went through it, studying the photos and the old newspaper articles, fixing every detail in his mind while he tried to read between the lines. The facts were thin on the ground and the police had been cautious in what they'd said publicly, not wanting to encourage idle speculation.

Harry already knew that he would spend the whole weekend on this case, trying to prise some daylight from the darkness of the tragedy. Not that he had anything better to do. His social diary was about as thrilling as a rainy day in lockdown. How long since he'd last been on a date? Months. After Valerie – and that was over two years ago – there hadn't been anyone serious. Women came and went, none of them wanting to stick around. Surprising really, considering his quick wit and sparkling personality.

He sent up a silent prayer of thanks that the worst of the pandemic now appeared to be over, and business was picking up again. There was a limit to how much time you could spend in your own company and with zero income coming in. Although it was a while since restrictions had been lifted, it still felt like something of a novelty to leave the confines of his flat, the four walls he'd grown so sick of, and to be out in the world again.

Harry checked his watch, stretched out his left leg and flexed his ankle. He stood up and looked out of the window again. The crowds at the bus stop had thinned out and he now had a fairly clear view of the florist's. The outside display had been completed and the space in front of the shop was awash with colour. No sign of the girl, though. He shrugged. 'Give it a rest, Lind,' he murmured. 'She's not your concern.'

He turned from the window, walked across the room, put his overcoat back on and set off to see Mrs Mortlake.

6

Harry shut the front door behind him, swung a left and strolled along Station Road until a gap in the traffic enabled him to cross over. He had deliberately gone further than necessary so that he didn't need to go past the florist's and face the temptation of peering inside and trying to catch a glimpse of the girl, and now had to double back until he came to the lane that led through to the cemetery.

A fifty-yard walk brought him to an entrance that was rarely used, and from here he cut between the old crumbling gravestones and made his way across the wet grass to the main path. This short-cut to the south side of Kellston had the advantage of being quiet and peaceful, giving him the opportunity to think about what he'd say to Celia Mortlake. It was a week since he'd taken on the case, and he still thought now what he'd thought then – that there wasn't a hope in hell of finding out anything new. He had relayed this information to her – albeit in more diplomatic terms – but she hadn't been deterred.

'Humour me, Mr Lind,' she'd said. 'I'm an old woman. This could be my last chance to find out what happened to Christine.'

In truth, Harry felt guilty about even billing her for work he was sure would lead nowhere. It had been fifty-one years since Christine, Celia's twelve-year-old daughter, had disappeared. She had set off down the road to visit her friend, Amy Greer, one Sunday afternoon in August 1971, and not a trace of her had been found since. Not that anyone other than him was looking. Although the police investigation was still officially open, the files hadn't been read for decades. The senior officer who had been in charge was deceased, and Harry was still trying to track down someone more junior to aid his probably hopeless inquiries.

It was a sad, dreadful, tragic case. Harry sighed as he strode along the path, wondering how Celia Mortlake had coped for all these years with the not knowing. No body, no explanation, no resolution. But perhaps that was what had kept her going: the thought that one day her daughter might be found, dead or alive, and she might finally get some answers.

Despite his belief that he was unlikely to uncover anything new, Harry was still determined to go through all the evidence with a fine toothcomb, to double-check everything the police had done, to track down everyone still living who had given a statement at the time, and to explore every possibility that was open to him. He would do as thorough a job as possible with what was available to him, but whether this would yield any new light on Christine's disappearance was doubtful.

Harry's eyes skimmed over the gravestones and their inscriptions. Reflected within the lines was the great lottery of life: who died at six months, who lived to be ninety-six. Was it random or predestined? Was your future, or lack of it, laid out for you, even at the very moment you were being born? He frowned and shook his head. He needed more caffeine before even beginning to ponder on such questions.

It was the thought of that coffee, always freshly ground, always strong, that put an extra spring into his step. Within ten minutes he was out of the cemetery, and five minutes later he was on Magellan Street. It was a street that had once been grand, lined with large detached Victorian houses, but which over the years had become run-down and shabby with most of the properties subdivided into flats or bedsits and the front gardens turned into parking spaces.

At first sight Mrs Mortlake's house was imposing – three storeys high, clad with ivy, and with sections of stained glass in the upper parts of the windows. It was only on closer inspection that the signs of neglect became apparent: the rotting window frames and peeling paintwork, the crumbling mortar and over-flowing gutters. He opened the gate, walked up the path and rang the bell.

It was the housekeeper who answered the door, a small plump woman who wouldn't see sixty again. She gave him the same look she had on the previous occasions he'd visited: abject disap-proval, as if he was some shyster lowlife, a master of exploitation only there to rip off her employer. Harry didn't entirely blame her for the attitude.

'Good morning, Mrs Feeney,' he said cheerfully.

Mrs Feeney's expression remained dour. 'She's in the drawing room. You know your way.'

Harry made a point of wiping his feet on the mat before advancing indoors. Mrs Feeney was already disappearing into the depths of the house, her flat-soled shoes slapping against the parquet flooring, a low grumbling escaping from what he imagined to be a very pursed pair of lips. As he closed the door behind him and advanced into the hall, he was assailed by an old-house smell of stale air and mildew. It was as chilly inside as it was out, and he didn't hang about.

The drawing room was off to the right, and he walked there at speed along the gloomy, rather depressing hallway. The door was ajar, but he still knocked lightly before going in. This room, thankfully, was lighter and warmer, and smelled pleasantly of beeswax and coffee.

'Ah, Mr Lind. You're here at last.'

'I'm sorry, I'm not late, am I?' Harry said, even though he knew he wasn't. He had made sure he arrived punctually.

'Come and sit down. I'll pour you some coffee.'

Harry did as he was told, lowering himself cautiously on to a pale-yellow brocaded chair that had spindly legs and dubious stability. He noticed her hands shake a little as she lifted the pot, but otherwise, on first sight, Celia Mortlake didn't bear much resemblance to the average octogenarian: she was tall and upright, her spine ramrod straight. Her hair, pure white, was cropped short and her ear lobes were adorned with small emerald earrings. Today she was dressed in a tweedy outfit, old-fashioned but probably stylish in its time. There was something of the headmistress about her, a natural authority, a sternness that made him faintly wary, as if she might issue a detention if his work didn't come up to scratch.

'Thank you,' Harry said as she passed the coffee to him. It was in a porcelain cup so delicate he feared breaking it, and he put it down quickly on the side table next to his chair. 'I'm afraid I don't have much to report. We're still trying to track down Amy Greer. There's every chance she got married, which makes it that bit harder. But we'll keep going. Are you certain you can't think of anyone round here who might know where the family went?'

'Unfortunately, all my old neighbours are long gone. The Greers moved away a few months after Christine disappeared.

I've never been entirely decided as to whether that was understandable or suspicious.'

'Did you suspect them?'

'Of course,' she said. 'Naturally. Well, someone was lying, and it wasn't us. But obviously I don't know anything for sure. Perhaps they were completely innocent, as much in the dark as we were.'

Harry knew there were three main possibilities as to what had happened that day: that Christine had never left home; that something had happened to her at Amy's house; or that she'd been intercepted and abducted on the short walk to the Greers'. There were other options – that she had run away or deliberately gone somewhere she wasn't supposed to be going – but with her twelve-year-old face plastered all over the papers, it seemed unlikely that she could have stayed at large for long.

'What did you think of them, the Greers?' Harry said. 'I mean, before Christine's disappearance.'

'I didn't know them well. Hardly at all, in fact. He was the local greengrocer.'

Mrs Mortlake's voice was high and thin, and Harry thought he detected a note of condescension. But then she came from a time when class had been more important, when one's status in life depended on where one stood on the social ladder. It was probably still true today but not to the same extent. The Greers would have fallen into the category of 'trade' while the Mortlakes had been upper middle class.

'Yes, on the high street,' he said. 'George and Pauline.' Not having access to the original case files (he was still working on that), he had fallen back on trawling through the newspaper reports of the time, gleaning what he could from them. Sadly, other than a few minor details like these, factual information was thin on the ground, the papers resorting instead to carefully worded conjecture. 'And Amy? What was she like?'

Mrs Mortlake hesitated before she spoke. 'The truth? I didn't care for her much. She was one of those noisy, over-confident girls, older than her years. And she had a way of looking at you as if everything you said amused her in some way. A smirking sort of girl, sly. I thought it was nerves the first time I met her but she was always like that.'

'Were they close, she and Christine?'

'No, I don't think so. They didn't even go to the same school. It was more a matter of convenience. Christine's other friends lived across town and Amy lived down the road. What's the common parlance these days? They just used to "hang out" together. Mainly in the holidays, a few hours here and there. They were company for each other, I suppose.'

'But Amy wasn't expecting her that Sunday?'

'Not according to Amy.' Celia Mortlake's voice was full of scepticism. 'She said they hadn't made any plans.'

'But it was quite normal, was it, for one or the other to just call round? It didn't need to be pre-arranged?'

'I suppose not,' Mrs Mortlake said. 'With them living so close to each other . . . but I definitely got the impression from Christine that an arrangement had been made, that Amy was expecting her.'

An impression, of course, wasn't the same as a fact. Harry nodded. He had asked most of these questions before, but it never did any harm to go back over old ground. Memory was a strange thing: sometimes, from nowhere, it could dredge up something new, a tiny pearl from the depths.

'And Christine left here after lunch. What time would that have been?'

'Two o'clock or thereabouts. I told her to be back by six. That was when we had supper.'

Which was why the alarm hadn't been raised until six thirty

when Mrs Mortlake, thinking that Christine must have lost track of time, had called Mrs Greer to ask her to send her daughter home. Harry could imagine what that moment must have been like, those few horrifying seconds while Mrs Greer explained that Christine wasn't there, had not been there at all, that Amy had spent the afternoon on her own. His stomach lurched at the thought of it.

'And what happened next?'

'Arthur went round there, just to check, you know, to make sure there hadn't been a misunderstanding.' Celia Mortlake's lips twisted a little. 'But they were sticking to their story. Amy claimed she'd been in the garden all afternoon. Mr and Mrs Greer backed her up, swore that none of them had seen Christine, that she definitely hadn't been there.'

Harry glanced at the photograph of Arthur Mortlake on the mantelpiece, a thin-faced, serious-looking man who stared back at him through dark judgemental eyes. An accountant for some big City firm, Harry remembered from the papers. 'And then?'

'Arthur came home, told me what they'd said, and then went out again to search for her. While he was gone, I rang round all her other friends. By now it was getting on for seven – she'd been gone five hours – and so I called the police. She wasn't the sort of girl to just wander off, Mr Lind. She was sensible, reliable. I don't recall a single time she ever got home later than she'd promised.'

Harry nodded again. It was only when you looked more carefully that Celia Mortlake's age became apparent. She was like the house, he thought, deceptively solid until you got up close and observed the papery thin skin of her face and the lines that creased along her cheeks. 'Did you see her leave that afternoon?'

'No, but she came in here to say goodbye and then I heard

the front door shut. You can't see the street from this room, but I'm certain that she left.'

'But not what direction she went in?'

'Towards Amy's,' she said, almost fiercely. 'Which other way would she have gone?'

Harry didn't press it. But he knew that even 'sensible' girls didn't always do what was expected of them. There was a short silence when all he could hear was the ticking of the ancient radiators. He waited.

Celia Mortlake's gaze dropped to the floor. 'It killed him, losing Christine like that. She was our only child. He died six years later, you know? A heart attack. Every waking hour he spent trying to get to the truth. He never gave up. He refused to believe that the culprit would never be brought to justice.'

'And you? What did you believe?'

'That something terrible had happened in that house.' Her eyes flew up sharply, but her voice wavered. 'Find out what it was, Mr Lind. Please. If you can. Find out what happened.'

Harry didn't make any false promises, only saying what he always said, that he would try his very best, that he would do everything he could. He didn't stay much longer. After providing her with a quick update on his lines of inquiry, he finished his coffee, said his goodbyes and saw himself out.

He didn't go straight back to the office but instead strolled to the end of the street where the Greer house, smaller than the others, had been squashed in like an afterthought. Even this property had been converted into flats. The house and the garden must have been thoroughly searched, but there had been plenty of time to get rid of the evidence – if there had been any evidence to get rid of.

Harry stood for a while, gazing up at the windows. He'd already spoken to all three of the tenants but, unsurprisingly, none of them had heard of the Greers. He'd done a door to door on every other house in the street too. And drawn a blank. Fifty-one years was a long time. People moved on, downsized, died. Had Christine come here that day? If only walls could talk. He put his hands in his pockets, wondering how far away he was from finding out the truth. A long way, he decided, a *very* long way.

7

Phillip Grosvenor woke up with the hangover from hell. He had passed out in the early hours and slept awkwardly, his neck twisted, one leg hanging over the edge of the sofa. Cautiously he opened his eyes and squinted into the morning light. The bottle of whisky, almost empty, was on the coffee table beside his laptop. A trio of Chinese takeaway cartons, one containing a fork, were on the floor. Two cigar butts lay in the ashtray, their stale tobacco reek adding to the putrid atmosphere of the room.

He was cold and shivery, with an ache in his head that hammered his temples. Aspirin was what he needed, aspirin and water. And a pee. And probably something to eat if he could face the prospect. There was a bad taste in his mouth, a metallic tang. He propped himself up on an elbow and checked his watch: ten forty. Why had he got so damn drunk? Writer's block, that was why. He glared at the laptop, wondering if there was anything worth reading on it. Doubtful. Anyway, he wasn't going to take a look until he was feeling less fragile.

It was icy in the room. Through the window he could see a

square of sky that was gunmetal grey and full of rain. Another dreary day. He had to turn the central heating on. Phillip slowly shifted his body round, placed his stockinged feet on the floor, and tentatively stood up. Instantly a wave of nausea washed over him. He wobbled unsteadily, his legs like jelly. Perhaps he had alcohol poisoning. Perhaps he would die in this godforsaken place, keel over and expire on the threadbare carpet.

Eventually he made it to the bathroom, where he emptied his bladder, washed his hands, threw some water on his face and brushed his teeth. Did he feel any better? No. He should take a shower and change his clothes, but he couldn't be bothered. And what did it matter if he smelled? There was no one else here to complain about it.

In the kitchen he turned on the heating then took two aspirin and washed them down with water. He made coffee and took it through to the living room. He should tidy up: the flat was a tip. He'd do it later. He wandered over to the window and looked down on the estate. The sight that met his eyes gave him a start. The place was swarming with police. What the . . . ? He blinked twice, not quite believing it. Squad cars were lined up outside the building and an army of uniformed officers was spreading out between the three towers.

He frowned, trying to make sense of it. Typical, he thought, that something bad – and it must be seriously bad – had happened while he was flat out on the sofa. He pressed his nose against the glass, trying to figure out what was going on. Should he be taking notes, taking pictures? An event like this could be useful for his book. But he didn't have the energy. Instead, he stored up the images in his head, saving them for when he finally got his whisky-addled brain back into gear.

Phillip watched for the next few minutes, fascinated by what was unfolding in front of him. It was the most interesting thing that had happened since he'd moved here. Then, because he had to know more, he snatched up his phone, scrolled down through the numbers and pressed. It rang a few times before it was answered.

'Hello?'

'Hello, Mrs Floyd. It's Joe Chapel here. Sorry to bother you but I just glanced out of my window and saw the police everywhere. Do you have any idea what's going on?'

Phillip could almost hear Edna Floyd lick her lips. Passing on information, rumour and gossip was her *raison d'être*. She would cease to exist, explode in a puff of smoke, if such opportunities were denied to her. He'd been cultivating her ever since he'd found out that she was the fount of all knowledge on the Mansfield, making himself useful by running errands, doing her shopping and picking up prescriptions.

'It was last night,' Mrs Floyd announced. 'A murder! Can you believe it? Right here on the estate. They didn't find the body until half an hour ago. She was lying behind the bins.'

'Gracious,' Phillip said, feeling that Chapel was the sort of man who'd say that sort of thing. 'A murder?'

'Stabbed to death,' she said, almost gleefully. 'A young woman. Coloured.'

Phillip rolled his eyes. Edna Floyd was a terrible bigot, disliking anyone who wasn't the same pasty shade of white that she was, of a different religion or nationality, or inclined towards anything that could roughly be described as liberal.

'How terrible,' he said, although a part of him – a part he was not especially proud of – was rather excited by this unexpected occurrence. There was often trouble on the estate – brawling and drunkenness, knife crime, the occasional gunshot – but murder was something else. 'Do you know who it was?'

'Charlene something or other. She works in that charity shop on the high street. Or used to.'

Phillip's innards did a roll. Charlene? Jesus! One of his own intended 'victims'. Perhaps his swift intake of breath was audible, or the following silence betrayed him, because Mrs Floyd was quick to pick up on what she must have sensed was a change in mood.

'Are you all right, Mr Chapel?'

'Oh, yes, yes, it's the shock, that's all. It's just sinking in. That poor girl. You don't expect it on your own doorstep, do you? Murder, for heaven's sake. I don't know what the world's coming to.'

'The police are doing the rounds, talking to everyone. For all the use it will be. The only sort likely to have been out at that time of night are the sort who are up to no good themselves. This place is going from bad to worse. We're not safe in our beds anymore.' She made a low tutting sound before quickly adding, 'Why don't you come down and have a cuppa?'

Phillip had to think on his feet. Apart from the fact he had a stinking hangover, if the police turned up at Mrs Floyd's when he was there, he'd be asked for his name, and he didn't want to lie about it. But then he would have to explain to her why he'd been going under a pseudonym for the past six months and she wouldn't appreciate the deceit. He wouldn't trust her to keep quiet about it either, which would mean his cover being blown.

'I'd love to, Mrs Floyd, but I've been sneezing all morning and I've got a bit of a sore throat. I wouldn't want to pass anything on to you.'

'Oh, best not, then,' she said quickly, the fear of Covid or flu forever in the forefront of her mind. 'You should stay in and drink some hot water and lemon.'

'Yes, I'll do that.'

Phillip hung up and exhaled a breath. Charlene, for God's sake! That was about as weird as it got, almost as if he'd willed it to happen, as if his psychopath had flown off the pages and become a real-life killer.

Right on cue, Chapel piped up. 'Don't start playing the blame game. *You* can't even remember what you did last night.'

Phillip stared at his alter ego who was lounging in the arm-chair with his feet up on the coffee table. 'What are you saying? Of course I remember. I was here all night. I didn't set foot out of the door.'

'So how did you get the Chinese?'

Phillip's gaze swung to the empty cartons with their greasy stains and remnants of noodle. 'Delivered,' he said confidently.

Chapel laughed, throwing back his head to reveal a row of small white teeth.

'What's so funny about that?'

'They don't deliver to this estate. You know that. Come on, what's the matter with you? They haven't delivered for months. Not since that bloke on his moped got jumped.'

Now he mentioned it, Phillip did recall. So had he gone out? He must have done, probably when he was halfway down the bottle of whisky and hunger pains were gnawing at his guts. He frowned, straining to recollect his trip to the high street, but there was a fog in his head where the memory should be.

'If you can't remember that, what else can't you remember?' Chapel said, raising his eyebrows.

'What's that supposed to mean?'

'I'm only saying. People do all kinds of things when they're drunk. Stupid things, out-of-character things, *murderous* things.'

'*I* didn't kill her,' Phillip said incredulously, but his lips were suddenly dry, and the words came out like a croak. Tiny snatches of last night were gradually coming back to him: the cold whip of the air, the rain, the smell of the Chinese takeaway, the loneliness of the streets. He had been walking behind someone, a good way behind, and had followed them back to the Mansfield.

'You look like you need a drink,' Chapel said. 'Go on, have one. Hair of the dog. It'll do you good.'

Phillip picked up the bottle and unscrewed the lid. The smell made him want to gag but he tipped back the bottle and took a swig anyway. The neat spirit burned his throat and made him cough. 'It wasn't me,' he insisted. 'I wouldn't forget something like that. I couldn't.'

'Two minutes ago, you couldn't remember that you'd left the flat.'

'That's not the same.'

Chapel shrugged. 'I mean, it would have been like fate, wouldn't it? Charlene there all on her own, not even any druggies around. The rain pouring down. The whole place deserted. She was virtually asking for it.'

Phillip's head was spinning now, and not just from the whisky. 'Stop it! Stop winding me up. She was stabbed, Mrs Floyd said. Where would I have got a knife from?'

Chapel looked towards the kitchen. 'There's plenty in there.'

'Okay, but why would I have even taken a knife with me? Why would I?'

'Who wouldn't if they were walking through the Mansfield late at night? This place is a jungle. You were pissed. You were probably worried about being mugged.'

Phillip passed the palm of his hand over his forehead. He was sweating, one half of him saying that this was all ridiculous, the other part afraid – no, terrified – that he had drunkenly crossed that line that no human being is ever supposed to cross. 'I didn't do it.'

'It's not me you need to convince. Maybe you should check out that laptop, see what's written on it, before the law get here.'

But Phillip was too scared to open it up, too scared of what he might find there. Instead, he went to the kitchen and opened the cutlery drawer. There were several possible candidates, all sharp and shiny, all capable of slicing through human flesh with ease. He pulled them out and laid them side by side on the counter. His hands were shaking, his mind in tumult. It couldn't be true. It *couldn't*.

Chapel lounged against the door jamb, watching, waiting, like he didn't have a care in the world. 'Could have been any one of them. I dare say you cleaned it when you got home. That's *if* you brought it home. Are any of them missing? You might have dumped it.'

'Nothing's missing.'

'Well, that's good. You don't want to leave a murder weapon lying around. What about your clothes? You should put them in the machine. They can find the tiniest speck of blood these days.'

Phillip looked down at his sweater, his trousers, his socks – his shoes were still in the living room – but there were no visible signs of blood. But then there wouldn't be because he hadn't killed anyone. Chapel was just being a shit. Calm down, he told himself. Don't play the game. Don't let him manipulate you. He tried again to resurrect last night, to bring back the details of exactly what had happened. But he only got as far as seeing the girl in front of him, her shoulders hunched against the cold, the hood of her coat pulled over her head.

'Stop fucking about,' Phillip said, clattering the knives back into the drawer.

Chapel's smile was thin and sly. 'I'm only trying to help, Phil. I wouldn't want to see you behind bars just for the sake of a touch of carelessness.'

'Don't call me Phil. You know I hate it.'

'Freya used to call you Phil.'

'Freya was a bitch.' Phillip's third wife, who had disproved the theory of third time lucky, had lasted five years. Five miserable, emasculating years until he couldn't even bear to be in the same room. He could have happily killed *her*, wrung her scrawny neck, and not had a second's regret over it. He slammed shut the cutlery drawer. 'Go away and leave me alone.'

'I can't leave you in this state.'

'I'm not in a state.'

'So why are you shaking like a little girl?'

Phillip *was* shaking, his entire body vibrating. He could imagine his internal organs dancing around like jumping beans. Even his teeth were chattering. He couldn't think straight, that was the trouble. Nothing was clear. He wanted to lash out, hit Chapel right in the mouth, shut him up until he'd worked things out. 'Sod off.'

'That's no way to speak to a pal.'

The doorbell rang, two long rings. Phillip jumped.

'Don't answer it,' Chapel said softly. 'It'll be the law. You don't want them to see you in this state. They'll have you tagged as guilty as soon as they look at you.'

'They'll come back.'

'Sure, they'll come back, but not for hours. This evening probably. By then you'll be showered and shaved and not smelling like something that got pulled out of a drain. And you'll have your story straight.'

'There is no bloody story.'

The bell rang again, another two rings.

'They'll clear off soon enough,' Chapel said.

Phillip held his breath, afraid that someone had seen him last night, that what the police were doing was not routine. His fingers gripped the edge of the counter. Sweat slid down the back of his neck. He waited for the bell to go again, but there was only silence. Ten seconds passed, twenty. He expelled his breath in a hiss of relief. 'I need to get out of here,' he muttered.

'Don't be stupid,' Chapel said. 'If you run, they'll know it's you.'

8

Jem got through the rest of the day with nothing untoward happening. She had glanced across the road on more than one occasion but had not seen Harry Lind again. There had been no sign of Moses either, although she'd be keeping her eyes peeled from now on. She didn't want a repeat of this morning's performance. It seemed to her that London was full of odd people, and she wondered if the city made them strange or if their strangeness drew them to the city.

There was a small rush at the florist's just before closing time, and then she was free to go. It was still cold outside, and a thin drizzle was falling. The streets were full of weary-looking people on their way home. As she tramped towards the Mansfield, she couldn't glance in a shop window without being reminded that Christmas was rapidly approaching: the displays all full of fake snow and tinsel and flickering lights. When she was a kid she'd made paper chains with her mother, clumsily linking the strips of paper – pink and blue and yellow – until they had strings long enough to hang from one side of the room to the other and her mouth tasted of glue.

This afternoon Stefan had asked what she was doing for Christmas Day and, worried that he might take pity on her and issue an invitation to join him and Al, she had quickly announced that she was going to spend it with a friend. It wasn't that she disliked the couple, far from it, but she knew that this would be their first Christmas together and she had no desire to gatecrash the celebrations.

Anyway, this wouldn't be the first Christmas she'd spent alone. She wasn't looking forward to it, that was for sure, but she knew it was survivable. Just one day and then it was done. Somewhere, in the back of her mind, it seemed to her that she deserved those twenty-four hours of unrelenting misery, that she had made mistakes in the past that needed to be paid for, that it was, in a way, a kind of penance. She knew that she would think too much about the absent ones – her mother, her grandparents, Georgia – and that there would doubtless be tears.

Jem strode on, trying not to dwell on it. She had plenty of things to be grateful for – a roof over her head, a job, some money in the bank – and most of all, no Aidan. At least not for now. Her body stiffened at the very thought of him. The street was slick with rain from an earlier downpour and the cars whooshed past, their wheels sending sprays of water across the pavement. Not wanting to be soaked, she kept close to the shops, her eyes drawn again and again to the festive decorations.

She wasn't far from the estate when she noticed the two kids in front of her. Kayleigh and Kit. They were lugging three large carrier bags – the girl with two, the boy with one – and clearly struggling with the weight of them. Jem's first instinct was to hang back so she wouldn't need to talk, but then felt instantly guilty for it. They were only kids, for God's sake, not spies or Aidan's little helpers. She had to stop being so damn paranoid and start being more neighbourly.

When the kids reached the main gate they paused, hefted the carrier bags on to the low wall and took a breather.

'They look heavy,' Jem said when she caught up with them. 'Would you like a hand?'

Kayleigh gave her a wary look, as if she suspected ulterior motives. 'They're not that bad. We can manage.'

'Course you can, but we're going the same way so let me carry one at least.'

Kayleigh thought about it, shrugged, and eventually relinquished what appeared to be the heaviest of the bags – full of tins and packets and a large container of milk.

'Ah, you've been shopping,' Jem said.

'Mum's got the flu. She can't get out right now.'

'Oh dear, is she all right?'

Kayleigh's voice took on a distinctly defensive edge. 'It ain't Covid or nothin'. She did a test. She'll be fine in a day or two. She's already on the mend, but she can't go out yet. That's why we're doing the shopping. She'd do it herself but . . . '

'Well, that's good to hear. That she's on the mend, I mean.'

Kayleigh frowned, took Kit's bag off him, and the three of them went through the main gate and started walking towards Haslow. It was only then that Jem noticed the police tape fluttering in the wind and a couple of squad cars parked up outside the tower. 'Looks like there's been trouble.'

'Haven't you heard?'

Jem shook her head. 'No, I've been at work all day.'

Kayleigh hesitated, gave her brother a small push in the back and said, 'Run on ahead, Kit, and see if you can find us a lift that doesn't stink.'

'What's happened?' Jem asked as soon as he was out of earshot, thinking it was probably down to the usual gang strife, a row that had escalated and turned into something nasty.

'A woman got murdered. They found her this morning.' Kayleigh nodded towards the side of Haslow. 'Over there by the bins. She was stabbed in the heart.'

'Jesus,' Jem said. 'That's dreadful.'

'Everyone was talking about it at school. Well, the older kids. I don't think Kit knows. I'm going to have to explain to him later.'

'Maybe your mum could do that.'

Kayleigh gave her a glance, frowning again. 'Oh, yeah, I guess. If she feels up to it.'

Jem's gaze strayed over to the flapping police tape, and she inwardly flinched. Some poor woman killed and left like a pile of old rubbish. It was gross. It was vile. It was frightening. A few bunches of flowers had been left against the wall, incongruous flashes of colour in a grey landscape.

'Her name was Charlene,' Kayleigh said. 'She lived in our block, up near the top somewhere.'

'Did you know her?'

'Only to see her around. I won't be doing that anymore.'

There was something curiously matter of fact about the way Kayleigh said it, as if sudden and violent death was nothing unusual on the Mansfield. Or perhaps it was just her way of protecting herself. Jem tried to sound confident when she replied, 'I'm sure the police will catch who did it. Maybe they already have.'

They passed through the door into the lobby, where Kit was waiting. There was a strange atmosphere about the place this evening: a combination of subdued excitement and sombre contemplation. The people gathered there talked in low voices, their eyes darting over and over again to the door at the back that led to the bins.

The lift Kit had chosen didn't seem any cleaner than the

others but then the task he'd been given was probably an impossible one. The pungent smell of cannabis accompanied their journey upwards.

'You never told me your name,' Kayleigh said.

'Didn't I?' Jem said, feigning surprise. 'It's Jem.' And then she quickly shifted the conversation on in the hope that Kayleigh wouldn't go so far as to request a surname too. Not that she'd give her the right one, but it grew tiresome having to lie all the time. 'So have you lived here long?'

'Ages. Forever. Ever since I was born.'

'Oh, right. I've only been here a few months.'

'I know,' Kayleigh said. 'Al used to live in your flat.'

'He did.'

'Is he coming back?'

'I don't know,' Jem said. 'Maybe some day.'

Kit stared up at her with his wide blue eyes, mute as last time. Jem smiled at him. He didn't smile back. There was something disturbing about his silent watchfulness, something that set her on edge. The lift ground to a halt and they all got out.

'So, what are you having for your tea tonight?' Jem said with forced cheerfulness as they walked down the corridor. It felt wrong, inappropriate somehow, to be talking about food when she'd just heard about the brutal murder of a fellow resident, but she could hardly embark on a conversation about *that*.

Kayleigh glanced at her. 'Tea?'

'Dinner, I mean,' Jem said, rapidly correcting herself. She was still getting used to the north/south divide when it came to the terminology of mealtimes. 'Anything nice?'

Kayleigh shrugged her skinny shoulders. 'Dunno.'

'I don't suppose your mum feels like cooking much at the moment.'

'No. Well, she can do fish fingers. She's okay.' They stopped outside Kayleigh's flat, and she held out her hand for the bag Jem was holding. 'Ta,' she said.

'Are you sure you don't want me to bring it in?'

'No,' Kayleigh said too quickly. 'We can manage from here. I don't want to wake up Mum, not if she's sleeping.'

'If you're sure. See you around then.'

'See you.'

Jem glanced over her shoulder as she walked away. She saw Kayleigh put down the bags, unlock the door, gently propel Kit inside, pick up the bags again and disappear into the flat. Was it odd that the girl hadn't wanted to let her in? Perhaps not, not if the mother was ill. Unexpected guests were probably the last thing she needed. But something still bothered her. Those kids were too pale and thin, and not dressed for the winter cold. She had the distinct feeling that something wasn't right.

9

Kayleigh released a sigh of relief as she closed the door behind her. What was wrong with the woman? She'd gone from being the least friendly person in the world to Neighbour of the Month in the space of twenty-four hours. All those stupid questions. *Have you lived here long? What are you having for your tea?* She hoped she wasn't going to be another Mrs Floyd, always poking her nose in and interfering in things that weren't any of her damn business.

Unsurprisingly the flat was dark and cold and empty – still no Nola – and Kayleigh swore softly under her breath. Earlier today, when she'd heard about a body being found on the estate, her stomach had dropped like a stone, and she'd broken out in a cold sweat. She had been so afraid that she'd thought she might faint. Her head had gone fuzzy, her heart banging in her chest. But now she knew it wasn't her mum she could afford to be angry at her again. And yet a small sliver of ice still slivered down her spine. What if she *never* came back? What if this time, like Dad, she was gone for good?

Kayleigh lugged the bags through to the kitchen and hauled them on to the counter. With no electricity there could be no hot food, but at least there was bread and cereal and spread and peanut butter and bananas. She had given the staff at the food bank the same story she'd given the woman – her mother too sick to go out – and thankfully they'd taken her word for it.

She found a fresh candle – only two left – lit it and began unpacking the bags. 'Here, Kit, help me with these. I'll pass them to you, and you put them in the cupboard under the counter.' It was frustrating having baked beans and tinned soup and pasta and not being able to eat any of it. She had to sort out the leccy problem, and fast.

'Did you see the police tape outside? A woman had an accident, but it wasn't Mum so it's nothing for you to worry about. She'll be home in a day or two.' How many times had she said that to him now? Empty promises. Nola was a shit for leaving them like this. Three days, for God's sake. They could starve to death for all she cared. And freeze to death too, come to that.

Kayleigh rubbed her hands together, trying to get them warm. She left the loaf of bread on the counter. It would be sandwiches again but at least they could eat more than one. Neither of them would go to bed hungry tonight. She wished they could watch the telly; there would be nothing to do all evening except sit around wrapped in blankets, playing cards and hoping that Nola would come back with some cash in her pocket.

The doorbell rang and Kayleigh started. Who was that? No one came to the flat other than the social and the occasional mate of Nola's. She wasn't going to answer it. If it was the social, then she and Kit would be out of here in the time it took for a phone call to be made and 'alternative arrangements' for their care put in place. Unless Nola had lost her key. But their mother had a pair of lungs on her: she'd beat on the door and holler until they let her in.

The bell went again.

Kayleigh put a finger to her lips. 'Don't move,' she whispered to Kit. 'Don't make any noise.' They stood in the flickering candlelight and listened. Perhaps it was the woman from along the landing, come back to check on them. She'd given them a funny look when Kayleigh had refused to let her in.

Eventually, whoever it was gave up and went away. Kayleigh sighed and set to work on the sandwiches. 'We need a plan,' she said. 'We can't carry on like this. We need to find Dad.'

10

It had been a long day. Phillip Grosvenor had showered and shaved, put on clean clothes, and gone through his story with Chapel a hundred times. 'Be relaxed,' Chapel kept saying. 'If you look guilty, then they'll think you are.' Which was all very well for him to say in that smug way of his: he wasn't the one in the firing line. He wasn't the one with the hangover from hell, either.

Matters hadn't improved in the late afternoon when Phillip discovered a reddish stain on the cuff of his anorak. Blood? It could be. Except it couldn't be. He hadn't killed Charlene, hadn't gone near her. Well, not near enough to stab the girl. He could swear to it, even if his memories of last night were a little on the fuzzy side. A person knew instinctively what they could and couldn't do.

But then a dreadful thought had occurred to him. What if the cops noticed the discolouration and hauled him down to the station? Forensics would prove it wasn't *her* blood, probably not blood at all, but by then the whole block would know about him being arrested. No smoke without fire and all that. He'd be the subject of gossip, of rumour, of sly insinuations. Which was why he'd put the coat through the washing machine and although the stain had gone a blurry pink colour it was still there, and now he was weighing up whether to get rid of the coat or not. Which presented an entirely new problem: if he dumped it and it was found, and they managed to trace it back to him, that would make him look even more guilty.

Phillip stared down at the anorak, now lying damply on the kitchen counter. He had just spent half an hour scrubbing at the cuff, but the stain wasn't coming out. It was useless. He swore softly, imagining Freya's glee if he *was* arrested. She'd be straight on the phone to all her shitty friends saying that she'd always known there was something off about him.

'Why would they even look at your coat?' Chapel said. 'They're not going to do that unless they have good reason to suspect you.'

'If I admit I was out last night, out at around the time she probably died, they *will* suspect me. I was walking behind her, for God's sake.'

'Well, you're not going to tell them that.'

'I can't deny I went out. What if someone saw me? What about the people at the takeaway?' Phillip's voice was rising in pitch, taking on that strained squeaky sound that had always made Freya roll her eyes. 'What about the CCTV?'

'Okay. Calm down. What I meant is that you're not going to tell them about *her*. Going out for a Chinese doesn't make you a murderer. And they won't know exactly what time she died. There are people constantly coming and going on this estate. They'll only have limited coverage on camera: the takeaway, the high street, Mansfield Road perhaps. None of the cameras work on the estate.'

This was true, Phillip thought. Hadn't Edna Floyd said as much? She was always complaining that as soon as they were repaired, they were down again. The council, sick of throwing good money after bad, had finally given up. There were too many people on the Mansfield who had a vested interest in keeping their activities private.

'What are you going to do with *that*?' Chapel asked, staring at the anorak. 'Might be best not to leave it lying around. Not if plod decide to come in.'

Phillip, who'd been hoping that any kind of exchange would be conducted at the front door, looked up at him sharply. 'Why would they come in?'

'They probably won't, but just in case. Best put it somewhere out of sight, huh? Otherwise, they might wonder why you felt the urge to wash it today. The law have got very suspicious minds.'

Phillip felt a flurry of panic. He looked at his watch. Should he screw up the anorak and hide it? Cut it into tiny pieces? Try and burn it? But the damn thing wasn't going to burn while it was wet. And anyway, the pungent smell of burning was bound to alert the cops. In the end he went through to the bedroom and hung it in the wardrobe. He stared at it for a long while wondering, if they searched the flat, how the hell he'd explain away a wet coat on a hanger but couldn't think of what else to do and so left it there.

In the living room, he sat down and flipped open his laptop. He'd already cleared his search history – too many articles on how to murder without getting caught – but knew that any police computer geek could probably retrieve it without too much trouble. That was a worry. He'd also transferred what he'd written last night on to a tiny memory stick that he'd hidden in a CD of Mahler's fifth symphony. Chapel said he should be arrested just for having CDs, but Phillip couldn't be doing with iPods or online streaming or anything else that was supposed to enhance his listening experience.

Some of what he'd written in his drunken state was a rambling disaster but there were parts that might be salvageable. The drugging of a woman, the torture, the slow painful death. He knew it was only wish fulfilment, a description of what he'd like to do to Freya if his middle-class morality didn't stand in the way of outright murder. Chapel would have done it without a flicker of remorse, but then Chapel was capable of anything.

By seven o'clock Phillip was starting to wonder if the police were going to bother coming back. By ten past he had his answer. Two long rings on the doorbell made him jump. He was tempted to ignore it, to pretend he wasn't home, but then he'd have to spend all of tomorrow in a state of trepidation. He glanced around for Chapel, but he was nowhere to be seen. He stood up and took two deep breaths. Better get it over and done with.

The uniformed policeman was young – although everyone looked young to him these days – with reddish brown hair, long arms and legs that gave him an odd, gangly appearance, and a weary smile. He was carrying a clipboard and the kind of expression that suggested he'd been asking the same questions for hours and getting pretty much the same answers.

'Good evening, sir. I'm PC Liam Hanks. I'm sorry to disturb you but we're investigating the death of a young woman on the estate last night.'

Phillip's mouth was dry, his pulse racing. 'Yes, I heard about it. Terrible business, just terrible.'

'Charlene Ellis,' Hanks said. 'Did you know her at all?' He held out a photograph, a picture that showed her in happier times, smiling widely, oblivious to what was just around the corner.

Phillip took the photograph and made a show of looking at it properly. He'd been worried that his hands might shake, but thankfully they held steady. 'She's vaguely familiar. Did she live in Haslow?'

'On the fifteenth floor.'

'Right, yes. I think I've seen her around, but I never knew her to talk to.'

'Did you see her yesterday or last night?'

Phillip shook his head as he handed back the photo. 'No, I don't think so. I mean there are so many people living here . . . but no, I don't recall seeing her.' He was about to nervously elaborate on the vastness of the estate when Chapel hissed in his ear: *Shut up now. Don't say any more than you have to.*

'Did you ever see her with someone else? Not just here but anywhere?'

'No,' Phillip said. 'I don't believe I did. I'm sorry I can't be of more help.'

PC Hanks, his pen poised over the clipboard, nodded. 'Can I just take your name, sir?'

'Phillip Grosvenor. That's Phillip with two Ls.'

Hanks wrote it down. 'And do you live here alone?'

'Yes.'

'Well, thank you for your time, Mr Grosvenor. If you can think of anything that could be useful, however small, please don't hesitate to get in touch.' Hanks passed him a photocopied leaflet showing Charlene's face and a number to ring.

'I will.' Phillip could feel his spirits rising. Was that it? Was it over? He tried not to look relieved. 'I hope you catch whoever did it.'

But then Hanks said casually, 'I don't suppose you were out last night at all?'

Phillip could feel his insides freeze. 'Last night?' He wanted to lie, to say no, to deny ever having left the flat, to swear that he was working for the entire evening. The temptation rose in him, but he pushed it back down. 'What sort of time?'

'Any time, sir.'

'Well, actually I was, briefly. I went for a takeaway at about . . . I'm not sure when exactly, probably about ten o'clock. The Chinese on the high street. I was only gone about fifteen minutes.'

'And did you see anyone on the way there or back?'

'There were some people, a few, but it was raining so I wasn't taking much notice. No one that I recognised.' Phillip paused and then added, 'Is it important? Was that around the time she was . . . ?' He raised a hand to his chest as if he was shocked. 'Heavens! I don't remember anyone in particular. I just wanted to get back as quickly as I could.'

'Do you have a phone number I could take, sir, just in case we need to contact you again?'

'Yes, of course.' Phillip's stomach was sinking as he reeled off the number. Now he was on the radar, on the list, a man who could, at the very least, be a witness, and at the very worst, a suspect.

PC Hanks thanked him again, said good night and moved off along the corridor. As he closed the door, Phillip put a hand to his chest. He wouldn't be surprised if he had a heart attack or a stroke right this minute. Clammy hands, shallow breathing, his mouth as dry as sandpaper. He could drop dead, and no one would be any the wiser. He could lie undiscovered in this flat for months. It took an effort just to walk back into the living room.

Chapel, who was reclining on the sofa, gave a snort. 'That's just fear,' he said. 'It's panic. Pull yourself together. Take a few deep breaths. Have a drink.'

'He took my number, for God's sake. He asked me if I was out last night.'

'So what? Even *they* won't believe that you killed her. What did you do? Put your noodles down while you were stabbing her to death?'

Phillip stared at him. He hadn't really considered the logistics before. Could he have held the takeaway in his left hand while he stabbed her with his right? It would have been an unwieldy way to go about things. He *could* have put the bag down. But would he have done that? Put his dinner on the filthy Mansfield ground where all the germs would have been free to congregate inside? Even blind drunk he found it hard to believe that he could have been that reckless. He was a man who valued hygiene, who regularly washed his hands, who still had the rules of Covid firmly entrenched in his brain.

Phillip went through to the kitchen, placed the leaflet on the counter, put on his rubber gloves and rummaged in the bin. He pulled out the crushed takeaway bag and held it up, examining it. No sign of any obvious dirt on the bottom, or blood come to that.

'Jesus, Phil, what the hell are you doing?'

'What does it look like?'

'Like you've lost the plot.'

'There would have been stains on this bag if I'd put it down. It was raining last night; the ground was wet.' Phillip held out the bag. 'You see? Nothing. There's nothing on it.'

'Well, it would have dried off by now.'

'I didn't kill her. I didn't go anywhere near her.'

Chapel smirked. 'You must have thought about it, though. Don't tell me it didn't cross your mind. Opportunities like that don't come along every day.' He picked up the leaflet and flapped it under Phillip's nose. 'She was wearing that red coat, remember, the one with the hood?'

Phillip did remember, in a washed-out, distant kind of way.

He'd always liked her in that coat. But Charlene hadn't been a friendly girl: he'd smiled at her once in the lobby, said a cheerful good morning, but she'd looked straight through him as if he wasn't there. Not very neighbourly. Still, she'd been on the list even before that unfortunate episode. He'd already singled her out as worthy of attention.

'So, it looks like you're off the hook,' Chapel said. 'No jail for you today.'

'I'm not off the hook yet. The police have still got me out on the estate when Charlene was murdered.'

'Nothing to worry about *if* you're innocent.'

Phillip didn't like the way Chapel put the emphasis on 'if' as though there was still some doubt about the matter. 'Haven't you ever heard about miscarriage of justice? Or the police framing people? Or just being in the wrong bloody place at the wrong bloody time?'

'You should use all this in your book,' Chapel said. 'It might supply some of that authenticity you're after.'

'I'll write you out of it if you're not careful. There's plenty more psychopaths where you came from.'

But Chapel was unmoved by the threat. He slithered back into the living room, laughing softly.

11

By eight o'clock on Friday morning Harry was in the office studying the photographs of the two twelve-year-old girls laid out side by side on his desk. He'd had one of those restless nights, his head full of the Mortlake case, and now a low-level ache throbbed gently in his temples. The coffee wasn't helping, but starting the day with anything less than a strong dose of caffeine was beyond him.

The photographs were school pictures, taken a month or so before Christine had disappeared. Amy Greer – fair-haired, grey-eyed, a wide smile for the camera – had been the more conventionally pretty of the two. Christine had taken after her father, her features heavy, her hair and eyes both brown, but there was something more interesting about her face – something thoughtful, wary, secretive. Or was he just imposing impressions with the benefit of hindsight? School photos did not provide the best insight into a person's character. He could still remember his own stiff, formal portraits that had never quite looked like he did in real life.

It was Amy that he needed to track down, but there was every chance, even after all these years, that she didn't want to be found. The backlash from Christine's disappearance – the suspicion, rumour, gossip – would have been enough to send the family into hiding. He could imagine the pressure they'd been under and how life in Kellston would have become intolerable for them. When they'd moved, they would have changed their surname and tried to make a fresh start. He made a quick note to check out Pauline Greer's maiden name; people tended not to stray too far from what was familiar to them.

For all the problems he was faced with, Harry had at least received one piece of good news: Mac, with his vast network of police contacts, had managed to track down a former officer called Alec Beddows who had worked on the Mortlake case back when he was a DC. Long retired, he now lived in Maidstone, and had agreed to meet at eleven o'clock this morning. Harry glanced at his watch. He had plenty of time, but he'd set off at nine just to allow for any hold-ups.

Harry sat back in his chair, leaned forward again and took another look at the photographs. It seemed barely possible that Christine Mortlake was still alive. The only question was how she'd died and why. And where her body was, of course. Did Amy know anything? Did her parents? Mr and Mrs Greer could be dead by now, and Amy, if she was still alive, would be about sixty-three.

Not for the first time, Harry had the feeling he was chasing after shadows. He wondered if Christine could have had a boyfriend. Celia Mortlake had dismissed the idea – *She was only twelve, Mr Lind* – but parents didn't always know what their children were up to. However, it had been a different world back then: no social media, no mobile phones and no pressure to grow up faster than you should. Not to mention neighbours who would happily squeal on you at the first opportunity. So, it was probably unlikely, but he couldn't entirely dismiss the possibility.

The neighbours. Was it odd that none of them had seen Christine walk along the road? Maybe they were all still eating their Sunday lunch. Or maybe the front walls and hedges had been higher then with less visibility. Depending on the pace she walked, it would have taken her about three to four minutes to reach the Greers' house, a slim window for any opportunistic pervert passing in a car.

Harry had checked out the large but neglected rear garden on his second visit to see Celia Mortlake. The beginning of December was not a good time for any garden but this one had looked especially bleak with its long grass, weeds, brambles and general air of abandonment. It ended in a six-foot red brick wall, the sort of wall he could easily have scaled when he was twelve – there were plenty of footholds – but which might have been an obstacle too far for Christine. The garden backed on to Lisburn Street from where she could have made her getaway – if getting away was what was on her mind.

Harry pushed back his chair, stood up and looked out of the window. Across the road the door to the florist's was still closed, but the light was on. He could see the bloke moving around inside, shifting buckets of flowers. No sign of his nameless girl yet. Commuters were passing in and out of the station, crowding the pavement and hurrying to the café to buy coffee and hot bacon rolls.

He shifted his gaze to the Fox pub, where last night, tired of his own company in the flat upstairs, he had whiled away a couple of hours listening to varying opinions on the state of the economy, the NHS and the murder of a local woman on the Mansfield. The latter had given him a jolt – it was the first he had heard of it – and for a few seconds he had wondered if it was *her*, the mystery girl, the girl he had saved from Moses. It hadn't been, of course, that had soon become evident, but the possibility had shaken him.

Harry didn't even know if she lived on the estate. He didn't know anything about her, other than that she worked across the road and was jumpy around strangers. And now he was back to letting his imagination run riot, creating a story for her that probably wasn't even close to the truth. Moses would be enough to make anyone jumpy. He needed to keep things in perspective.

However, thinking about the religious zealot sparked an idea in his head. How long had Moses lived here? Long enough, perhaps, for him to remember the Mortlake case. Back in the seventies Kellston must have been a different place, a more close-knit community, with everyone knowing everyone else's business. Whether Moses could bring anything new to the table was another matter altogether, but he could be worth talking to. With so little to go on, Harry was willing to clutch at even the unlikeliest of straws. Any bit of background, any small detail, could be useful.

Harry scoured the street, checking out the crossing at the traffic lights, but the old man was nowhere to be seen. A busy time last night, perhaps, harassing the Albert Road toms. He was either having a lie-in or peddling his faith elsewhere. The conversation would have to wait. Moses, he was sure, wasn't going anywhere.

He was about to leave the window and resume his examination of the slimmer-than-it-should-be Mortlake file, when he noticed the girl arrive at the very spot where he had seen her yesterday. He saw her glance around, wary no doubt of bumping into Moses again. Her shoulders were up, hunched against the cold, and she shifted impatiently from one foot to the other while she waited for the lights to change.

Harry watched her cross over and walk towards the florist's. She was almost at the door when she suddenly turned her head and looked straight up at him. Taken by surprise, his instinct was to step back, but he forced himself not to. That, he felt, would only make it seem like he'd been watching her – which he had been – rather than gazing idly out of the window. Their eyes locked. He smiled and raised his hand. She hesitated, frowned and looked away.

Harry grimaced, and quickly sat back down at his desk. Well, that could have gone better. He should have had the wit to glance to the side, to pretend he was looking someplace else, but it was too late now. Her reaction had said it all. Now she probably thought he was some kind of creepy stalker following her movements from his office window.

So, not the most auspicious start to the day. He stared down at the file, drank some coffee, and tried to concentrate on the job in hand. It was Christine Mortlake he should be thinking about, a different girl, a different problem. He went through the pages, re-reading what he'd already read ten times before. He attempted to look at things from every which angle. A person couldn't just disappear into thin air. Concentrate, he said to himself. But no matter how hard he tried, his mind kept drifting back to the girl across the road.

12

The journey to Maidstone took just over an hour. Harry arrived early, found the bungalow in a long line of identical bungalows and then doubled back to where he had noticed a café. Here he ate a cheese toastie and drank more coffee while he went over the list of questions he wanted to ask Beddows. He hoped he was the kind of ex-cop who had a decent memory and a helpful disposition. The day had started badly – coming all this way for nothing was the last thing he needed. Still, the very fact that he'd agreed to see him boded well.

When it was ten minutes to the appointment, Harry put his notepad back in his pocket, paid, left the café and drove back to Greenleigh Close. It was a quiet tree-lined road, but there was something about bungalows, especially rows of them, that always depressed him, as if they were places people went to die. The front gardens were all neat and tidy, the flower beds raked over and planted with winter pansies. He parked, got out of the car and strode up the drive.

The door was answered almost as soon as he'd rung the

bell. Alec Beddows was a tall, lean, slightly stooped man in his mid-seventies. He had a thick shock of grey hair and shrewd grey eyes. Holding out his hand, he said, 'Mr Lind? Pleased to meet you.'

'Call me Harry. Thanks for agreeing to see me. It's good of you.'

'The pleasure's all mine,' Beddows said as he led him through to the living room. 'I've been looking forward to it. I don't often get the chance to talk shop these days. It makes a pleasant change. Take a seat. I made some tea, but if you'd rather have coffee?'

Harry sat down on the sofa. 'Tea's fine. Thank you. White, no sugar, please.'

A tray was already sitting on the coffee table. Beddows settled himself into the armchair, poured out two cups and passed one over. Harry glanced around the room, which was neat and tidy and had all the small touches that a woman brought to a place – matching cushions, ornaments and family photographs – and yet there was a sense of absence too.

'My wife died a couple of years ago,' Beddows said, as if he had picked up on Harry's train of thought. 'It makes for long days sometimes.'

'I'm sorry to hear it.'

'You never want to be the one who's left behind.' Beddows sighed, inclined his head, paused for a few seconds and then gave a brisk smile. 'But you're here about the Mortlake case. I've been thinking a good deal about it since Mac called. How can I help? What is it you'd like to know?'

'Everything, anything,' Harry said. 'Celia Mortlake has hired us to take another look at Christine's disappearance but we're talking over fifty years ago. It's proving hard to find anyone who was around at the time.'

'Well, I'll tell you all I can remember, but we never got any-where, Harry, and that's the honest truth of it. I was a young DC then – it was one of my first cases – and I know we must have missed something. The DCI, Jim Sharp, was convinced that Greer had taken her, but there wasn't any evidence.'

'Why George Greer?'

'There were a limited number of suspects, unless we were looking at a complete stranger. One family or the other was lying, and Sharp reckoned it was the Greers. He didn't have any-thing to base it on other than his own class prejudice – Mortlake was a well-paid accountant, Greer was a greengrocer – and he reckoned one could be trusted a lot more than the other.'

'But you didn't agree with him?'

'I didn't think we should dismiss Arthur Mortlake just be-cause he had the good fortune to be better off. Money doesn't enter into it when it comes to circumstances like these, or at least it shouldn't. And I'm pretty sure they were both Masons, Sharp certainly was, and that lot always watch each other's backs.' Beddows gave a wry smile. 'Or am I showing my own prejudices now?'

Harry shrugged. 'We all have them. What did you think of Mortlake?'

'Arrogant, entitled, demanding. He constantly pushed for Greer to be arrested, made it clear to anyone that would listen that the man was guilty of abducting his daughter. He made Greer's life hell, even though there wasn't a shred of solid ev-idence. I mean, I understand that he was devastated – who wouldn't be? – but I felt that he influenced Sharp in his think-ing, pushed him in a single direction, closed him off to other possibilities.'

'And the other possibilities were ...?'

'That Mortlake himself was the guilty one. Or that there

could have been a third party involved. Maybe Christine didn't go to Amy Greer's. Maybe she went somewhere else entirely.'

Harry, whose thoughts had run along much the same lines, gave a nod. 'But she didn't have any other friends in the district, did she?'

'Not that we knew of. Her best friend lived in Bloomsbury. Vivienne something. I can't recall her surname right now: it'll come back to me. But, anyway, Vivienne had been with her family all afternoon, and said she hadn't heard from Christine for a few days. They'd talked on the phone the previous Thursday, but Christine hadn't said anything about what she was doing at the weekend.'

'What had she said? Any family rows, anything like that?'

'No, just school stuff, according to Vivienne. And she couldn't think of anywhere Christine might have gone. I think she was telling the truth.'

'And Amy Greer. What did you make of her?'

Beddows paused and scrunched up his brow, as if trying to find the right words. 'She was an odd kid. No, not odd, that's not the right word. She just seemed a bit indifferent to it all, as if we were making a fuss over nothing. She wasn't worried, not like her parents. But then she was only twelve. I suppose she might not have fully understood the implications of Christine being missing for hours.'

'Celia Mortlake didn't like her. She thought she was sly and overly confident.'

Beddows picked up his cup and sipped some tea. 'She must be getting on now, Celia Mortlake.'

'In her late eighties,' Harry said. 'One last chance to get some answers.'

'I understand that. All these years and . . . I always thought Christine's body would turn up one day. It's one of those cases that stay with you. Do you know what I mean? Yes, of course you do. Mac told me you used to be in the force.'

'You were always convinced she was dead, then?'

'Not at first. Girls take off, go places they shouldn't or run away from home. And although Christine didn't seem the type to do that, it wasn't an impossibility. I was hoping she might still show up, but after a while ... well, there were a few false sightings and that was it.'

'Disappeared into thin air,' Harry said. 'Except someone knows where she is. Or someone did.'

'They could be dead and buried by now.'

'Is George Greer still alive?'

Beddows shook his head. 'I've no idea. Sharp grilled him for days, really put the thumbscrews on, but he wouldn't confess. And other than some fairly dodgy circumstantial evidence – the fact that Christine *said* she was going to Amy's – he couldn't find any reason to charge him. Both the mother and the daughter backed up his story, adamant that she hadn't been there, and without a body ... '

'I'm presuming the houses were thoroughly searched?'

'Top to bottom, everywhere, the attics, cellars and the gardens. Nothing. But both men had transport, and the time to get rid of her body. We talked to the neighbours but none of them had seen Mortlake's car or Greer's van leaving – and there was nothing incriminating in either of the vehicles. Christine's hair was found in Mortlake's but that was only to be expected.'

'It must have been frustrating.'

Beddows gave a hollow laugh. 'It was that all right. And the longer it went on, the more obvious it became that we weren't going to find her, alive *or* dead. Sharp had been so fixated on Greer being guilty that he'd given the real culprit time to cover his tracks.'

'And you think the real culprit was Arthur Mortlake?'

'I'm not sure what I think anymore. It's true that I didn't take to the man, that I felt we should have looked more closely at him, but over the next few years he made Greer's life hell, following him wherever he went, haranguing him, harassing him, trying to force him into a confession, to tell him what had happened to Christine.'

'Not the actions of a guilty man. Unless he was going out of his way to prove his innocence.'

'That's what I thought at first, but it didn't stop. The Greers had to keep on moving just to get away from him.'

'Do you know where they went?'

'Essex at first. Chelmsford. Then it was Lincoln. Then Oxford or Cambridge.' Beddows gave a light shrug. 'I don't remember which. What I do know is that Greer made several complaints of harassment to the local police. They contacted Cowan Road, but Mortlake had friends in high places. Nothing was ever done about it.'

'Any idea where the family ended up?'

'Sorry. Greer must have been always looking over his shoulder, though, always wondering when Mortlake would catch up with him again.'

Harry pondered on this for a few seconds. 'I don't suppose you know if they changed their name, the Greers?'

'I imagine so, although I couldn't tell you what to. And it didn't seem to stop Mortlake tracking them down again and again. Private detectives, probably. He had the money.'

Harry made a mental note to ask Celia Mortlake about the detectives. If the company kept records, it might be possible to find out the Greers' last known location. It was a long shot – after fifty-one years the company probably didn't even exist anymore, and the files would have been destroyed – but he was prepared to follow up on any lead no matter how tenuous it seemed. 'The other thing, surely, is that Mortlake couldn't have killed Christine without Celia knowing? And if she does know, why would she employ me to find out what happened?'

'Unless she didn't know. Those big old houses have all sorts of hiding places. I'm not saying we didn't give it a thorough search, but we could have missed something.'

It seemed to Harry that Beddows couldn't make up his mind whether Arthur Mortlake was guilty or not. It was clear that he *wanted* him to be, but that the evidence wasn't really there to back up his suspicions. 'Tell me about George Greer,' he said.

'He seemed a decent sort. Scared, naturally. He could see how it looked; he knew he was going to get the blame. My instinct was that he was telling the truth, that he hadn't seen Christine that day, but Sharp thought otherwise. Well, I've already told you that. He had no criminal record, not even a parking ticket, and there was no suggestion that he'd ever showed an unnatural interest in young girls. He seemed credible to me, but I wasn't the one leading the investigation.'

'Maybe there was an accident, Christine died, and they all panicked. Greer could have decided to try and cover it up. Maybe Amy did something that led to her death. As her father, he'd have wanted to protect her.'

'Except Amy was the least worried of them all. She seemed convinced that nothing bad had happened, that Christine would turn up before too long. Unless she was the world's best actress – and she was only a twelve-year-old, remember – I can't see her being able to lie so casually about the death of a friend.'

'Do you think she knew something? Where Christine had actually gone, perhaps? That could explain the lack of concern.'

'It's possible. But she was questioned several times and always stuck to her story. That's not easy when you're an adult, never mind a kid.'

'Although later, when it was clear that Christine *wasn't* coming back, she might have been too scared to tell the truth about whatever it was she did know.'

'*If* she knew anything.'

A silence fell over the room.

'Which leaves a third party,' Harry eventually said. 'There are eighteen houses between the Mortlakes' and the Greers' if we count both sides of the street. Were they all searched?'

Beddows made a derisive sound in the back of his throat. 'Not as soon as they should have been. Sharp was so focused on Greer that it was a few days before he decided to extend the search. By then, if Christine had been in any of them, there had been plenty of time to dispose of the evidence.'

'Any likely suspects?'

'No one that stood out. And no one with any kind of record.' Beddows sighed into his tea. 'And no one who admitted to seeing Christine in the street that afternoon. But this was before computers and cross-referencing and the Sex Offenders Register so it would have been easy enough for someone to slip through the net.'

'It's still possible that Christine called round at Amy's, didn't get any answer to her ring on the bell – they might not have heard it out in the garden – and decided to either go home again or to take a walk someplace. If it was the latter, then she could have ended up in any of the surrounding streets, or even in the centre of Kellston. It was a Sunday, so I doubt there'd have been much in the way of public transport, and I don't suppose she had money for a cab. Wherever she went it was likely to have been on foot.'

'She could have bumped into someone she knew along the way.'

'She could have.'

Both men fell silent again. It was all conjecture, but they had nothing else to go on. Harry was aware of the flimsy nature of the inquiry, of evidence worn thin, and clues eroded by the passing of the years. Christine Mortlake seemed to be receding further and further into the distance. He felt a spurt of anger that someone had got away with it.

'Was there anything else? Anything that you think should have been followed up and wasn't?'

Beddows gave another of his sighs. 'It was a botch job, Harry. That's the beginning and end of it. Sharp has a lot to answer for. Well, perhaps we all do, everyone who worked on that case. If we'd been better organised, more on the ball, we might have caught the bastard who took her.' His face, dark and serious, suddenly brightened. 'Vivienne Bayle! That was her name. Bayle with a y. Christine's friend. I knew it would come back to me. She became an actress.'

'I've never heard of her.'

'Oh, nothing big, not famous or anything, but she had some minor parts on TV. I think she did some theatre work too. I remember seeing her name on a poster once. She shouldn't be too hard to find. If you track her down, she'll be able to tell you more about Christine.'

Harry wrote the name in his notebook. 'Thanks. That could be useful.'

'I wish I had more to tell you. I've racked my brains, gone over it again and again, but I still can't put the pieces together.'

Harry, sensing that Beddows had told him as much as he could, stood up, took a business card from his wallet and laid it on the coffee table. 'You've been very helpful. If you think of anything else, do give me a call.'

'Good luck. Let me know if you manage to find out anything.'

At the door the two men shook hands, made a little small talk about the state of the weather, and parted company. Harry got in his car and set off back to London. He had not got the breakthrough he'd hoped for – the chances of that had always been slim – but at least he'd learned a few things and was in possession of a fresh lead. Whether any of it would take him where he wanted to go was another matter altogether. Sharp had screwed up the investigation, leaving most stones unturned, and on paper the trail was as cold as the grave.

13

Jem spent the whole day with one eye on the job and the other on the office across the road. She saw Harry Lind go out half an hour after she'd spotted him gawping at her, and he didn't come back until after one. Was she making something out of nothing? Her nerves were so frayed that she couldn't differentiate between what was normal and what was suspicious. There had been the calling out of her name, the incident with Moses, the intervention by Lind, the meeting with the strange kids, and then the murder of the young woman, all combining to throw her off-kilter.

While Lind was away, she made up three bouquets of birthday flowers – Stefan, who liked to get out and about, would deliver the bouquets to their happy recipients – and then set to work on orders for the cemetery. Alone in the shop, she dealt with the customers and tried to look confident and cheerful. The Christmas wreaths were selling well, along with the holly and mistletoe.

Jem was all right when she was busy, able to keep the worst

of her fears at bay, but when her hands were idle her mind wandered into dangerous territory. Aidan seeped into her head like poison. Before she knew it, she was back in Lytham, back to being fifteen again, slowly sliding into a pit of violence and abuse. A tremor ran through her body. She didn't want to be this person, always afraid of her own shadow, but didn't know how to escape from her either.

At quarter past three she saw Harry Lind leave his office again, turn right, and saunter along Station Road towards the traffic lights, glancing around as if he was looking for someone. She watched him through the plate-glass window while she pretended to arrange a bucket of yellow chrysanthemums. He had a limp, something she hadn't noticed before, which affected his gait and gave it a slightly rolling appearance, like he was walking on the deck of a ship.

She was about to turn away when she saw the dreaded Moses loom into view. Instead of trying to avoid him, Lind did the very opposite, placing a hand on the old man's shoulder and drawing him to one side so they didn't block the pavement. That was odd. For the next five minutes the two of them were deep in conversation. Jem leaned in closer to the window as if those fractional inches might give her a better idea of what they were talking about. She stared at the pair, transfixed. Then Lind reached inside his pocket, took out his wallet and passed something over. Money? It had to be.

Moses grabbed whatever was on offer and scuttled off. Lind watched him for a second or two and then strolled back towards the office. Jem drew back from the window. She was rapidly joining the dots, her pulse beginning to race. Hadn't she suspected a set-up the moment Stefan had told her that Harry Lind was a private detective? And now she had witnessed the proof. Moses had just received payment for accosting her, for getting her in a state, so that her knight in shining armour could step in and save the day. His plan being ... what? To establish that she really was Jem Byrne and then to pass that information on.

Of course she didn't know any of this for sure, but what other motive could Lind have for talking to the crazy man? No one in their right mind would voluntarily engage with him. Not unless they had good reason. And Lind, she presumed, had not suddenly seen the light, found God, or undergone a miraculous conversion on the road to Kellston station. No, it was the anti-Christ he was in league with, a devil called Aidan Hague.

Fortunately, Stefan was on the phone and too preoccupied by some last-minute changes to a wedding order to notice her own distraction. She was already making plans for packing up and moving on, for getting out of Kellston as fast as she could. The idea of it filled her with dread, but not as much dread as the thought of Aidan being hot on her heels. Where to next? She would keep going south to Hampshire or Devon or Cornwall, keep going until she fell off the very edge of the country. Or was pushed.

Almost as soon as the idea of leaving entered her head, she railed against it. She was too tired to keep running, too sick of always being on the back foot. And besides, she liked it here, liked working in the shop at least, with its heady smell of lilies and its general air of peace. Calm had been in short supply over the past year, and she was reluctant to relinquish it. But if she was right, if Aidan wasn't far away, what choice did she have?

14

Harry's afternoon had been relatively productive. On returning from Kent, he had put Lorna to work on tracking down
Vivienne Bayle – if the actress didn't have an internet presence,
there was always Equity – while he called Celia and found out
the name of the detective agency her husband had retained back
in 1971.

Lorna's job had turned out to be straightforward. Vivienne
had a public Facebook page and a message had been sent to her
explaining the situation and asking if she'd be prepared to talk
about Christine Mortlake. They were still waiting for a reply.
Chasing down the detectives was proving more problematic.
The firm had been called Currans but was now, unsurprisingly,
defunct. Celia had not been able to tell him much other than
that it had been located in Kellston.

Harry, after a fruitless search online, had resorted to the more
traditional method of getting information: local knowledge.
He'd been intending to talk to Moses anyway, and after a short
search had found him on the high street. For a man who was

overly preoccupied with God, sin and redemption, Moses had proved equally well informed about certain secular matters too.

Of course, getting him to concentrate on these distant local issues had been a problem in itself. No sooner had Harry taken him aside and mentioned the Mortlake case, than Moses was looking him in the eye and saying, 'The evil deeds of the wicked ensnare them; the cords of their sins hold them fast.'

'Yeah, I'm sure you've got a point, but do you recall a detective agency here in Kellston? Currans they were called. Does it ring any bells? We're talking the seventies, early seventies. Around the same time as Christine went missing.'

Moses peered at him, his wrinkled forehead forming ever deeper grooves. 'Currans,' he repeated.

'Yes, do you remember them?'

The old man's attention was distracted by a couple of young women approaching, one with a baby in a pram. His tongue darted out, moistening dry lips. His eyes slid away from Harry and focused on the approaching prey.

'Moses!' Harry snapped, before he lost him to the cause. 'All those sinners are still going to be there after we've finished. Five minutes of your undivided attention. I'll make it worth your while.'

Although Moses was theoretically above worldly gain – surely sinful in itself – times were tough, a man had to eat, and the state pension didn't go far. Reluctantly his eyes focused back on Harry, and he let the women pass by without haranguing them.

'The Currans?' Harry prompted.

'What do you want to know about all that for? It was years ago, old history. Why are you digging up the past?'

'Because I'm being paid to dig it up. And if you want to be paid too, you'd better get on with it.'

'Two brothers,' Moses said quickly. 'Geoff and David.

Ex-army. Military police. Long gone now. They had an office on the high street.'

'Both dead?'

'Years ago.'

'What about family? Is anyone still around – widows, sons, daughters, grandkids?' Harry had already checked the Electoral Register and tried calling a few phone numbers he'd been able to find, but without any luck. 'Someone who was related?'

'Could be.'

'But you don't know for sure?'

'There were a couple of daughters. I couldn't say if they're still around. Might be, might not. I don't keep track of all the comings and goings.'

'But you could find out?'

Moses gave a shrug. 'Those Currans were tough boys, hard as nails.' He gave Harry a quick up and down as if, with his limp, he might not quite shape up in the macho stakes. 'Mortlake took them on to flush out George Greer.'

'Was that common knowledge?'

'Mortlake made sure everyone knew how he felt about Greer. Anyone who'd listen. Guilty, that's what he reckoned, guilty as—'

Before Moses could embark on yet another pithy quote from the Bible, Harry swiftly interrupted him. 'Was that the general opinion at the time Christine went missing? Did a lot of people think Greer was responsible?'

'Enough to drive the family out of Kellston.'

'And what did you think?'

'No smoke without fire. That girl went to their house and the next thing she's gone.' Moses clicked his fingers. 'Gone, just like that. Disappeared without a trace. I mean, you've got to draw your own conclusions, Mr Lind.'

91

'And I'm sure everyone did.' Harry took out his wallet and gave Moses a twenty. The information wasn't worth that, but he wanted to keep the old man interested. 'There's more where that came from if you can find a relative of the Currans. And sooner rather than later would be useful.'

'Blessed is the man who remains steadfast under trial,' Moses said. He grabbed the note, buried it quickly in the pockets of his overlarge overcoat, and scurried off to find the next target for his religious fervour.

Harry watched him, wondering what had happened in his life to make him what he was today. Perhaps the obsession with sin was down to some kind of repressed sexuality. Moses only ever approached women, and usually the young ones. Or maybe he was overthinking it all. It could just be that women were less likely to punch him in the face, although from what he knew of the Albert Road lot that was hardly a given.

15

When Harry got back to the office, Lorna was in the process of putting on her coat and preparing to leave. Her desk was clear, and everything was tidy. The room smelled of vanilla as if she'd given it a final squirt of air freshener to see it through to the end of the working day. 'Right, I'm off to feed the hungry ones.'

'You spoil those kids,' he said.

'Apparently, they don't thrive unless you feed them regularly.'

Harry grinned. 'Who knew?'

'Have a nice weekend. Don't spend it all here.'

'As if. You have a good one too. I'll see you on Monday.' Harry went through to his office and settled down at his desk where the Mortlake file was still open, the mystery still as obscure as it had been this morning. Although some progress had been made. Baby steps, but every little helped.

Over the next hour Harry typed up what he had learned from Alec Beddows, printed it out and added it to the file. Everything was on the computer, but he liked to have a hard copy, something more tangible that he could lay out in front of him, unexpected connections sometimes coming from a random rearrangement of papers.

He was still sifting through the information when the front-door buzzer went. Rising to his feet he walked into reception, pressed the button on Lorna's desk and spoke into the intercom. 'Hello?' There was no reply, only a thin crackle and the sound of traffic. 'Hello?' he repeated. This time he thought he could hear a distant voice, but it might just have been someone passing on the street. Hoping it was Moses, he released the lock to let him in.

'Push the door when you hear the click.'

Harry left the office door ajar and waited for his visitor. The footsteps coming up the stairs were light and not just one pair but two. He got a surprise when two scruffy kids, a girl of about ten and a younger boy, walked in. His first thought was that they'd made a mistake and come to the wrong place.

'Hello. Can I help?'

The girl had her school bag flung over her shoulder. 'You Mr Mackenzie?' she said.

'No, I'm the other one. Harry Lind.'

'You look for people, right. You're a detective?'

'Sometimes,' Harry said. 'I mean, sometimes I look for people.'

The girl nodded. 'Good. I need you to find my dad. His name's Ray Dunn.'

'Okay,' Harry said, perching on the edge of Lorna's desk so that he didn't tower over them. 'Well, we could try and do that, only I'd need permission from your mum first. Does she know you're here?'

'She's sick. She's got the flu. That's why she couldn't come with us.' Then before Harry could say anything else she quickly continued. 'Dad used to work at Froome's in Hackney. They sell

94

second-hand motors. He left there one day, a few years back, and never came home. The police reckon he just did a bunk, walked away and left us, but he wasn't like that, Mr Lind. He was a good dad, the best. He always took care of us.'

Now Harry was wishing that Lorna was still here. She knew how to deal with kids, and with tricky situations. He could see that the girl was upset although she was doing her best to hide it. 'Well look, why don't you get your mum to come and see me when she's feeling better. I can talk about it with her. I'm really sorry about your dad. We can certainly look for him but unfortunately there will be some charges involved.'

The girl's face fell but then instantly brightened again. 'Dad can pay you when you find him. He's got money. I know he has.'

'It doesn't quite work like that.'

'Then Mum can sort it out. But you can get started, can't you? If you find him, he can be home for Christmas.'

'What's your name, love?' Harry asked.

'Kayleigh Dunn.'

Harry looked at the boy. 'And yours?'

'He's Kit,' Kayleigh said. 'There's no point asking him, he doesn't talk.'

'You're the quiet one, huh?'

But Kit didn't respond, not even a smile. He just stared at him through wide blue eyes. He looked like one of those kids in the cheap living-room pictures you used to be able to buy in Woolworths, a street urchin with a solemn, almost angelic, face. Harry turned his attention back to Kayleigh.

'Okay, I think the best thing is for you to go home and chat to your mum. You know where I am. She can give me a call or just drop by.'

Kayleigh shook her head. She played with her lower lip for a while, as if trying to decide what to do next. 'Mum won't come here. She thinks he left us, but I know he didn't. Not deliberate like. Can't you help, Mr Lind? Can't you do something? He didn't take nothing with him when he left, not even clothes, not even his leather jacket and he loved that jacket.'

Sadly, leather jacket or not, Harry knew that some men had a tendency to scarper at the least hint of trouble, when a relationship turned sour, or the responsibility got too much, or they just couldn't be bothered anymore. 'So you haven't heard from him in the past few years?'

Kayleigh hesitated. 'Only a note three weeks after he left. It said sorry. And a bit of money, but that's all gone now. He probably thinks Mum's still mad at him, but she'd take him back, I know she would. She can't manage on her own. It's hard for her with the two of us. You should talk to that Carl Froome. I bet he knows where Dad went.'

'What makes you say that?'

'Because he was all shifty and angry when Mum went to see him. Swore blind he didn't have a clue where he was or why he'd left, but I reckon he was lying. He had one of those lying faces. Do you know what I mean?'

'Yeah, I know what you mean,' Harry said. Carl Froome was a piece of work, a nasty sod. He was also hand in glove with Danny Street, the local criminal psychopath. Street was into everything he shouldn't be – drugs, prostitution, extortion – and the proceeds were laundered through small businesses like Froome's.

'It would only take you five minutes,' Kayleigh said. 'How much would that cost?'

Harry had to give her ten out of ten for persistence. He grinned. 'To be negotiated ... with your mother.'

Kayleigh pulled a face. 'If I leave it up to her, we'll never find him.'

'You should go home before she starts worrying about you.'

'She won't worry. She thinks we're at the library.'

While Kayleigh was talking, Kit clung on to her hand, studying Harry intently as if he might be forced to answer questions about him later. Harry got to his feet, hoping to bring the exchange to an end. He felt sorry for them both but there wasn't anything he could do. He couldn't take instructions from a child even if he wanted to.

'Do you live on the Mansfield?' he said, although he didn't really need to ask.

'Yeah.'

Harry edged towards the door. 'It's dark. You should be getting back.'

'I ain't afraid of the dark,' Kayleigh said defiantly.

'Yes, but with . . . ' Harry stopped, not wanting to scare them with a reminder of what had just happened on the estate, but at the same time wanting them to take some sensible precautions. 'Still, it's getting late.'

'It's five past five,' Kayleigh said, glancing at the clock on the wall. 'That ain't late. It's still daytime.'

Harry remained firm, completing his walk to the door and opening it. 'I'm sorry I can't be of more help right now, but if your mum changes her mind, you know where I am.'

'Carl Froome,' Kayleigh said again as she and Kit left the office. She raised her face to him, her eyes bright and pleading. 'If you bump into him, accidental like, you could still ask, couldn't you? He might tell you something.'

Harry gave a vague smile, refusing to commit himself. 'You take care of yourselves.'

'And there's Dad's mum too. Margaret Dunn she's called. She lives in Essex someplace, but I don't know where. Mum had a row with her over Dad leaving and they don't talk no more. She might know where he is.'

'Essex is a big place.'

'You're a detective. You can find her.'

After the kids had gone, Harry sighed and wandered back to Lorna's desk. To him it seemed a sadly straightforward case of abandonment. The note and the money ruled out foul play, suggesting only a man with a bad conscience. But that was hardly something you could explain to a ten-year-old girl without smashing all her hopes and dreams.

Harry swore softly and then said, 'You've got a lot to answer for, Ray Dunn.'

16

Jem had spent the afternoon in a state of nervous tension. The sky darkened, dusk fell, and the streetlamps came on. Her gaze kept flying towards the window as if Aidan might suddenly appear, as if her worst nightmare might turn into reality. At half past four the door to Lind's office opened and a fair-haired middle-aged woman stepped briskly out, put up her umbrella, and jaywalked across the road to the Fox car park. Business partner, secretary, client? Not the latter, she thought, unless she'd missed her going in.

Twenty-five minutes later there was a more dramatic development. Just as Jem was starting to wonder if she might have overreacted to Lind's encounter with the God-botherer, she was astonished to see the two kids, Kayleigh and Kit, come trudging along the road, stop outside the office, stare at the door for a moment, press the buzzer and then walk in. What? She could hardly believe what she was seeing and suddenly all her worst fears were confirmed. She might have jumped to conclusions as regards Moses, but this was a coincidence too far.

Jem's hands curled into two tight fists. Was everyone in Kellston conspiring against her? Anger and fear churned her guts. She felt panic rising in her chest. She had to think. She had to do something. It was time to take a stand.

Customers were coming and going, and she tried to keep an eye on Lind's door as she wrapped flowers and took the money. The kids weren't there for long. Ten minutes after they'd entered the office, they were out again, turning right and walking towards the high street. What other reason could they have had for visiting other than to snitch on her, to tell Lind that her name was Jem, to sell her down the river?

Unless they were *his* kids. Could that be possible? But she instantly dismissed the idea. Why would they be living on the Mansfield, half starved by the looks of it, if they were his own flesh and blood? No, that didn't make any sense at all. She had been right all along about Lind. He was in league with Aidan Hague, and she had to do something about it.

The shop, after a brief flurry of activity, had gone quiet and so she asked Stefan if she could leave. Her hours were flexible, and she would always stay when she was needed, but business wasn't really brisk enough to justify the two of them being there. As soon as he agreed, she was in the back taking off her tabard and shrugging on her coat. She had to do it *now*, before she lost her nerve and skulked home to the Mansfield with nothing more than a Friday night full of fear and misery to look forward to.

Jem shot across the road, only narrowly avoiding an approaching cab. The driver honked his horn and glared at her. He probably swore at her too, but the traffic was too noisy for her to hear. She hurried over to the door of the private detective, saw the plaque with the names Mackenzie, Lind, and promptly jabbed at the intercom button.

There was a short delay before a voice responded. 'Hello?'

'I need to speak to Harry Lind,' she said as calmly and politely as she could. It took an effort but what she didn't want was for him to refuse to let her in, to leave her seething on the pavement with everything still unsaid. But she needn't have worried.

'Push the door when you hear the click.'

As soon as she heard the lock being released, Jem rushed inside. She stormed up the stairs, taking them two at a time, and burst into the reception area with her heart pumping and her eyes wild with anger.

Harry Lind was waiting for her. He smiled and said, 'Oh, hello, it's you.'

Jem, without even pausing for breath, launched straight into him. 'Are you proud of yourself, using kids to do your dirty work? I hope you're paying them well.'

To give him his due, Lind made a good job of looking shocked. 'What? I'm sorry, but I don't have a clue what you're talking about.'

'Don't give me that. First Moses and now Kayleigh and Kit. I'm not completely stupid. I know what you're doing, or at least what *he's* asked you to do: find out where she lives, what she's calling herself, what she's doing. Does it make you feel good spying on innocent people? Do you sleep well at night? Well, of course you do. Men like you, like *him*, don't have a conscience.'

Harry Lind raised his hands, palms out. 'Hey, slow down. Can we take a few steps back here? I don't know what you think you know, but you're completely wrong.'

'I know you're working for Aidan Hague. I know you're using those kids to get information on me. There's no point in denying it. Why can't you just be straight with me? Why can't you be honest about it?' Jem paused but only for a second. All her fears and frustrations were rising to the surface and spilling out. 'No, I suppose it's too much to ask. I mean, you make your living out of this kind of stuff, don't you? Well, I've had enough. I'm not just going to sit back and—'

'If you'd just calm down for a moment.'

Which was the kind of comment guaranteed to inflame Jem even more. 'Why the hell should I calm down? Who are you to tell me to calm down? This is my life we're talking about, or are you too stupid to realise that? I can't just—'

'Do you want to know why the kids were here? If you'll shut up for two minutes, I'll tell you. I think we need to sit down. Come into my office and we'll finish this conversation – if it can be called a conversation – there.'

Harry Lind walked off to the rear of reception, went into his office and sat down behind his desk. With little other choice, Jem followed him, still steaming and sure that all he was doing was playing for time. She ignored the chair that he gestured towards and remained standing with her arms folded across her chest, her eyes blazing.

'So?' she said. 'Have you worked out your story yet?'

Lind's eyebrows shifted up. He looked at her with an infuriating hint of a smile playing around his lips. 'Well, normally I'd quote client confidentiality to you, but seeing as those kids are way too young to be clients, I don't suppose I'm bound by that. You seem to have them pegged as some kind of informers but actually they're just looking for their dad. It's as simple as that. He took off three years ago. That's why they came here, to see if I could track him down.'

'And why should I believe that?'

'Because it's the truth. You clearly know the kids. Ask them. Have you seen their dad around recently?'

'I don't *know* them,' Jem said. 'They just live along the corridor from me.'

'So what makes you think they're spying on you?'

'Because they've been asking me questions, asking what my name is, and I keep bumping into them and . . . ' Jem could hear how weak it sounded when she spoke her suspicions out loud. 'And now they've been in here talking to you.'

'That's what kids do, ask questions. There's nothing odd about that.'

Jem felt herself on the back foot, but quickly rallied. 'So what about Moses? One minute he's on my case and you're helping to get rid of him and then the two of you are having a cosy chat in the street. And you're giving him money. You did give him money, didn't you?'

Lind sat back and put his hands behind his head. 'I think we could ask who's actually been doing the spying here.'

'I can't help it if I look out of the window and see you. And you're not answering the question. You did pay him, didn't you? What did you pay him for?'

'I paid him for information. Not that he told me much, but I'm hoping he'll come back with more.'

'What sort of information?'

'Nothing to do with you, if that's what you're thinking. It's for a case I'm working on, a missing girl, local.'

'I've not heard about any missing girl.'

'You wouldn't have. She disappeared a long time ago, over fifty years. A little before your time – or mine, come to that.'

Jem glanced down at the open file on his desk. There was a picture of a dark-haired girl in school uniform. 'Is that her?'

Lind's only answer was to flip shut the file.

'Why is someone looking for her after all this time?'

'Because someone still cares. And, returning to the subject, if I wanted to confirm your identity, I have better ways of doing it than hiring a couple of kids to provide me with information. Haven't you ever heard of the camera? What's to stop me taking a photograph of you and sending it to this Aidan Hague? It would seem a simpler option, and a cheaper one.'

Jem didn't like the smug look on his face. But what she liked even less was that he was right. Why the hell would he need to use Moses, use the kids, when all he had to do was pick up his camera and click? But she wasn't backing down right away. She was still too worked up to throw in the towel. 'Because . . . because I don't look the same. And for all I know you already *have* sent a photo, but he wants to be sure.'

'Ah, so you're a master of disguise.'

'Don't laugh at me,' she said, seeing his lips twitch again. 'None of this is funny.'

'No, it's not. You appear to be accusing me of all sorts of unpleasantness. If I was the sensitive type, I might take offence. Why don't you tell me why this Aidan Hague is looking for you.'

Jem shook her head. 'Why should I trust you? You could just be telling me a pack of lies.'

'I could, but I'm not. We're a respectable business, ex-cops, both of us. All legal and above board. And we don't go looking for anyone, especially women, unless we're sure of the client's intentions.'

'Cops aren't whiter than white,' Jem said. 'Plenty of them are bent or vicious or greedy.'

'You say that like you've had experience of it.'

'I read the papers. I hear things.'

Lind frowned, his fingers tapping out a gentle beat on the top of the brown folder. 'So where do we go from here? All I can do is give you my word. What you do with that is up to you.'

Jem stared at him. 'I don't know what to do with it.'

'If you tell me about Aidan, I might be able to help.'

'You can't help, no one can.' Jem's response was instinctive, automatic, her voice rising in pitch at the same time as her conviction that Lind was complicit in Aidan's vendetta was beginning to drain away. She glanced around the office, at its white walls and filing cabinets, at the dark oblong of evening visible behind Lind's head and knew that her paranoia had made her jump to unfortunate conclusions. She'd been wrong, she realised, about Lind, wrong about everything. Paranoia had overtaken take her, swamping all reason.

'You know my name,' he said. 'Why don't you tell me yours?'

'Jem,' she said. 'Jem Byrne.' She had a sudden sense of hopelessness, a wave of despair flowing over her. Slumping down in the chair, she put her head in her hands. 'I can keep running but he'll find me eventually. He'll never stop looking, you see.'

'Let's have some coffee,' Lind said. 'I think we're going to need it.'

But Jem, regretting her moment of weakness, quickly leapt to her feet. She couldn't face talking. She had learned not to do it, to keep her mouth shut, to stay in the shadows. 'Sorry,' she muttered, before fleeing from the office. She dashed through reception and clattered down the stairs like she had the devil at her heels.

17

Kayleigh didn't need to switch on the hall light to know that her mother was home: she could smell the pervasive stink of weed as soon as she entered the flat. Relief and anger surged through her. Dumping her school bag on the floor, she stomped through to the living room to find Nola curled up on the sofa wearing her dressing gown and watching TV. There was a half-drunk bottle of wine on the coffee table and an ashtray with the remains of a couple of joints.

'Where have you *been*?'

Nola stared at her through stoned eyes. 'What kind of greeting is that?' She looked round her to Kit and smiled. 'Hey, little man. Did you have a good day at school?'

'Since when did you care?' Kayleigh said. 'You left us with no leccy and no food. We could have starved to death.'

'Don't be so bleedin' dramatic. I've only been gone a day.'

'Three days!' Kayleigh retorted. 'What's wrong with you?' Not that she needed to ask. Once her mother got off her head, she had no idea of time. Still, at least she'd returned without any obvious bruises this time. 'If the social had come round, we'd be in care by now.'

'If the social had come round, you wouldn't have answered the door.'

Kayleigh knew this was true, but she rolled her eyes anyway. 'You can't just clear off and leave us here alone. It ain't safe. There's a girl that got killed here yesterday. Charlene her name was.' She would have liked to say more, to lay it on thick, but she had to be careful in front of Kit. 'Did you buy any food?'

'It's in the kitchen.'

Kayleigh went through to take a look. There was an un-packed carrier bag on the counter and inside were sausages, spuds, a bottle of milk and a pack of defrosting peas. She opened the fridge and bunged the peas in the icebox. It was typical of Nola that she couldn't even be bothered to put the shopping away.

After turning on the grill, she checked the leccy meter and saw that it was on just over nineteen quid, enough to keep them going for three or four days, but not much longer. The next government voucher should be coming soon and Nola, if she was around, would be able to top-up. The storage heaters ate money, but it was good to be warm again.

While the grill was heating up, she put the kettle on and peeled some potatoes. Had Nola been any kind of decent mother, she would be the one in the kitchen making dinner, but Kayleigh knew better than to wait for that miracle to happen. If they wanted to eat any time soon, she'd have to do the cooking herself.

Back in the living room Kit was sitting on the sofa, curled up beside Nola while she blew smoke over his head. Kayleigh leaned against the door jamb and frowned. 'Keep that stuff away from him. You want to get him stoned?'

Nola gave Kit a squeeze. 'Your sister's turning into a right old nag.'

'I have to go out later,' Kayleigh said. She'd promised Dion to be at his flat by six. That was when people got home from work or from wherever they'd been all day and decided that a bit of weed was what they needed to get them through the night. 'You're going to stay in, ain't you? You won't leave Kit on his own?'

'Where are you going?'

'Tracey's. We've got a project to finish for school.'

'You can do that over the weekend.'

'We can't. She's going to her gran's tomorrow.' Kayleigh knew that Nola wouldn't check, didn't know what number Tracey's flat was, didn't even know that they weren't really mates anymore. 'I won't be late.'

Nola's voice grew whiny. 'Why can't you do your project thing here?'

Kayleigh guessed that she wanted to sod off down the pub later and leave her to look after Kit. 'Because I can't. It's all arranged. Everything's at her place.'

'All right, but home by nine, yeah?'

Kayleigh went back to the kitchen, put the spuds on, and placed the sausages under the grill. While she was watching everything cook, she thought about Harry Lind. He could track down her dad; she was sure of it. He looked like the kind of bloke who could find people. Would he give it a shot? He'd said he wouldn't, not unless her mum went to see him, but she still had a glimmer of hope.

Kayleigh returned to the doorway of the kitchen, folded her arms and said casually, 'How come we never see Nana Dunn these days?'

'You know why not.'

'I don't remember.'

Nola sighed and raised her eyes to the ceiling. 'Because the old cow wouldn't tell me where your dad had gone. And don't say she didn't know because she damn well did. That woman would do anything to protect her precious little boy, even if we all had to suffer because of it.' She took another long pull on the reefer before stubbing it out in the ashtray. 'So that's why you don't see her no more. Because she chose him over us, chose him over her own grandkids. I mean, have you seen her knocking at the door recently? No, she doesn't give a damn if we're dead or alive.'

'Where does she live?'

Nola's eyes narrowed. 'What do you want to know that for?'

Kayleigh shrugged. 'I just wondered.' Her memories of Nana Dunn, Margaret, were starting to fade. She had been a big, noisy woman, always clashing heads with Nola, the two of them bickering from the moment she got through the door to the moment she left. But she'd usually brought sweets with her, big bags of Maltesers or Revels or Haribos.

'Well, you don't need to wonder. That bitch is never setting foot inside this flat again.'

Kayleigh decided that she'd check Nola's phone later, just in case there was an old contact number on it.

They ate their dinner on their knees, watching TV: bangers and mash and baked beans. Nola didn't ask where the beans had come from, probably didn't even think about it, as if tins of baked beans just appeared by magic in the kitchen cupboard. Kayleigh wanted to have another go at her about leaving them alone in the dark and the cold, about what a shitty thing it was to do, but Kit looked so content she couldn't bring herself to raise the subject again. She wasn't going to let it go, though. They'd have round two later, when he was in bed.

Just before six, Kayleigh grabbed her school bag, put on her coat and yelled goodbye from the front door.

'Nine o'clock, remember?' Nola called out to her.

Kayleigh didn't answer. She could have told Dion that she couldn't make it tonight, but she wanted the money. There was no knowing when Nola would do another disappearing act and leave them in the lurch again.

18

Kayleigh took the stairs down to the sixth floor, checked that the landing was clear and then walked quickly to Dion's and rang the bell.

'Hello, hon,' he said when he answered the door, his eyes automatically glancing left and right along the corridor. 'How are you doing?'

'Good, ta,' she said, gazing up at him. He was almost as tall as Harry Lind but dressed more casually in a pair of navy-blue joggers and a white vest. 'Got everything ready for me?'

'Sure,' Dion said. He reached out to a table just inside the door and picked up a small pile of envelopes, took another swift glance left and right and handed them to her. 'Eight in all. Six here and two for Carlton.'

Kayleigh was already opening her school bag. She deposited the envelopes and quickly pulled the zip across. Carlton House was next door, a tower identical to Haslow and connected by various walkways and tunnels. Good for keeping out of the rain if you didn't mind taking your chances with the muggers.

'Fast as you can,' he said. 'There'll be more by the time you get back.'

Kayleigh nodded.

'And watch out for the filth,' he added. 'They were here earlier, asking about that dead girl. Make sure you keep out of sight.'

Kayleigh walked to the top of the stairs, checked that no one was around and opened her bag. There were eight envelopes inside, each with a letter and number in the top right corner, and another number in the bottom left. The letter denoted which tower it was – Haslow, Carlton or Temple, the first number was the number of the flat, and the number at the bottom the amount of money that was owing. Most of the latter were tens and twenties, the residents of the Mansfield not having much cash to splash and just wanting a small amount of weed to see them through the weekend.

Kayleigh never worried about getting caught, partly because she was always careful, but mainly because she couldn't envisage her life being much worse than it currently was. Anyway, the law had other things on their mind right now. And they weren't much interested in the little dealers: it was the chiefs they wanted, the ones at the top of the tree, the Mr Bigs like Danny Street.

Kayleigh worked at speed, up and down in the lifts, knowing exactly where she was going. The transactions were fast too, a quick furtive exchange of cash for goods. She knew all the regulars, but no one stopped to chat. All the time she was wondering if Nola would stay put or if she'd clear off before she got back. It could be knocking on ten before the deliveries finished, and it wasn't beyond her mother to put Kit to bed and then go out.

There had been times in the past when Kayleigh had been faced with the choice of leaving Kit on his own or bringing him with her. But she'd always been too afraid to leave him. What if something happened? What if the flat burned down? She'd never forgive herself. She made sure he stayed out of sight of the customers though, and out of sight of Dion too.

While Kayleigh worked, she was careful to divide the money she took, half in her bag, the other half in the inside pocket of her jacket. That way, if she ever got robbed, she'd only lose half the cash. It was a trick Dion had taught her. Fortunately, no one had ever thought to try and snatch the takings: schoolkids don't usually walk around with anything worth stealing, and the other dealers hanging around near the entrances to the tunnels, watching out for the law, didn't look at her twice.

The hours passed quickly. She had just arrived back from another trip to Carlton House when she walked slap bang into Mrs Floyd in the lobby.

'And what are you doing out at this time of night, young lady?'

It was only half past nine. To hear her talk you'd think it was midnight or after. 'I've just been to see a mate.'

'You shouldn't be wandering round on your own. It's not safe, especially at the moment. And where's that little brother of yours?'

'Fast asleep, I should think,' Kayleigh said, even though the chances of it were slim. 'At home with Mum.'

'How is your mother?'

Kayleigh didn't like being interrogated. She didn't like being held up either. But she knew better than to get on the wrong side of the old bat and so didn't let her irritation show. 'She's okay. She's fine, ta. I'd better get back or she'll start to worry.'

Mrs Floyd's doubting expression implied, quite rightly, that Nola Dunn didn't do much worrying about her kids. 'I haven't seen her for a few days.'

'Oh, yeah, she's not been out much. She's had the flu.'

Kayleigh got in the lift with Mrs Floyd. The old woman was small and stooped and walked with a stick. She smelled of lavender and cough sweets. Her face was heavily wrinkled, her hair white as snow, but her eyes were sharp and bright.

'Flu, eh? There's a lot of it about. Mr Chapel was only saying yesterday that he thought he was coming down with something.'

Kayleigh was glad when the lift doors closed and they began the ascent. She'd had to press the button for the eighth floor just to prove that she was going where she said she was. 'I don't know him.'

'Balding,' Mrs Floyd said, 'but nice enough. He's always very helpful. I dare say you've seen him around. Fifty-odd, glasses, usually wears a beige anorak. He's not been here long, less than a year.'

But Kayleigh never took much notice of balding middle-aged men in anoraks. She shook her head, eager to get away and finish her work.

'Up on the sixth,' Mrs Floyd said.

Kayleigh gave a start. That was the same floor as Dion. She didn't like the idea of one of the old lady's spies being so close. 'Oh, what number's that then?'

Mrs Floyd, suddenly suspicious, inclined her head and frowned. 'Now what would you want to know that for?'

'Just wondered,' Kayleigh said, which was her go-to answer to any question she didn't want to answer directly.

'I can't recall offhand. My memory's not what it was.'

Which Kayleigh didn't believe for a minute. The woman was old – she looked about a hundred – but she still had all her marbles. And what did Mrs Floyd think she'd do with the information? Maybe ring the bell and run away, which was a common pastime for some of the kids in the block.

The lift stopped and Mrs Floyd shuffled out. 'Give my best to your mother, dear,' she said, and somehow made it sound more like a threat than a pleasantry.

'Yeah, I will.'

Kayleigh was glad to see the back of her. As the doors were closing, she quickly pressed the button for the sixth floor. But as she travelled up, she began to fret about this Chapel bloke. If he noticed her going to and fro from Dion's, he might mention it to Mrs Floyd. She got out of the lift and walked along the corridor, glancing sideways at every door she passed. He could be behind any one of them. She was relieved that this had been her final run. Once she'd handed over the cash, she could collect what was due to her and get going.

But then the unexpected happened. A few yards from Dion's, she noticed that his front door was ajar. She stopped dead in her tracks. *Damn.* Did he have a visitor? Should she wait for them to go? Or, knowing that she was due back shortly, had he left the door open for her? Except he'd never done that before. She stood in a state of indecision, unsure as to what to do next.

Thirty seconds passed and nothing changed. She glanced up and down the corridor. She went a little closer. The sound of Marvin Gaye's 'Let's Get It On' was coming from the flat – she knew it was Marvin because her dad had liked him too – but no other voices. Her instinct was to walk straight past, to go and wait on the stairs until the coast was clear, but she was impatient to get home.

Kayleigh stopped again by the flat, leaned in and listened. Just the music, nothing else. If someone was there, she'd hear them talking, wouldn't she? She gave a short ring on the bell. No one came. Perhaps he was having a wee. Perhaps he had fallen asleep. She nudged the door with the toe of her shoe and stepped inside.

'Dion?' she called out softly.

No response.

At first, because she was looking straight ahead, she only caught it out of the corner of her eye – a shape lying in the shadows of the long, narrow hallway that led off to the right. She turned her head and abruptly it came into focus. Her hand rose instinctively to her mouth. A gasp, a stifled scream, died on her lips. Her heart began to hammer. The rest of her froze.

Dion was flat on his back, his left leg twisted, his eyes wide and bulging. One smooth brown arm was bent at the elbow, one hand reaching for his throat. There was a ribbon of red wire embedded in his swollen neck. She went cold. She felt sick. She wanted to cry. She had watched enough cop shows on TV to know when someone was dead, when they were beyond help, when there was nothing that could be done.

And then, just as she was absorbing the awfulness of it, the horror, she thought she heard a sound. Something that cut through the music. Another thought leapt into her head: what if the killer was still here? He could be in the living room, the bathroom, anywhere. He could be watching her right now. That was when the adrenaline kicked in. On shaky legs, she backed out of the door and fled.

Kayleigh sprinted up the stairs, her feet barely touching the concrete, her right hand sliding along the rail. Panic surged through her. She couldn't think straight, couldn't breathe properly. *Dion was dead. Dion had been murdered.* How was that real? It couldn't be real. She had the image of him in her head, not the lifeless Dion – she couldn't bear to see that again – but the man he had been earlier, the man with the navy-blue joggers and the white T-shirt, the man who was young and alive and smiling. None of it made any sense. She prayed that she wouldn't bump into anyone, that no one would see her.

By the time she reached the eighth floor her lungs were

pumping, her heart pounding. But she didn't even pause. She ran to the flat, rummaged for the key with shaking hands, unlocked the door, closed it behind her and rushed into the living room. Had her mother been awake, she would have blurted out everything, told her the whole lot, but she was fast asleep on the sofa with her snores vying with the noise from the TV. Kayleigh picked up the remote and turned the volume down.

Then she stood, trembling, not knowing what to do next. Should she call 999? Nola's phone was sitting on the coffee table. But then she would have to explain what she was doing at Dion's, and she didn't reckon the law would take too kindly to her weed deliveries. In fact, they would probably drag her away and put her in some kids' home. Not prison, she was too young for that, but something that wasn't far off.

A fresh wave of panic swept over her. Would they know she'd been at Dion's flat? Had she left fingerprints? No, she hadn't touched anything, and she was sure she'd nudged open the door with her foot. But what if someone had seen her? Well, Mrs Floyd had, but that had been down in the lobby. Would the old bat tell? Would she make the connection? If Kayleigh was questioned, what would she tell the law? If she said she'd been at Tracey's and they checked, they'd soon find out that it was a lie. She would have to think of another story, but what?

She rubbed her face and ran her fingers through her hair. Her pulse was still racing, her breath still jagged. And then there were the customers, all the people she'd delivered to tonight. But they weren't going to admit to buying weed, were they? At least they weren't going to *volunteer* the information. She didn't think so. Which meant they wouldn't grass her up either.

Kayleigh stared down at her mother, sighed and retreated to the bedroom that she shared with Kit. He stirred in his sleep but didn't wake up. She left the door half open so that some light filtered in from the living room. Her heart was slowing now, the sweat cooling on her back, but her teeth had started to chatter. She clenched her jaw and tried to fight off the fear.

It was only as she slumped down on the bed that she remembered she still had the cash from the deliveries. She couldn't give it back, not now. And it was a lot. The last run had been longer and busier than the others. She took the money from her jacket pocket and the bag, and carefully counted it out. Two hundred and twenty pounds. She would never have stolen from Dion, but this wasn't stealing, was it? The cash was no use to him now. Poor Dion. She didn't like that many people on the estate, or anywhere come to that, but he'd always treated her fairly. And now he was gone. Gone, like her dad. Well, not exactly like her dad because he was still alive somewhere. And that was when the idea came to her. If Harry Lind needed money before he started searching, then she had some right here.

19

It had happened ten minutes ago. Phillip had been on his way back from the bog when he heard the footsteps out on the landing, the quick slap of soles against lino, coming towards the flat. His first thought was the police, and he froze by the door waiting for the bell to ring. He held his breath. This was what he'd been dreading, a return visit, a proper interrogation about his movements on the night Charlene had been murdered. Perhaps they would even arrest him.

But the bell hadn't gone. The footsteps carried on and then abruptly stopped. Phillip exhaled softly, leaned in towards the door and peered through the spyhole. Nothing but an empty bit of corridor. Whoever it was must be just out of sight.

Chapel had come out of the living room and said, 'What's going on?'

Phillip had turned and put a finger to his lips. He'd waited until the footsteps had resumed before quietly opening the door a crack and peering out. Hell, it was just a kid! One of Nola's brats, the girl with the long brown hair. He followed her progress almost to the end of the corridor where she stopped by the flat of the young black guy who lived there. Dion something his name was. Phillip was sure he was a dope dealer. Once, in the lobby, he'd seen him pass a tiny package to someone and palm some cash in return.

Phillip had watched as the girl went into the flat, stayed there for a minute, and then hurried off towards the stairs. He'd closed his own door and said to Chapel, 'She must be picking up some weed for that deadbeat mother of hers.'

'Who?'

'Nola Dunn's kid. She's just been to that Dion's flat.'

'Mrs Floyd would have something to say about that.'

Phillip reckoned she would, but he wasn't going to share the information with her. He didn't want her passing it on, saying that Mr Chapel had told her this or told her that, as before long he'd become known as a gossip as big as she was. 'Mrs Floyd isn't going to find out. Well, not from me, at least.'

'Probably wise. She'd only shoot her mouth off. You don't want social services knocking on your door as well as the law.'

They had come back into the living room and now Phillip drifted over to the window. Earlier in the day, he had seen Nola Dunn tottering through the estate on her stiletto heels, her bare legs thin and pale, her miniskirt barely preserving her modesty. The rain had been coming down hard, plastering her peroxide blonde hair to her skull. She'd had a fag in one hand and a carrier bag in the other.

Chapel yawned, not bothering to cover his mouth. 'Yeah, you should keep quiet about the tart, especially if she's next on the list.'

'There is no list. Forget about the list.'

'Don't tell me you're getting cold feet, Phil? Jesus, we've barely got started. I never took you for a quitter.'

'It's not to do with being a quitter.'

'What is it to do with then?'

But Phillip didn't see why he should have to explain himself to the likes of Chapel. He sat down at the table and stared at the screen of his laptop. Maybe he should dump everything he'd written up till now and start a new book. What about *Death of a Psychopath*? Yes, that had a certain ring to it.

'What, trying to get shot of me now?'

Phillip ignored him.

'You know you need me, mate. I'm the only real friend you've got.' Chapel leaned down and whispered in his ear. 'One murder isn't enough. We should do Nola next. I mean, what kind of mother gets her kid to buy weed for her? It's immoral, shameful. In fact, it's pretty much your civic duty to eliminate the whore. It's only what she deserves.'

'Easy for you to say. You're not the one who'll be spending the rest of your life in jail. And I didn't kill Charlene, so you can drop all that "one murder isn't enough" business.'

'Come on, there's got to be some jeopardy, Phil. Otherwise, what's the point? Use your imagination. You've just got the jitters. They'll settle down in a day or two.' Chapel gave a light laugh. 'You remember what Freya used to say?'

Phillip scowled, preferring not to think about his ex-wife. 'She said a lot of things.'

'She said you had no balls, Phil. You don't want to prove her right, do you? You want to give up at the first hurdle? What kind of a book is this going to be if you're going to run and hide at the first sign of trouble?'

'No one's hiding.'

'You could have fooled me. If you're trying to act like an innocent man, then holing up in this flat isn't doing you any favours.'

'I've got a book to write.'

'You need to get rid of that anorak. And buy some more whisky. You always write better when you've had a few. Like Hemingway. I don't mean that you *write* like Hemingway – that would make you a bloody genius – just that he used the booze to oil the cogs.'

Most of Phillip's cogs had ground to a standstill since Charlene had been murdered, and the only ones still moving were too preoccupied with the police, with the fear of being accused, to concentrate on anything more literary. He was almost convinced that he was innocent, but a small, disturbing element of doubt remained. There was still that blank in his memory, that black hole between passing through the gates of the Mansfield and waking up the following morning.

Phillip, frightened by the stain, had already ordered another anorak off the internet, one that was similar although not identical to his old one. He'd have to scruff it up when it arrived, make it look less new. He didn't want Mrs Floyd noticing and wondering why he'd suddenly replaced a perfectly good coat. 'How am I going to get rid of it? I can't put it in the bin. The police might still be going through the rubbish.'

'Put it in a bag and take it into town tomorrow,' Chapel said. 'Dump it there. You could do with getting out.'

But Phillip had visions of bumping into Mrs Floyd in the lobby, of her eyeing up the bag and asking what was inside. It sounded ridiculous but he wouldn't put it past her. The woman had no boundaries. She thought it was her right to interfere, to ask anything she liked, to poke her nose into everyone's business. Or, even worse, what if the police stopped him? What if they were waiting for the killer to do something stupid? He could be caught red-handed, trying to dispose of the evidence.

'For God's sake,' Chapel said. 'Pull yourself together. You're being pathetic.'

20

Shortly after ten, Harry Lind locked up the office and crossed the road to the Fox. He was in a decent frame of mind, not overjoyed but not in the depths of despair either. Earlier in the evening an email had arrived from Vivienne Bayle, agreeing to a meeting and suggesting a café in Covent Garden at midday tomorrow. It was another of those small steps but one that could prove useful. If anyone had known the real Christine, what she would and wouldn't have been capable of, it was probably her best friend.

When he finally got served, he ordered a pint of Guinness and stayed by the bar to drink it. The usual crowd was in – people celebrating the end of the working week, meeting their mates or drowning their sorrows – and every table was taken. He preferred to stand anyway, to stretch his legs after sitting at his desk for so long. With his height he had a good view over the main room.

Harry liked the Fox. It was the one redeeming feature of Kellston's otherwise inner-city bleakness, a warm and welcoming oasis. There was no TV, no pool table or fruit machines, and the music was played low enough to enable you to think. Since he'd last been in, the decorations had gone up and now a Christmas tree, festooned with tinsel, baubles and fairy lights, dominated the far corner. There were bunches of holly on the walls and sprigs of mistletoe hanging from the ceiling, the latter unlikely to be of much use to him unless his love life took a sudden turn for the better.

Harry's mind should have been on the Mortlake case but instead he was thinking about Jem Byrne. After she'd taken off so abruptly, he'd been left with enough unanswered questions to prompt him to do an internet search. Aidan Hague, it transpired, had been convicted of the murder of a girl called Georgia Mason – deliberately mowing her down in the street – and of the attempted murder of Jemima Byrne, his former girlfriend. He'd been given fifteen years, which meant, if he'd behaved himself inside, that he was probably free now. Which would tally with Jem's concerns about him being on the hunt for her. Concerns? The word hardly covered it, he thought. Blind terror was closer to the mark.

Harry didn't come across many Jemimas in his line of work. He'd found an old photograph of her, taken after the sentencing, looking very young and blonde and fragile. Eighteen she'd been then. She looked different now, but not unrecognisable. Hague had changed his plea at the last minute to guilty. There were photos of him too, a tall, fair-haired, handsome man who looked more like a Californian surfer than a drug-dealing killer from Blackpool.

Further online searches hadn't produced anything more recent, no Facebook or Instagram or Twitter accounts for Hague. Nothing for Jem Byrne either. Both of them keeping a low profile but probably for very different reasons. He considered giving Valerie a call to try and get more information on

Hague – she was working up in Manchester now, which wasn't *that* far from Blackpool – but couldn't decide whether he wanted to hear her voice again or not.

Since the end of their relationship Valerie had moved on in every way: new job, new location, new partner. She was a DI now. It probably wasn't a good idea to get in touch. Harry didn't like to dwell on the past but sometimes it crept up on him all the same. He'd been hell to live with after he'd come out of hospital, bitter at his inability to do his job, resentful that *she* was still leaving for work every day, too wrapped up in his own anger and self-pity to see the wood for the trees. Everything she'd said and done had been wrong, because there'd been nothing to say or do that would have been right.

Harry wasn't proud of any of it. That she'd stuck around for as long as she had was a credit to her. But everyone has their breaking point. Hers had been reached and the relationship had crumbled. It would be true to say he had regrets, but he knew they were pointless.

He was still pondering on whether it was his place to interfere in Jem Byrne's business when he noticed Carl Froome sitting with a mate at a table near the Christmas tree. Fate, a sign, co-incidence? No, none of those. He'd seen Froome in here before. But what were the odds of seeing him on the very same day that Kayleigh and her brother had turned up uninvited at his office? Not that long, he thought. The Fox was the best pub for miles around and anyone who wanted a decent pint on a Friday night was likely to show up here.

Harry only knew Froome by reputation, and that reputation wasn't a good one. There were plenty of rumours about him and his dodgy motors: that some of them were cut-and-shuts – two cars that had been written off and welded into one – and that the rest were either overpriced or nicked. Then there was his connection to the infamous Danny Street. The Street family had ruled Kellston for years but now the old patriarch, Terry, was past his prime, and past being able to control his psychopathic son too. Danny ran most of the girls on Albert Road and supplied most of the drugs in the area. He was a law unto himself: brutal, nasty and vicious.

Harry surreptitiously studied Carl Froome, being careful not to keep his eyes on him for too long. The car dealer was a small but muscular man in his forties with brown receding hair, a pasty complexion and a lurid collection of tattoos. He looked like he spent half his life down the gym and the other half putting coke up his nose: there was something hyper about him, something over-confident. Why was he even watching the bloke? It wasn't as if he was going to approach him. Except Kayleigh's pleading voice had crept into his head. *If you bump into him, accidental like . . .*

Harry felt sorry for the kids, abandoned by their father and with a mother who, reading between the lines, was probably not coping too well with the joys of single parenthood. He understood how relationships broke down, how people could no longer bear to live together, but what he couldn't understand was how men – and it usually was men – walked away from their children too. What sort of bloke dumped his own flesh and blood? Deadbeats, he decided, wasters who didn't deserve to have kids in the first place.

But it wasn't any of his business. Don't interfere, Harry told himself. He hadn't been officially hired and it wasn't his place to go poking his nose in, even if Kayleigh's plea had pulled on his heart strings. At the very moment that this thought was going through his head, Froome's mate rose to his feet, picked up two empty pint glasses and made his way over to the bar. While the bloke was waiting to be served, Harry made a snap decision, swallowed down the rest of his Guinness, put aside his misgivings and quickly strode over to Froome.

'Sorry to disturb you, but could I have a quick word?'

Carl Froome looked up at him and scowled. 'You the filth?'

'No.'

'You smell like the fuckin' filth.'

'A private investigator,' Harry said, taking a business card from his wallet and laying it on the table.

Froome nudged the card into a puddle of beer and smirked. 'Same thing, ain't it?'

Harry kept his expression neutral. He pulled out the vacant chair and sat down. 'I'm making some enquiries into the disappearance of Ray Dunn. I understand he used to work for you.'

A hint of something – surprise, anxiety? – flickered across Froome's face, but then as quickly disappeared. He laughed artificially. 'Jesus, don't tell me that fuckin' tart Nola Dunn is at it again?'

Harry neither confirmed nor denied it. 'Again? When was the first time?'

Froome hesitated, as if in two minds whether to be cooperative or not. Then, unable to resist the opportunity for a spot of badmouthing, he said, 'Right after he scarpered. Three years ago, or so. And not just once. She was round the lot four, five times, shooting her mouth off, screaming at me like some bloody banshee, calling me a liar and a load more too. The first time right in front of her kids and all. I mean, what kind of mother behaves like that? And how the hell would I know where he'd gone? I was as much in the dark as she was. One minute he's there and the next . . . he left me right in the lurch, pissing off like that. Then I had the law on my back too, wanting to look at the CCTV, giving me hassle when it was nothing to do with me. I mean, how is it my fault if he decided to do one?'

Harry thought Froome was talking too much, which could have been down to the coke or, just as likely, because he had something to hide. Up close he could see the pinprick pupils of the man's eyes and a sheen of sweat on his forehead. 'You've no idea why he left so suddenly?'

'I'd have done a bloody runner too if I was married to *that*.'

'But no other reason that you know of? Nothing out of the ordinary happened at the lot that day?'

'What other reason did he need?' Froome shrugged his muscular shoulders. 'No, nothing happened, or if it did, he never said nothing to me. Mind, he wasn't what you'd call the chatty sort. He kept himself to himself when he wasn't flogging motors.'

'Was he a good salesman?'

'Average. But he turned up every day, which was more than some. I'd have called him reliable until he did what he did. He went for his lunch at one o'clock and that was the last we ever saw of him.'

'Where did he usually go for his lunch?'

'No idea, mate.'

'Weren't you concerned when he didn't come back? That he might have had an accident, perhaps?'

Froome shook his head. 'He would have called to tell us. Or someone would have. Maybe he had a fancy piece tucked away, decided the grass was greener someplace else. I dunno. But you can tell Nola bloody Dunn that it was nothing to do with me. I know as much as I did three years ago, and if she even thinks about coming round the car lot again—'

Harry interrupted before he could complete the threat. 'Was he the type to just leave his kids like that? Three years is a long time to have no contact.'

'How the hell would I know?' Froome was getting agitated

now, irritated by the questions. 'He worked for me, that's all. I never knew the ins and outs of his private life. Look, are we done here? I've got better things to do on a Friday night than talking about that waste of space.'

Harry could see the mate approaching with a couple of fresh pints, and guessed he wouldn't get anything more out of Froome. 'Thanks for your time. My number's on the card. If you think of anything useful, give me a call.'

'Yeah, well if you do catch up with the bastard, tell him I want my fuckin' Nissan back. He still owes nine payments on that motor.'

'I'll be sure to pass the message on.'

Harry returned to the bar, where he ordered another Guinness and thought about the exchange. He suspected Froome of lying, or at the very least of avoiding the truth, but that was probably his natural character. Was the bloke just irked at Ray Dunn for leaving him in the lurch, for bringing down the wrath of Nola, or was there something more? He glanced over at the table where the two men had their heads together, talking quickly, their expressions sour. Harry had the feeling that he'd ruffled a few feathers, and that was never a bad thing.

21

It was early Saturday morning, and Jem wasn't due in work for another hour. She had eaten breakfast, had two cups of tea and now she was killing time until she could leave the flat. Her night had been restless, filled with frantic dreams. Fragments floated back to her, faint and yet threatening, wispy tendrils that coiled around the inside of her head. She tried to push them aside. There was enough to fret about without her unconscious joining in too. She regretted having told Harry Lind about Aidan, regretted crossing over the road to see him, regretted the moment she had let her fear get the better of her. Lind might be all he said he was, but even one person knowing her secret felt like one too many.

While she fought against the temptation to pack up her things and run, she was sketching out a picture on her pad, a drawing of two children holding hands. Like Hansel and Gretel, she thought, except the girl was the older one in this story. And the kids weren't alone in the wood but walking through the concrete jungle of the Mansfield estate. They also looked suspiciously like Kayleigh and Kit.

She could imagine the finished painting, most of it in shades of grey, with brief pops of colour from the children's clothing. The sky would be dark, low and ominous. Haslow House would loom over them, emphasising their smallness: two tiny figures abandoned by their parents and left to fend for themselves in a dangerous place. Of course Kayleigh and Kit had a mother – but was she a good one? – and only their father had deserted them.

Jem immediately thought of her own dad. He had not abandoned her in the conventional sense, but he'd been relieved, she was sure, when she had chosen to live with her grandparents. Although the awful, shattering loss of her mum had temporarily crushed her, she had learned to live with the pain as she got older. Consolation had been found in the unconditional love of her grandparents, and sanctuary in the little shop they owned.

The shop, set just off Lytham seafront, hadn't been anything fancy, just a small store selling affordable jewellery and offering repairs on necklaces, bracelets, clocks and watches. There had been nothing she had liked better than to sit beside Gramps and watch him as he worked, his nimble fingers restoring what had once been broken. He would sing while he worked, old Irish songs he had learned as a child, melodies that remained with her to this day.

Remembering made the breath catch in her throat. She wondered why it was that you could only see happiness in retrospect, that when you were in the middle of it, the contentment never registered properly. It was only later, looking back, that you realised how much you had lost. She lifted her head, pencil poised in mid-air, and reflected on the power of the past, on its ability to sweep right over you when you least expected it, to drown you in regret.

At fifteen she had been as happy as any teenager. Suffering from frustration, perhaps, from the ennui that comes from the longing for your real life to begin, from the claustrophobia of a small town, but not unduly miserable. Until . . . and there he was again, the loathsome Aidan Hague, slithering into her mind like a poisonous snake. She could try and try, but she could never free her head of him. He had blighted her life, terrorised her, tormented her and turned her into someone afraid of her own shadow. A fairy-tale villain if ever there was one, a wolf in sheep's clothing, her very own Pied Piper.

There was nothing extraordinary about her story. It was dull and banal, hackneyed, a tale played out a million times before by manipulative men and credulous girls. At fifteen she'd been ripe for the picking. The first time she'd seen him . . . why did she keep going over it? As if she could change the past, twist history, make it all never happen.

Aidan had given the impression of being both cocky and shy at the same time, which, to give him credit, was no mean feat. But then he'd had plenty of practice. She was hardly the first girl he'd led down the path to purgatory. And he'd set his trap skilfully, luring her in with the promise of romance, of tenderness and warmth, a happy-ever-after scenario that was about as far from reality as lies were from the truth.

Grooming was the name for it, but back then she'd called it love.

If Gramps hadn't died suddenly, if her gran hadn't coiled in on herself, if there had been someone there to look out for her, maybe things would have been different. But what ifs were pointless. And anyway, she was only making excuses. She could line up all those justifications in a row – youth, innocence, naïveté – and shoot them down like fairground ducks. She should still have seen him coming.

Jem glanced down at the drawing. Aidan had always mocked her watercolours. 'Why don't you paint something cheerful?'

132

he'd say, suspecting – quite rightly – that the gloominess of her artwork reflected her general unhappiness. Not that he would have cared about that. Causing unhappiness was Aidan's *raison d'être*. He was never more content than when he was inflicting pain on others.

Her face twisted. She despised the woman she'd become – weak, insular, afraid of anyone and everyone. For a decade, while Aidan was inside, she'd been able to build some semblance of a life, but all that had quickly disintegrated when she'd heard he was coming out. Perhaps she had never been able to truly move on. The few relationships she'd embarked upon had been brief, unsatisfactory affairs, her antennae poised for the first sign – real or imagined – of possessiveness or manipulation, at which point she had severed all ties and withdrawn back into herself.

For some reason, she suddenly thought of the missing girl Harry Lind was looking for. She had only caught a glimpse of her picture: about twelve or thirteen, dark hair, dark eyes. Lost for fifty years. Except lost wasn't the right word. Dead, in all likelihood. What had happened to her? Who had taken her? She couldn't see how he could hope to find out after so much time had passed. Some horrors stayed buried for ever.

Jem shivered, imagining what the girl had gone through. She knew what fear felt like, real fear, the sort of terror that turned your guts to liquid. She didn't want to look back – it revived too many horrors – but she couldn't escape the memories. They were imprinted on her, stained into her skin, as permanent as unwanted tattoos.

She frowned, put the pencil down and pushed the drawing away. How was it, she wondered, that Kayleigh, a mere child, had the nous and the courage to walk straight into a private detective's office and ask for his help? The innocence of youth, perhaps. Or the ignorance. She, on the other hand, baulked at even talking about her own problems. Maybe she should take a leaf out of Kayleigh's book. Maybe it was finally time to face things head on.

22

Harry was in Covent Garden by quarter to eleven. It was a busy place to meet, heaving with Christmas shoppers, tourists, mums and kids. An opera singer, watched by a shifting crowd, was belting out arias in front of St Paul's church, and he had to jostle his way across the piazza. Eventually he found the café, went inside, spotted an empty table, grabbed it, sat down and ordered a latte. He was early but he didn't mind. It would give him time to think about Vivienne Bayle and what he was going to ask her.

He had looked her up on IMDb, a website that provides lists of actors' credits, and discovered that she'd had a steady if not sparkling career, mainly minor parts in TV soaps and dramas. Her photograph – red hair, brown eyes, wide smile – didn't betray much of her character, although her face was a pleasant one. She was sixty-four or thereabouts and he wondered how much work she got these days in an industry that was so youth obsessed. He hoped she wasn't going to be one of those overly artistic types, all affectation and exaggerated gestures, the sort who called everyone 'darling'.

What he was really aiming for with this meeting was an insight into Christine Mortlake's personality, a different perspective from the one her mother had provided. Whether this would help in the investigation was debatable, but it might, at a stretch, cast some light on what she might or might not have done that long-ago Sunday afternoon. There were other matters too – he had a list in his head – which she could be able to help him with.

Harry was halfway through his coffee when the door to the café opened, and Vivienne Bayle swept in. She was one of those women who made an instant impact, not because she was beautiful or glamorous but because she carried about her an air of friendly exuberance. She was small, leaning towards plumpness, and was dressed in a camel coat with a silk scarf at her neck. He had the advantage of already knowing what she looked like and so immediately rose to his feet to save her the bother of searching him out.

'Mr Lind, I presume,' she said when she reached the table, smiling.

'Call me Harry,' he said as they shook hands. 'Thanks for coming. Can I get you a coffee?'

'Viv,' she said. 'Yes, a cappuccino would be great. I'm not late, am I?' She glanced at her watch. 'Sorry, I didn't realise what a scrum it would be out there.'

There was a short flurry of post-handshake activity while he got the attention of the waitress, and she removed her coat and hung it over the back of the chair before they sat down and faced each other again.

'Heavens,' she said, 'it gave me quite a shock when I read the email. Poor Christine. It's a terrible thing to admit, I feel bad even saying it, but I've hardly thought about her for years.'

'You shouldn't feel bad. We all have to get on with our lives, even when dreadful things happen.'

Vivienne sighed. 'It still makes you feel kind of treacherous somehow. Disloyal. And guilty. I don't know. So has something changed? Have you got new information?'

'Early days. As Lorna explained in the email, I've recently been hired by Celia Mortlake to take a fresh look into Christine's disappearance.'

'God, Celia must be a good age now. I didn't realise she was still alive.'

'In her late eighties, but she's still got all her wits about her. I did explain to her, at length, that the chances of finding out anything new were slim, but she insisted on proceeding. One last go, I suppose, at discovering the truth, however painful it might be.'

Vivienne put her elbows on the table, linked her fingers together and balanced her chin on the plateau of her hands. 'I can understand that. I'm a mum myself – two girls – and I'd never let it go, however bad the odds. It must have been awful for her, all these years of not knowing. I'm not sure how I can help, though. I mean, I'd like to, but I'm as much in the dark now as I was back then.'

'Maybe you can help in other ways. About Christine, for example. What was she like? What kind of girl was she?'

Vivienne left a long pause. 'Sorry,' she said eventually. 'I was trying to think of how to describe her. It's hard when it was all so long ago. I don't mean that I've forgotten but the picture gets kind of blurred, and you start to wonder if you're remembering properly.'

'That's all right. Take your time.'

'She was fairly quiet, I suppose. Well, in comparison to me. I was always the noisy one.' Vivienne gave a small self-deprecatory smile. 'So not an extrovert but not shy either. Somewhere in between, I suppose. And she was clever, good at school, naturally clever without ever having to try that hard. I don't think either of us really fitted in – I was too careless, she was too cautious – but maybe that's why we got on. We had a nice balance and we trusted each other. We had each other's backs.'

'What did you talk about back then?'

'God, now you're asking! What *do* twelve-year-old girls talk about? Nothing profound, that's for sure. Pop stars, I suppose, and actors, films, TV, teachers, other girls at school. Our lives weren't what you'd call a rich tapestry.'

'What about boys?' Harry suggested.

Vivienne laughed. 'Not in the sense you mean. Perhaps we would have done in a year or two but then it was just mild crushes on the unobtainable: David Cassidy, Donny Osmond, Michael Jackson. It was 1971, remember. Girls didn't grow up so quickly in those days. We might have dreamed of kissing David, but we'd have run a mile at the prospect of kissing a real boy.'

The cappuccino arrived, creating a break in the conversation. Harry waited until the sugar had been added, the drink stirred, before continuing. 'And her parents? What did you make of them?'

'They were pretty strict.' Vivienne held the cup to her lips and blew across the surface. 'Strict compared to mine, at least. They kept her on a short leash, as they say. She wasn't even allowed to go to the local youth club on a Friday night. Too many bad influences. Girl Guides once a week and that was about it. Oh, and Amy's of course.'

'Did that frustrate her?'

'Of course it did. That's why she liked coming over to mine. We could get out of the house, go for a wander in the park, go to the Wimpy and have a Coke. I know it doesn't sound like much, but it was a big deal to her. A bit of freedom.' Vivienne drank some more coffee. 'I didn't like him, if that's what you're asking. Her father. He was very old-fashioned, the type who liked to rule the roost, keep everyone in their place. Head of the household and all that. A bit of a tyrant if I'm being honest.' She pulled a face. 'I suppose I shouldn't speak ill of the dead. And I didn't see that much of him, so I'm basing most of my opinions on what Christine told me.'

'And what did she tell you?'

Vivienne left another of those pauses. 'Perhaps it was more what she didn't tell me. I got the impression that she was scared of him, although she never came right out and said it. She'd wrinkle her nose whenever his name came up, say something dismissive, but her face would go all pale and tight. And it's not the sort of thing you ask about, not at that age, not straight out. You haven't really got the words.'

'Scared, though,' Harry said. 'It's a strong impression.'

Vivienne's forehead creased into a frown. 'Maybe scared isn't right. Just intimidated. I don't know. I could be making too much of it. I don't want to mislead you.'

'And her mother? Celia? What was Christine's relationship like with her?'

'Oh, not too bad. Mums and daughters. There's always friction. But no, not too bad. Celia was a terrible snob, you know – appearances were everything – but she wasn't unkind, Overprotective perhaps, but some mothers are just like that. She was always nice to me.' A shadow fell across Vivienne's face. 'I suppose I should have made more of an effort to keep in touch. Mum did, for a year or so, but when nothing changes it's hard to know what to say. We moved to Richmond, and she gradually rang less and less until she stopped altogether. I know she felt guilty about that.'

'Did you move because of Christine?'

'Partly. My nan, Dad's mum, was getting on and the

Richmond house was too big for her. It made sense for us all to live together. Although I think my parents did get the jitters and decide that we should live somewhere greener, somewhere less dangerous. Not that Bloomsbury *was* dangerous, but you know what I mean. They had that fear that all parents have: that the same thing might happen to me. And I didn't mind moving because I didn't much like school without Christine, so I suppose it all worked out.'

'You liked it in Richmond?'

Vivienne gave a soft laugh. 'I must have done. I'm still there. I moved back in after my divorce, and I've stayed there ever since. Mum and Dad are dead now and my two girls have lives of their own, but I let out a few rooms to aspiring actors, and out-of-work actors, and various waifs and strays that come my way. It gives me some income and some company too.'

'Were your parents in the business? Acting, I mean?'

'Only Mum. She was quite well known for a while. Jackie Lister? The film actress? She flapped a hand. 'Before your time. She gave it up when she got married. It's odd to think of that now, isn't it? Women giving up their careers to stay home and clean the house and have a lovely dinner on the table for when hubbie gets home.'

'Happy days,' Harry said drily.

'The things we do for love.'

'What about your dad? What was his line?'

'Richard Bayle. He was a barrister.'

'You must have missed Christine back then. It's tough losing your best friend.'

Vivienne played with the teaspoon in her saucer. She glanced up at Harry. 'I've never really grieved for her, you know, not properly. In my mind she's still in a strange kind of limbo – probably dead, but not definitely – and grieving would be like

140

giving up on her. Hope springs eternal and all that. Or maybe it's just easier, less painful, not having to face it full on, putting it to one side until there isn't any doubt. Do you think she'll ever be found?'

'I don't know,' Harry said honestly. 'Sometimes when you stir things up, new evidence rises to the surface. Sometimes all you get is a big fat nothing. We'll have to wait and see. From what I've heard, the original police investigation wasn't all it could have been. They were so concentrated on the Greers, they didn't bother looking anywhere else. You knew Amy, didn't you? Were you friends?'

'I wouldn't say friends exactly. We didn't go to the same school. The only time I ever saw her was when I was round at Christine's. She was all right, quite funny, but I think we bored her.'

'What makes you think that?'

'She was . . . how shall I put it? A bit mocking. Like we were posh girls who needed taking down a peg or two. She was never directly hostile but there was always something there in the background, a kind of frisson of disdain. And she seemed older than us, even though she wasn't. More sophisticated. Is that what I mean?' Vivienne stroked her chin with a knuckle. 'I'm not sure. Just more streetwise, perhaps.'

'Did you ever go to her house?'

Vivienne shook her head. 'No, I only ever saw her at Christine's. I never met her parents either. It was bad what happened to the Greers, wasn't it? Mum said they were hounded out of Kellston, that Arthur Mortlake turned everyone against them. Which is pretty awful if they *were* innocent.'

'Did your mum believe they were?'

'On the fence, I think. She felt sorry for Celia, desperately sorry, but she sympathised with the Greers too. What if they were telling the truth and Christine had never been there? Nobody saw her go into the house. Nobody saw anyone leave. She could have gone somewhere else entirely.'

'She could,' Harry agreed.

'I think it annoyed my father, her saying that. He was of the same opinion as Arthur Mortlake: if Christine had said she was going to Amy's, then that's where she'd gone.'

'But did Christine always tell the truth?'

'Of course not,' Vivienne said. 'She was twelve. But she wasn't one of those girls who lied all the time. When she did, it would have been for a quiet life, so her mum didn't nag her, or her dad didn't lecture her. You know what I mean. The little things. Nothing really important.'

'Did she ever talk about running away?'

Vivienne looked startled. 'Heavens, no! Where would she run away *to*?'

'It was just a thought.'

'No, not Christine. I can't imagine it. And I don't remember her ever saying that she wanted to.'

'And she was sensible enough not to get in a car with a stranger, or go anywhere with a stranger?'

'She'd have never done that. We had it impressed on us as kids, the whole stranger danger thing. No. Is that what you think? That someone might have abducted her?'

'I've an open mind at present. Exploring all avenues.'

'Leaving no stone unturned.'

Harry gave a rueful smile. 'Something like that.'

'It must be hard after all these years. Sometimes I can't remember what I did last week, never mind back then.'

Harry, who had come here knowing that Vivienne was unlikely to provide any startling revelations, was still disappointed that he wasn't learning more. He was careful not to let it show.

'The last phone call you had with her. Do you remember any of that conversation?'

Vivienne gave a light shrug of her shoulders. 'The police asked me that. But it wasn't anything. Just casual chat, you know? Stuff about homework, what we'd done that day, what we were doing tomorrow. She sounded the same as always, not upset or anything.'

'No plans to meet up?'

'We had my nan over for the weekend and she wasn't going home until Monday. I said I'd call her – Christine, I mean – the following week. Mum usually gave me a lift to Kellston and picked me up at the end of the day. And Celia would give Christine a lift if she was coming here.'

Harry wondered if it was relevant that both Celia and Jackie could drive and then put it aside to consider later. 'She didn't say anything about going to Amy's?'

'No, she didn't mention it.'

Harry ran through a few questions, ones he didn't expect to get a positive response to but felt obliged to ask for the sake of covering all bases: if she knew Pauline Greer's maiden name, if she'd heard where the Greers had moved to, if she'd ever seen Amy again? No to all of them, which wasn't any big surprise.

'I'm not being very helpful,' she said. 'Sorry.'

'Don't worry about it. Just out of curiosity, what was your first thought when you heard that Christine was missing?'

Vivienne's eyes half closed as if she was trying to transport herself back to that moment. 'God, I don't know. I'm not sure I took it that seriously, not when Celia Mortlake made the first call. I think I just thought that she'd lost track of time, gone for a walk or something, and that she'd turn up before too long.'

'And later?'

'It was confusing ... and frightening. More real, I suppose.

The police had been called and I kept thinking that Christine was going to be in serious trouble when she got home. Except she never did get . . . well, of course she didn't. And then there was the business with the Greers, how Christine had said she was going to Amy's, how she never showed up – or so they said – and then my dad went over to help look for her.'

Harry's ears pricked up. 'I didn't know that.'

'He wasn't the only one. A lot of the neighbours rallied round to join the search, apparently. Word travels fast. He was there for hours just driving around Kellston, checking anywhere he could think of, returning to Magellan Street every half hour – there were no mobile phones back then – to see if she'd turned up.'

In the ensuing panic there would have been an opportunity, Harry realised, for someone, the local neighbourhood paedophile, perhaps, to dispose of Christine's body under cover of helpfulness. Another car going out to look for her wouldn't raise any suspicions. He made a mental note to ask Celia who else had turned out that Sunday.

Vivienne was still talking. 'It was late when Dad came home, and I was in bed. I heard them talking. Mum said, "You can't go jumping to conclusions" and he said, "If it looks bad it probably is bad. Why would she say she was going to Amy's if she wasn't?"' She stopped, frowning a little. 'It's odd what you remember. The next few days are a bit of a blur. I think Mum tried to prepare me for the worst without scaring me to death, but that was a tough balancing act. The longer it went on, the more everyone was convinced that she was dead. And convinced that George Greer had killed her. Do you think he did?'

'I wish I knew.'

There was a short silence before Vivienne pushed the cup aside and glanced at her watch. 'Thanks for the coffee. I'm sorry but I have to go. Will you let me know if you find out anything?

Please give me a ring if you need to ask anything else. I put my number in the email I sent.'

'Thanks for coming. It's been useful.'

Vivienne slipped into her coat. She hesitated and then said, 'Has it?'

'Of course. Everything helps.'

'Please give my best to Celia when you see her again.'

Harry sat for a while after she'd left, wondering how sane it was to try and solve a mystery that was over fifty years old. No one liked failure and the chances of his were high. Pessimism raised its ugly head before he could prevent it. But he couldn't afford to think that way. The meeting hadn't been a complete waste of time. Even snippets could be pieced together to form a bigger picture.

His eyes roamed around the busy café before coming to rest on a dark-haired girl who would have been much the same age as Christine when she disappeared. Had Vivienne Bayle been telling the truth? Perhaps as much truth as she could from the point of view of a twelve-year-old. Harry stared at the girl until he realised her mother was glowering at him. He quickly looked away.

23

After dithering all morning, Phillip had finally decided to head into the West End to dispose of the 'evidence'. It was nearing midday and he suspected that if he didn't go now, he never would. He'd spent the last hour scanning the estate looking for any signs of the police, but if they were around, they were keeping a low profile. No more procrastination, he told himself, it was time to act.

He stuffed the stained anorak into a thin carrier bag and then stuffed the carrier into a canvas shoulder bag. It looked bulky and bulging, like he'd tried to squeeze a duvet into a pillowcase. No, that wouldn't do. He quickly pulled out the wrapped coat and placed it instead in a large, extra-strong Sainsbury's bag. That was better. Now it looked more like shopping and less like the suspicious accoutrements of a man who'd committed murder.

'And why would you be carrying shopping *off* the estate?' said Chapel, who was never slow to have a dig at Phillip's reasoning.

'Don't start. You were the one who said I should get rid of it.'

'You don't need to go to the West End to do that.'

'Why not? It's as good a place as any.'

Before Chapel could introduce any more unwelcome doubts into his mind, Phillip went through to the hall and put on his flimsy raincoat. He wasn't looking forward to his journey across the estate, what could be – if he was being melodramatic – his last ever walk as a free man. The police could be skulking anywhere: in the corridor, the lobby, perhaps even by the gates.

If he was stopped and searched, what would he say? That he was dropping off the coat at a charity shop. Nothing wrong with that. Except, shit, Charlene had worked at the Oxfam on the high street. Too much of a coincidence? He could imagine their eyes narrowing, their expressions turning smug as they drew the offending item from the bag and saw the incriminating stain on the cuff. *If you could just accompany us to the station, sir.*

He opened the door, stepped outside and glanced left and right. The corridor was empty. Good. He was probably stressing over nothing. The police couldn't stop everyone leaving the estate – they didn't have the time or the manpower – and if he didn't act suspiciously, he should be all right. But it was, of course, hard to act normal when you were trying to act normal.

Phillip noticed that Dion's door was ajar again. More customers, he thought, as he headed for the lifts. The lazy bastard was probably on benefits too, getting everything paid for without the trouble of raising a finger. Had he ever paid tax in his life? No, he just expected the government to support him while he raked in the profits from his nice little sideline. And by government what Phillip really meant was himself, *his* taxes going into the pockets of endless people who didn't deserve it.

This inner diatribe kept him diverted while he travelled down to the ground floor. He was growing increasingly right wing as he got older, his once liberal views hardening into more extreme opinions. Or was it Chapel's influence? He had always thought of himself as a decent person, a fair person – a cheerleader for equality and human rights – but was starting to wonder if all that meant was lying down and being walked over.

Nerves assailed him again as the lift doors opened. There was the secondary worry now of bumping into Edna Floyd, a woman who seemed to be omnipresent. He scuttled across the lobby, keeping his eyes peeled, hoping that just for once she'd be safely ensconced in her flat and not lying in wait for someone to complain to. He made it out of the building and on to the path. He saw the flowers that had been laid out for Charlene. A trickle of sweat ran down the back of his neck.

The gates were his next hurdle. He strode towards them, the bag hanging at his side. There were plenty of other people around, coming and going, and he walked among them with a studied casualness, not too fast, not too slow, his eyes constantly scanning the space around the exit for any signs of police activity.

He felt more than relief when he passed through the gates without incident and on to Mansfield Road. A surge of exultant adrenaline flowed through his body. That was the first difficulty successfully negotiated. A pat on the back, Mr Grosvenor. Now all he had to do was to get some distance from here and get rid of the coat. Once that was done there would be nothing tangible to link him to the murder of Charlene.

Although deep down Phillip still believed himself to be innocent of the crime – he was, he had to be – that tiny doubt remained. And Chapel didn't help, forever whispering in his ear, making him question his own reason. Still, he told himself it was useful to experience what it felt like to be in the shoes of someone who *was* guilty. He would write all this down when he got back – the fear and anxiety, the damp clamminess of his hands, the frantic beating of his heart. Even a psychopathic murderer had to worry about getting caught.

He was surprised he hadn't heard from the police again. Maybe they'd established that the time of Charlene's death didn't tally with the time he had made his trip to the takeaway. After he'd seen her, she might have gone straight to her flat and been murdered there – the body later dumped outside – or she might even have gone out again to get rid of her rubbish or to meet up with someone.

He could already be off the hook.

Or were the police just biding their time? Playing with him?

Phillip walked to the high street and then down to Station Road where he joined the queue for a bus that would take him to the West End. He glanced towards the florist's and saw Gem inside serving a customer. Her head was bent over, her graceful fingers wrapping the flowers in paper. He tried not to stare. He was reminded of the hyacinths he'd bought, their scent already filling the living room.

'Nola's next,' Chapel said, suddenly appearing beside him.

Phillip frowned. '*I'll* decide who's next.'

'If we wait for you to make up your mind, we'll still be waiting this time next year. You're not what they call decisive, are you, pal? It's Nola, I'm telling you. And no one's going to be sorry when she's six feet under: she's hardly a productive member of society.' Chapel smirked. 'Not unless you count spreading your legs as a useful contribution to the country's wellbeing.'

'Some men might say so.'

Chapel gave a low, ugly laugh. 'Well, there's nothing to stop you having a bit of fun before you get shot of her. Or even after, if you fancy crossing that forbidden line.'

'What are you? Some kind of bloody monster?'

'Oh, don't pull that one! And don't give me any of your holier-than-thou looks. I'm what you made me, Phillip Grosvenor, so you can skip the shocked expression and all the other prissy outbursts that might be forming on your lips right now. If you haven't got the balls for it, we may as well go our separate ways. You either want this or you don't. There are no half measures. So if you've changed your mind ...'

'Did I say I'd changed my mind?'

'You're always taking one step forward and two steps back-wards, pal. It's half-hearted, lacklustre. Where's the passion, the drive, the determination? I'm not seeing it, I'm really not.'

The bus came and they both got on. Phillip found an empty seat near the front. Chapel sat down beside him and imme-diately splayed out his legs in the way that Freya had always found so infuriating. *Why do men have to do that? Take up three-quarters of the space as if it's their God-given right?*

'Now you're sulking,' Chapel said.

'I'm not sulking.'

'There's no rush with that one,' Chapel said, looking back towards the florist's. 'Your fancy piece isn't going anywhere. She'll still be here when you've done with Nola.'

Phillip wrapped his arms protectively around the bag. He didn't like it when Chapel had a go at him, like he was pull-ing all the strings, like it was *his* bloody book. Silence reigned while the bus trundled through the streets. He was annoyed at Chapel, but Chapel didn't care. The man was immune to un-comfortable silences and cold shoulders. Phillip tried to think about something else.

It occurred to him that the jacket might not be quite as easy to dispose of as he'd hoped. How did one dump a bulky item like this without drawing attention to oneself? All it took was one watchful pair of eyes, one grasping hand, and the bag could be retrieved as quickly as it had been deposited. And then there were the bins themselves. Ordinary litter bins only had slats in them – some kind of bomb deterrent perhaps – and the space was too small to squeeze the jacket through. He'd need something bigger, like one of those domestic wheely bins. Except that was asking for trouble. What householder, coming across uninvited rubbish, wouldn't pull out the bag and examine its contents?

'Now you're just inventing problems,' Chapel said.

'If it was left to you, nothing would be done properly.'

'No one cares about your bloody rubbish. So what if someone finds it? It's just some shitty old coat that nobody wants.'

Phillip shifted in his seat, tightened his hold on the bag and sighed. That was the trouble with Chapel: he never thought through the consequences. And okay, so it was unlikely that the jacket would be connected to a murder in Kellston, but why take the risk? He stared out of the grubby window as if fascinated by the festive decorations in the shops. Christmas. The season of good will. Not so far away now. Like a big black cloud looming on the horizon.

'There you go again,' Chapel said. 'Always looking on the bright side.'

'And what is the bright side of being on my own?'

Chapel raised his eyebrows. 'Well, thanks for that.'

'You know what I mean.'

'You can always invite Edna Floyd. I can just see the two of you sitting down to a lovely roast dinner ... turkey, spuds, parsnips, sprouts ... and a bottle of fizz, of course. It'll be your good deed for the year. Very Christian.'

'Yeah, funny. I've done enough good deeds for Edna Floyd, thank you.'

Chapel's face grew crafty. 'Or maybe you could get yourself

some more agreeable company over the festive period, someone more to your taste.'

Phillip thought about it. And then he thought about it some more.

24

'What's wrong with you?' Nola said. 'You've got a face on you like a smacked arse.'

'Nothing.'

'It don't look like nothing. Come on, spit it out. If you've got something to say, just say it. Is it about me having to go out and work for a living? Because if it is, there's not a whole lot I can do about that.'

Kayleigh, who'd been dwelling on Dion all morning and for half the night – had they found him yet? Had anyone seen her at the flat? – grabbed at the easy excuse Nola offered her. 'Three days,' she said. 'Do you want us put into care?'

'Jesus, you're like a dog with a bone. Stop being such a drama queen. I'm home now. What more do you want?'

A mother that doesn't go missing, Kayleigh might have said. *A mother that doesn't forget she's got kids at home. A dad who hasn't gone AWOL.* Instead, she kept quiet.

Nola joined her by the window. 'What's so interesting out there anyway?'

Kayleigh was keeping an eye on the estate gates – that was the way the law would come in – but there was no sign of any squad cars yet. Surely one of the neighbours would notice that Dion's door was open, *still* open, and go to investigate? She wouldn't like to be in their shoes when they stepped into the hallway. 'I saw Mrs Floyd last night when I was on my way back from Tracey's. She was asking about you. She said she hadn't seen you around in a while.'

'Nosy old bag. What did you tell her?'

'That you've had a cold. That you've been staying indoors.'

'Good girl. She should mind her own bleedin' business. It's like living with the Gestapo on this estate, like having twenty-four-hour surveillance. Hasn't she got anything better to do? You can't step outside your own front door without someone spying on you. I should report *her* to the social. It's harassment.'

'Yeah, well, that's just the way she is. Do you have any money?'

'What do you want money for?'

'It's almost Christmas. I want to get Kit a present.'

'That's not for weeks.'

'If you hang about, all the best stuff sells out.' Kayleigh knew how to strike when the iron was hot. Nola hadn't gone out to work last night, which meant she must have made some cash over the last few days. Had she been more with it, she'd have nabbed a share while Nola was asleep, but she'd been too preoccupied, too shocked by what had happened to Dion, to concentrate on the practical things. 'We need food too. I can go to the Spar while I'm out.'

Nola sighed, as if the expense of eating was a cost she could do without. She left the window, took her purse from her bag and pulled out a twenty. 'This'll have to do you. And don't go splashing a fortune on Kit. We can't afford it.'

Kayleigh wrinkled her nose. 'Twenty? Is that it?'

'I'm not made of money,' Nola said. 'And a thank you would be nice.' She reached out a hand as if to snatch the note back. 'But if you don't want it . . . '

Kayleigh quickly tucked the note into her jeans pocket. 'Ta.' There was still food in the cupboard, everything she'd got from the charity place, but that wouldn't last long if Nola disappeared again. And she couldn't go back to the food bank and claim her mother was *still* ill, not without someone smelling a rat. She began to doubt her decision to give Dion's money, or at least most of it, to Harry Lind. Was it a mistake? Was it too much of a gamble? She couldn't decide.

'What's wrong now?' Nola said.

'Nothing.'

'I need a pee,' Nola said.

While she was out of the room Kayleigh picked up her mum's phone from the coffee table and scrolled through the address book. Near the end of the list, she found an entry for 'Marge' and not having any paper to hand she rolled up her sleeve and copied the number on to her arm. By the time Nola returned the phone was back where it had been.

'I'll see you later,' Kayleigh said.

'Don't stay out all afternoon. I want you back before it gets dark.'

'Yeah, yeah.'

'I mean it. I don't want you ending up like that Charlene.'

What she really meant, Kayleigh thought, was that she wanted to get down to the Fox as early as possible.

25

Harry parked the car, walked over to the office and had barely got the keys out of his pocket when Moses sidled up. He brought with him the unwelcome aroma of bad breath and unwashed clothes.

'Got some information for you, Mr Lind.'

'What's that then?'

But Moses wasn't going to elaborate until he'd seen the colour of his money. Harry unlocked the door and ushered him in. Upstairs the office was cold. In what he was rapidly starting to think of as 'the good old days' he would have left the heat on while he went to Covent Garden, but now with the cost of living through the roof, he had to think less about comfort and more about the bottom line.

Moses didn't seem to mind. He shoved his hands deep into his shabby overcoat pockets and stood by Lorna's desk. 'Those Curran relatives you were after. I've found a daughter living local. Nancy her name is, Nancy Porter.'

'Excellent,' Harry said. 'And do we have a number for her?'

'I've got an address.'

Harry waited but the old man didn't go on. Taking the hint, he got out his wallet and passed over a twenty-pound note. 'You're costing me a bloody fortune.'

'Time is money, Mr Lind. I've done you a favour. This way you won't have to spend weeks looking for her.'

'What's the address?'

'Silverstone Road, number seventeen. One of them council places. She's Geoff Curran's daughter.'

Harry picked up a biro and wrote it down. 'Close by, at least.'

'Anything else you need, Mr Lind, let me know.'

Seeing as he'd just forked out another score, Harry thought he might as well try and get his money's worth. 'You remember Arthur Mortlake, don't you? What kind of a man was he?'

Moses shrugged and his expression grew sly. 'A rich one, Mr Lind. He didn't mix with the likes of me.'

'But you knew *of* him. What was his reputation? Was he liked? Disliked? What was the general opinion of him? I mean, before Christine went missing.'

'Same as any other rich geezer, no better and no worse. Liked to look down his nose at the little people, but that was nothing unusual. He were a man of his *class*, Mr Lind. He knew his place and he liked everyone else to know theirs too.'

Harry thought about how much things must have changed in Kellston over the past fifty years. Not human nature, that would never change, but the whole dynamic of the borough. Back then Kellston would have been more like a small town, with everyone knowing everyone else's business. These days half the people who lived here probably didn't even know their next-door neighbour's name.

'He might have gone to church every Sunday,' Moses continued, 'but he was still a sinner.'

'A sinner?'

Moses raised his right hand, rubbing his thumb and index finger together. 'Money. That's all his type really care about.' He scowled, took a deep breath and said, 'And Jesus entered the temple and drove out all who sold and bought in the temple, and he overturned the tables of the money changers and the seats of those who sold pigeons. He said to them, "It is written, My house shall be called a house of prayer, but you make it a den of robbers."'

Harry, confused about the pigeons, and sensing a sermon coming on, quickly interrupted. 'When did you hear that Christine was missing?'

'Huh?'

'When did you find out about it?'

'What's that got to do with anything?'

'I'm just trying to get a feel for that day, that evening. I was wondering when it became general knowledge, how fast the news spread.'

Moses considered this for a moment, scratching his head, as if trying to peel off the layers of his memory. 'It would have been when the Fox opened, so seeing as it was a Sunday, that would have been about seven. Yeah, that's when I heard. Everyone was talking about it. Some men went out to join the search. It was summer, still light.'

'But not you?'

'One more wasn't going to make any difference.'

Bearing in mind the old man's religious fervour, Harry didn't find this an especially Christian attitude. In fact, it was bordering on the callous.

Through his silence, Moses must have sensed an implied criticism. 'Do you think *he'd* have gone out to look if it was my kid who was missing?'

Harry heard a rancour in his voice, a bitterness that might have been directed specifically at Mortlake or, just as likely, at anyone from his class and position. 'I've no idea.'

Moses gave a snort. Then he shrugged, turned away and made off down the stairs.

Harry had wanted to ask him who else had been in the Fox that night, but the opportunity had slipped away. Instead, he went through to the kitchen, switched on the heating and the kettle, and retired to his office to write up his notes on the meeting with Vivienne Bayle while it was still clear in his head.

At two thirty Harry stood up, put on his jacket, locked up the office and went to retrieve his Audi from the car park at the Fox. With double yellow lines stretching along the length of Station Road, an arrangement had been made with the pub landlady which was beneficial to everyone: she received a weekly payment, and the workers at Mackenzie, Lind had the convenience of never having to hunt out a parking space.

Harry could have walked – Silverstone Road wasn't that far away – but the rain had started up again, and arriving on the doorstep looking like a drowned rat wasn't the best way to make a good first impression. He would have preferred to phone first, only a quick search of the internet hadn't yielded any useful results. If Nancy did have a landline, it must be ex-directory, but like so many people these days she probably just used a mobile.

As he drove away from the Fox, Harry glanced towards the florist's, wondering what to do about Jem Byrne. From this angle he could only see the outside display – a bright splash of colour – but no sign of Jem herself. Perhaps she wasn't even working today. Perhaps, like he'd already told himself, it was none of his damn business. Except he couldn't forget that look on her face when she had slumped down in his office – the hopelessness, the dreadful despair.

It was only a three-minute drive. Silverstone Road consisted of two rows of terraces, each house more or less identical to the next, apart from the addition of a porch or new windows or a couple of planters in the meagre front garden. Some of them, maybe most, would be privately owned now, the council tenants having grabbed the opportunity back in the eighties to purchase their properties at knockdown prices.

At the end of the road, effectively making it into a cul-de-sac, was the 'luxury' development of Silverstone Heights. High walls, cameras and a sturdy pair of wrought-iron gates meant that this community, with its convenient location for the City, wouldn't be blighted by any anti-social habits of the locals. Harry didn't like the place, didn't like the whole 'us and them' scenario, but he was long enough in the tooth to know that his opinion hardly mattered in the greater scheme of things.

Harry parked and stared for a moment at the imposing iron gates, more like the entrance to a prison than an exclusive estate. He wondered what the neighbours thought of it. Perhaps they were simply relieved to see the residents disappearing through the entrance in their swish cars, thus being spared the joy of having to look at their smug, superior faces for any longer than they had to.

He got out of the car, found number 17, walked up the short path and rang the doorbell. Immediately a dog started yapping, and immediately after that a woman started shouting at the dog. There was a short delay before the door was opened.

'Nancy Porter?' he asked.

The woman nodded. She was in her forties, a heavyset woman with an irritated expression on her face and a wide purple stripe in her dark hair. She was leaning over, holding on to the collar of a small terrier-type dog who continued to pull and bark, his ferocious eyes firmly fixed on Harry. 'Oh, shut up, Toby,' she said. 'Give it a rest.' And then to Harry, 'Sorry, don't mind him. He doesn't bite. He's just a noisy bugger.'

Harry introduced himself, raising his voice to be heard above the din of the dog, and showed her his ID. He began to explain what he was doing there but had no sooner mentioned the Curran detective agency than she swiftly interrupted him.

'God, Dad's been gone these past ten years. No, eleven, now I come to think of it. And Uncle David too.'

'Yes, I'm sorry. A Mrs Mortlake has asked me to look into the disappearance of her twelve-year-old daughter. It happened a long time ago, in 1971, and your father and his brother worked on some aspects of the case. I know it's a long shot, but I was wondering if you knew what had happened to their business records?'

Nancy, her curiosity piqued, dragged the dog back and said, 'A missing girl? You'd better come in.'

'Her name was Christine Mortlake,' Harry said, as he wiped his feet on the doormat and followed her inside. 'Her mother's very old now. She wants me to take one last look at the case.'

From upstairs, behind closed doors, came the muffled, conflicting sounds of Dizzee Rascal and Ed Sheeran. Harry went through to the living room where Nancy cleared a space for him on a sofa that was covered in discarded clothes and magazines. 'Teenagers,' she grumbled. 'They don't know the meaning of putting things away.' Harry suspected that Nancy spent a great deal of her time in a losing battle against the slovenly but not unusual habits of her children.

'Would you like a brew? It's no trouble. I've just put the kettle on.'

'Thanks,' Harry said. 'Milk, no sugar.'

161

Nancy disappeared into the kitchen. By now Toby had stopped barking but was still watching the intruder, a low growl emanating from his throat. Harry pulled his feet closer to the base of the sofa, hoping he wouldn't take advantage of Nancy's absence to launch an unprovoked attack on his ankles. Dogs usually liked him, but not this one. Perhaps he was losing his charm: first women and now dogs. It was all going downhill.

Harry was still musing on this when Nancy came back with the tea, placed his mug on the coffee table and sat down in an armchair.

'Thank you. So, did your dad ever mention the Mortlake case to you?'

Nancy shook her head. 'Not that I remember. It was before I was born though, so I suppose by the time I came along it was old news.' She raised a hand to her mouth and frowned. 'Oh, that didn't come out right. I didn't mean ... '

'It's all right. Life goes on, doesn't it?'

'I'm not sure if mine would, not if anything happened to one of my kids.' Her eyes took on an almost liquid quality. 'It used to be that mothers worried more about their daughters, but now, with all this knife crime and gangs and everything, the lads seem to be in as much danger as the girls. You worry every time they go out.'

'Yeah, it's changed a lot since our day.'

'So what happened then? What happened to Christine?'

Harry gave her a quick rundown of the circumstances surrounding Christine's disappearance – nothing that wasn't already public knowledge – and reiterated his hope that somewhere there might be information relating to the case. 'I know that your dad traced the Greers after they left Kellston. They moved several times, and it would be interesting to know where they ended up. I'm not saying the family had anything to do

162

with it, there's every chance they were entirely innocent, but I'd still like to talk to them.'

'Over fifty years,' Nancy said. 'How has that poor woman managed?' She shuddered, as if the very thought of it sent shivers down her spine. 'There's some old office stuff in the cellar but I don't know if it'll be of any use. Dad was a bit of a hoarder, never liked to throw anything away.'

Harry thanked God for hoarders. 'Would you mind if I took a look?'

'Of course not. It's a bit of a mess down there though. Charlie, that's my partner, he's always saying we should have a good clear-out.'

'I'm glad you didn't.'

'Well, you can take whatever you like if you think it'll help.'

The cellar was cold and musty, but it didn't feel too damp. A bare forty-watt light bulb hung from a central fitting casting shadows over the room. The place contained the usual array of discarded family items, as well as a multitude of tools. Nancy directed him towards the right-hand side, which was filled with various office paraphernalia: an old desk, a couple of telephones, a typewriter, a stained swivel chair and a stack of boxes that stretched from floor to ceiling. Harry's heart sank. It could take him hours to get through this lot, and even at the end of it he might not find anything pertaining to the case.

'I'll leave you to it. Give me a shout if you need anything.'

Harry took a swig of tea, placed the mug on the desk and set to work dismantling the tower. A few boxes were labelled, but time had rendered the writing virtually illegible. It soon became clear that he would have to examine them one by one, and this job was hardly helped by having to work in the twilight zone.

Harry worked quickly but methodically, opening each box and checking its contents, rifling through bills and invoices, tax returns and VAT, rental agreements and expense sheets. Eventually he discovered that inside some of the boxes were rows of green-coloured files, the type that fit snugly into a filing cabinet, and attached to these were the names of clients in alphabetical order. These were the ones he wanted, specifically the Ms, but to find them he had to keep on searching.

It was almost an hour before Harry discovered the fat Mortlake file. By then he was covered in dust and cobwebs, breathing heavily and thinking that he should take some more regular exercise. He was tempted to start reading straight away, to dive right in, but resisted the temptation. Patience. At least he'd found the damn thing; he'd been beginning to suspect that it might not even be here.

Harry returned the boxes to their place against the wall, stood back, made sure everything was much as he'd found it, and then climbed the steps to let Nancy know that he was done.

26

Jem had been watching the door to Mackenzie, Lind all afternoon. She had seen Harry leave in the morning, come back and
then go out again. Now, at almost three o'clock, she noticed his
Audi swing into the car park of the Fox. A few minutes later
he crossed the road clutching a large green file and let himself
into the office.

Last night she had come to the decision that she would hire
him to establish where Aidan was. She couldn't live with the not
knowing, with the need to be forever looking over her shoulder. At least this way she could be prepared. Although even as
that thought entered her head, she wondered *how* she could be
prepared exactly. Buy a knife? Buy a gun? There were probably
plenty for sale on the estate if you knew whom to ask. But she
didn't know. All she did know was that she was sick of running,
that she couldn't take it anymore, that she was sick of all the
sleepless nights, sick of the endless fear.

Perversely, despite her new-found resolution, she had still half
hoped when she'd come in this morning that Harry Lind might

not be working today, that she could put off until Monday what she'd intended to do today. Cold feet. But now she had flipped over again, anxious that he might leave the office and go home before she got the chance to talk to him.

Jem made a decision. She waited until Stefan was serving a customer, went to the toilet, took out her phone, googled Mackenzie, Lind, got the number and pressed 'call' before she could change her mind. He answered almost straight away.

'Harry Lind.'

She hesitated, gripping the phone, tempted to hang up.

'Hello?'

'It's me,' she said eventually. 'Jem Byrne.'

'Hello, Jem.'

She left another pause. 'Can I talk to you? I don't mean now. Later. Half five, say? Or just after. Would that be convenient?'

'Sure,' he said. 'I'll be here.'

'Okay.' Jem hung up. No going back now.

Kayleigh studied the row of night lights in the discount store, weighing up which one Kit would like best against which one, as she shared a bedroom with him, would be the least irritating. Did she really want to have to lie and stare up at the galaxy on the ceiling every night? Still, she could always turn it off once he was asleep.

She picked up the boxes and looked at the pictures on them. It was hard to decide. There was a cheap moon version – only £9 – but she thought it might get a bit boring after a while. Or, bearing in mind the price, just fall to pieces. The planets one was more interesting, and more expensive. But she had money. She had her mum's cash and Dion's. She didn't need to worry about the price.

Dion. Her stomach turned over. Would they have found

his body by the time she got home? Perhaps the law would be waiting for her, sitting impatiently in the living room while Nola circled round telling them that they'd got it wrong, that they were all fucking mad, that no daughter of hers could be involved in drugs and murder. There was still a chance that one of last night's customers had grassed her up, confessed to having bought the weed from her, volunteered her name and address. It wasn't impossible. But people on the Mansfield didn't usually do that kind of thing. People on the Mansfield hated the law.

With these conflicting ideas rolling around in her head, Kayleigh chose the night light with the planets design and went to pay at the till. Under different circumstances she might have tried to nick the light, but the way her luck was running she'd probably be nabbed by security. She was pleased with the gift. At least Kit would have something to open on Christmas Day. A better present, of course, would be if Dad came back. That would be the best Christmas ever.

Harry was still thinking about Jem Byrne's phone call as he made coffee in the tiny kitchen and took the mug through to his office. He was aware that he'd spent more time than he should have researching Aidan Hague on the internet. When he'd been a cop it had always been a relief to get men like that off the street – one less psychopath for the world to worry about – but now that Hague was out of jail there was no knowing what he'd do.

Her fear was understandable.

He thought about calling Valerie but decided to leave it until he'd talked to Jem again.

In the meantime, he had the Curran file to go through. Harry drank his coffee as he slowly turned over the pages. It was clear from the start that the only enquiries Arthur

Mortlake had wanted them to make were in connection to the whereabouts of the Greers. They'd been hired in March 1972, probably a few days after the family had packed up and left Kellston, to find out where they'd gone. It hadn't taken the brothers long to locate them. There was no indication as to why they had fled to Chelmsford – had there been relatives there, friends? – but the address had been passed on and the case closed.

If the retired cop Beddows was right, Mortlake had pursued the family, probably making some public accusations too, causing them enough grief anyway to move on again a few months later. The Currans had been re-hired in June, their job made trickier on this occasion by the Greers having changed their surname to Neames. More difficult but not impossible. Eventually they'd been located in Lincoln. Six months later, the Currans were looking for them again, this time running them down to Cambridge.

It had been a relentless game of cat and mouse with the Greers constantly moving, and the Currans persistently hunting them down. But George Greer, no matter how hard he'd tried, had never been smart enough to evade discovery. It was interesting, Harry thought, how quickly the brothers had always run him to ground. Either they had been remarkably lucky or, more likely, they'd had inside information – a contact, perhaps, in George Greer's bank or the phone company, someone who would tip them off (for a price) whenever he registered a new address.

Included in the file were a number of photographs paper-clipped to the reports. The first one, taken in Chelmsford, showed an ordinary-looking man of about forty, average height, slightly overweight, red cheeked, with thick brown hair. The jolly greengrocer. Except not so jolly perhaps. Already the strain was starting to show. In the picture George Greer was emerging from a modest semi-detached, his shoulders hunched, his expression almost furtive.

Harry read on. It was more of the same. Wherever the family moved to, the Currans weren't far behind. And this, no doubt, was soon followed by a visit from Arthur Mortlake, keen to tell the neighbours who they were living next door to, and to spread the word about the danger their daughters were in. For the Greers it must have been a living hell. George might not have been convicted of anything, but no smoke without fire and all that.

At the end of the file Harry came across a photo of George, Pauline and Amy sitting at a wooden picnic table with the sea in the background. Whitstable, 1977. No one was smiling. George looked at least ten years older than his actual age, his face thin and haggard, his eyes sunken. The chase had taken its toll. Pauline, short fair hair streaked with grey, was gazing out towards the horizon with a vacant expression on her face. Amy, who must have been eighteen by the time the photo was taken, was sporting the sulky look of a teenager. Except, of course, she had plenty to be sulky about. Six years of moving house, moving schools, of making new friends and having to leave them behind. By this point the family must have been desperate.

Harry leaned back. So, the Greers had ended up in Kent, but had they stayed there? He had no way of knowing whether Mortlake had got to them before he died, frightening them into moving on again. Still, at least he had a starting point with Whitstable, somewhere to begin looking.

He had already checked the electoral register for Greer on first taking on the case – no George, Pauline or Amy of the right age – but he would try again with Neames. If he had no joy with that, he would search for a death certificate, a document that would bear the name and address of whoever had registered the death.

Harry had just leaned forward again, pulled the laptop towards him and booted it up, when the buzzer went. He glanced at his watch. Too soon for Jem unless she'd come early. Standing up, he looked out of the window, across the road to the florist's, but the only person he could see was the bloke messing about with some holly.

The buzzer went again. Someone was impatient.

Harry left his office, walked into reception and spoke into the intercom. 'Hello?'

'It's Kayleigh,' a small but determined voice said. 'It's Kayleigh Dunn.'

Harry sucked in a breath. He'd been hoping in a fairly hopeless sort of way that she might have given up or that when she *did* come back it would be when Lorna was here. 'What do you want, Kayleigh?'

'Can I come up?'

'Is your mum with you?'

'It's raining, Mr Lind. I'm getting well soaked out here.'

Harry reluctantly pressed the button to release the lock on the front door, wondering what was worse – condemning a child to pneumonia or inviting one in who had no right being here. These days you had to be careful about being alone with pre-pubescent girls, or any young girls come to that. He would try to get rid of her as quickly as possible.

27

Harry sighed as he heard Kayleigh Dunn scamper up the stairs. She entered the office swinging a carrier bag at her side. Her long brown hair was damp from the rain, and he was struck by how thin she was, like she hadn't had a square meal in weeks.

'Hiya,' she said, grinning at him, as if they were the best of mates.

Harry didn't smile back. He tried to do his stern-but-fair cop voice. 'You shouldn't be here on your own. What did I say about bringing your mum with you?'

Kayleigh flapped her free hand as if what Harry said was neither here nor there. She put the bag down on the floor, rummaged in her pocket, produced a roll of notes and placed it on Lorna's desk. 'Two hundred quid,' she said triumphantly.

'Where did you get that from?'

Kayleigh looked at him, and then away, and then back at him again. 'Mum told me to give it to you. Is it enough? We ain't got no more at the moment. She couldn't come today, she's still sick, but she wants you to have it so you can start searching properly for Dad.'

'You told me last time that your mother wasn't interested in finding him.'

'She changed her mind.'

'Okay,' Harry said, not believing a word, 'but I'll still need her signature on the contract, still need to see her face to face. I can call in if that makes it easier. What's the address?'

Kayleigh shook her head. 'You can't do that.'

'Why not?'

''Cause she's sick, ain't she? She can't be doing with all that signing business.'

Harry suppressed a smile. Kayleigh was like one of those kids who'd had to grow up too fast, a curious mixture of little adult and child. 'Where did you really get the money?'

She opened her mouth as if to protest – you calling me a liar? – but then promptly shut it again.

'Kayleigh?'

'I saved it up,' she said. 'Christmas and birthdays. I've been saving for ever.'

Harry didn't believe that either. 'Well, I can't take it from you. Sorry, but that's just the law. I can't have a contract with a minor.'

Kayleigh's mouth twisted in frustration. 'All I want to do is find my dad. You seen that Carl Froome yet?'

Harry knew that he should just say no and bring this exchange to an end. But he didn't have the heart. Her pleading eyes were fixed on him again. 'I have, as it happens. I bumped into him in the Fox and asked if he knew anything about your dad's disappearance.'

'What did he say?'

'That he didn't.'

'What else?'

172

'Nothing else. Sorry.'

Kayleigh stared at him. 'And you believed him?'

'I didn't say I believed him, only that that's what he said.'

'I told you he was a liar.' Kayleigh's gaze roamed over the desk. 'You got a pen? And something to write on?'

Harry passed her a biro and a notepad. He thought she was finally going to reveal the details of her address but instead she rolled up the left sleeve of her jacket and copied down a mobile number that was scrawled on her arm.

'This is Nana Margaret's number,' she said, pushing the notepad towards him. 'Can you find out where she lives from it?'

'Why don't you just call her?'

'Because I reckon Dad might be there. I can't think where else he'd be. If I call, then she'll tell him, and he might do a bunk again.'

'Why would he do that?'

''Cause he's worried about Carl Froome catching up with him. Bound to be. Something happened at work that day. It's obvious. There weren't no row at home or nothing. If I call, he might think Mum's using me to flush him out, and that she'll tell Froome where he is – her being so mad at him and all. So can you get an address from that number?'

Had Harry not witnessed Froome's somewhat shifty behaviour he might have dismissed Kayleigh's theory as wishful thinking – a means of explaining away her father's abandonment – but now he wasn't so sure. Perhaps there was something in it. And Ray, after three years' absence, could have decided that it was safe to lie low at his mother's.

'That depends on whether she's got a contract or not,' Harry said. 'If the phone's a pay-as-you-go, it's going to be untraceable.'

Kayleigh winced at the word 'contract' coming up again, as if it was her deadly enemy. 'And what if she has got one?'

Harry shrugged. 'Then maybe.'

'Good,' she said, as though it was a done deal. 'Ta.'

'I didn't say I was going to do it.'

Kayleigh, ignoring the comment, picked up the money and put it back in her pocket. 'Essex,' she reminded him. 'Somewhere in Essex.'

'Look, Kayleigh . . . '

But she'd already grabbed her carrier bag and was heading for the stairs. She stopped briefly by the door and glanced over her shoulder. 'Ta, Mr Lind.'

Harry perched on the end of the desk and listened to the sound of her footsteps on the stairs. A moment later the front door banged shut. He found himself wondering, not for the first time, how he'd been outmanoeuvred by a ten-year-old.

28

Jem was putting on her coat, getting ready to leave, when Stefan came into the back.

'Hey, have you thought any more about Christmas?'

Jem had thought some more and had come to a decision. The lie slipped from her lips as easily as every other lie she'd ever told. 'Oh, yes, thanks for the offer, it's really sweet of you, but I'm going to spend it with a friend of mine. Lisa. She's just divorced and having a bit of a bad time.'

She had thought Stefan would be relieved – no third wheel to spoil a cosy couple's Christmas – but instead he looked genuinely disappointed. His face dropped, his mouth drooping at the corners.

'Well, if you change your mind. Only Al's invited a bunch of mates from work.'

Jem wasn't sure what Al did exactly – something to do with the theatre, stage design perhaps – but she could tell from the way Stefan spoke that he wasn't best pleased at the prospect of spending the day with Al's friends. 'Not that bad, are they?'

'They're just so bloody ... *arty*.'

Jem glanced over his shoulder at the shop full of flowers, and grinned. 'You're not exactly *un*arty yourself.'

'Believe me, I'm positively pedestrian compared to that lot. To hear them speaking, you'd think they'd invented drama. They're always quoting Shakespeare and Ibsen and Strindberg and making all those little in-jokes that you don't have a clue about. Patronising sods. I was hoping that I'd at least have you to talk to, someone normal.'

Jem laughed at that, knowing that she was as far from normal as a person could be. 'Can't you tell Al you'd rather spend the day just with him?'

'Too late for that now. He's already invited them, hasn't he?'

Jem was starting to regret that she'd turned down the offer. What else was she going to do on Christmas Day? Spend it in solitary confinement, feeling sorry for herself. If she'd known that it was going to be more of a gathering, she wouldn't have been so hasty. Although it was hard to backtrack now that she'd made the excuse, she made a faint stab at it. 'Mind, Lisa is a bit of a flake. She could have changed her plans by this time next week.'

Stefan perked up at this. 'Do you think? The invitation's open. Just let me know.'

'I will. Thanks.'

Outside it was dark and cold. Rain was coming down in a drizzly, lacklustre fashion, the drops pattering on the ground and dancing in the orange halos of the streetlamps. Jem put up the hood of her coat. As she crossed the road, zigzagging around the traffic, she almost had a spring in her step. She was thinking that, after a decent interval of time, she might accept the offer after all, thus killing two birds with one stone: sparing herself the loneliness of spending Christmas Day on her own and providing some moral support for Stefan. Even if the other guests were beyond pretentious, *he* was good company, and they could get pleasantly pissed over one too many bottles of fizz.

But this wasn't the only reason for her positive frame of mind. Now that she had finally decided to do something about Aidan she felt as if a weight had been lifted from her shoulders.

Jem pressed the buzzer at Mackenzie, Lind without any hesitation, heard the click of the door as it unlocked – no voice on the intercom, but then he was expecting her – and went inside. She climbed the stairs, resisting the temptation to run. Harry Lind was waiting in reception. The room was pleasantly warm. Last time she had barely taken any notice of her surroundings, so intent had she been on confronting him, but now she appreciated the clean, airy feel of the place, the white walls, the comfortable sofa, the tidy polished desk with its phone and computer and printer.

'Good to see you,' he said. 'Come on through to the office.'

The office was less tidy but had the reassuring look of industriousness with files and folders stacked on his desk, and papers spread out beside a laptop. There was a large, framed map of Kellston on the wall, one of those old maps dating back to the 1850s and showing an area with a lot more green space than it had today.

'Grab a seat,' he said, as he pulled out his chair and sat down. 'Would you like tea, coffee?'

Jem shook her head. Now that she was here, she wanted to get it over and done with. 'I want you to find out where Aidan Hague is, if he's still in Blackpool or not. Can you do that?'

'You reckon he might not be?'

He hadn't answered her question, not directly at least. 'I'm *worried* that he might not be. Wherever I go, he finds me eventually. It's relentless. There was this time in Aston when …

Anyway, I've been followed while I've been here, I'm sure I have, for the last few weeks. Not all the time, just sometimes. And I heard someone call out my name when I came back from work last week. I think it was my name, I don't know. I might be wrong about that, but not about someone following me.' Jem sensed that she was in danger of rambling and so took a moment to draw breath. 'It would help to be sure of where he was. Put my mind at rest. Or not. It's the not knowing that gets to me, wondering if I'll go home one day and find him sitting in my living room.'

Harry nodded. 'What will you do if he isn't in Blackpool?'

'Move on,' she said. 'Maybe. No point in making it easy for him.'

'Have you told the police? I presume he's still on licence.'

Jem gave a hollow laugh. 'Tell them what? That I think my psychopathic ex is on the hunt for me? Except I haven't got any actual proof. You know how it works. You used to be a cop. There's nothing they can do unless *he* does something, and Aidan's too smart to get caught in the act. By the time he does make a move, it'll be too late.'

'So you're just going to keep running?'

'Unless you've got a better idea?' she snapped, and then quickly rubbed her face with her hands. 'Sorry. I didn't mean to . . . It's frustrating, that's all, and exhausting. So can you find out where he is, Mr Lind? Is that possible?'

'Call me Harry,' he said. 'Yeah, I can put in some calls. I've got contacts up north. I'll see what I can find out.'

'Thank you.'

The next few minutes were occupied by the signing of a contract, providing details of her address and phone number, and the handing over of a deposit. Jem hoped that the final bill wouldn't be too exorbitant. Her savings were getting low – it was expensive to keep moving – but it would be worth every penny to be one step ahead of Aidan.

'Is there anything else you need to know?'

Harry shifted some of the papers on his desk, shuffling them into neat piles. Then he leaned back, put his hands behind his head, looked at her and said, 'Would you like to get out of here for a while? Go for a drive?'

The question startled her. 'A drive?'

'Not far. Just round Kellston. I'm sick of these four walls. What do you say? You can tell me a bit more about Aidan. I think better when I'm driving.'

'It's raining,' she said stupidly, still not sure how to react.

'It's waterproof,' he said. 'The car.'

Jem smiled, despite herself. With another bloke the suggestion might have set off alarm bells, but she didn't think that he had ulterior motives. Harry Lind was simply a man who didn't enjoy being cooped up. And what else was she going to do? Go home to an empty flat. Or, even worse, go home to a flat that *wasn't* empty.

Harry drove the Audi out of the Fox car park, turned left and then left again, until they got away from the evening traffic and were winding through the backstreets of south Kellston. The rain smattered against the windscreen, and the wipers swished back and forth in a smooth, almost hypnotic movement. So she didn't feel the need to explain the whole back story, he told her how he'd looked up Aidan Hague on the internet and read the news reports.

'You knew I'd come back then,' she said.

'No, I was just curious. I can't help myself when it comes to a mystery. It's like a compulsion. I have to find out the details or I can't sleep at night.'

She glanced at him as though she wasn't sure how serious he was being. 'You must think I'm a fool for getting involved with him in the first place.'

Harry kept his eyes on the road. 'I think you were young. Men like that are clever. They know how to manipulate, to take advantage. Don't go blaming yourself.'

'But I *am* to blame,' she insisted. 'Partly. If it hadn't been for me, Georgia would still be alive. I was the one he was trying to run over. She was just ... well, Aidan would have called it "collateral damage". There was always a lot of collateral damage when he was around.'

They were quiet for a while. Harry didn't want to press too hard, to ask too many questions. After a while she seemed to relax, to lose the tension in her shoulders, and he thought there was something about the confines of a car, about sitting next to him without having to look at him, that made things easier for her.

'You're not from round here, are you?' she said. 'Not from London, I mean. Somewhere up north. Lancashire?'

Harry was surprised that she'd realised. She must have a good ear. He'd been in London for over twenty-five years and didn't think much remained of his original accent. 'Morecambe,' he said, 'but I left a long time ago.'

'And never looked back.'

'No, I never looked back. I like London. I like its ... ' Harry wondered what he *did* like about it – not the pollution or the constant noise or the bad-tempered inhabitants – and paused for a moment. 'Oh, just its anonymity, I suppose. You get used to a place after a while. So, where will you go if you get this Aidan business sorted?'

'I haven't really thought about it. Go home, I guess. I miss the sea.'

'Yeah, you don't get much sea air in Kellston.' Harry gestured towards the street. 'Now this is the posh part of Kellston, or it used to be. Most of the houses have been converted into flats and bedsits now.'

Jem pressed her face against the window and gazed out at the big old buildings with their chimneys and gardens. 'I didn't even know this part existed. It must have been quite grand back in the day. It's sad when places get shabby.' She paused, sighed and then said, 'Just in case you think I'm completely paranoid, I have seen Aidan since he came out of jail. I'm not just being a crazy woman.'

'I didn't think you were. Are you talking about Aston?'

'I'd only been there a month and I got home from work one day to find him parked outside the block of flats I was living in.'

'What did you do?'

Jem gave another of her empty laughs. 'Scarpered before he noticed. I was lucky. I saw him before he saw me. I booked into a cheap hotel, got up at the crack of dawn and went back to the flat. Aidan was never the patient sort so I figured he wouldn't have made a night of it. He likes his home comforts too much. As soon as I was sure he'd gone, I went in, packed up – I travel light these days so it didn't take me long – and got out of there as fast as I could.'

'You could have reported him for that.'

'For what? The coincidence of being in Aston at the same time as I was? Anyway, he'd have only denied it. I didn't have any proof. I didn't even get the registration number of the car.'

'How do you think he found you?'

'That's the million-dollar question. I suppose someone might have recognised me and tipped him off. Or maybe by some other means. I try to keep as little as possible in my name, but there are still ways of tracking people down. Well, you know all about that.'

'It's hard to keep under the radar these days. There are all these privacy laws, but people find ways to get around them.'

'And it wasn't just Aston. I saw him again in Bedford. He only ever seems to be one step behind.' Then, perhaps to take her mind off her own troubles, she asked, 'How are you getting on with the missing girl?'

'Christine Mortlake. It's a tricky one. Fifty-one years is a long time. You can't rely on most people's memories from last week never mind half a century ago. But I'm still digging. Something will come to light eventually.'

'Fifty-one years,' she murmured. 'Did she live round here?'

'Not far.' Harry took a left, then a right, before turning into Magellan Street. He drove slowly along to the end before pulling into the kerb and, with the engine idling, gestured towards the house. 'That's where Christine was supposed to be going on the day she disappeared, visiting her friend Amy. The Mortlakes lived at the other end of the street – a three-, four-minute walk on a sunny Sunday afternoon.'

Jem stared at the house for a while. The front garden had been concreted over to make room for parking spaces. There were a few lights on behind pulled curtains, some signs of life. 'God, if walls could speak. Poor kid. It creeps me out thinking about what might have happened in there.'

'*If* anything happened.'

'You don't think so?'

'I'm keeping an open mind. The Greers all swore she wasn't there that day, that they never saw her. They could have been telling the truth. The police tore the house apart, but they didn't find a shred of evidence.'

'Someone could have moved the body.'

Harry shrugged. 'They could. But this used to be a close neighbourhood, and no one noticed Greer's van leaving the premises.'

'Do you have a theory?'

'Several,' Harry said, 'none of which would stand up to close examination.'

Jem glanced over her shoulder, back towards where he'd said the Mortlake house was. 'Tell me.'

'It's all the obvious stuff.' Harry used the fingers of his left hand to count them off. 'One, Christine never left her own house that day. Two, she was killed at the Greers'. Three, a person or persons unknown snatched her off the street. Four, she left of her own accord.'

'Ran away, you mean?'

'It's not impossible. Unlikely, but I can't rule it out.'

'You got a favourite?'

'Not yet.'

'I can see why it's tricky. Are her parents still alive?'

'Only her mother.'

Jem nodded. 'Was she the one who hired you?'

Harry drummed his fingers lightly against the steering wheel. 'She's getting on now, wants some answers before it's too late.'

'Poor woman.'

He checked his mirror, indicated and set off again. It was only then that he noticed the silver-grey Beamer, parked a hundred yards down the street, pull out too. And suddenly he had a memory of a similar car – the same car? – following him out of the Fox. Just to be sure, he made some turns, three lefts going round in a square, until they were almost back where they started, and he was certain that they had a tail.

'Don't look now,' he said. 'But I believe we have company.'

Jem stiffened, made to look over her shoulder but stopped herself. 'What? We're being followed?'

'Looks that way.'

Her voice had grown small, slightly hoarse. 'Who . . . who is it?'

Although Harry couldn't see the driver clearly through the rain, there weren't that many silver-grey Beamers roaming the streets of Kellston. 'Don't worry, it's nothing to do with Aidan. Hold on. Let's get rid of them.' He accelerated, took a sharp right without indicating, roared up Henley Street, took a left and pulled into the driveway of a house in darkness and quickly killed the lights. The Beamer went past about ten seconds later. Harry reversed out and took off in the opposite direction.

Jem looked over her shoulder. 'I don't see them.'

'Job done then.'

'It *could* have been Aidan. What makes you so sure it wasn't?'

'Have you ever heard of a man called Danny Street?'

Jem shook her head, then glanced over her shoulder again. 'Should I have done?'

'His father, Terry, used to run this manor – drugs, girls, pubs, clubs, extortion – the usual gangster stuff. Terry's getting on now and not too well by all accounts, so Danny's stepped into his shoes, or tried to. There's another son called Chris but he's keeping his head down these days.' Harry continued to glance in the rear-view mirror just to make sure their unwanted tail hadn't got lucky and found them again. 'Trouble is, Danny's not smart like his dad, and he hasn't got his charm either. In fact, he's got a screw loose – well, a whole toolbox of screws – and he's a law unto himself, that law being that he does what he wants when he wants and doesn't much care who gets hurt in the process. Anyway, to cut a long story short, he has a car just like that one.'

'But why would he want to follow you?'

'Because he's interested in something I'm doing. I just have to figure out what. I've been mainly working on the Mortlake case, but I can't see why that would bother him. He wasn't even alive when Christine went missing.' Harry thought some more while he drove the car in a wide arc heading towards the Mansfield estate. 'No, I think it might have to do with a conversation I had in the Fox with an acquaintance of his.'

'And who was that?'

'A guy called Carl Froome, a second-hand car dealer. Kayleigh's dad used to work for him. I asked if he had any idea where Ray might have gone, and the question seemed to unsettle him.'

So what's the connection between this Froome and Danny Street?'

'Rumour has it that Danny launders some of his ill-gotten gains through the business.' Harry checked his mirror again. 'Good, I think we've shaken them off. Yeah, Froome was on edge, like he wasn't sure how much to say. He was unconvincingly insistent that he had no idea why Ray had gone missing and seemed to think that Kayleigh's mum had hired me to look for him.'

'Hasn't she?'

'Huh?'

'You said it like she *hasn't* hired you.'

Harry grinned. 'Officially speaking, she hasn't. It was Kayleigh who came to see me and asked if I'd try and find him. To be honest, I'm not sure Nola's even interested. I think Ray burned his boats when he walked out on them. Good riddance and all that. What's she like, Nola? Do you know her?'

'No, I don't think I've ever seen her. I only met Kayleigh and Kit recently.' Then, frowning a little, she said, 'So why were you asking Froome about Ray if you haven't been hired?'

'Curiosity,' Harry said. 'An impulse. I don't know. I saw him in the pub and . . . I feel sorry for the kid. Obviously I can't take her on as a client, but I reckoned I could spare five minutes just to see how he reacted. Kayleigh was convinced Froome knew more than he was saying when Ray disappeared – better that than him having simply walked out on them, I suppose – but I thought it was just wishful thinking. Now I'm starting to wonder. Maybe I touched a nerve with the delightful Mr Froome.'

'I still don't get why they're following you.'

Harry was trying to figure this out too. 'Either because they're hoping I'll lead them to Ray, or they've got some reason why they don't want me to find him.'

Jem raised her eyebrows. 'So are you going to keep looking?'

'I should think so.'

'Even though you're not being paid?'

'It's not all about money.'

Jem looked at the road behind and then looked at him. 'I wish you'd told me earlier that you were such a soft touch.'

Harry's mouth widened into a smile. 'Now that's not a rumour I'd want getting around. I'm just curious, that's all.'

'One of those unsolved mysteries.'

'Yeah, something like that.'

By the time they reached the Mansfield it was getting on for six thirty. It was clear, even as they passed through the gates, that something was going on. Lights, noise, activity. The police were everywhere, a uniformed invasion, and a line of squad cars sat in front of Haslow House.

'Looks like there's trouble,' Harry said. 'Again.'

'Just another Saturday night. Perhaps they've caught whoever killed that poor girl.'

Harry took the car as close as he could to the tower. 'You sure you'll be all right? Do you want me to come in with you?'

Jem had already unbuckled her seatbelt and had a hand on the door. 'What, in case something happens, and I can't find a policeman? I don't think that's going to be a problem.'

'Well, you take care of yourself. I'll call as soon as I get any news on Aidan.'

'Thank you.'

Jem got out of the car and didn't look back. In a few seconds she was swallowed into the crowd and Harry could no longer see her. All that was left was the faint scent of perfume.

29

Jem manoeuvred through the gawping crowd and made her way into the lobby, passing from cold and wet air to warm and damp-smelling. It was busy here too with residents gathered in groups, talking in low voices while the police tried in vain to encourage them back into their flats. Among the faces she recognised the old lady she had gone up in the lift with the first time she'd met Kayleigh and Kit. Mrs Floyd, wasn't it? A gossip, Kayleigh had said. Well, that could be useful.

With curiosity overcoming her usual restraint, Jem walked over and asked, 'Excuse me, but do you know what's going on?'

Mrs Floyd seemed pleased by the enquiry, glad to have some fresh blood to share the news with. Her tongue ran over dry lips while her eyes crinkled at the corners. 'There's been another murder, dear. On the sixth floor.'

'It's a terrible business,' the middle-aged man beside her said. 'Strangled in his own home, garrotted. You'd think—'

'Dion, his name was,' Mrs Floyd interrupted, shooting the man a warning glance as if to establish who had precedence in the gossip stakes. 'Dion Dixon. Killed last night, they say, although no one found him until this afternoon. I've heard he was a drug dealer. He lived on the same floor as Mr Chapel here, but you didn't see anything odd, did you?'

Mr Chapel shook his head. 'Not a thing. Mind, his flat is at the other end of the corridor. I've no reason to go past it.'

That word *garrotted* was still revolving in Jem's head. Aidan had tried to strangle her once, put a belt around her neck and pulled it tight. That awful sense of hopelessness, of fighting against what couldn't be fought against, of grasping wildly with useless hands, of feeling your life slowly ebb away.

Mrs Floyd must have seen her go pale because she patted her on the arm and said, 'It'll be a gang thing, no doubt. Drugs. Nothing for the rest of us to worry about. You're new here, aren't you?'

'Fairly new,' Jem agreed.

'You must feel like you've moved into the Wild West. Two murders in three days. Who'd have thought it? And this used to be such a nice place back in the sixties when I first moved in. You wouldn't believe the changes.' Mrs Floyd lowered her voice. 'It's full of coloureds now, of course, full of all sorts. You wouldn't think we were even living in England. Not that I've got anything against them, but it won't be long before we're in the minority.'

Mr Chapel looked uncomfortable and said with fake joviality, 'Variety is the spice of life. Isn't that what they say, Mrs Floyd?'

Mrs Floyd didn't seem to embrace the idea. 'I'm as tolerant as the next person but there has to be a line drawn somewhere.' Then, turning to Jem, she said, 'I'm Mrs Floyd and this is Mr Chapel.'

'Joe Chapel,' he said, giving her a nod.

'Jem. Pleased to meet you.' Discomfited by Mrs Floyd's casual racism, she glanced towards the lifts, noticing that the police appeared to have commandeered two of them. Brisk men and women in white coveralls stepped out at regular intervals, their faces stern, their hands full of plastic bags. A uniformed officer stood guard. Of the lifts that were left, one was out of order, and the others were busy ferrying people up to their flats.

'Mr Chapel hasn't lived here for long either,' Mrs Floyd said.

'Long enough,' Mr Chapel said ambiguously.

Jem wasn't sure whether he meant *too* long or long enough to be used to the place. 'Oh, right.'

One of the available lifts finally made its way down to the ground floor, the occupants spilling untidily into the lobby. Jem was hoping that her new acquaintances might be staying to watch the ongoing spectacle, but they appeared to have tired of it. The three of them got into the lift along with two studenty-looking girls who, either oblivious or indifferent to the murder, were conducting an avid exchange about a third girl whose ears would currently be burning.

'What floor?' Mr Chapel asked, his hand hovering over the buttons.

'Four,' one of the girls said.

'Eight, please,' Jem said.

The doors closed and the lift began its juddering ascent. Mrs Floyd looked at Jem through sharp shrewd eyes, like an employer trying to assess a candidate's potential. 'Eight,' she repeated. 'That's Nola's floor. Do you know Nola Dunn?'

Jem was instantly reminded of Harry, who had asked the very same question. 'No,' she said. 'Sorry.'

'Blonde girl, loud voice. You'll hear her coming before you see her. She's got a couple of kids, a boy and a girl.'

Jem smiled faintly and shook her head as if she'd never set eyes on Kayleigh and Kit, deciding it was easier to claim ignorance than to get embroiled in the old lady's gossip. Thankfully, she was saved from any further interrogation by the lift coming to a halt on the first floor. Mrs Floyd exited with a breezy wave as if another murder on the Mansfield was all part of life's rich fabric.

The girls departed on the fourth floor, still badmouthing their 'friend' with seemingly endless bitchiness. And then there was only her and Joe Chapel. He cleared his throat, gave a deep sigh and said, 'Two killings. It's really quite distressing. You wonder where it's going to end.'

'Yes, it's awful. Did you know him?'

'Not really. Nodding acquaintance, that's all. But it's still been a dreadful shock.'

Jem tried to place his accent – predominantly working-class London but underlain by something more middle class – and might have wondered what his story was if she hadn't been preoccupied by the murder of yet another Mansfield resident. Chapel was in his fifties with thinning brown hair, small brown eyes and plump lips in a rather fleshy face. He was slightly overweight and not very tall. She noticed his clothes – discount store – and his shoes with their worn heels. A man down on his luck.

'Yes,' she said. 'Dreadful.'

'Perhaps it's best not to think about it too much.' Chapel shuffled from foot to foot, as if eager to follow his own advice but unable to do so. 'These things happen, I suppose, even if we wish they didn't.'

Jem could see his anxiety, more obvious in the confines of the lift than it had been down in the lobby. She thought she could detect the sharp tang of sweat, although it was hard to tell above the usual stink of dope and urine. 'Are you all right?'

'Oh, yes, quite all right. Well, I will be in a while. It's the knowing it happened just along the corridor that's so disturbing.'

'Too close for comfort.'

'Exactly. Too close for comfort.'

The lift stopped at the sixth floor, the doors opening to the sound of activity, footsteps and voices. Chapel gave her a nod. 'Goodbye, then. Take care.'

'Goodbye.'

Chapel stepped out, turned to look at her and seemed on the verge of saying something else, but the doors were already sliding shut and whatever he'd meant to say remained unspoken. Jem went on up to the eighth floor, walked along to her flat, went inside and instantly forgot about him.

Kayleigh was in the living room chewing on her nails while she watched TV with Nola and Kit. Some game show that she wasn't even following and certainly didn't care about. The laughter of the audience grated on her nerves. She knew that Dion's body had been found, had seen the law descend on the estate, and now she could only wait and see if anyone pointed the finger.

Last night she'd had bad dreams, the sort that had stayed in her head all day and wouldn't leave her alone: Dion running wide-eyed along the corridor with red wire around his neck; her pockets so full of weed that she left a trail wherever she went; standing by the lift and the doors opening to reveal nothing but a yawning black hole. She had tossed and turned, slept and woken up in a cold sweat, convinced that her secret wouldn't be a secret for long.

The doorbell went, two loud rings, and Kayleigh jumped. She looked at her mother.

'Get that, will you, love,' Nola said, leaning forward to grab another cigarette.

Kayleigh would have told her to get it herself if her mind hadn't been preoccupied by more serious matters than Nola treating her like a personal slave. She got up and padded to the front door in her rabbit slippers, nervously wondering if it would be the law, dreading what they'd ask, what she'd say back, how the hell she was going to explain about Dion and the weed.

Then, when she opened the door, it was like all her worst fears made real. A uniformed cop, a young woman with cropped red hair, was standing there holding out her warrant card with one hand and clutching a clipboard with the other.

'Hello,' she said, smiling. 'I'm PC Liv Maddison. Is your mum in?'

They didn't ask about dads on the Mansfield – there weren't many of them around. What Kayleigh wanted to do was slam the door in her face but instead she simply nodded as she backed away. 'Wait there. I'll go and get her.'

'Mum, it's the law.'

'What do they want?'

Kayleigh hovered by the sofa. 'I dunno. It's probably about that guy who was murdered.'

When Nola dragged herself off the sofa, Kayleigh waited a couple of seconds and then followed her as far as the living room door, keeping to the side so that the cop couldn't see her. Her palms were damp, and she could feel her heart beating in her chest. The constable told Nola about the murder of Dion Dixon and asked if she'd been in last night.

'Where else would I be with two kids to take care of?'

The constable, who was used to low levels of politeness, kept her voice genial and asked if she'd seen or heard anything unusual between the hours of nine and twelve.

'I was watching the telly. And it's two floors down. How would I have heard anything? You lot need to get your act together. It's a bloody disgrace. This estate ain't safe for decent people.'

'Did you know the victim? This is a picture of him.'

There was a pause while Nola looked at the photo. 'No, I don't know him.'

Kayleigh knew this was untrue because her mother had sometimes bought her weed from Dion, but like his other customers – or *hopefully* like his other customers – she wasn't about to admit it. Kayleigh's guts were still churning, though. Her lips were dry, and she ran her tongue over them. She was waiting for that moment when the cop would mention that someone (Mrs Floyd) had seen Kayleigh in the lobby last night. Or, just as bad, that Nola might mention her visit to Tracey's.

'That it?' Nola said. 'Only I've got things to do.'

The cop handed her a small card. 'If you think of anything, there's a number on here you can ring.'

'Sure.'

Kayleigh's fingers slowly uncurled. She needn't have worried. Her mother had no interest in helping the police with their enquiries or of encouraging them to linger on her doorstep any longer than was strictly necessary. As the door closed, she relaxed. For once in her life, she was grateful for Nola's ability to lie through her teeth.

Phillip Grosvenor's end of the corridor hadn't been taped off but even as he was putting the key in the lock, he was approached by a police officer who asked him his name and if he had seen or heard anything unusual last night.

'No, nothing, nothing at all,' he said, with perhaps an excess of vehemence. 'Sorry. I wish I could help. What a dreadful business.'

'Did you know Mr Dixon?'

'Only by sight. I've never talked to him.'

'And you're sure you didn't hear anything, anyone coming or going?'

Phillip could have told him that Dixon was a dealer – did

they know that already? – and that the Dunn girl had been there buying dope for her mother. But he knew better than to draw attention to himself, especially after the business with Charlene. A low profile was what was needed now. Play the ignorance card, keep his head down, pretend to know nothing. But he could feel his pulse accelerating, feel the burn of his reddening cheeks. Withholding information was what they called it.

There were a few more questions and then he was free to enter his flat.

'Jesus, your bloody face,' Chapel said as they went inside. 'You're supposed to be a smooth-talking psychopath, not a little boy quaking in his boots.'

'There wasn't any quaking.'

'You should pour yourself a drink. You look like you need it.'

Phillip did pour himself a Scotch, a big one, and then he put the heating on. He took his drink over to the table and sat down by the window to watch the police activity in front of the block. He could hear them along the corridor too, their great boots clumping back and forth, their voices filtering through the thin walls. It was a good thing, he thought, that he hadn't investigated Dion's open door this morning. What if he'd discovered the body? That would have meant him being connected, if only in a slight way, to both of the killings on the estate. Enough to raise a few suspicious eyebrows.

At least his quest to get rid of the anorak had proved successful. After much traipsing about – along Regent Street, Shaftesbury Avenue and Charing Cross Road – he'd eventually come across a large flip-lid bin outside a supermarket on Tottenham Court Road and had dropped his parcel in along with a newspaper and an empty bottle of water. The damn coat was gone now and hopefully he'd never see it again. One less thing to worry about.

'All that effort and for what?' Chapel said. 'A complete waste of time.'

'You're the one who said I should get rid of it.'

'And if I said you should throw yourself in the river, would you do it? For Christ's sake, Phil, you need to start thinking for yourself. I'm not always going to be here to hold your hand.'

Phillip drank his Scotch, staying calm and not rising to Chapel's taunts. It was in the man's nature to be contrary, to say one thing one minute and the opposite the next. He was just a wind-up merchant. Phillip was still convinced he'd taken the right action – better to be safe than sorry – and now he could relax.

It had all been rather different fifteen minutes ago when he'd walked from the bus stop and come back on to the estate. His guts had turned to jelly at the sight of all those cops and he'd known with a sudden certainty that they were there to arrest him, to cuff him and read him his rights, to charge him with the murder of Charlene. His first instinct had been to turn tail and run, to get off the Mansfield as fast he could, but that would have been the action of a scared and guilty man.

Instead, he had used his brains and slowed his pace while he'd carefully looked around, trying to process what he was seeing and to make better sense of it. And gradually the truth had dawned. The boys in blue weren't there for him at all. There were too many of them coming and going. It didn't take half the local police force to make an arrest. Something else had happened.

As soon as he'd walked into the lobby, he'd come face to face with Mrs Floyd. She'd taken up a prime position by the lifts and her beady eyes were busy drinking in the drama.

'Feeling better, Mr Chapel?'

'Much better, thank you. What on earth is going on?'

And that was how he'd found out about the murder of Dion Dixon.

'Ah, she's a right tattler, that one,' Chapel said, joining him at the table and pouring himself a drink. 'I hope you didn't tell her about Nola's brat.'

'Of course not. I didn't tell her anything. You think I want the police knocking at my door again? Anyway, that wasn't the good bit. Guess who else came into the lobby and wanted to know what was happening?'

'I've no idea,' Chapel said. 'The prime minister? Joe Biden?'

'The flower girl! The lovely Gem. We came up in the lift together.'

'Did you ask her what she was doing for Christmas?'

'Don't be ridiculous.' Phillip swigged his Scotch, feeling the soft anaesthesia as it slid down his throat. Already he was regaining his confidence, recovering from the shock of Dion's death and from finding the police in occupation. He had been nervous in the lift with Gem but thought he had hidden it well. Now they'd been introduced, now they were on neighbourly terms, he'd have every excuse to talk to her again.

'Yeah, trust,' Chapel said. 'That's what it's all about. Once you get them to trust you, it's all plain sailing.'

30

Back in his office Harry stood in darkness, staring out across the road at the Fox. The silver-grey Beamer was parked at the far end of the car park, its driver probably in the pub and not best pleased at having been given the slip. He couldn't put his hand on his heart and swear that it had been Danny Street, but the chances were high. What was the psycho playing at? His money was still on Ray Dunn as being the motive for the tail.

The rain began to thrash harder against the glass, obscuring his view. His thoughts ran on to Jem Byrne and the fear that she existed with. Enough to send anyone crazy. She was a peculiar mix of defiance and defensiveness – he remembered the way she had stormed into his office when she'd believed that he was working for Aidan Hague – with an edge of vulnerability thrown in. He didn't know why he'd taken her to south Kellston or why he'd shown her the house where the Greers had lived.

Before leaving the Mansfield, Harry had stopped by the gates, asked a group of lads what was going on, and found out there had been another murder. This time the victim had been a dealer by the name of Dixon. He hadn't been shocked – the estate was hardly renowned for its peace and harmony – but the fact Jem was living there gave him a more personal interest. If the killing was gang related, one murder could easily trigger another and before you knew it innocent victims were getting caught in the crossfire.

Harry sat down and turned on the Anglepoise lamp. It was still early, just after seven, and although it was tempting to while away the rest of the evening over a few pints, he had work to do. First on the list was a call to Gerry Whitelaw, his go-to man for when he needed access to the kind of information that mobile phone companies wouldn't give out to private detectives. How Gerry got his information didn't bear close examination, but he was fast and reliable and didn't give a damn as to why you wanted to know.

'Evening, Harry. I won't ask why you're working on a Saturday night. I'm sure it's no reflection on your social life.'

'Yeah, great to talk to you too.'

'What can I do for you?'

Harry could hear music in the background, voices and the chink of glasses. 'I need an address for a mobile number in the name of Margaret Dunn. It's in Essex somewhere. You got a pen?'

'A pen? Jesus, man, what age are you living in? Fire away. I'll put it in my phone.'

Harry, duly admonished for being a technological dinosaur, passed on the number, spent a couple more minutes in idle chit-chat, and then hung up. He took a moment to consider what Gerry, the geekiest guy he knew, had said about his social life and decided he probably had a point.

Next on the list was Pauline Neames. He opened the laptop, switched it on and waited for the miracle that was Microsoft to do its work. A search of the electoral register came up with a number of women called Pauline Neames but only one was around the right age and living in Whitstable. The address was for a residential care home called 'Seaview'. He jotted down the details and moved on to the database of births, marriages and deaths.

After half an hour of searching he eventually came across a death certificate for George Neames, who had died in a Kent hospital over fifteen years ago. The death had been registered by a Pauline Neames, living in Whitstable but at a different address. Putting these pieces of information together, he came to the conclusion that he'd either stumbled on a complete coincidence or that he'd found Amy Greer's mother.

Harry did another search, this time for Amy Neames, looking for a marriage or death certificate, but this produced no useful results. She wasn't on the electoral register under Neames either. It was possible that she'd gone abroad, married abroad, or simply changed her name.

This created a problem. Harry couldn't just rock up to 'Seaview' unannounced. For all he knew Pauline could have dementia or some other debilitating illness. And even if she was still sound of mind, he was loath to question a seventy-nine-year-old woman about events from the past that must have caused considerable anguish. No, he had to give this some more thought. He'd discuss it with Mac and Lorna on Monday.

Only one task left to complete, the one he'd been putting off since he got back from the Mansfield. Harry picked up his phone and put it down again. He turned and looked out of the window. The rain had eased off. He stared at the locked-up florist's and the café, the Fox, the station, and then dropped his gaze to watch the people passing by. Procrastination is the thief of time. Why didn't he want to call? It wasn't that he didn't *want* to call, only that he feared it would be awkward.

Harry couldn't remember the last time they'd spoken, but it must be getting on for nine months. Sometimes he did that dreadful snooping thing of checking out her Facebook page – they were still 'friends' apparently, despite everything that had happened – but, being a cop, she was always careful what she posted. He had, however, seen some pictures of the current man in her life, holiday photos taken in June on the Greek island of Naxos, showing a suntanned Jake drinking white wine at a taverna while the sun went down over a shimmering sea.

Jake was a doctor at a Manchester hospital. When it came to relationships, were doctors a better bet than cops? Or ex-cops, come to that. Probably. Not quite so screwed-up by everything they'd seen, not quite so cynical, not quite so battered by the knowledge of what human beings were capable of. Unless they were working in A & E. He had made, of course, the inevitable comparisons. Was Jake better-looking than him? Was he better in bed? Did he make her laugh the way *he* had before it had all fallen to pieces?

Although he accepted that it was over between him and Valerie, that it would never work out between them, he still found it hard to accept that she had moved on. He grimaced. Jesus, was he turning into one of those men who only ever want what they can't have? Before he could dwell too much on that unwelcome thought, he snatched up his phone again, found her number and pressed the button.

Valerie answered almost straight away. 'Hello, stranger,' she said.

'Hi, how are you doing? Is this a good time or would you like me to ring back later?'

'No, it's fine. I've got five minutes.'

Making it clear that five minutes was all she had to spare. Make it short. Make it snappy. Better get straight to the point before the clock timed him out. 'I've got a favour to ask but don't worry if you can't help.'

'I won't,' she said.

'You won't help, or you won't worry?'

Valerie's voice took on an exasperated edge. 'Just tell me what you're after, Harry.'

'Okay. I've got a client who's worried about a psycho ex coming after her. Name of Aidan Hague. He lives in Blackpool, so I wondered if you had any contacts over that way, someone who'd know whether he was currently there or not. He came out of jail just over a year ago after a long stretch for murder. He tried to run my client over but killed her best friend instead.'

'He sounds a peach.'

'He certainly is. She thinks he's coming after her – old scores and the rest – so it would be helpful to know his exact location at the moment. She's already seen him, not in London but in Aston where she used to live, and now she's convinced that it's only a matter of time before he shows up in Kellston.'

'All right,' Valerie said. 'I'll see what I can do. I can make a few calls, but it won't be until Monday when I'm back at the station.'

'Monday's fine. Thanks, I appreciate it.'

'Always glad to help.'

As Harry reckoned he still had three minutes of his allocated five left to him, he quickly asked, 'So how are things with you? Everything going well in sunny Manchester?'

'Yes, good, thanks. No problems other than the usual misogynist crap. Nothing I can't deal with, although it would make life a damn sight easier if I didn't have to. How about you? How's the business doing after the delights of Covid?'

'Oh, picking up again, thank God. Yeah, we're pretty busy.' In the old days he could have discussed his cases with her, asked for her opinion and valued it. He missed that. There was a pause as if she was trying to think of something else to say and so he filled the gap with a couple of stupid questions. 'How's whatsisname? You two still together?'

'You know what his name is, Harry. *Jake*. And yes, we're still together. And yes, he's fine. Thank you for asking.'

Harry pulled a face, wishing that he hadn't gone there. He had just lost the battle in that tactical war between exes, making the rookie error of pretending to forget their current partner's name. As if you didn't care. As if it didn't bother you. Jesus, he was such a moron. 'Good, good. Well, I won't keep you. Thanks again for the Aidan favour.'

'I can't guarantee anything.'

'No, I get that.'

After they'd said their goodbyes and hung up, Harry raked his fingers through his hair and wondered how he'd become such an imbecile. Why had he had to go and ask about Jake? Because he was hoping that things might have fizzled out, that Valerie might have discovered that the grass isn't always greener, that she might still have some feelings for him. And then what? He was only hankering after the past, a past that had ended acrimoniously and would, in all likelihood, end the same way again if they replayed the relationship.

And now he was feeling sorry for himself. Never a good thing. Should he go across the road and have a pint? Why not? It was Saturday night and he had nothing better to do.

31

Harry squeezed his way through the crowd in the Fox and waited to be served. Once he'd arrived at the front of the queue, he ordered a pint of Guinness and, as the landlady was pouring it, leaned forward a little and said, 'Maggie, if I wanted to know about something that happened in Kellston a long time ago, like fifty years back, who would I ask?'

'What sort of something?'

'A girl who went missing. Christine Mortlake.'

Maggie thought about it. 'You could try Lionel and Betty. They've lived round here all their lives. You'll find them in the back, far right-hand corner.'

'Ta. It's appreciated.' Harry passed over a note and said, 'Keep the change.'

He carried the pint carefully through to the far room, trying to avoid spilling any as he manoeuvred through the crowd. Concentrating on the Mortlake case was a good way of not thinking about Valerie. He already had a lead – finding Pauline

Greer was a step forward – but he had the feeling that the answer to everything lay right here in Kellston.

It wasn't hard to spot the couple, who looked to be in their late seventies, both small and grey-haired, smartly dressed in their Saturday glad rags. She had on a flowery dress, and he was wearing a suit. Their winter coats were hung over the back of their chairs. They were not talking to each other but instead were people watching, their eyes flitting from one person to the next, as absorbed by the comings and goings as by a nightly soap opera.

Harry approached them, apologised for interrupting, introduced himself, said he was a private investigator and held out his ID. 'Maggie said you might be able to help me. I'm looking into the disappearance of a girl. It was a long time ago, over fifty years and—'

'You'll be talking about the Mortlake girl then,' Betty interrupted.

Harry nodded. 'Yes, Christine Mortlake. You were living here when that happened?'

'Oh, yes. I remember it like it was yesterday. I mean, you don't forget things like that in a hurry. A dreadful time, truly dreadful. It shook everyone up. We had kids of our own, you see, and we worried that they might be next. Didn't dare let them out of our sight for months.' Betty paused, gazing up at him. 'You'd better sit down, or I'll get a crick in my neck.'

Harry took a stool from a nearby table and then remembered his manners. 'Can I get you a drink before we go on?'

Lionel, who had kept quiet until now, perked up at this. 'A pint of mild would go down nicely, thank you. And the missus here will have a port and lemon.'

Harry went back to the bar, queued up again and put the order in. He took the drinks back to the table and sat down.

'Thanks for this. Really, I'm just trying to get a feel for what the general opinion was at the time. I know what Arthur Mortlake was saying, who he was accusing, but did everyone believe him? Did you? Did you think George Greer knew more than he was saying?'

Betty, who was clearly pleased by this interruption to their usual Saturday-evening routine – perhaps people rarely asked their opinion these days – was quick to respond. 'It was hard to know what to believe. How does someone just disappear like that, in broad daylight and all? It was only down the road, wasn't it? I said the same to Lionel. "How can that happen?" I said. "One minute she's there and the next she's gone."' Betty shuddered. 'Lord, it doesn't bear thinking about.'

'Did you know the families, the Mortlakes and the Greers?'

'The Greers,' she said. 'Now I knew them pretty well. I always bought my veg from his shop. He struck me as a nice man, decent, but you can never tell. I wanted to believe he was being truthful, that Christine had never gone to his house, but once you've got doubt in your mind you just can't get rid of it. And I wasn't the only one. People round here were all suspicious.'

Lionel spoke up for the first time since Harry had brought the drinks back. 'Not everyone. He had a raw deal, that man. The whole family did. I understand why Arthur Mortlake behaved how he did, but I still think he got it wrong.'

'Lionel used to be pals with George,' Betty explained.

'We weren't pals exactly, but we'd have a drink together from time to time. I like to think I'm a good judge of character. He didn't have it in him to hurt anyone.'

'You can't know that, not for sure. You can't ever know what goes on behind closed doors,' said Betty.

Lionel shook his head. 'People should have had more faith in him. That man wouldn't have harmed a fly. He didn't do anything wrong, and I'd bet my life on it. He was a scapegoat, that's what he was, a bleedin' scapegoat.'

Harry wasn't learning anything new, but he nodded and listened, waiting for the opportunity to move the conversation on. 'Was anyone else under suspicion? Any other names being bandied around? I mean, apart from the Mortlakes themselves. Usually in situations like this there are certain people who spring to mind when these things happen.'

'I don't think so,' Betty said. 'I don't remember if there was. It all seemed very cut and dried – either the Greers were lying or the Mortlakes were.' She turned to her husband. 'Can you think of anyone else, love?'

Lionel's shaggy eyebrows knitted together. 'If you ask me there wasn't much of an investigation. The law made their mind up and that was that. They couldn't prove anything but mud sticks, doesn't it? George Greer was never charged – there was nothing to charge him *with* – and yet they made it known that they weren't looking for anyone else. That's as good as saying that they think he's guilty, but they just can't prove it.'

'I agree,' Harry said. 'They were only looking at two options and Arthur Mortlake was never a serious contender. His wife was there all day and she heard Christine leave so unless she was lying ... but they didn't think she was.' He drank some Guinness and put the glass down. 'I understand there was a search that evening, that some of the locals got together and scoured the streets.'

'That's right,' Betty said. 'They set off from here and looked for hours. Lionel went with them.'

Harry looked at Lionel. 'Can you remember who else was there? How many?' There were some perpetrators who liked to be close to the action, just for the thrill of it. They couldn't resist the temptation to be at the centre of it all without anyone suspecting them.

'There were about eighteen, twenty, I reckon. But when it comes to names . . . it was a long time ago.' Lionel scratched his chin and thought about it. 'John Lake, Richie Boothroyd, Sam Middleton. There were some I only knew by sight and others I'd never seen before, friends of friends, people who'd just come in for a drink but who offered to help.'

'There was a man called Bayle,' Harry said. 'The father of one of Christine's friends.'

'I don't recall him.'

'And Moses was in the Fox too, wasn't he? You know who I mean?'

'Everyone knows old Moses,' Betty said.

'Did he go out on the search?' Harry asked, even though he knew the answer.

Lionel shrugged. 'He might have.'

'I don't think so,' Betty said at the same time. 'He had troubles of his own back then.'

'What kind of troubles?'

Betty gave Lionel a quick look as if she wasn't sure whether to say anything more. But then she made up her own mind. 'It's no secret. You'll find out anyway. He'd lost his own daughter and his wife a few weeks earlier. A hit and run on Violet Road. Eleanor and little Annie. She was only six. Whoever it was just drove off and left them there in the road.'

'Jesus,' Harry said. 'And did they find out who did it?'

'Never,' Betty said. 'He was in a bad way. Who wouldn't be? He spent most of his time in the pub – well, I suppose it was his way of coping – until he found God, or God found him. So when it came to searching for Christine, I doubt he was sober enough to put one foot in front of the other, or even care that much that she was missing.'

'That's a bit harsh,' Lionel said.

208

'I don't mean he was an uncaring person, just that he was taken up with his own grief. He didn't have room for anything else.'

Harry was thinking how easily grief could turn to anger, and anger to some kind of retribution. Had Moses suspected one of the Mortlakes of killing his wife and daughter, and killed Christine in revenge? Or just lashed out at any girl? It wasn't impossible. But then again, there was no real evidence for it either. Maybe his imagination was running away with him.

Betty began reminiscing, talking about how Kellston used to be, how people always looked out for others, but Harry was only listening with half an ear. He wondered why he was so keen to put Moses in the frame. Did he have some kind of unconscious prejudice because the bloke was a religious nut? Or maybe not unconscious at all but a perfectly conscious bias against anyone who tended towards the extreme.

But Moses had given him the information about Nancy, Geoff Curran's daughter. Why would he do that if he had something to hide? Perhaps because he knew the brothers had only been hired to chase after George Greer and not to investigate the disappearance of Christine. By being helpful he could deflect suspicion from himself and make a few quid at the same time.

When Betty came to a natural halt, Harry asked, 'So is Moses his real name, or just some kind of nickname?'

'Michael Moss,' she said. 'That's his real name. But everyone started calling him Moses when he went all religious. I mean, he always went to church – we all did in those days – but he wasn't so . . . what's the word I'm looking for, Lionel?'

'Fanatical,' Lionel said.

'Yes, that's it.'

Harry's mobile beeped, telling him there was an incoming text message. 'Sorry about this,' he said as he took it out of his jacket pocket.

'You youngsters and your phones,' Betty said, but not with any irritation. 'You're never separated from them.'

Harry smiled, wondering when he'd last been described as a youngster. It was all relative, he supposed. The message was from Gerry, an address for a Margaret Dunn in North Weald. He texted back 'Ta' and put his phone away. That was his Sunday sorted, a trip out to Essex and probably a long day waiting for Ray to put in an appearance.

'Is there anything else you remember about that evening?' he asked, looking from Lionel to Betty. 'Anything at all could be useful.'

They both shook their heads.

'I haven't thought about it in a long time,' Lionel said sadly.

And Harry felt a twinge of guilt at resurrecting bad memories that had perhaps been best left buried. He couldn't think of anything else to ask and so he stood up, thanked them for their help and left his business card on the table. 'Give me a call if anything comes back to you.'

It was getting noisier in the pub now, the sound increasing as sobriety levels fell. He considered having another pint at the bar but decided against it. Suddenly he wanted to be away from the crowd, back in his flat with just his own thoughts for company. He was heading for the door when he saw Danny Street sitting to the side of it. Their eyes locked and Danny smirked. There was something about that smirk that got under Harry's skin.

On impulse he stopped by the table and said, 'Do you want my itinerary for tomorrow? Save you having to follow me.'

'Huh?' Danny said, all mock innocence. 'No idea what you're talking about, mate.'

'Ray Dunn.'

'Who?'

'You know who he is.'

Danny folded his arms across his chest and grinned. 'Why should I be interested in that stupid bastard?'

Harry remembered what Froome had told him about Ray taking off in a car that hadn't been paid for. 'Because he robbed you.'

A flash of anger lit up Danny's dark eyes. 'Not me, mate. No one robs me. Not if they want to rest easy in their bed at night.'

'Robbed your mate, then. Carl Froome.'

Danny's expression instantly changed, the grin returning. His whole posture relaxed as if he'd just got away with something. 'That's his business, not mine.'

'So what's with the tail?'

'What tail?'

Harry knew this conversation was going nowhere, but at least he had the satisfaction of having given him the slip earlier. That must have riled him. Danny was sitting with a vacant-looking blonde with a Barbie figure. She was half his age and was drunk or stoned, possibly both, and kept narrowing her eyes as if she was trying to bring Harry into focus.

'Early start tomorrow,' Harry said. 'Sheffield. You'd better make sure you have a full tank.' And then before Danny could respond he walked on, pushed open the door and went out into the night.

Getting the last word was gratifying, but as he jogged across the road Harry was certain that Ray Dunn had crossed Danny over something more serious than a second-hand motor. Why else would he be so interested in finding him? But he was getting sidetracked. It was Christine Mortlake he should be concentrating on. Celia was the one who was paying, not Kayleigh. He sniffed the cold night air – diesel fumes and rain – and tried to focus his mind. He could almost imagine the sound of men tramping these streets all those years ago, calling out for

Christine and to each other, every one of them knowing that the chances of finding her were getting slimmer by the minute.

An ominous feeling wormed its way into Harry's guts. He knew there could be no happy ending to this case, that whether the truth was discovered or not, it was all going to end badly.

32

Phillip's fingers flew across the keyboard while he tried to capture his protagonist's feelings as he came back on to the estate. Not *his* feelings, not the stress and the fear and the worry that he was about to be arrested, but Joe Chapel's more arrogant reaction. Chapel would have been confident, even cocky, pleased to find the police there and to know that his latest killing had been discovered. Two murders now and more to follow.

He stopped to take a gulp of whisky. He was quite drunk, he thought, but the words were flowing. The day had been an eventful one. Finally, the police had gone, leaving in their wake strings of tape and a trail of muddy footprints. The woman who'd discovered the body – she lived down the hall, almost opposite Dion's flat – had told a neighbour about the red wire around his neck, and the neighbour had told Edna Floyd and now everyone knew.

'Where did the wire come from?' Chapel said.

'How would I know? A hardware shop, an electrical store, the back of the cupboard.'

'You need to know. If you don't, who does?'

'I'll get to it. It's not essential to the plot right now.'

'It's the random nature of it all,' Chapel said. 'That's the brilliance of it. What connects Charlene and Dion? Nothing – other than the fact they both lived in Haslow House.'

'Dion lived on the same floor as me. And I followed Charlene home from the takeaway. *There's* a connection, two connections, in fact.'

'Hundreds of people live in this block. And if the law had you in the frame, they'd have been back by now. No, to them you're just a boring middle-aged geezer who happened to be out that night. Ordinary. Mundane. They probably ran you through the computer to be sure, but once they saw you were clean, they'd have placed you way down the list of suspects.' Chapel took a swig from the can of beer he was drinking. 'You see, people don't just start murdering for the hell of it. Especially at your age. They've nearly always got form – a history of violence or abuse, a row of glaring red flags.'

Phillip's fingers paused on the keys. Why was Chapel always using words like 'boring' or 'middle aged' when he referred to him? Little digs he slid into the conversation, put-downs to make him feel bad. Just like Freya used to do.

'This is all her fault,' Chapel continued. 'Freya was the one who brought you to this, always criticising, always undermining you. She was a bloody ball breaker.'

'And now you're doing it too.'

Chapel was affronted. 'What's that supposed to mean? Fuck, man, I'm the only one looking out for you. I don't see any of your other so-called mates queuing up to spend the evening here.'

'Forget it,' Phillip said, wanting to get on with the book. He could never win an argument with Chapel, no matter how hard he tried. 'I need to get this chapter finished.'

'I need to get this chapter finished,' Chapel mimicked in a high-pitched girlie voice that was nothing like Phillip's.

'Give it a rest, can't you?'

'What you need, mate, is to start appreciating what I do for you, and stop being so bloody negative. Have you even thought about that whore upstairs?'

'There's time enough for that. The police may have left for now, but I bet they'll be back.'

'Good things come in threes. You need to get your act together, pal. It's part of the fun, doing it right in front of their noses.' Chapel finished his beer and crushed the can between his fingers. 'I'm ready to do whatever you want. You just have to tell me.'

Kayleigh watched as Nola put on her make-up: some concealer under her eyes, a layer of foundation across her face, eye shadow, eye liner, mascara, and finally, with a flourish, some bright red lipstick. Her mother leaned back and viewed the effect in a mirror she had propped up on the coffee table, inclining her head as if to examine the transformation from a different angle. She smelled of cigarettes and perfume.

'Do you have to go out?'

'It's only for a couple of hours, love. I won't be late.'

'Do you promise you'll come back?'

Nola gave her a sideways glance. 'Where the hell else would I go?'

But Kayleigh knew that Nola wasn't reliable, that she said one thing and did another.

Jem poured herself a glass of wine, took a sip, and stared at the TV. She didn't drink much these days, too anxious about Aidan turning up to voluntarily impair her mental faculties with

215

alcohol, but tonight she was feeling more relaxed. Harry Lind would find out if Aidan was in Blackpool or not.

Then she wondered what difference it would make if he *was* in Blackpool. It wouldn't mean he'd always been there or always would be. Tonight, tomorrow, he could jump in a car and before she knew it be right here in Kellston. It was possible that he was using a private investigator to track her down, one who wasn't quite as fussy as Lind about the clients he took on, one who wouldn't think twice about handing over her address to a convicted criminal who had already killed one girl and wouldn't think twice about killing another.

It was warm in the flat, but she still shivered.

Damn it! She'd been calm a moment ago and now her brain was going into overdrive, planning what she'd do if Aidan *wasn't* in Blackpool. She could move again, keep on running, or she could stay and make a stand. Quite what this stand looked like she hadn't even begun to figure out. In fact, it sounded more like a suicide mission than a plan.

Think about something else.

And not about the two murders that had recently been committed on the Mansfield. First Charlene and then, last night, the man called Dion. She had fled violence in one place only to encounter it in another. The atmosphere on the estate was charged, fizzing with a curious mix of fear and excitement. She recalled the look in Mrs Floyd's eyes as she'd recounted the grisly details.

Think about something else, *someone* else.

Harry Lind. She'd felt oddly at ease with him while he took her on a guided tour of south Kellston. He was easy to talk to, quite funny in a dry sort of way. She liked men who had a sense of humour. And men who didn't patronise. Or knock you about. Or get that cold look in their eyes just before . . . No, she wasn't going there. She wasn't going to dwell on *that*. Instead, she forced herself to focus on the case Lind was working on, the missing girl who'd disappeared all those years ago. Christine Mortlake. She had seen a photo the first time she'd gone to his office: a pale, dark-haired girl who would never grow up. A short walk from her house to her friend's on a sunny Sunday afternoon. And a mother waiting at home for a daughter who would never come back . . .

Jem's mobile rang, cutting across her reflections. She picked it up and stared at the screen. There weren't many people who had this number, only her dad (who never called), Stefan, Al, her doctor and dentist. It had flashed up as an unknown number. Probably someone trying to sell her something, or to scam her out of her life savings. She was about to reject the call when she wondered if it could be Harry Lind. She had taken his card earlier but had not yet transferred the details into her phone.

Jem hesitated but her need to know if he'd found out anything about Aidan outweighed her concern about the anonymity. She pressed the button and held the phone to her ear.

'Hello?'

There was background noise on the other end of the line – the hum of conversation, the clink of glasses, like the caller was in a pub or a restaurant – but no one spoke.

'Hello?' she said again.

Jem thought she could hear breathing, but she wasn't sure. And then suddenly the line went dead. Just a wrong number, she told herself, nothing to worry about. She put the phone down, picked up her glass and took a gulp of wine. Her hand was shaking. Her lips had gone dry. If there was nothing to worry about, why did she feel so afraid? Like the past was catching up with her. Like ice was travelling down her spine.

33

Harry was up early, showered and shaved before his watch showed seven o'clock on Sunday morning. Before leaving he made a flask of coffee and some ham sandwiches, knowing he could be sitting outside the house for hours. Surveillance could be tedious at the best of times, and he wasn't even getting paid for this stake-out. He hoped there was somewhere to park that wouldn't make him stand out like a sore thumb, and that the neighbours weren't the suspicious sort.

Harry decided to take the Mortlake file with him too, something to peruse while he was waiting and watching. He still had Moses on his mind but maybe he was making something out of nothing. As Betty had said, the man was grieving at the time and someone else's missing child had been the least of his concerns. But he wasn't going to dismiss him out of hand. It was someone else to add to a very short list of suspects.

It was still dark when he crossed the road to the Fox car park. He looked around for unwanted company, but the only other cars present were Maggie's red VW and a white Peugeot that had probably been left last night by someone who'd had too much to drink. No sign of the Beamer. Harry's black Audi – dented and scratched – was parked at the rear. Although the bodywork was old, the engine was souped up and almost new. A perfect example of never judging a book by its cover.

The car park lights were off, and the streetlamps weren't bright enough for him to be able to see clearly. He unlocked the Audi, took the torch from the glove compartment, and kneeled to examine the undercarriage and the wheel wells, checking to make sure that Danny Street hadn't put a tracker on the car. Harry could have used the bug finder they kept in the office, but he didn't entirely trust the machine to take the place of a proper manual search. It could pick up signals from mobile phones and other random places, providing a false positive and leaving you searching for non-existent trackers for half an hour.

Within a couple of minutes Harry was on the road, keeping a close eye on the rear-view mirror in case Danny or Carl were using the old-fashioned method of tailing him. With the light Sunday-morning traffic, they'd find it tricky to stay out of sight. He thought it more than likely that the delightful duo had staked out Margaret Dunn's house on more than one occasion, but maybe not for a while. With Ray being gone for so long they would have given up on him ever returning to within spitting distance of London.

Harry put on a Tom Waits playlist, some gravelly blues, and sang along as he drove out of the East End and headed for Essex. It was pleasant cruising through the streets without the usual chaos on the roads. Dawn was brightening the horizon, bringing distance into focus, and the sky was turning to a pink-striped inky blue. He had that bunking-off feeling, a sensation of stolen hours, of liberation. He should probably be working on the Mortlake case but even a private detective deserved a day off every now and again. Not that this was a day off exactly, but it wasn't something he was being paid for.

As he grew closer to North Weald, Harry started thinking about what he'd do if he did find Ray at Margaret Dunn's house. Talk to him? Tell him his children wanted him home? Ask him what the hell he'd done to upset Danny and Carl so much? Whatever their reason for wanting to find him, it was connected to more than a second-hand car. But Ray was a flight risk. If Harry did make an approach, there was every chance that the bloke would be packing a bag and bidding a fond farewell to his mother as soon as he'd left.

So he'd have to think about it. Decide what course of action to take. If any. And it didn't help that he had no idea what Ray looked like. What if Margaret had other sons? A son-in-law? He could have asked Kayleigh to give him a description but that would have been like making a deal with her, agreeing to look for her dad, creating an obligation where he didn't want one. He wondered again where she'd got that two hundred quid from, a large amount of money for a ten-year-old to have.

Harry found a place to pull in, switched off the music and keyed Margaret's postcode into the sat nav. For the next ten minutes he was guided through the streets by a supercilious female until he reached his destination and could thankfully turn her off. The houses along Larch Avenue reminded him of the properties in Silverstone Road, as if they'd all been built to the same spec: uninspiring two-up, two-down squares with pebbledash exterior walls and spare front gardens.

He did a drive-by, clocking number 26 before circling round and finding a place to park that was close enough to provide a clear view of the front door but far enough away not to arouse suspicion from anyone glancing idly out of the window.

It was seven minutes past eight.

Harry saw that the curtains were open and hoped that meant someone was up and about. Perhaps Ray, if he was there, might come out and head down the road for a paper or a pint of milk or some fags. Or maybe there was a dog that needed walking. Although the rain could be a deterrent in that respect: it had started coming down in long slanting arrows, bouncing off the windscreen and gathering in the gutters.

He drank some coffee and listened to the news – a nurses' strike, more rail strikes, the economy on the rocks – and felt like he'd been transported back to the seventies. It was only a matter of time before the lights went out and the rubbish started piling up in the streets. So much for progress.

Larch Avenue was quiet, with only the occasional car going by. While he was waiting, he used his phone to do a search of the archives of the *Kellston Gazette* and the *Hackney Herald*, but neither of them went back as far as he wanted. He was looking for further information on the hit-and-run involving the wife and daughter of Moses. When a general google search came up with nothing either, he sighed with frustration.

With nothing better to do, Harry embarked on some fresh searches on the Greers and the Mortlakes, but didn't come up with anything new. The Bayles offered more fertile results – Richard's successful career as a barrister, Jackie's brief fame as an actress – but he couldn't see either of them as being likely candidates for Christine's disappearance. Vivienne's mother had been a good-looking woman, a striking redhead and, purely in the interests of research, he took a few moments to study her Rosetti-like face and hourglass figure.

But he was getting distracted. Harry's eyes flicked between his phone and Margaret Dunn's house. No change. No activity. Was it too early to eat a sandwich? He could be here for hours, and it made sense to ration his provisions. He reached out for the Mortlake file lying on the passenger seat, placed it on his lap and opened it.

Trying to imagine that hot summer's day when it was currently lashing down outside wasn't easy. How many times had he gone over it in his head? Not as many times as Celia, that was for sure. He felt pressure to provide some kind of resolution for her. But the years had done a good job of covering up the evidence, layer upon layer of accumulated dust, of long-lost clues and fading memories.

He hoped that Pauline Greer, if he ever got to see her, could shed some light on it all. And Amy too if she was still around. Especially Amy. Had anyone even listened to them back then? Listened to them properly? The police had been so focused on the family as suspects that they hadn't been able to see beyond it. Alec Beddows had been more open-minded, but he'd been too junior to have any influence.

Harry was silently cursing the incompetence of DCI Sharp's investigation when his phone rang. It was Valerie.

'I didn't wake you up, did I?' she said, as soon as he picked up.

'Only from a very boring surveillance job.'

'Ah, poor you. Anyway, I've got some good news about your Aidan Hague.'

'That was fast.'

'I put in a call last night to a colleague. Your client can rest easy. Hague isn't in Blackpool or anywhere else. He was murdered a few days ago.'

Harry pressed the phone against his ear. 'What? Are you sure?'

'No, I'm just making it up for the fun of it. Of course I'm sure. A bullet through his head, and then the vehicle was set on fire.'

'And this was in Blackpool?'

'Yes, but they've only just identified him and released his name so there hasn't been anything in the media yet. Well, there might be by now, something on the internet at least. Anyway, good news for your client, not so great for you. This must be the shortest case you've ever had.'

'I can live with it. Has anyone been arrested?'

'Not yet. Although come to think of it,' Valerie said, only half-jokingly, 'I hope your client has a decent alibi for Thursday night.'

'I'll be sure to check. Can't see her committing cold-blooded murder, though. Sounds more gangland style to me.'

'Ah, Harry, you always underestimate the vengefulness of women.'

'Do I?'

Valerie gave a light laugh. 'Okay, I've got to go. Enjoy your stake-out.'

'Thanks for the information.'

Harry hung up and considered if he *was* the master of under-estimation. Her comment, even if it hadn't been entirely serious, got him thinking. For a moment it crossed his mind that Jem could have gone to Blackpool on Thursday evening – on the train, in a car – did she even have a car? – shot Aidan Hague and returned to London. But then why employ him to look for Hague? No, it was ridiculous. She wasn't capable of murder. And she hadn't faked that scene in his office, or the terror when she was talking about him.

Harry found her number on his phone and was about to call when he decided it would be better to do it face to face. It wasn't as if she was in any danger now. If Aidan Hague had been on her trail, he'd been stopped in his tracks. He would tell her the good news when he got back to Kellston.

34

Phillip already had the hump by the time he went out to buy a paper. For one he had another hangover – a deep throbbing in his temples that felt like a hammer beating on his brains – and for another, he had just looked at Freya's Instagram account and found that she was currently on holiday, pre-Christmas skiing in Austria. And not just in any resort but in bloody St Anton. How much was that costing her? Or, more to the point, how much of *his* money was she spending on it? The divorce settlement still rankled: the cheating bitch hadn't deserved a penny. And now there she was, dressed up to the nines, drinking cocktails in some fancy bar overlooking the white glittering slopes.

He stomped off the estate on to Mansfield Road and then turned left on to the high street. The rain had eased off to a drizzle, but dark storm clouds were starting to gather again. He glanced up at the sky, hoping he'd make it there and back without getting a soaking. No soft flurries of snow here, no beautiful mountains, no panoramic views to swell the soul. A quiet rage was bubbling inside him.

At the newsagent's he bought a copy of the *Observer* and a can of Coke. He toyed with the idea of buying *The Times* instead, of shifting his allegiance to something more right wing, but old habits die hard. What would Chapel read? Probably the *Sun on Sunday*.

Phillip had just got back, had just entered the lobby, when he spotted Nola Dunn approaching the lifts. She looked as rough as he felt. It was obvious that she'd been out all night with her creased clothes and smudged mascara. Like something the cat had dragged in. He hurried over to join her. 'Morning,' he said.

Nola gave an ugly grunt. She didn't smile. She barely even glanced at him.

'Good night was it?' he persisted, if only to let her know that he was perfectly aware that she had only now got home.

Nola's eyes narrowed as she glared at him. 'Did you want something?'

Phillip didn't like her tone. He didn't like anything about her. She was a cheap little tart who didn't even have a civil tongue in her head. 'Just being neighbourly.' And then, channelling his inner Chapel, he asked provocatively, 'How are the kids?' Doubtless she had left them to fend for themselves while she went out whoring.

Nola glared at him. 'What the fuck have my kids got to do with you?' she said loudly. 'What are you, some kind of paedo?'

Phillip felt something in him snap. Everyone passing through the lobby could hear her. This was how rumours started, how perfectly innocent people ended up being labelled as perverts and hounded out of their homes. His cheeks burned bright red. He wanted to put his hands around her throat, shove her hard against the wall and shatter that empty skull of hers. Instead, he pushed his face close to hers and hissed, 'You should be careful what you say, Nola Dunn. If it wasn't for me keeping my mouth shut, you and your daughter would be down the nick right now.'

Nola snorted. 'You got a screw loose or what?'

'I saw her on Friday night. Kayleigh, isn't it? I saw her at Dion's flat buying your weed for you. I don't suppose that would go down too well with the police – or the social come to that.'

'You're talking crap,' she said. 'Kayleigh was nowhere near that Dion's.'

'If you say so.'

'She was in all night with me.'

Phillip drew back from the dirty tart – he could smell her stinking breath, her stale perfume – and gave her a smug smile. 'Must have been her twin sister, then.'

'I'm telling you, my Kayleigh didn't go nowhere near him,' Nola repeated. She jabbed at the button to open the lift doors and stepped inside.

Phillip followed her in. 'You can deny it as much as you like but I saw her with my own eyes.'

'Then you should get your fucking eyes tested.'

'You should be grateful that I've kept you both out of it. There's plenty who wouldn't have.'

Nola, her hands on her hips, stood by the doors as the lift travelled up. 'I don't know what your game is, mister, but you're playing it with the wrong person.'

Phillip was reminded again of Freya, of his ex-wife's ability to lie through her teeth, to blatantly refute his accusations, to try and make him think he was imagining things, to make him question his own sanity. Gaslighting – wasn't that what they called it? Well, he wasn't going to take it from this little tramp. 'A thank you would be nice.'

'Fuck off.'

The lift reached the sixth floor, stopped, gave a small ding and slid open its doors. Phillip stared at her as he stepped out. 'You'd better hope I don't change my mind. It's only a short walk to Cowan Road.'

But the doors were already closing and if Nola had anything to say in response it was swallowed up by the screen of metal. 'Bitch,' he muttered as he walked towards his flat. What was the point of women like Nola Dunn? They were only good for one thing and in her case even that was questionable. Who'd want to screw that filthy tart? Chapel was right. She didn't deserve to live. She was vile and disgusting, scum of the earth. He unlocked his door and slammed it shut behind him.

35

Kayleigh was in the kitchen making lunch for herself and Kit. Fish fingers under the grill and baked beans in the pan. Last night she had lain awake until the early hours, listening for the key in the door, but her mother hadn't come back. Here we go again, she'd thought, doing mental calculations as to how long the money would last. Getting up to a Nola-less flat, she had given Kit the usual spiel about how she must have got delayed, that she'd be home before he knew it, that there was nothing to worry about. Did he worry? Maybe, like her, he was used to it now.

As she was stirring the beans to stop them sticking, she heard the front door open and close. She relaxed. For once her fears had been unjustified. Her relief didn't last long, however.

'Kayleigh Dunn!' Nola yelled. 'I want a fucking word with you.'

Kayleigh braced herself. 'I'm in here.'

Nola stormed through, throwing her bag on the counter. She glared at her daughter. 'I've just had some bloody scumbag telling me that you were at that Dion's on Friday night.'

'What?' Kayleigh said, attempting to look confused. 'Dion's? Who told you that? I never went near him. I don't even know where he lived, not which flat or nothing. I was at Tracey's.'

'You'd better not be lying to me.'

'Who said I was there?'

'Some balding piece of middle-aged crap. Going on about how he could have gone to the law. Said he saw you with his own eyes. Why would he say that if it wasn't true?'

Kayleigh frowned, remembering what Mrs Floyd had said about the bloke called Chapel, the one who lived on the sixth floor. Damn it, damn it, damn it! He must have seen her at the flat. She took a deep breath and shrugged. 'I dunno. He's got me mixed up with someone else.'

'What, some other ten-year-old who looks exactly like you?'

'I was at Tracey's. We were doing that project. Go and ask her if you want.'

'Oh yeah, as if she's going to tell me the truth.'

'What would I be doing at Dion's?' Kayleigh said, turning away to stir the beans. 'I didn't even know him. Maybe that bloke just saw me when I was coming home.'

'If you've been up to something, Kayleigh Dunn, you'd better tell me right now before the law turns up on our doorstep.'

Kayleigh glanced over her shoulder. 'What could I have been up to? I was at Tracey's. I swear. Do you want some of these fish fingers?'

'No, I don't want any bloody fish fingers. I want to know why some random is claiming my daughter was at Dion Dixon's flat on the night he was murdered.'

For one crazy moment Kayleigh considered a confession – she wanted to tell someone, anyone, about the awfulness of finding Dion's body – but the desire was short-lived. Not only would telling the truth mean admitting to having lied for the past two minutes, but it wouldn't take Nola long to work out that if she'd been delivering for Dion, she'd have been collecting cash too. And from there it would be one short step to seeing all her money disappear into Nola's purse. 'How would I know? Maybe he was just winding you up.'

Nola opened her mouth but swiftly closed it again. She seemed to have run out of steam. She went over and put the kettle on, took the coffee jar out of the cupboard and got some milk from the fridge. Her movements were slow and measured like she was learning to make instant coffee for the first time.

Kayleigh switched off the grill and plated up the food. 'Kit! Your lunch is ready.'

Nola's gaze swung between the kettle and Kayleigh. 'If you're lying to me,' she said, 'you'll bloody well regret it.'

'I'm not.'

Kayleigh wondered if Harry Lind had found the address for her nan yet. Maybe they could go and live with her in Essex. Would the house be big enough? She and Kit didn't take up much room. It would be nice to live in a place where you didn't have to worry about where the next meal was coming from, or being left alone, or having clean clothes to wear, or even, God forbid, getting murdered.

Nola shambled into the living room with her coffee, muttering under her breath.

Kayleigh was glad she hadn't come clean. Her mother couldn't be trusted with secrets. Her mother couldn't be trusted full stop.

36

Shortly after midday, Harry's patience was rewarded. The man who emerged from number 26 was tall, thin, with cropped light brown hair. He was wearing a grey sweatshirt and black joggers and had a furtive look about him. In his early thirties, Harry estimated, which put him in the right age bracket to be Kayleigh's father.

Harry pretended to be checking his phone as the man passed by on the other side of the road. He waited until Ray – if that's who it was – had turned the corner, and then slipped the Mortlake file under his seat, got out of the car, and followed at a distance. Once he had him in sight again, he kept his face averted, gazing off to the left in case the man glanced over his shoulder.

Two minutes later, his target pushed through the door of the Royal Oak. After waiting for several minutes Harry followed him inside. He still had no clear idea of whether he was going to talk to him or not. For now, he was just playing it by ear, trying to get a feel for the situation. The pub was quiet, with only a handful of customers. It was one of those country-style places with beams, a wood floor and a log fire burning in the grate. There was a lunch menu chalked on a blackboard and he felt his stomach rumble. Two ham sandwiches weren't enough to keep an adult male's hunger at bay.

Harry spotted the man straight away, sitting in the corner with a pint in front of him. Waiting for someone? It was hard to say. He was hunched over the table gazing into his glass, as if some answers could be found in its beery depths. Harry didn't stare. He ordered a tonic and lime, paid and stayed at the bar. From here he had a good view of most of the pub, and especially of the person he was interested in.

Over the next ten minutes the place began to fill up. Harry sipped his drink and surreptitiously watched. He had to make a decision soon. The bloke might only stay for one pint before he went home again, and once he was back in the house, Harry had no way of getting to him. If Margaret answered the door, she could easily deny that her son was there – and by tomorrow, maybe even tonight, he could have scarpered. Harry didn't want to approach him in the street either; although he didn't look to be in the peak of fitness, the man had two fully functional legs and could probably still outrun him.

Harry thought about Kayleigh. What was the point in even coming to North Weald if he wasn't going to follow through? But there was reason behind his hesitancy. He didn't want to have his worst suspicions confirmed – that Ray was a deadbeat, that he didn't care about his kids – and then have to diplomatically pass on the bad news that Daddy wasn't coming home.

But what was the alternative? Let sleeping dogs lie? No, he'd come here for a purpose, so he might as well grab the opportunity of asking some questions while he could. Decision made, Harry drained his glass, left the bar and sauntered down the centre of the pub as if he was looking for someone or was on his way to the gents. He stopped by the man's table and smiled.

'Hey, Ray Dunn, isn't it?' he said, in a pally sort of way as if they'd met before.

Ray, caught off guard, looked up sharply and stared, frowning, trying to place him. But he didn't deny his name. At least not immediately. There was a moment's thought – Harry could almost see the cogs in his brain revolving – before he said, 'Sorry, mate, but I think you've got the wrong person.'

Harry pulled out a chair and sat down opposite him. 'Come off it, Ray. I'd know you anywhere. It's been a few years, mind, but I never forget a face.'

Ray's gaze darted around the pub, focusing briefly on the door – calculating whether he should make a run for it, perhaps – before settling on Harry again. He shrugged, still trying to play the mistaken identity game, but his body language gave him away. His shoulders were tight, his jaw clenched, his eyes full of fear.

'Don't worry,' Harry said. 'Danny Street hasn't sent me. Or Carl Froome, come to that.'

Ray flinched at the names. 'I don't know who—'

'Oh, cut the crap, Ray. I haven't come all this way to listen to your bullshit.'

'So what the fuck have you come for?' Ray Dunn might have pulled the bravado out of the bag, but he still looked like a cornered animal, tightly coiled and waiting for the killer blow.

Harry took his ID out of his wallet and slid it across the table. 'To be honest, I didn't think it would be this easy to find you. If I can do it, so can they. I mean, your mum's, for God's sake. It's hardly the most original place to hide out.'

Ray picked up the ID and stared at it. His pale, blotchy face took on an expression of petulance. 'I've only been here a couple of weeks. She moved from Romford, didn't she? A couple of years ago now. After Carl kept showing up on the doorstep and shouting the odds. He hasn't been back, so I reckon he doesn't know where she is.' He passed the ID back to Harry. 'So if it's not Carl, who are you working for?'

'Three guesses,' Harry said.

Ray's sigh was one of resignation. 'Nola.'

Harry didn't immediately put him right. 'The past always catches up with you in the end. You never thought of giving her a call, letting her know you were still alive?'

'I tried, a few weeks after I'd left, but she'd changed her number. Mum said she didn't want anything more to do with me – or with her, come to that. And once Nola makes her mind up, that's it. Can't say I blame her. I fucked up good and proper.'

'Want to tell me about it?'

'Why should I?'

Harry raised his eyebrows. 'Because it's only a matter of time before Carl and Danny track you down. And yeah, you can take off, go somewhere else, but you'll always be looking over your shoulder. Is that how you want to live for the rest of your life?'

'Can't see I've got much choice.' Ray sounded sulky, like a child. He drank some beer and put his glass down on the table. 'Why's Nola so keen to get hold of me all of a sudden? Are the kids all right? Has something happened?'

'It wasn't Nola who asked me to look for you.'

Ray tensed and his eyes filled with suspicion again. 'What? Who then?'

'It was your daughter, Kayleigh.'

'But she's only . . . ' Ray had to pause to figure out her age in his head. 'She's only ten.'

'Good of you to remember.'

Ray shot him a look, but whatever retort he may have

234

considered died on his lips. Perhaps he thought he deserved the jibe.

'She came into the office,' Harry continued. 'She's a smart girl, your daughter. Of course, I couldn't take her on as a client, her being the age she is, but I figured it wouldn't do any harm to put out a few feelers. Anyway, as you can see, you weren't too hard to find.'

'So what does Nola think about all this?'

'I've no idea. I got the impression Kayleigh hadn't told her. She did say it was hard for her though, being a single mum. I suspect things aren't entirely rosy on the home front.'

Ray put his head in his hands and groaned. 'I wanted to go back but I couldn't. Danny Street would have killed me. I figured it was better for everyone, for Nola, for the kids, to just stay away.'

'Is that what you told yourself?'

'It's the truth,' Ray said vehemently. 'You know what he's like.'

'And what had you done, exactly?'

Ray shook his head, unwilling to spill.

Harry pushed back his chair and got to his feet.

'What are you doing?' Ray said.

'Leaving,' Harry said. 'I've got better things to do with my Sunday afternoon than sit here listening to you. I'll tell Kayleigh I couldn't find you. It's probably best all round, don't you think? I wouldn't want her imagining that you simply don't care.'

'Who said I didn't care? I sent Nola money, five grand to tide her over, just until I got myself sorted. Once the dust had settled, I was going to get them all up to join me, only ...'

'Only?'

'Things didn't pan out like I'd hoped.'

'Clearly,' Harry said. 'But as you obviously don't want my help, I can't see any point in hanging around.'

'And how *are* you going to help? Unless you've got a spare thirty grand in your back pocket. And even then, Danny Street's not going to forgive me for nicking from him in the first place.'

Harry, sensing that Ray finally wanted to talk, sat back down again. 'Tell me what you did.'

Ray ran his tongue along dry lips. 'How do I know I can trust you?'

'You don't. You'll just have to take a leap of faith. What have you got to lose?'

Ray obviously thought he had plenty to lose – he played with his glass, turning it around in his hand – while he considered his options. This didn't take long. His options were limited, and he knew it. 'It was a spur-of-the moment thing. I didn't plan it or nothing. One of Danny Street's goons had come to the show-room in the early afternoon, carrying a holdall full of money.'

'How did you know there was money in it?'

'Because it arrived every four weeks or so. Usually, it was Danny Street who did the delivery, but he was inside then, doing a short stretch for assault. I saw Carl emptying the money into the safe once. Bundles of readies, like thousands of pounds. Carl would put it through the books – sales from imaginary cars, I'm guessing, although I don't know all the ins and outs, only that Danny brought the cash round and Carl banked it as income from the business.'

'So you knew something dodgy was going on?'

'Nothing to do with me,' Ray said. 'I wasn't going to start asking questions. It might not have been the greatest job in the world, but it was still a job. I couldn't afford to lose it.' He took a couple of large swigs from his pint, then went quiet.

'And?' Harry prompted.

Ray took a deep breath and exhaled. 'The goon had just left when some punter started kicking off out in the yard, shouting about a motor he'd bought that kept breaking down. Carl went to deal with it. I was passing his office – I was on my way out to lunch – when I saw the holdall on his desk. It was still zipped up. He hadn't even opened it. Like I said, it was a spur-of-the-moment thing. The office door wasn't locked, and I went in and grabbed the bag, went out the back door, got in my car and cleared off.'

Harry raised his eyebrows. 'I can't see Danny being too pleased about that.'

'Yeah, but he was banged up, wasn't he? Not much he could do about it. Anyway, I drove and kept on driving. I knew I had to get away as fast as I could.'

'I won't ask what you were thinking.'

'I wasn't bloody thinking. Well, if I was, it was just that I was sick of it all, the daily slog, the scrimping and saving, the always struggling to make ends meet. Suddenly there it was – a way out. A bag full of money that I could use to start a new life. I knew I'd never get an opportunity like that again.'

'A new life without the wife and kids.'

'No,' Ray said, shaking his head. 'It wasn't like that. I swear. Not that everything was brilliant between me and Nola, but that was mainly down to money. I just didn't have time to stop and pick them up. She was at work and the kids were at school and nursery. I was going to ring her later, tell her where I was and what was going on, but then I thought it would be better if I left it for a while, made it look like I'd done a runner. That way Nola and the kids wouldn't get any grief. The less they knew about it all, the better.'

Harry didn't believe him. He was more inclined towards a story where Ray *had* done a runner, had stared temptation straight in the face and been unable to resist. Act first and think later. 'Bit risky, wasn't it? Leaving her to deal with the fallout?'

Ray's face tightened. 'Carl isn't the violent sort. I knew he'd panic, but he wouldn't hurt her. He wouldn't go to the law either. How could he when the money I'd nicked was dodgy to start with? Nah, he'd go round to the flat and see if she knew anything, but he wouldn't push it. He'd just try and suss out if I'd done the dirty on her too.'

'So why send her all that money? Why not just give her enough for the train fare and ask her to join you, to bring the kids to wherever you where?'

'Glasgow,' Ray said. 'That's where I ended up. And I needed some time to get things sorted, to find another job, to get us somewhere to live. And anyway, I knew Carl would be watching her, waiting to see if she took off too. I had to wait for everything to calm down, until it was safe for them to leave.'

Harry got the impression that Ray was rewriting history, telling it like he wanted it to be, trying to put himself in a better light. There was a weakness about him, something pathetic. He knew he'd made a huge mistake, but he wasn't prepared to own it.

'When I did try and call,' Ray continued, 'the number wasn't working. I got Mum to go round, to find out what was going on, but it turned into an unholy row and Nola chucked her out.'

'Does she know what you did? Your mum, I mean? Did you tell her?'

'At the beginning I told her that we'd had a falling out, me and Nola, and that I'd gone away for a while. Some space, you know? She was never that keen on Nola anyway. She only put up with her because of the kids.'

'And when Danny and Carl showed up on her doorstep?'

'Yeah, she was none too pleased about that. It was about three months later, when Danny had got out and was looking to get his money back. Though I reckon he'd have made Carl pay him anyway just for being so bloody careless. They must have got her address from Nola. It's the sort of thing she'd do.'

Personally, Harry didn't blame her. By then she'd have realised that Ray must have taken off with a large sum of money – only some of which had come her way – and that he wasn't coming home anytime soon. Concern for her husband's welfare, or her mother-in-law's come to that, was probably the last thing on her mind. 'What did your mum tell them?'

'That she didn't know where I was, that she hadn't seen me in months, that she'd call the law if they kept on harassing her. Not that that stopped them. In the end she decided that the smartest thing to do was move.'

But mothers were more forgiving than wives, Harry thought. They'd stand by their kids no matter what. He felt pissed off at Ray for leaving Nola to deal with everything alone. Being on the wrong side of Danny Street wasn't a good place to be. 'You could have written to Nola, told her what was going on.'

'I'm not much of a letter writer. And anyway, she'd already made up her mind that I'd left her. *She* was the one who changed her phone number and wouldn't even tell Mum what it was. There didn't seem to be a way back. If I even set foot in Kellston again, I know Danny will have me.' Ray paused, drained his glass and then heaved out one of his self-pitying sighs. 'Twenty-five grand sounds like a lot but it doesn't last long, not with the price of everything these days. It took me ages to get another job.'

'Didn't you worry about how Nola was coping? It's not cheap having to feed and clothe two kids.'

'Course I worried. That's why I came back. I miss the kids. I want to see them again.'

Harry thought three years was a long time to be missing your kids and not do anything about it, but he kept his opinion to himself. He suspected Ray had only come back because things had gone wrong in Glasgow. Despite the risk of Danny Street finding him, he'd been forced to break cover and seek refuge at his mother's.

'So how did you find me?' Ray said. He was fidgeting, glancing around the pub, afraid that his enemy might walk in through the door. 'Like you said, if you can do it, Danny can too.'

'Kayleigh gave me Margaret's number – Nola had it on her phone – and we traced the number to the North Weald address.' Then, because he didn't want Ray getting spooked and doing another runner, he added, 'If Danny had been able to do that, he'd have done it by now, so I wouldn't worry too much on that score.'

'Why didn't Kayleigh just call my mum?'

'Would your mother have told her you were there?' Harry didn't wait for a reply. 'Kayleigh thought you'd just run off again.'

Ray shifted his shoulders and scratched his chin. He looked simultaneously downcast and rattled, as if running off seemed a pretty good idea right now. 'So what next? How the hell do I get out of this mess?'

Harry didn't have an answer to that, at least nothing that sprang instantly to mind. 'Just sit tight for the moment. Keep your head down and don't do anything stupid.'

37

Jem could hear what Harry Lind was saying but it wasn't really sinking in. That's because she didn't believe it. He'd called five minutes ago, said he was passing the Mansfield and that he had some information for her. Now he was standing in the living room telling her that Aidan was dead, but she knew that he wasn't. She felt it in her gut, in the very core of her. If Aidan had really gone, she would be feeling it in her soul, in her heart; she would be feeling that darkness lifting to reveal a light she hadn't seen for so long.

'He can't be.'

'I know it's hard to process but it's true. You don't need to worry anymore. I got the information from a police contact in Manchester. There's no doubt about it.'

'How? How did he die?'

'He was shot in the head. In his car.'

She sensed there was more, stuff he wasn't telling her. Sparing her feelings. 'When?'

'Thursday night. He's been identified.'

'It can't be him,' she said. 'He called me last night.'

Lind looked startled. 'What? You talked to him?'

'No, he didn't speak, but I know it was him.' She could see Lind watching her, could almost see the thoughts whirring through his head: that she was in denial, that it was all too much for her, that she couldn't grasp the reality of what had happened. 'I'm sure of it.'

'It could have been a wrong number.'

'It could have been, but it wasn't.' She knew she must sound crazy. Maybe she *was* crazy. How could she explain about the quality of that silence, the creepy lightness of breath, the venom leaking down the line? Sometimes you just knew things without being able to explain them properly. 'Who identified him?'

'I don't know. The police, I presume. Dental records.'

'Why would they need dental records?'

Lind briefly looked away as if unwilling to share this final unsavoury piece of information. 'The car was set on fire after he was shot.'

'Ah,' she said. 'So he was unrecognisable.' And there it was – the flaw to the story. She smiled thinly. If it *had* been Aidan, she might have taken some satisfaction from the thought of him burning in hell. It was the very least he deserved. But she wasn't convinced that he had gone to meet his maker, even if his maker was Satan himself.

'I'm sure they'll have checked and double-checked.'

'Aidan's clever. You've no idea what lengths he'd go to. It might suit him for everyone to believe he was dead.' Suit him, she thought, because dead men couldn't commit murder. They were invisible. They could walk around, make phone calls and dispose of their enemies in whatever fiendish ways they wanted. But then, because Lind was looking so dejected – he had come here thinking he was delivering good news – she felt suddenly guilty about pouring cold water on everything he'd said. 'I'm sorry. It's just the shock. I can't ... I can't take it in just yet. Thank you for coming to tell me. I appreciate it.'

'I understand. You'll need some time to get used to the idea.'

'Yes. Yes, that's true.'

As she walked with him into the hall Lind was saying something about giving him a call if there was anything else she needed to know, but she was only half listening, her head too full of Aidan's 'death' to concentrate on anything else. Aware that she was chivvying him along, she opened the door, quickly thanked him again, said goodbye, closed the door and leaned against it. Outside she heard his footsteps on the lino as he headed for the lifts.

Jem had longed for the day when Aidan would no longer occupy her thoughts or terrorise her dreams, but that day wasn't today. She was sure of it. She felt it in her bones, in every doubting, mistrustful part of her body. There was no sense of relief. Aidan may have managed to fool the police, but she hadn't been taken in.

She pushed herself off the door and went through to the living room. Here she paced from one side to the other, unable to stay still. Dental records? They could be faked, couldn't they? He could have paid off a dentist or, if the dentist was a woman, used his charm to persuade them to swap his records for someone else's, the someone else who was probably lying in the morgue right now. A man of about the same age and height, a man who in a charred state could easily pass for Aidan Hague. Complicated but not impossible. Although if she was to go down a simpler route, he could have just bribed a cop to switch the evidence.

Jem kept coming back to that phone call. What if it *had* been a wrong number? What if Aidan had screwed with her head so much that even after he was dead, she was unable to believe it? That would mean her looking over her shoulder for the rest of her life. Although that might not be too long now that he was free to do as he liked.

She wrapped her arms around her chest, stopped by the window and looked down on the estate. Quiet apart from some kids kicking a football around, and a few dealers looking to provide relief from Sunday boredom. Her gaze strayed to the gate and lingered there for a while. It would have amused Aidan to have faked his own death, hoping to lull her into a false sense of security. But she wasn't going to drop her guard. If anything, she would be even more vigilant now, even more careful.

38

The Monday-morning meeting was a casual affair with the three of them – Harry, Mac and Lorna – gathered round the desk in reception. They drank coffee and caught up on the events of the previous week. Mac, who had always thought the Mortlake case was more trouble than it was worth, raised his eyebrows when Harry revealed that he'd finally tracked down Pauline Greer – or Pauline Neames as she was currently known.

'And what's she going to say that's any different to what she's said before?'

'I'd still like to hear it from her,' Harry said. 'And to get hold of Amy if I can.'

Lorna suggested that it might be better if she made the phone call to the home in Whitstable, that on the whole people were less suspicious about women asking questions than men. 'I'll get the visiting times and make some enquiries about Pauline's health. There's no point going all the way to Kent if she's not well enough to see you.'

Mac shifted his bulk and stared longingly at the empty paper bag that had contained Harry's breakfast. He had lost weight, over a stone, since Lorna had put him on a strict diet after his heart attack, but he wasn't immune to temptation. 'Did Beddows have anything to bring to the party?'

'Only that DCI Sharp wasn't as smart as his name suggests. He was completely focused on the Greers to the detriment of the entire investigation. Tunnel vision. He wasn't prepared to accept that anyone else was involved.'

Mac leaned back in his chair, put his hands behind his head and nodded. 'Yeah, some cops are like that. How long are you going to spend on this, Harry? And don't say as long as it takes. I don't want a complaint from Celia Mortlake that we've been taking her money and getting zero results. It might start to look like we're taking advantage.'

'She won't complain. She's not a fool; she knows the chances are slim. Once I've exhausted all avenues, I'll call it a day. A couple of weeks, maybe.'

'By Christmas, then?'

'Yeah,' Harry said, 'by Christmas.' He didn't mention Moses or his chat with Leonard and Betty in the Fox or any of his wild suspicions. It was all too vague right now, too blurred around the edges. He had the feeling there was something just beyond his grasp, a clue that he couldn't quite get hold of. It was like spotting a movement out of the corner of his eye, only every time he turned his head there was nothing there.

The talk moved on to an insurance case Mac was working on and shortly after that the meeting broke up. Back in his office, Harry glanced across the road at the florist's as he sat down. He hadn't seen Jem arrive this morning and there was still no sign of her now. Then he remembered that she worked on Saturdays and so probably had Mondays off.

He had thought a lot about her reaction to the news but

hadn't come to any firm conclusions. It was understandable that she hadn't immediately been able to accept Aidan's death – her fear of him had become entrenched, a part of her life – but he hoped she would come to believe it eventually. Otherwise, she would be living in a strange kind of limbo, unable to relax, always looking out for ghosts.

Now that Aidan Hague was dead, the case was finished before it had even got going. He'd return her deposit – it hardly seemed reasonable to charge her for a single phone call – and close the file. He had no reason to see her again, although as she worked across the road it was not beyond the bounds of possibility that they would bump into each other from time to time. He could go into the shop and buy some flowers but that might send out the message that he had someone to give flowers to. A Christmas wreath, perhaps. He'd think about it.

At twenty past nine, Harry heard Mac leave the office and half an hour later Lorna knocked on his door. She poked her head in and said, 'I've been in touch with Seaview. What would you like first, the good news or the bad?'

'Always the bad.'

'Pauline has Alzheimer's, not in the later stages yet but she does tend to get confused. The good news is that her daughter visits frequently. I've left a message with the home for Amy to call me urgently. No details, just my name. If she does ring, I'll put her through to you.'

'Thanks. It's going to be tricky getting her to agree to meet.'

'You'll just have to use your charm.'

Harry smiled thinly. 'I suspect it'll take more than that to talk her round. I'm sure the last thing she wants to hear is that someone's looking into the Mortlake case again.'

Lorna came into the office and perched on the edge of his desk. 'You're not bothered by what Mac said, are you?'

'No.'

'What's on your mind, then? Something's bugging you.'

Harry could have picked from a list – Jem, Val, Moses, Celia, the seemingly impenetrable circumstances surrounding Christine Mortlake's disappearance – but in the end he chose Kayleigh Dunn. Lorna needed to know about her anyway in case she called by the office when he was out. He gave a quick rundown of the girl's visits, how she was searching for her father, and explained about speaking to Carl Froome, about Kayleigh giving him Margaret's mobile number and what had happened with Ray yesterday.

'You're getting soft in your old age,' Lorna said. 'If word gets around half the kids on the Mansfield will be queuing up for free Dad-searching services.'

Harry, who didn't want to come across as a complete push-over, said, 'Well, I was at a loose end and fancied a drive so North Weald seemed as good a place as any. It wasn't as if he was hard to find.'

'Are you going to tell her?'

Harry shook his head. 'Not yet. It's all a bit complicated, isn't it? I need some time to think it over.'

'Perhaps you should talk to her mum.'

'I would, but if I tell Nola where he is, she might just pass the information on to Danny Street. There's no love lost between her and Ray, not after he abandoned her like that.'

'Got you,' Lorna said. 'And you don't want to get on the wrong side of Danny Street.'

'I think that ship might have sailed already. We had words in the Fox on Saturday night. Mind, he looked like he was off his head so he might not remember.'

'What sort of words?'

'The sort you exchange when you've noticed Danny Street's

car following you. Before I went to the pub, I went to take another look at Magellan Street and found Street's Beamer on my tail.'

'You think he's interested in the Mortlake case?'

'I can't see why he would be. He wasn't even born when Christine went missing. No, I reckon Froome told him about me asking after Ray, and Danny thought I might know where he was. Or perhaps he was just trying to intimidate me into giving out an address. It wasn't what you'd call a subtle tail.'

'Does Danny Street do subtle?'

'Yeah, I'm not sure it's in his repertoire.'

'You should watch yourself, Harry. It might not be such a great idea to get involved in this Ray Dunn business.'

'Bit late for that.'

Lorna stood up and smoothed down her skirt. 'Well, just watch yourself, okay? I haven't got time for hospital visiting.'

Harry grinned. 'Are you suggesting that I couldn't take Danny Street?'

'That man doesn't play by the rules. All I'm suggesting is that you might not see him coming.'

'Don't worry. If he wants to find Ray, it's to his advantage to keep me in the best of health.'

'Let's hope you're right.'

Lorna returned to reception. Harry, after some brief reflection on what she'd said, tried to put it aside, opened the Mortlake file and began flicking through the pages. But he couldn't keep his mind on the job. His thoughts kept going back to Ray Dunn and the stupid mess the man had got himself into. Even if Ray had the money – which he clearly didn't – paying back the debt would never be enough. Danny Street wouldn't let people get away with ripping him off; it was more than his reputation was worth. He would demand some form of retribution and that would involve, at the very least, broken bones and a rearrangement of Ray's already less than lovely features.

Harry wondered if some kind of on-the-quiet access to the kids could be arranged through Nola, the occasional day in North Weald, perhaps. But he couldn't see her agreeing to that. Not unless Ray was about to step up and start paying for his offspring. And even if he did, how long would it take for Danny Street to figure out that he was back on the scene?

Harry shook his head, placed his elbows on the table and stared down at the Mortlake file. What was he missing? The evening of the day Christine had disappeared was of interest: the locals going out to search for her, Moses staying in the pub. The summer light would have been fading by then, the temperature dropping, hope slipping away with every minute that passed.

He would have liked to go back to Magellan Street, to walk between the two houses again, to try and shift whatever was lurking in the back of his mind, but he was afraid of missing a call from Amy. Which meant he could be stuck in the office all day. The thought was not an appealing one. Despite the filthy weather, the cold and the rain, he still preferred to be outside than in.

In the event, he needn't have worried. The staff at Seaview were more efficient than he'd expected. Someone must have rung Amy to let her know about the urgent call, or she made morning visits to see her mother. Either way she was on the line less than an hour after Lorna had left her message. The phone buzzed and he answered it.

'I've got Amy Bolton for you,' she said. 'Pauline's daughter.'

'Thanks. Put her through.'

Harry took a deep breath, thanked Amy for returning their call, introduced himself and said, 'I know this may come as a bit of a shock, but I've been asked by Celia Mortlake to look again into the disappearance of Christine.'

A noise like an angry hiss travelled into his ear. 'Oh, for God's sake!'

'Please don't hang up,' Harry said quickly. 'Just give me a minute. I know you all had a terrible time back then, that the police treated you very badly and—'

'Not just the bloody police,' she interrupted.

'No, Arthur Mortlake as well. I'm aware of that. Between them they must have made your lives a misery. I can't change any of that, but I am trying to find out what really happened.' Harry was hoping she wouldn't terminate the call while he was still talking, so tried to get her on board as fast as he could. 'The police investigation was a travesty. I've been going back over it all and I can see how biased and incompetent it was. I'm not coming at it from the same angle. I don't have any preconceived ideas.'

'You might be saying all the right things, Mr Lind, but you're still working for that woman. She's the one who's paying you.'

'To find out the truth,' Harry said. 'Nothing else. Whatever she thinks won't affect my judgement. But it would be useful, very useful, if I could talk to you and your mum.'

Amy's voice lifted in pitch. 'Don't you dare go near my mother! She's not well. She can't deal with all this being brought up again. I'll ring the police if you even try and go near her. It's harassment.'

Harry rapidly attempted to calm and reassure her. 'No, I won't. I swear. You have my word. I understand that she's unwell. But it would mean something, wouldn't it, if I could clear your family for once and for all?'

'Too late for my dad,' Amy said bitterly.

'But not for you and your mum. I can't promise anything, though. Only that I'll do my best and I'll do it objectively. A lot of time's gone by and people's memories fade. Perhaps the chances are slim of finding any new evidence but it's not impossible.'

Amy thought about this for a moment. It was doubtful that she trusted him, but the possibility of the family name being cleared tempted her – enough to overcome her suspicion of him. 'So what is it you want to know?'

'Not on the phone,' Harry said, wanting to see her face to face when he asked his questions. That way he could watch her reactions and form a judgement as to whether she was lying or not. 'Could we meet? I'm happy to come to Whitstable.'

'Today?'

'If you like.'

Amy hesitated. 'I suppose I could do this afternoon. About two? There's a café at the harbour called the Blue Yacht. I'll meet you there.'

'Thanks,' Harry said. 'I appreciate it.' But before he could say goodbye she'd already hung up. He replaced the receiver, sat back and wondered if this was the breakthrough he'd been hoping for. Surely Amy would have something to add to the investigation, or at the very least to what had been going on in Christine's life? That's if she turned up. With three hours to go before the appointment she had plenty of time to change her mind.

39

Kayleigh couldn't concentrate on what the teacher was saying. Nouns, verbs and adjectives were bobbing around on the periphery of other more dominant thoughts. What was Nola doing? Would she drink a bottle of wine, get in a funk, find Joe Chapel and confront him about Friday night? The booze always put her in a mood. And what if Nola *did* ask Tracey, or Tracey's mum, about whether she'd been at their flat doing her project?

Kayleigh glanced across the classroom at Tracey. They didn't sit together now. They'd been best mates once, tight, but now they barely spoke to each other. All that was down to Nola too: she was absent so often these days that Kayleigh was forever looking after Kit and couldn't meet up with Tracey after school or at weekends. Well, not without taking Kit with her and that had always gone down like a lead balloon. So in the end she'd just started making excuses and Tracey had drifted off, making friends with other girls.

Although she'd never admit it out loud, the split had upset her. She pretended she didn't care but she did. School was boring, *more* boring, without someone to hang out with. Could she ask Tracey to cover for her? No, she'd want to know why, and Kayleigh couldn't think of a good enough reason. Not the truth, that was for certain. She didn't trust Tracey to keep her big gob shut. She'd just have to cross her fingers and hope that Nola let it drop.

At break, the boys had been talking about the murder of Dion. One of them, a tall, loud oaf called Ben Higgins, said that he'd been wasted by Danny Street as a punishment for dealing on his patch. Kayleigh was afraid that she'd been seen by Danny, that he'd still been there when she'd gone inside the flat. If that was the case, would she be punished too? Or maybe he would just want the money she'd collected. She had the bundle of notes in her school bag, safe from Nola's grasping hands, but perhaps not from Danny Street's.

Kayleigh couldn't work out if Ben was making it up or if he really did know something. He came from a criminal family – his dad was doing a fifteen stretch for armed robbery, his older brother five years for assault – so maybe he got to hear things that others didn't. She almost envied Ben for having a dad in prison; at least he always knew where he was and got to visit once a month.

She wondered how Harry Lind was getting on. Would he have found out Nana Margaret's address? Was it too soon to go round to the office again? She worried that he might just ring the number and that Nana would come to the flat, and there'd be another row like last time where Nola called Nana a lying bitch, and Nana called Nola a cheap little slut, and there was a lot of shouting before Nana finally left and never came back.

But even all that faded into insignificance beside the threat of Danny Street. Everyone knew he was a monster, a man with a black heart. Just thinking about him made the hairs on the back of her neck stand on end. And if he had killed Dion, he could kill her too.

Jem, with nothing else to do other than fret over Aidan, had taken her paints and brushes out of the cardboard box and set to work on the Hansel and Gretel watercolour. Something to calm her mind, to keep her sane while she tried to figure out what to do next. Her first instinct was always to run, but she didn't want to listen to that voice whispering in her ear, the one that kept saying, 'He's coming for you, girl.'

Maybe she *was* nuts. Maybe Aidan had made her that way. She wanted to believe he was dead, but she couldn't. He was clever, sly, malevolent and, above all, vengeful. She quietly cursed that his 'death' held so much ambiguity, that it had not been clear and straightforward. How much better if he'd been shot in the street or stabbed or strangled. Then there would have been a recognisable body, no doubts remaining. The burnt-out car scenario stank of deceit and duplicity, of something staged, of something advantageous and all too convenient.

Jem wondered what kind of a person she'd become to sit here mentally listing the preferred methods of a man's death. A damaged one, probably. God, there was no probably about it. She had long ago moved beyond normality into the dim, shadowy world of the victim. It was hard to live with constant fear without it chipping away at your sanity.

Somewhere from the past, from five or six years ago, a banal male voice rose up from the swamp of her memory. *You're only a victim if you choose to be, Jem.* Spoken by an ex of hers – he'd become an ex shortly after providing this unhelpful comment – and his take on the situation had made her cringe. He had probably thought he was being supportive or uplifting but had only succeeded in shoring up her belief that she had terrible taste in men.

It wasn't that she wanted to be a victim – who did? – but neither did she need some amateur shrink suggesting that she should (in as many words) just get over it. How the hell could she get over Aidan Hague when he was obviously spending his every waking hour thinking of ways to get his revenge on her? Even though she had not given evidence against him it was enough, she knew, that she'd been prepared to. He had only pleaded guilty at the last minute, albeit with the claim that he had not been in his right mind at the time (when had he been?) and was full of remorse. As if he even knew the meaning of the word. The judge hadn't bought it.

Jem had known there were ways, even from inside prison, to wreak revenge on the people you perceived as having wronged you. It was only after several years had passed, years of looking over her shoulder, of waiting for the worst to happen, that she'd realised that Aidan would never delegate something so important to anyone else. He would want to be there, to inflict the pain himself, to watch her die with his own eyes. Once she'd grasped this basic fact and accepted that it was a postponement rather than a cancellation, she'd been able to relax a little, even if she was on borrowed time.

Jem laid a grey wash over the paper in long easy strokes. Here, now, at this very moment, she had control – where to put the paint, what shade to use, how to alter the light and the dark – but outside in the real world she was still at the mercy of a psychopath. She didn't care what the police thought, *she* knew him better than anyone.

Her phone rang and she jumped. For a second, she thought it was Aidan again, but then she saw that the caller was Harry Lind. Last night she had added his number to her very short address book. She considered not answering, letting it go to voicemail, but then she wondered if he'd got more information about the 'murder'.

'Hello?'

'It's Harry,' he said. 'How are you doing?'

'Good, thanks,' she said, trying to sound upbeat, trying to sound like someone who actually believed her tormentor was dead. For some reason, and she wasn't sure why she cared, she didn't want him to think that she was some mad woman in denial. Not that she'd made a very good job of that when he'd first broken the news.

'I was thinking about what you were saying the other day, about missing the sea.'

Had she said that? Maybe she had. 'Yeah?'

'I'm about to go to Whitstable – a work thing, a woman I have to talk to – and wondered if you'd like to come along for the ride? There's sea there, apparently. You could have a walk on the beach while I'm seeing her, or a look round the harbour.'

Jem hesitated. 'Whitstable?' she repeated, playing for time. The invitation had come out of the blue, and she wasn't sure how she felt about it. Was it some kind of date or just a pity excursion for the crazy girl who liked to throw her toys out of the pram?

'Kent,' he said. 'It's only an hour or so away. But don't worry if you can't – I know it's short notice.'

As if with her overstuffed social diary, she might not be able to fit in a jaunt to the seaside. She glanced out of the window at the grey sky, and down at her painting with the grey wash, and suddenly thought how nice it would be to walk on yellow sand and breathe the fresh salty air. 'Okay,' she said. 'Why not? When were you thinking of leaving?'

'Half an hour all right for you? I'll pick you up from the Mansfield.'

Even as she was hanging up, Jem was starting to regret agreeing. She began a small internal argument with herself. What if he *did* think it was a date? She wasn't in the market for a new relationship. Although she could do worse. Well, she had done worse. But perhaps he was just being kind, wondering if she might like a change of scene. Which was true. And it would be lovely to get out of London for a while. But she didn't want to give him the wrong idea. 'Oh, for God's sake,' she said, getting to her feet. 'Stop overthinking everything.' She went to the bedroom to find a sweater and a sturdy raincoat.

Phillip was working on the novel, typing at the living room table, drinking lukewarm coffee and trying not to think about Freya living it up in St Anton. How was it that she could cheat on him, screw around behind his back, and still come out of the divorce with the Camden house and enough cold hard cash to make his eyes water? And it wasn't just the money that infuriated him; she had taken most of his friends too. With his career in freefall and hers in the ascendency, his so-called pals had deserted him in droves.

'Not this again,' Chapel said. 'You're beginning to get tedious.'

'Well pardon me for breathing.'

'It's not the breathing I'm bothered about. It's the endless self-pity. Droning on and on like you're the first man to have been screwed over by a woman. I mean, Jesus, you should be used to it by now. Why don't you channel your anger into something more positive? Take some action instead of sitting there like a limp fucking lettuce, bemoaning your life but doing nothing about it.'

'This isn't nothing,' Phillip said, nodding towards the laptop. 'As near as.'

Phillip's guts gave a twist. 'What, you think it's no good?'

'I didn't mean that. It has some credit but it's still a little soft around the edges. It lacks a certain gritty realism, wouldn't you say?'

'No, I wouldn't say. I've spent six months in this hellhole immersing myself in bloody grit.'

'You've been watching, yes, I don't deny that, but you haven't been participating, mate. It's all from a distance. You need to be more ... more hands-on.'

Phillip's fingers were still poised above the keys, his confidence in freefall, when the doorbell went. The police again? He glanced at Chapel, unsure as to whether to answer it or not.

Chapel shrugged. 'It's your place, mate. Do what you want.'

What Phillip wanted was to be left alone, to get on with his writing before doubt destroyed what little was left of his faith in the plot. If Chapel was right – could he be right? – then his future was in the balance. This was his last-ditch attempt to restore his reputation. And his finances. Every time he looked at his bank statement his heart fell. If the novel wasn't a success, he might have to sell the Primrose Hill flat. And then what? He would have to leave London and find somewhere cheaper to live. And that, let's face it, was the very epitome of failure.

The doorbell went again, followed by a flurry of raps on the door. Whoever it was wasn't going to go away. Reluctantly he got to his feet. It had to be the police. No one else ever came here, not even Mrs Floyd. Whenever *she* wanted something – which was more often than was usually convenient – she would phone him up and ask if by any chance he might be going to the shops that day, not to worry if he wasn't but she was almost out of milk/tea/washing-up liquid or was down to her last few pills. He never said no. Keeping Mrs Floyd sweet was essential if he wanted to keep abreast of the latest gossip.

Phillip walked to the door expecting to find a uniform on the other side of it. He was anxious about this but not as anxious as he'd been after Charlene's murder. The killing of Dion Dixon had nothing to do with him and whatever questions they wanted to ask he could answer without fear. Unless they were here about Charlene ... Fresh worry ran through him, a shudder of apprehension, but it was too late to change his mind now. He pulled back the bolt and opened the door with trepidation. But it wasn't the police. His jaw dropped when he saw who it was. *Nola bloody Dunn.*

The woman was drunk, completely pissed. He could smell the fumes coming off her, great drifts of alcohol, as if she'd taken a shower in the stuff. Although her eyes seemed unfocused, her mouth was set in a tight straight line and her expression was fierce.

'You!' he said. 'What are you doing here?'

Nola pushed roughly past him into the flat. 'We need to talk, mister.'

With little other choice, Phillip closed the door and followed her into the living room where she stood with her hands on her hips and a face like thunder. She was wearing a pale blue minidress with a thick, tattered cream cardigan over the top. Her legs were bare, and she had a pair of silver flip-flops on her feet. Hardly sensible clothing for a December day, he thought, but then the words Nola and sensible were rarely uttered in the same sentence.

'How can I help?' Phillip said softly, not wanting another confrontation. The sooner he got her out of the flat, the better.

But this gentle enquiry only seemed to infuriate her. 'Help? You can bleedin' well help by keeping your nose out of my business. Don't start dragging me or my daughter into this Dion business. It weren't nothing to do with us.'

'Did I say it was?'

'You said my Kayleigh was there at his flat. Well, she damn well wasn't. She was with me all night so don't you go saying nothing different. I don't need trouble from the likes of you.' She looked him up and down and snarled like a wolf. 'What's the matter, man? Is your life so fucking pathetic that you need to go messing up other people's? Or are you just after a freebie, is that it? Fancy a quick fuck without paying for it, do you? I know your sort.'

Phillip stared at her, willing her to shut up. As if he'd want to fuck *that*. He couldn't even begin to imagine the diseases she must be carrying. Like a walking advertisement for the venereal clinic. 'Have you quite finished?'

Nola stuck her face into his, giving him a close-up encounter with her boozy breath. 'I've not even begun, mister. Nah, you're not after a freebie with me. I'm too old for you. It's the young ones you like, ain't it? The little girls like my Kayleigh. Well maybe I'll take a walk down Cowan Road myself and tell them how you've been watching her, offering her sweets and trying to get her into your flat. Let's see how the law feel about that!'

'Don't be ridiculous. The police aren't going to believe you.' Although even as he was saying it, Phillip wondered if it was true. How could you prove a negative? He felt a shiver run through him.

'Maybe they will, maybe they won't, but either way it's going to be all over the estate that they took you in for questioning. They don't like kiddy fiddlers on the Mansfield. I mean, shit, nobody likes them anywhere. Before you know it, they'll be spraying "paedo" on your door and shoving crap through your letterbox. Your life won't be worth living.'

The little grey cells in Phillip's brain were starting to fizz. He could feel the colour rising in his cheeks, could feel the burn of rage and indignation. Already he could imagine being in some small brightly lit room down the police station trying to prove that he had perfectly normal sexual desires and had never been aroused by the sight of a child. The very thought of this ordeal made him want to be sick. 'You're nuts,' he said. 'Crazy! Get out of my flat and go and sober up.'

But Nola stood her ground. Then she started to laugh. It was a vile, disturbing sound, devoid of any humour. 'I'm not going nowhere, hon. I reckon I deserve some compo for all the grief you've put me through. What shall we say? Fifty quid? Yeah, that sounds about right. Fifty quid so I keep my mouth shut about you and my Kayleigh.'

'You're not getting a penny out of me, you lying tart!'

'Have it your own way.' Nola started to walk towards the door, swinging her skinny hips as she flip-flopped away from him. 'You'll be sorry, though. I'll make sure of it.'

The rage rose inside Phillip, constricting his chest. Suddenly Nola Dunn felt like the embodiment of every woman who'd screwed him over, every bitch who'd trodden him underfoot, every conniving cow who'd made his life a misery. It was then that his gaze fell on the blue hyacinths sitting on the table. He had put them in a cheap ceramic bowl that he'd bought from the market and his hand reached out to grab it. Two steps, three, and he was right behind her. She had her back to him and didn't see it coming. He brought the bowl down on her skull with the full force of all his anger and frustration, and it shattered into pieces – soil and hyacinths spilling over the carpet – as she crumpled to the ground without a sound.

Then there was an eerie silence. Phillip stared at her lying spreadeagled on the floor. He couldn't move. His feet were rooted to the spot. His lips opened but no sound came out. What had he done? Jesus, what had he done? Panic washed over him. There was red in her bleached blonde hair, crimson blood leaking from the cut in her head. He retched and the taste of vomit came into his mouth. He couldn't think straight. This couldn't be happening. The hyacinths, he noticed, were almost the same colour as her dress; they lay to one side of her like a sad sort of wreath. Her legs were pale, almost white. One of her flip-flops had come off, a flash of silver on the dark brown carpet.

Chapel came and stood over her, peering down. 'Is she dead?'

'I don't know.'

'No, I think she's still breathing. Look, you can see. You've just knocked her out.'

Phillip finally got his legs to move, and he crouched down beside her. Thin whispery breaths, too shallow to be comforting, escaped from her lips. How serious was it? She could be dying. Her life could be slowly ebbing away.

'It looks nasty, mate. What are you going to do?'

'I don't know,' Phillip said again. 'I'd better ring for an ambulance.'

Chapel sucked in a breath. 'Are you sure? What are you going to tell them when they get here? That she threatened to expose you as a paedophile and so you hit her over the head with a bowl? That's not going to go down too well.'

'Don't say "expose". She wasn't going to expose me. I'm not a bloody paedophile.' Phillip clambered to his feet, rubbed his face with clammy hands and tried to pluck a story out of the air. 'I'll . . . I'll just say she slipped and hit her head.'

'And what will *she* say when she comes round?'

Phillip was going hot and cold, his pulse racing, his heart thudding in his chest. He knew what she'd say, and it would be the end of him. He could see his future flashing before his eyes, the shame and humiliation, the handcuffs, the police interviews, her word against his, a short road to prison.

'Maybe you should finish her off.'

'What?'

Chapel put his hands in his pockets and rocked back on his heels. 'It might be for the best. The minute she opens her mouth, you're done for.'

40

The drive to Whitstable was passing quickly. Jem had been worried that Harry Lind might want to talk about Aidan, might want to make sure that she wasn't caught in some nightmarish fantasy about him still being alive (she was), but his name wasn't even mentioned. Instead, they chatted about London, about work, and about the people they worked with – Stefan and Mac and Lorna – and it was all very calm and easy.

Now that they were no longer in a private detective/client relationship, she supposed that she should call him Harry, but as she hadn't quite got used to this change and wasn't exactly sure *what* they were – not romantically involved and not close enough to be described as friends – she avoided calling him anything at all.

It felt curiously liberating to be out of the city, to be passing green fields, to know that shortly they'd be on the coast. The rain was still coming down, but she didn't care. She'd come prepared in jeans and boots, in a sweater and a hooded rain-coat. Nothing the weather could throw at her could make a difference. She had grown up by the sea and knew how to dress for it.

'So this person you're going to meet. Are they involved in the Mortlake case?'

Harry hesitated as if in two minds whether to tell her or not, but then he shrugged and said, 'Her name's Amy Bolton, formerly Greer. She's the girl Christine was going to see on the day she disappeared.'

'Ah,' Jem said. 'She could be useful then.'

'I hope so.' Harry gave her a sideways glance. 'Girls tell each other stuff, don't they? When they're mates?'

'It depends on how close they are. Were they close, Christine and Amy?'

'Not according to Celia Mortlake, but she's something of a snob. She wouldn't have wanted Christine being best buds with the local greengrocer's daughter. According to her it was more a friendship of convenience. You know, with the two of them living so near each other. I got the feeling Celia didn't care much for Amy. Well, actually, it's not even a feeling; she called her sly and over-confident.'

'Hardly a ringing endorsement.'

'But I'm not sure how much parents ever know about their kids and their mates.'

Jem nodded. 'Just because someone lives nearby doesn't mean you're going to spend time with them. Especially when you're that age. Christine must have liked her – at least some of the time.'

'Yeah, that's what I reckon too.'

'It's sad, though, isn't it? All those years of not knowing what happened to her. You wonder how people endure it. Did Celia have any other kids?'

'No, Christine was an only child.' Harry glanced at her again. 'I am too. Do you have any brothers or sisters?'

'Three half-brothers and a half-sister. They're all much younger than me. My dad married again after Mum died. Quite soon after. They moved to Sydney, so I don't get to see them much. I stayed with my grandparents in Lytham. My choice.'

Jem wasn't sure why she was telling him all this when a simple no would have sufficed. Perhaps she felt the need to return the favour when it came to confidences. He had told her about Amy, about the case he was working on – information he perhaps wouldn't normally have shared – and she in return was giving him a riveting precis of her family history. Still, there was probably a rule when it came to these situations: what was said on the A2 stayed on the A2, or something like that.

'Sydney, huh? Sun, sea and a handsome opera house. You've never thought about joining them?'

'It's never crossed my mind.' And then before he could delve any deeper into what must appear a somewhat perverse decision in light of all her Aidan troubles, she quickly asked, 'So how's it going in the search for Kayleigh's dad?'

Harry didn't answer straight away. He was pretending to check out the road signs while he weighed up the pros and cons of telling her. She knew all about the art of evasion.

'Oh God,' she said. 'You've found him, haven't you?'

'What makes you think that?'

'It's written all over your face. How did you manage that so quickly?'

'Well, I'd like to put it down to my incredible powers of detection, but actually he was pretty easy to track down. He was at his mum's of all places. You mustn't say anything to Kayleigh, though. If Danny Street finds out where Ray is, he'll be dead meat.'

'So what are you going to do?'

'Nothing for now. I need to give it some thought.'

Jem pondered on why things were always so complicated, how people made bad decisions (she knew all about that) and then compounded those bad decisions by making even more. 'I won't breathe a word. I promise. So what's Ray like? Does he want contact with his kids?'

'Yeah, he says so. Although not at the expense of getting his head kicked in, or worse. He's not a bad bloke, just a stupid one. And I'm not sure if Nola would welcome him back into the bosom of the family. Three years is a long time to be AWOL.'

'I've still not met her. Mrs Floyd – the local gossip according to Kayleigh – says I'll hear her coming before I see her. She doesn't sound like the sort of woman you want to get on the wrong side of.'

'All the more reason to tread carefully,' Harry said. 'I don't need Nola Dunn on my back as well as Danny Street. Anyway, we're almost there. Whitstable. Now all we have to do is find somewhere to park.'

In the event, Harry didn't have to worry about parking. He found a spot near the harbour in a road that would no doubt be bumper to bumper in the summer but was pleasingly quiet in December. The rain had stopped, the grey clouds drifting apart to reveal a glimmer of winter sun. Because he didn't need to be at the café until two, he suggested a fish-and-chip lunch – his treat – and they took the polystyrene containers and the wooden forks down to the seafront where they found a bench on the beach and settled down to eat.

Harry couldn't remember the last time he'd been by the sea or, more interestingly, when he'd last had lunch with a woman who didn't make him want to run a mile. He had reached that age, in fact he'd probably reached it a while ago, where most of the women he dated were looking for commitment and looking for it in a hurry. It was disconcerting to be asked if you wanted children, if you'd considered moving out of London, what your plans were for the future, before you'd even hit the second course. And it wasn't that he was afraid of commitment – he'd been with Val for years – only that he didn't like to rush into things.

Not that this was a date, of course. He didn't really know what it was to Jem; just a jaunt out of London perhaps, an opportunity for a change of scene. She was hard to read. And then there were the trust issues. He didn't know all the ins and outs of what had happened with Aidan Hague, but he was sure that none of it had been good.

While these thoughts were going through his head, *her* mind was clearly on something else entirely. 'What do you think Amy will be able to tell you after all this time?'

Harry ate a chip and savoured the salt and vinegar on his tongue. 'Maybe nothing, nothing new at least. But I'd like to get her take on it all. Christine still feels a bit . . . elusive. I can't quite get a grip on who she was.'

'Most twelve-year-old girls aren't that complicated.'

'She seems to have been smart and sensible, not the type to do anything reckless. I can't see her going off with a stranger. But then it was a Sunday, quiet. She could have walked on from the Greers and been bundled into a car or a van, and no one would have been any the wiser.'

'Or gone to see someone else. Did she have any other friends that lived nearby?'

'No one Celia knew about.'

The seagulls whirled around overhead, screeching into the wind. A couple dropped down on to the sand and hopped eagerly towards them.

'Watch your food,' Harry said. 'Our feathered friends are on the prowl.'

269

'You're supposed to look them in the eye,' Jem said. 'They don't like it when you're watching them.'

Harry stared at one of the gulls. It stared resolutely back with what might have been a slight sneer on its face. He ate some more chips and a portion of fish. 'Is that true or just one of those stories?'

'I read it somewhere. I think it's to do with predators. If something's watching you, it's probably lining you up for a meal.'

Harry instantly thought of Danny Street. Perhaps it was true of humans too. Except if you stared at Danny Street for too long, he'd probably just punch your lights out. 'It's a dog-eat-dog world,' he said. 'Or am I mixing up my wildlife?'

Jem smiled. 'Why do fish and chips always taste better by the sea?'

'I don't know. It's one of the mysteries of life.'

They lapsed into a comfortable silence. Jem gazed out towards the horizon while she ate, and Harry stayed on gull duty. Weirdly, the birds did seem to keep their distance when he kept his gaze on them. The beach was almost deserted with only a couple of stalwart dog walkers making their way across the sand. There was a chill gusty wind, but the hot food and the thin sun took the edge off it.

'Should we meet at the Blue Yacht?' Harry said. 'About three?'

Jem nodded. They had passed the café earlier when they'd bought the fish and chips. 'Will that be long enough? I don't mind if you want to make it later.'

'From how Amy sounded on the phone, I think I'll be lucky to get an hour. What are you going to do with yourself?'

'Oh, don't worry about me. I'll just have a wander round the town and the harbour. I'll be fine. I like exploring new places.'

Harry did worry, though. He had worried from the very first moment he'd seen her, when Moses had fastened his hand on her wrist and panic had spread across her face. Now that Aidan Hague was dead, she had nothing to fear any more, but fear wasn't easy to get rid of. It hung around like a bad smell, like a ghost that refuses to stop haunting. 'I'll keep my phone on,' he said.

41

Harry was ten minutes early for the meeting. He had his choice of tables – there were only three other customers in the café – and picked one by the window where he could look out at the boats while he waited. He was still not entirely convinced that Amy Bolton would show or even that she'd let him know she wasn't coming. She had been taken by surprise this morning, jolted back into the past, and that, he suspected, was not a place she wanted to revisit.

He ordered a latte, sat back and gazed out on to the harbour. A fleet of small boats were moored and bobbing prettily on the grey water, their multicoloured flags flapping in the wind. He had never been into sailing – he preferred his feet firmly on dry land – but presumed there was a certain peace to be found in it: the open sea, the wind in your hair and all that. He thought about Jem. He thought about Celia Mortlake. He thought about Ray and Kayleigh. When he'd exhausted most of his thoughts, he let his mind empty of everything but the vastness of the sky, the wheeling gulls and the disturbing notion that maybe nothing he did made a jot of difference.

Harry sighed, shifted in his seat, extended his long legs and tried to move his head space to somewhere more optimistic. He knew how easy it was to slip under that black cloud of depression, to let small setbacks get the better of him. It was never a good way forward. He couldn't change what he couldn't change and just had to be acceptant of it.

By quarter past two his worst fears seemed to have been confirmed. He would hang on to half past before he tried to call, although he doubted if Amy would pick up. He finished his coffee and ordered another one. He kept his eyes on the door, praying that his journey hadn't been a wasted one.

Eventually, five minutes later, Harry's prayers were answered. Amy Bolton strode into the café, her eyes quickly scanning the room until they came to rest on him. She was a tall, thin woman with a hollowed-out face and dark shadows under her eyes, wearing black trousers and a black wool coat; her clothes had a funereal air to them. Did she always dress like that, or had she picked these garments especially for the occasion? He smiled and gave her a wave.

'I wasn't going to come,' was the first thing she said when she got to the table.

Harry was already on his feet, hand outstretched. 'I'm glad you changed your mind. Thank you. Let me get you a drink. Tea, coffee?'

Amy's handshake was brief. She hesitated, perhaps not intending to stay long enough to drink anything, but then nodded and said, 'All right, I'll have a tea.'

Harry summoned the waitress, put the order in and then sat down. Amy sat opposite. Her expression was fierce, as if this was just the latest in a long series of encounters she hadn't wanted to have, as if he'd forced her to come here and she resented him for it. There was a hard edge to her, a simmering anger. She glared at him.

'I know how hard this must be for you,' he said.

'No, you don't. You've no idea. Were your family hounded out of their home, accused of murder, forced to move from place to place, to change their name, to live with the constant fear that *that* man would catch up with you again?'

'No, sorry. I didn't mean to be glib.'

'And you say you want to speak to my mother. As if she hasn't been through enough. I'm only here to keep you away from her.'

'And I appreciate it,' Harry said calmly. 'I promised I wouldn't approach your mother and I meant it. It's you I really wanted to talk to anyway; you're the one who was friends with Christine. I couldn't find you because of the name change.'

'I got married. It didn't last but I kept the name.'

'I thought that might be the case, only I couldn't trace any record of your marriage.'

'I lived in Jersey for nineteen years. I only came back because Mum was getting on and I wanted to be closer to her.' She glanced out of the window and then back at Harry. 'I'd never have come back to England if I'd had a choice. You can change your name, but you can't change the past. I hate this country.'

Harry could see that she had not aged as well as Vivienne Bayle, that the stress and anxiety of her life had taken its toll. Her face was heavily lined, and her earlier prettiness had faded although there were echoes of it in the high cheekbones and grey eyes. She had kept her fair hair long, but it now had a dyed appearance, dry and brittle, and was tied back with a dark grey chiffon scarf. 'I get that,' he said.

Amy gave him the kind of look that suggested he didn't get it at all.

The waitress arrived with the tea and there was a welcome pause in the conversation. After she'd gone, Harry said, 'As I told you on the phone, Celia Mortlake has employed me to go over the circumstances surrounding Christine's disappearance. I was hoping that—'

'Why should I do anything to help that woman?' Amy interrupted sharply. 'Why the hell should I? Give me one good reason.'

'For closure?' Harry suggested. 'To clear your family's name once and for all?'

'Closure,' she repeated scornfully. 'What use is that? It's just a word that's bandied around so people will forget about the awfulness of it all. What use is closure to my dad? He's six foot under because of the Mortlakes. He lost everything – his business, his pride, his self-respect, even the bloody will to live. He only kept going for me and Mum. It killed him being under suspicion like that, with Mortlake pointing the finger, constantly accusing him of something he hadn't done. Can you imagine what that was like? He was a happy, decent, hard-working man and it was all taken away from him.'

Harry felt that he was serving one purpose at least – allowing her to vent her rage and frustration, to speak openly about what she'd been forced to keep secret for so long. A kind of catharsis, although he wasn't sure she would thank him for thinking it. He decided to move things on before she decided to walk out on him. 'What was Christine like?'

Amy, taken by surprise by the question, gazed down at the table for a while. She must have been holding her breath, because she suddenly let it out in a long exhalation. 'Do you really think you can find out what happened after all these years?'

'I'm going to do my best,' Harry said.

'Even though no one else has been able to solve the case?'

'I don't think anyone else has ever tried that hard. The police investigation was a shambles and by the time they realised there was no evidence to charge your father, the trail had gone cold. DCI Sharp blew it. He couldn't get beyond his own simplistic conclusions, couldn't see the bigger picture. I don't have access to the police records, and Sharp is dead now, but I have spoken to a junior officer who worked on the case.'

'I told the police everything I knew,' she said. 'Which was nothing. Christine never came round that day, and I wasn't expecting her to.' Her voice, edged with frustration, rose a fraction. 'I mean, how could they think that my dad had done anything? He wouldn't have touched a hair on her head. He was a good man, gentle, not some murderous pervert.'

'None of it added up,' Harry said.

'That didn't stop Arthur Mortlake from spreading it round the neighbourhood, though. He put Dad firmly in the frame. Like Christine had *said* she was coming to see me, therefore she must have done. Even though she hadn't. Even though not a single person saw her.'

Harry tried again with his original question. 'So tell me about Christine. What was she like?'

'Oh, I don't know. Quiet, reserved, not the sort to push her-self forward. She was nice, though. I suppose I liked her mainly because she seemed to like me. It's enough at that age, isn't it? We weren't close or anything, not best friends, but we got on okay.' Amy put some sugar in her tea, stirred it and took a sip. 'Celia, on the other hand, didn't like me at all and never tried to pretend she did. She thought I was common and didn't really want me hanging out with her daughter but couldn't ban her from seeing me, not without making herself look bad. She used to flinch every time I opened my mouth, like my London accent was some kind of personal insult.'

'Snooty,' Harry said.

Amy smiled for the first time, although it wasn't much of a smile, just a temporary widening of her lips. 'Yeah, she was that all right. And to be honest, I played up to it a bit, the whole pushy working-class thing. She was always looking down her nose at me, at all my family, as if anyone who made a living from selling cabbages and spuds was beneath her.'

'That can't have been pleasant.'

Amy shrugged. 'I didn't care, not really. It just got on my nerves sometimes, that's all. She thought because she had money, she was better than us. Superior. And I think she suspected me of being a bad influence on Christine.'

'In what way?'

'In every way.'

Harry thought that Christine had chosen two friends – Amy and Vivienne – who were both very different from her, opposite in every respect. But maybe that was quite normal. Like didn't always attract like. 'How did Christine get on with her parents?'

'Oh, I don't know. They were strict, overly protective perhaps. I didn't see much of *him*. But when he was there, he always had straying eyes. You know what I mean?' She glanced down towards her chest. 'I was well developed for my age. He used to stare. It made me feel uncomfortable.'

Harry had no way of establishing whether this was true or not, or if it was just a bomb Amy had decided to throw into the mix. She had made no attempt to hide her loathing of Arthur Mortlake. 'Just staring or was there more?'

'No, there wasn't any more. I wouldn't have let him. If he'd laid a finger on me, I'd have screamed blue murder. That doesn't mean he didn't want to, though. He was a creep, that man. And I'm not just saying that because of what came later.' Amy paused again, raising the mug to her lips. 'I never understood how he kept on finding us every time we moved. Even after we'd changed our name. Do you know how he did that?'

'Private detectives,' Harry said. 'He employed a company in Kellston called Currans. They're not around now but I imagine, at the time, they had contacts inside the banks and utility companies. Things weren't as strict then about personal data or confidentiality. Your father would have had to inform certain people about his change of name, address, etcetera, and someone, for a price, has passed that information on. It wouldn't have taken long for Currans to track you down.'

'Private detectives,' she muttered, throwing Harry a dirty look.

'We're not all the same. Mackenzie, Lind would never pursue anyone like that.'

'And yet you're here,' she said sourly.

Harry nodded as if to acknowledge the logic of her argument. 'Only to get your take on things. But yes, I can see that it must feel like that. Sorry, you must have had enough of it all. More than enough. It's just that there's only half a story without getting your side. You were a victim too in all this. I was hoping you might be able to help me fill in some of the missing pieces.'

Amy gave a snort. 'Then you've had a wasted journey. Nothing I can tell you will help with finding out what happened to Christine. Don't you think I've been over and over it in my head? All I know is that she didn't come round to the house, or if she did, we didn't hear her. We were out in the garden and had the radio on, not too loud but probably loud enough to drown out the sound of the doorbell.'

'I believe you. Was there any access to the back garden from the front?'

'There was a side gate, but it was locked.'

'Can you think of where else she might have gone after she'd called round at yours? *If* she even called round. Any other friends in the area? Anywhere she liked hanging out?'

'Not that I know of. We used to walk down to Woolworths sometimes, buy sweets, but that wouldn't have been open on a Sunday. I don't think she had many other friends, no one she talked about anyway. Only that Vivienne who lived in the West End someplace. They went to that posh school together.'

'Did she ever hang out with you and Christine?'

'Not often.' Amy pursed her lips. 'I didn't get invited round when Vivienne was there.'

Harry thought of that saying – three's a crowd – and wondered if Christine had preferred to see her schoolfriend alone. Or was it Celia who'd tried to keep the greengrocer's daughter at a distance? 'What did you make of her, of Vivienne?'

Amy shrugged. It was warm in the café, but she hadn't taken off her coat, hadn't even unbuttoned it. 'I didn't see much of her. Confident, lots of red hair, freckles. That's about it. I don't think she liked me.'

'What makes you say that?'

'Whenever the two of them were together, they always made me feel . . . I don't know, like an outsider, I suppose, not part of their cosy little friendship. Exchanging glances when they thought I wasn't looking, that kind of thing. I remember Vivienne going on about her birthday meal, about going to Chinatown, even though I hadn't been invited. That was what she was like. Perhaps she saw me as a threat.'

Harry detected a strong hint of jealousy, of resentment, despite her claims that she and Christine hadn't been especially close. 'Did you expect to be invited?'

'No, of course not, but she didn't need to bang on about it. I mean, I didn't even want to go. What's so special about a Chinese meal? I just thought it was mean.'

279

Harry didn't really know where he was going with any of this. He was just throwing things out there and seeing where they landed. 'That must have been upsetting, feeling that you were excluded.'

'I didn't care,' she insisted. 'Why should I care?'

Despite her denial, he heard the hurt in her voice, and for the first time wondered if something *had* happened between her and Christine that Sunday afternoon. 'When was the last time you saw Christine?'

Amy screwed up her eyes, trying to recall. 'A few days before, the Wednesday or Thursday afternoon. Wednesday, I think.'

'And how was she that day?'

'The same as always.'

'She wasn't worried about anything?'

Amy gave a soft laugh. 'She was always worried about something. She was that sort of girl. Serious, you know? A bit religious. Always nervous in case God was watching her. She went to church and helped out with the Sunday-school classes for the little ones.'

'What church did she go to?'

'St James's, down by the cemetery. We used to go sometimes, Christmas and Easter, times like that, but not regularly. The Mortlakes were there every Sunday morning. They liked to pretend they were good Christians, but they weren't, were they? Good Christians wouldn't have behaved the way they did.'

Before Amy could disappear down the black hole of seething resentment, Harry quickly asked, 'So you don't think Christine was worried about anything in particular that Wednesday you saw her?'

'If she was, she didn't say. And before you ask, we didn't arrange to meet up again on Sunday.'

Seeing as Amy had raised the subject, Harry wasn't slow to

follow up on it. 'What did you think when you first heard that Christine had gone missing?'

'I thought it was a lot of fuss over someone who was only an hour or so late home. It was still light. I thought she'd just lost track of time. Celia rang first and then about five minutes later Arthur Mortlake came round. We all said she hadn't been at the house, but he didn't believe us. He even started shouting her name in the hall as if we might have locked her up somewhere.'

'And then the police arrived.'

'Yeah, asking the same questions over and over again: if I'd been expecting Christine, if Mum and Dad had been in the garden with me *all* the time, if I had any idea where she might be. Meanwhile the house was being searched, top to bottom. I could see how anxious my parents were getting but I didn't really understand why. I just thought it was because they were worried about Christine – which they were, of course – but it was more than that. They could see where it was all going, that they were suspects, that Mortlake wasn't the only one not believing them.'

Harry thought that Amy was consistent at least. Her story was the same one Beddows had heard. 'But you weren't worried?'

'Not then,' she said. 'Not at the beginning.'

'You didn't think it was out of character for Christine not to go home on time?'

Amy raised her hands, palms up, in a gesture of exasperation. 'It was. Of course it was. Looking back, I can see that now. But I was twelve and I didn't have those awful fears that parents have. And Christine never wore a watch. I kept thinking the phone would ring and Celia would say she was back, panic over. Except she never did.'

Harry nodded. 'No, she never did. And later, when it became apparent that Christine had definitely gone missing, what did you think might have happened?'

'I don't know. I suppose, at first, I thought that maybe she was afraid to go home, that she knew she'd be in trouble, but then . . . ' Amy's voice trailed off. She was quiet for a moment. 'It was hard to accept. It didn't seem real. And then the pressure from the police just got bigger and bigger, as if we were all lying, and *we'd* done something dreadful to her. I probably shouldn't say this but there were times when I hated Christine. Almost as much as I hated Arthur Mortlake. I knew, deep down, that it wasn't her fault but . . . Does that sound awful? Of course it does. It *is* awful. I just kept thinking that if she hadn't gone wherever she'd gone, then my family wouldn't be going through this.'

'I can see how you'd feel that way,' Harry said.

Amy narrowed her eyes and stared at him. 'You're just saying what you think I want to hear.'

This was true, although Harry wasn't about to admit it. Anyway, he didn't think it was that unnatural for Amy to have those feelings. When the world crapped on you from a great height you didn't always have room for empathy. 'None of us know how we'd react in a situation like that. Not until it happens. Your own family was caught up in the middle of a nightmare. I'm not sure I'd have felt that differently.'

Amy picked up her mug and continued to stare at him over its rim. Her face was full of distrust. 'You're not going to tell Celia where we are, are you? I don't want her turning up in Whitstable. If people find out about Christine, they'll treat Mum differently. No smoke without fire and all that.'

'I don't think Celia would do that. It was Arthur who drove the pursuit and it stopped when he died.'

'You don't *think*,' she said. 'That isn't good enough, Mr Lind. And you haven't answered the question.'

'I'll have to tell her that we met, but no, I won't tell her where you are.'

'And what if she demands to know? She's paying you, isn't she? She's the one with all the power.'

'She's paying me to find out what happened to Christine, not to track you down. Where you live, what your name is now, is irrelevant. She isn't about to hotfoot it to Whitstable and start accusing you again.'

'You know that for a fact, do you?'

Harry didn't, of course, but he hoped that this wasn't Celia's intention. Concerned that Amy might get spooked and take off, he said, 'She's had years to think it all over, to consider other possibilities. All she wants now is the truth.'

'That woman wouldn't know the truth if it was staring her straight in the face.'

The café door opened and a couple more customers hurried in. The sky had darkened again, great grey clouds rolling over the harbour. Drops of rain fell against the window. There was about to be a downpour. This was a good thing, he decided. Amy would be less inclined to do a runner while it was pouring down. But, just in case, he rapidly moved on to a subject she was bound to have an opinion on.

'Going back to Arthur Mortlake and his straying eyes, you didn't notice anything inappropriate in his behaviour towards Christine, did you? Was she ever nervous around him, scared? Did you ever get the feeling that something wrong was going on there?'

A light came into Amy's eyes at this new opportunity to badmouth her enemy. 'It's possible. You never know what goes on behind closed doors. Do you think he could have been . . . ? God, I wouldn't put it past him. There was definitely something creepy about that man.'

'But Christine never said anything to you?'

'No, but she wouldn't, would she? Girls who are being abused don't go around shouting about it. And she was the type who kept things in.' Amy stopped and considered it some more. 'So *he* could have killed her. Maybe she never even left the house. Is that what you're thinking?'

'I've got an open mind,' Harry said. 'Although that doesn't really tally with how he chased your family around the country for years. Why spend all that money on private detectives? Why pursue you so relentlessly if he knew you were innocent? He was never going to get a confession.'

'A guilty conscience,' Amy said. 'He couldn't face up to what he'd done and tried to shift the blame on to us. Or maybe he was trying to prove to Celia that he didn't do it. That's possible, isn't it? She could have had suspicions.'

Harry lifted and dropped his shoulders as if he wasn't completely dismissing the idea. He had considered these possibilities and more or less set them aside – for him, they just didn't add up – but he was happy to leave them on the table, mainly to prove that he wasn't Celia's stooge. It was probably too much to ask that Amy would trust him, but at least she could see that he didn't have an agenda, that he wasn't here to put her family firmly back in the frame.

Amy looked out at the rain, falling more heavily now against the glass, obscuring the view of the harbour. 'He could have done it,' she murmured. 'That bastard could have killed her.'

Harry got the feeling she was talking to herself as much as him. He left a few beats before moving on. 'I've just got some general questions to run by you if that's okay. Did Celia have her own car, or did she and Arthur share one? Do you remember?'

'No, she had her own, a little silver one. I don't recall the make. He drove a Merc, a big flashy thing. Dark green. Is it important?'

'I don't think so. I'm just putting the basic details into place.

And your dad had the van, right? Was that the only vehicle your parents owned?'

'Yes.' Suspicion clouded her face again. 'The police checked the van,' she said sharply. 'They didn't find anything.'

'I know.'

'So why are you asking?'

'To make sure I've got my facts right.' Harry thought Amy was like a tightly coiled spring, forever on edge, her emotions too close to the surface. 'Like I said, just the basic details. I've got most of my information from Celia and so I'm simply double-checking.'

Amy looked partly placated, although the suspicion didn't leave her eyes.

Harry went down a different road. 'Does the name Michael Moss mean anything to you? Or Moses? That was his nickname. Although it might not have been back then.'

Amy shook her head, frowning. 'Never heard of him. Who is he?'

'His wife and daughter were killed in a hit-and-run in Kellston a few weeks before Christine's disappearance.'

Amy's expression suddenly changed. 'Hang on. I do remember something. A little girl. What was her name? Annie, that was it. Yeah, little Annie. Christine was really upset about that. Annie used to be in her Sunday-school class.'

Harry nodded, trying not to appear *too* interested. He didn't want Amy jumping to any unfortunate conclusions. It was a link, a tenuous one, but it didn't necessarily mean anything. Although if Christine had known Annie, she might have known Moses too. Well enough to go somewhere with him if they met on the street? It wasn't beyond the bounds of possibility.

'What's the connection?' Amy said.

'I don't know if there is one. Probably not. I've just been

looking at events that happened around the same time. Background stuff. Do you know where the family lived?'

Amy shook her head. 'Not exactly. Off the high street somewhere, one of those side streets up by the Mansfield.'

Harry stored this new information away. Tomorrow he would try and get some newspaper reports on the accident. 'Did you know there was a search party on the night Christine disappeared? Neighbours and the like, people from the Fox.'

'Yes, we heard about it. Dad wanted to go out and help but the police wouldn't let him. They took him down Cowan Road shortly after that and later they took me and my mum too. They wouldn't let Mum sit in with me – I suppose they didn't trust her not to influence me in some way – and so I had a middle-aged social worker who kept telling me not to worry, just to tell the truth and I'd be fine. Ha! Nothing was fine, not ever again. The shits weren't interested in the truth, only in proving their own stupid theories. They kept Dad down there for hours, didn't let him go until the next morning. He had to spend the night in the cells.'

'It can't have been an easy time.'

'Well, if we thought that was bad, it was nothing compared to what came next. Do you know what it's like to have people constantly pointing the finger, talking about you, boycotting your business because they believe you did something terrible to a child? For as long as the police didn't charge anyone, Dad remained the only suspect. And Arthur Mortlake made sure that everyone knew who *he* thought had done it.' Amy paused and swallowed hard. 'It was a nightmare that just went on and on and on.'

'I'm sorry,' Harry said. 'It must have been awful.'

'It's never stopped being awful. And now Celia's raking it all up again. I bet she still believes Dad did it, doesn't she?'

'It's hard to know what she believes,' Harry lied.

'Is it?' Amy said scornfully. 'I doubt if the years have done much to change her mind.'

'She's had time to reflect.'

'Yeah, right.'

Harry felt sorry for Celia Mortlake – who couldn't feel sorry for a woman who had lost her child in such terrible circumstances? – but he understood Amy's bitterness too. Both women were victims in their different ways. 'She's very old now. This could be her last chance to find Christine, and to find out who took her.'

'And here you are wasting your time on me.'

'It's not a waste of time, Amy. Every bit of information, no matter how irrelevant it seems, can be useful.'

Amy rolled her eyes, glanced at the clock on the wall and pushed her mug away. 'If you say so. Are we done here?'

'It's still raining. Why don't you stay and have another tea?'

'No, thanks. I have to go and see Mum. She frets if I'm late.'

Harry took out one of his business cards and passed it across. 'Thank you for coming. I appreciate it. If you think of anything else, just give me a call.'

'Like what?' Amy said, getting to her feet.

'Like anything.'

'And you'll stay away from Mum? You promised.'

'I'll stay away,' Harry said.

Amy gave him a thin smile. She took a couple of steps from the table and suddenly turned around. 'If you find out about Christine, will you let me know?'

Harry nodded. 'Sure.'

He watched as Amy left the café, putting up her umbrella in the shelter of the doorway. Then he sat back and thought about the conversation they'd just had. Was her desire to keep him away from her mother driven purely by love, a desire to protect her from the horrors of the past, or had there been another motive? A fear, perhaps, that Pauline would say something she shouldn't.

There had been nothing new in what Amy said about that Sunday, nothing to convince him that Christine *had* been at her house that day, nothing to suggest that she'd lied all those years ago, and yet he couldn't be entirely sure of her innocence. Clearly there had been friction in the friendship, tensions between the three girls, small sparks of hostility that could have exploded into something disastrous.

Then there was the business of Arthur Mortlake. If she had told the truth about his lecherous looks, that was something else to think about. And that one small snippet about Annie Moss could have provided him with the clue he needed – a tenuous link between Moses and Christine, but a link all the same.

42

Jem had spent forty-five minutes wandering around the streets of Whitstable, lazily pottering from place to place and peering in the shop windows. It was a pretty town, especially on the front with its pastel-coloured beach huts. She had come across several art galleries, gone inside, and had an enjoyable time perusing the displays. Could she live here? She thought she could. Away from the bustle of the city – although it was bound to be busier in summer – and with the peace that comes from sea and sky and soft horizons. She could start painting again, maybe even sell some stuff. It was all just a dream, but she indulged herself in imagining a life without fear, a life without Aidan.

With fifteen minutes left before she was due to meet Harry in the Blue Yacht, she decided to spend them on the beach. The sky was looking ominous, great storm clouds gathering overhead, but she walked back to the shore anyway. The sea was slate grey, the waves laced with white. She could smell the tang of the salt air and could almost imagine herself back home in Lytham. Would she ever go back? Maybe you *could* never go back, not really. Maybe what was lost was lost and there was no point in trying to find it again.

Jem strolled along the beach, feeling the gentle crunch of the shingle under her feet. She didn't want to go too far and so she stopped and gazed out at the sea, happy just to look at it, to smell it, to feel it seeping into her senses. London felt like a long way away. The Mansfield estate – with its dirty concrete towers, its poverty and deprivation, its constant air of menace – retreated from her mind and was replaced by the fresh, sharp air of Whitstable.

It was cold, though. She was glad she'd brought a scarf. The wind whipped at her face and made her hunch her shoulders. Standing braced against the weather, her feet firmly placed, her hands in her pockets, she was pleased that Harry had phoned this morning and that she hadn't turned down his offer. What would she be doing instead? Only sitting in her flat and stressing over Aidan. Now, here, she could be free for a while, could breathe again, could relax.

The minutes passed. The sky grew darker, and a few drops of rain began to fall. Jem was so deep in thought that she didn't hear the approaching footsteps. Before she knew it, a man had appeared at her side, too close for comfort, his elbow almost touching hers. She jumped, startled, and turned to face him.

'Sorry, love,' he said, smirking. 'Did I give you a fright?'

Jem instinctively shifted away, one step to the side. He was a stranger. She didn't recognise him, had never seen him before. He was dark-haired and in his early forties, handsome in a ravaged kind of way, and with an odd expression in his eyes. As if he was high on something. Or drunk. She quickly scanned the beach – only three or four other people who were already heading for shelter from the rain – and looked at the man again. 'Do I know you?'

'Jem, ain't it?' he said.

She flinched, alarmed at him knowing her name. 'And you are?'

'Danny,' he said. 'Danny Street.'

Jem must have sucked in an audible breath because he smirked again. So this was the man Harry had been talking about, the one who had followed them when they'd been driving round south Kellston, the one who had a screw loose, the one who was trying to step into his gangster father's shoes. 'What do you want?'

'Now that's not very friendly, love. I just came over to say hello, us both coming from the same place and all. Fellow Kellston residents. Fancy bumping into you in Whitstable. Who'd have thought it? Small world, eh?'

Jem knew that he must have tailed them here unless someone from Harry's office had leaked the information. The latter, however, didn't seem likely. Had he been hoping they'd lead him to Ray Dunn? If so, he'd had a wasted journey.

'Nice to get a breath of sea air,' Danny continued. 'Invigorating. Blows all those cobwebs away. Are you having a good day?'

Jem, who didn't want to antagonise him – no one wanted to antagonise a man like Danny Street – gave a nod and started to walk back towards the harbour. 'Lovely, thank you.'

Danny, unsurprisingly, fell into step beside her. 'That boyfriend of yours still tied up?'

'Who?'

'Harry Lind.'

'He's not my boyfriend.'

'Is he still busy with that woman?'

What's it to you? she wanted to say, but she didn't. She pulled up her hood and increased her pace. 'I've no idea.'

'Shame on him,' Danny said. 'Leaving a pretty girl like you all on her own. Anything could happen.'

Jem heard the inherent threat in his words, in his tone, and shuddered. She stopped again, glared at him and, forgetting all about her non-antagonistic intentions, said fiercely, 'And what the hell is that supposed to mean?'

'Hey, no need to take that attitude, sweetheart. I'm just looking out for you. Girls aren't safe anywhere these days, even in a nice place like this. You never know who's around. There are some real arseholes in the world.' He left a pause before saying smugly, 'Still, you'd know all about that, wouldn't you?'

Jem blanched. 'Would I?'

'That shit, Aidan Hague. Now he was a piece of work. Bet you wish you'd never set eyes on *his* face. Still, I heard he got what was coming to him. What goes around comes around, huh?'

'How . . . how do you know about Aidan?'

'I know everything, love. I make it my business to. I've got to say, I didn't take to him. Had a bit of an attitude if you ask me. Still, ten years in the slammer will do that to a man.'

Jem's mind was reeling. She wanted to tell Danny Street to clear off and leave her alone, but she had to find out about Aidan. 'Was he in Kellston? Did you see him there? Is that what you mean?'

'Oh, did he not drop by? I got the impression he was looking forward to seeing you again.'

'When?' The thought of Aidan being in Kellston made her blood run cold. 'When was he there?'

Danny gave a shrug. 'What does it matter? You don't need to worry about him anymore. Although . . . '

Jem's stomach turned over. 'Although what?' she said through clenched teeth. There was something bad coming, something even worse than standing on this beach with a crazy Danny

Street. She could feel her pulse start to race, could feel her heart banging in her chest.

'Let's just say I heard he made some contingency plans. You know, in case his past caught up with him and he couldn't finish what he started.'

'What does that mean?'

Danny gazed out at the horizon for a moment like any old day tripper admiring the view. Then he fixed his weird eyes back on her. 'He was a man on a mission, your Aidan. Ten years to brood on how he'd ended up behind bars. Ten years to chew over what he'd do when he got out. He wasn't going to take any chances.'

'You're talking like he's dead but there's no real proof of that.'

'Would you rather he was alive?' Danny inclined his head and studied her. He gave a nasty laugh. 'No, I don't think so. Maybe we could help each other out, you and me. There are things you want to know and there are things I want to know. Sounds like a deal could be made.'

'A deal,' she repeated numbly.

'Yeah, a deal. You tell me where Ray Dunn is, and I'll tell you about the little legacy Aidan Hague left behind.'

Jem felt her heart miss a beat. 'What legacy? What are you talking about?'

'Ah, come on, sweetheart. You know how a deal works. I tell you something, you tell me something, and everyone's happy.'

'I don't know who Ray Dunn is,' she lied. 'I've never heard of him. How would I know where he is?'

'Maybe not, but your boyfriend does. Ray Dunn. Remember the name. Have a word with Harry. I'm sure he'll want to help you out.'

'He's not my boyfriend. I've already told you that.'

Danny grinned. He lifted his head to the skies and the rain ran down his face. 'Shit day,' he said. 'You should get inside before you catch your death.'

293

43

Jem was drenched by the time she got to the Blue Yacht. On the doorstep she shook herself like a wet dog before going inside. Harry was sitting alone by the window staring out at the harbour, and she hurried over to join him, leaving a trail of damp footsteps on the wood floor. She was breathing heavily, partly from the run to the café, but mainly from the fear that was still coursing through her veins.

He looked up and grinned. 'You didn't escape the rain, then?' But seeing the expression on her face, he wiped the grin and said, 'What's wrong? What's happened?'

Jem took a moment to try and get herself together. She shrugged off her raincoat and hung it over the back of the chair. She sat down, put her elbows on the table and waited for her breathing to slow. Then, finally, she spoke. Her voice was shaky, a pitch or two higher than it usually was. 'I've just seen Danny Street.'

'What? Christ, you're kidding? He's here? He must have followed us. And I didn't even notice. Why didn't I notice?

Maybe he used more than one car. Yeah, that's possible. Even so, I should have ... '

'I haven't just *seen* him,' she interrupted. 'He came up to talk to me on the beach.' She gave him a fast summary of the exchange, her eyes widening as she related the details. 'A contingency plan. What's that supposed to mean, for God's sake? And Aidan must have been in Kellston or how else would Danny know about me?' She gave an involuntary shudder at the mere thought of her ex being so close. 'I told Danny I didn't know who Ray Dunn was, but I'm not sure if he believed me.'

Harry was quiet, taking it all in. A few seconds passed before he replied. 'He could be bluffing, trying to take advantage of the situation.'

'That doesn't explain how he knows who I am. No one in Kellston knows that apart from you.'

'And I haven't told anyone, in case you're wondering.'

'No, I wasn't. I believe you. But Aidan *must* have been in Kellston, *must* have talked to Danny, it's the only explanation. Only if he was there, why didn't he ... ' Jem felt a tightening in her chest as she thought of those occasions when she'd been followed. 'If he came all the way to London, if he knew where I was, then why did he go back to Blackpool again?'

'Pressing business?' Harry suggested. 'Once he knew where you were, there wasn't any hurry. He could come back at any time.'

Jem's hands clenched into two tight fists. If that was true, then she'd had a close call. 'The kind of pressing business that got him killed,' she said. Only now was she considering the possibility that Aidan really was dead. But what horrors had he left behind? 'Contingency plans. That can only mean one thing. He's arranged for someone else to do what he wasn't able to. That means a contract, doesn't it? A hit. Christ, is there a bloody price on my head? I'll have to get out of Kellston, move somewhere else. I'll have to . . . '

Harry reached out a hand and placed it over her wrist. 'Hey, slow down. We don't know anything for sure. Danny Street could just be messing with us. When we get back to London I'll talk to the crazy bastard, see if I can find out what's going on.'

'He won't tell you anything unless you tell him where Ray is – and you can't do that. A quid pro quo is what he's after. You scratch his back and he'll scratch yours.'

Harry pulled back his hand, picked up his mug and drank the rest of his coffee. 'There isn't going to be any back scratching. There's every chance that Danny's trying to play us. Maybe he did meet Aidan – it's possible – but the rest of it could just be bullshit. He's a devious sod. If he sees a chance to get what he wants, he'll grab it.'

Jem shook her head. 'No, he couldn't just invent something like this. It's too . . . too extreme. And it's just the sort of thing Aidan *would* do. If he knew his own life was in danger, he'd make damn sure he didn't leave any loose ends behind.'

'I'll talk to Danny,' Harry said again. 'Let's find out what's really going on before we start jumping to conclusions.'

Jem was vaguely comforted by that 'we'. As if she wasn't in this on her own now. As if she had an ally. But she still felt sick to her stomach. 'Okay.'

'Even if it is true, I don't think you're in any imminent danger. If Danny Street wants to make a deal, he's going to make sure nothing happens to you in the meantime. I don't suppose that's much of a comfort but at least it gives us an opportunity to find out what's going on. We can go to the Mansfield and pick up your things when we get back to London. I think you should stay at my place for now.'

'I can't do that,' Jem said.

'Why not? At least it's an easy commute to work. I live in the flat above the office, and I've got a spare room. It's nothing fancy but you'll be safer than on the Mansfield.'

'I couldn't put you out like that.'

'You're not putting me out. To be honest, you'll be doing me a favour. I'll worry about you less if you're staying at mine. There's good security there. No one can get in unless we let them in.'

Jem opened her mouth to protest but swiftly closed it again. She wasn't going to argue with him. This wasn't the time for pride or any of those *I can take care of myself* sort of thoughts. She knew she was an easy target on the Mansfield, a sitting duck for anyone with a mind to murder. There had been two killings there already, and she didn't want to be a third victim. 'All right,' she said. 'Thanks. But just until this mess is sorted.'

44

Phillip had gone into a panic – what if Nola died? What if Nola *didn't* die? – and these two alternative outcomes had felt almost equally terrible. If she died, then he would be a murderer. If she didn't, then she'd report him to the police for assault and God knows what else. He had waited, staring at her unconscious body, not sure what to pray for.

'You should tie her wrists and ankles,' Chapel said. 'Stop her doing a runner when she wakes up.'

'And what if she doesn't wake up?'

'Then you've got a different problem.'

In this event Phillip considered doing a runner himself, packing a bag, grabbing his passport and getting the hell out. How long before anyone noticed his absence? He'd have a few days, he thought, before Edna Floyd raised the alarm. He could be clean away by then. No one here knew his real name, not even the bloke he'd rented the flat off. He could disappear and that would be that.

'The law know your real name,' Chapel reminded him. 'You gave it to them when they came to talk about Charlene.'

Phillip had forgotten about that. He felt his guts tighten.

Nola came round, grunting and groaning, about five minutes after she'd hit the floor. She slowly pulled up her knees and forced herself into a sitting position. With her right hand she gingerly touched the back of her head and winced. Her fingers had blood on them. Glaring at him through slightly unfocused eyes, she said, 'You hit me, you fucking bastard!'

Thus, any vague hope that Nola Dunn, if she recovered, might be suffering from memory loss, was instantly extinguished. 'You slipped,' Phillip said. 'You've been drinking, and you tripped on those stupid flip-flops and cracked your head on the coffee table.'

'Like fuck I did,' she said.

'You're pissed.'

Nola staggered to her feet and swayed unsteadily. Her hand kept rising to touch the wound he'd inflicted on her, to see the blood on her fingertips. 'I should be in hospital. You've put a goddam hole in my head.'

'Don't be so dramatic. It's only a little cut. They always bleed a lot.'

Nola bared her teeth. 'You're for it now, mate. They're going to lock you up and throw away the fucking key.' She had started backing away, moving towards the door. 'You're a fucking nutter.'

And Phillip knew then that he couldn't let her go. Not until he'd persuaded her to keep her big mouth shut. Although how he was supposed to do that, he had no idea. And how long would it be before Kayleigh reported her mother as missing? According to Edna Floyd, she often left the kids on their own so her absence might not be that unusual. And they'd be at school now – at least he hoped so – which meant they couldn't know that she was here.

Chapel was standing by the window, arms folded across his

chest. 'Are you going to let her talk to you like that? The little tart needs to learn some respect.'

Phillip, still in a panic, stepped forward, grabbed hold of Nola's elbow and roughly pushed her down on to the sofa. 'You're not going anywhere. And don't even think about screaming or I'll finish you off. Do you understand? Do you get it?'

Nola laughed, a mocking sound. 'You can't keep me here. People are going to be looking for me.'

'Oh yeah, and what people would that be then?'

'My bloke's waiting in the flat. I told him I was coming to see you. He's going to rip your fucking balls off.'

Chapel grinned at Phillip. 'What self-respecting bloke would shack up with a whore like that?'

'Bullshit,' Phillip said to Nola. 'No one knows you're here. No one's going to come looking because no one gives a damn. Even your kids don't expect you home.'

For the first time he saw a glimmer of doubt, of fear, on her face. 'You wait and see. He'll be here.'

Phillip looked down on her, savouring this change in the balance of power. He was still afraid, his nerves still jangling, and at a loss to how this was going to pan out, but at least he'd bought himself some time. She couldn't be mouthing off to the police while she was here. She couldn't be ruining his life while he held her captive. He saw her glance over her shoulder towards the door, and quickly said, 'It's locked, love. You're not going anywhere.'

'You'll have to tie her up,' Chapel said. 'And put a gag on her. I don't want to listen to her vile, whiney voice any more than I have to.'

Kayleigh, with Kit in tow, got home from school at half past three. The heating was on, but the flat had an empty quality. As

300

they hung their coats on the pegs in the hall, Kayleigh called out 'Mum?' No answer. They went through to the living room where there were signs of recent occupation: a packet of fags sitting on the coffee table along with an empty bottle of wine and Nola's mobile phone. Well, she couldn't have gone far, not without her phone and fags. Perhaps she'd just nipped down the offie to replenish supplies.

Kayleigh put the TV on, tuned it to CBeebies and left Kit on the sofa while she went into the kitchen. There was a dirty plate, a mug and some cutlery sitting beside the sink. She dropped them into the washing-up bowl and ran some water over them to soak. Then she opened the fridge, took out the milk, poured two glasses and took these along with a packet of chocolate digestives back into the lounge where she sat down beside Kit and stared at the cartoon without really watching it.

Half an hour later, Kayleigh was starting to feel ripples of anxiety. What if Nola had got it into her head to go and interrogate Tracey's mum about Friday? It was the kind of thing she'd do when she'd had a skinful. If she found out that Kayleigh hadn't been where she said she'd been, there'd be hell to pay. She glanced at her school bag where she'd stashed Dion's money. Perhaps she should look for somewhere safer to hide it.

But would Nola even remember where Tracey's family lived? She'd never been pals with Tracey's mum – Susannah, she was called – and so probably didn't know for sure that it was the third floor, number 31. Kayleigh had a horrible image of her banging on doors until she found the right flat. Susannah wouldn't appreciate a drunken Nola breathing cheap red wine all over her and demanding to know if her daughter had been there on Friday, and Tracey wouldn't be slow to tell the whole sordid tale to all the other kids at school.

Kayleigh shifted on the sofa, unable to sit still. She stood up and walked over to the window where she looked down on the estate, hoping to see Nola tottering through the gates with a bag full of booze and the firm intention of coming home. Not that she wanted her to drink so much, but better here than down the Fox.

It didn't take half an hour to go down the offie. Come to that, it didn't take half an hour to go round to Tracey's, not unless she was still searching for the right flat. And she couldn't have gone out for the night, not without taking her mobile. All this put Kayleigh on edge. She couldn't settle, couldn't concentrate. Unless Nola *had* gone to work and just forgotten the phone. That was possible if she'd been pissed. Anything was possible when she'd been on the lash.

Kayleigh was hungry. What to make for dinner? Baked potatoes, perhaps, and beans. She could put three large spuds in to cook and Nola might be back before they were ready. Kit wasn't fussy. He usually ate what she put in front of him. She went to the kitchen, turned on the oven, got the potatoes out of the cupboard, gave them a wash under the tap and used a fork to pierce the skins. When it came to cooking, she had a limited repertoire, but she had learned the basics through trial and error.

While she waited for the oven to heat up, she went and fetched Nola's phone. She stared at Nana Margaret's number for a moment or two, tempted to call but knowing that she shouldn't. Instead, she googled Mackenzie, Lind, found the number and keyed in the digits. A woman answered the phone.

'Could I speak to Mr Lind, please?'

'I'm sorry, he's not in the office. Can I take a message?'

'No, ta,' Kayleigh said and hung up, disappointed.

She would drop by the office tomorrow to see if he'd made any progress in the search for her dad.

302

45

Harry's flat was what Jem would have called minimalist: white walls, a leather sofa, a couple of lamps, a coffee table, a book-case and a TV. It was curiously impersonal with no pictures or photographs. Clean and tidy, it had the feel of a hotel room, of a place someone was just passing through. The two wide windows of the living room overlooked Station Road with a view of the Fox over to the right.

Jem wondered how much time he spent here, and suspected it was very little. She followed him into a small back bedroom where he put her hastily packed bag down on the floor and said, 'There you go. I hope it's okay.' Looking round as if he'd never seen the room before. 'Sorry, there's not much space.'

'It's fine,' Jem said. 'Thank you.'

'Good. The bathroom's next door. There are towels in the cupboard. I'll put the kettle on and leave you to unpack. Remind me to give you a key.'

As soon as he'd gone, Jem sat down on the single bed and examined her surroundings. This took even less time than in the living room. One single bed, one small chest of drawers, a bedside table and a lamp. But none of that mattered; she wasn't here to write a Tripadvisor review. She was here because . . . well, because she was beyond terrified by what Danny Street had said. Even thinking about it caused her body to go rigid, her pulse to race. And now she was trusting a man she barely knew to protect her from a grotesque threat that she wasn't even sure was real or not. She *could* trust him, couldn't she? Harry Lind was a private detective, an ex-cop, but none of that meant anything. There was constantly stuff in the news about cops abusing their position when it came to women.

Not wanting to think too much about this, Jem jumped up from the bed, took off her damp raincoat, hung it over the warming radiator and set about the business of unpacking. Five minutes later she was done. She hadn't brought much, just the essentials to get her through the next few days. She changed out of her damp jeans and hung them over the radiator too. Then she pulled on a pair of black joggers and went through to the kitchen.

Harry had coffee on the go, the percolator dripping. She sat down at the table as he got two mugs from the cupboard and a carton of milk from the fridge.

'Everything okay?' he asked.

'Sure. Thanks again. I appreciate it.' Jem felt awkward being here, like she was imposing on him, even though he was the one who'd offered. 'When do you think you'll be able to talk to Danny?'

'Later this evening. He'll show up at the Fox at some point. I'll keep an eye out for his Beamer and once it's in the car park I'll go across.'

'Should I come with you?'

Harry shook his head as he poured out the coffee. 'No, it's better he believes you don't know anything about Ray Dunn.'

A sliver of suspicion slipped into Jem's head again. Was that the real reason or was he trying to control her, to keep her out of the loop? God, she had to stop double guessing everything he said to her, or she'd go crazy. He wasn't Aidan. She couldn't judge him by that man's lack of moral rectitude. But on the other hand, she didn't want to make the same mistakes twice.

'Maybe you should take a few days off work until all this is sorted,' Harry suggested.

Jem hesitated, tempted by the idea, but then shook her head. 'I can't do that. It wouldn't be fair on Stefan. It's the busiest time of year. He can't cope on his own; someone needs to be in the shop while he's making deliveries. And anyway, what would I do here? Just stare at these four walls all day? I'll only be across the road.'

Harry put a mug of coffee in front of her. 'Let's see what Danny has to say, but yeah, you're probably safe enough for now.'

For now. Those words were guaranteed to send a chill through her. Not wanting to dwell on her own precarious situation, she changed the subject and asked, 'So not much joy from Amy Bolton, then?' Harry had touched briefly on the meeting on the way home, but they had passed most of the journey in silence, both preoccupied by their own thoughts.

'She's sticking to her original story,' Harry said, sitting down opposite her. 'I'm pretty sure she's telling the truth; either that or she's a damn good liar. But there were a couple of interesting things. She reckoned Arthur Mortlake had an unnatural interest in young girls, that he used to stare at her breasts whenever she went round.'

Jem pulled a face. 'Delightful. I know it's a bit of a leap, but do you think he might have been abusing Christine?'

'It's not impossible. But if he killed her, then why pursue the Greers for so long? I can see that he might have been trying to prove his innocence, but once he'd driven the family out of Kellston, why carry on?'

'Unless he was in denial about having done it. Or he just enjoyed tormenting people. Or it was just for show – proof to the world that he couldn't be guilty.'

'So how did he get rid of her body?'

Jem, grateful for the distraction, considered the question. 'Well, from the sound of things, the police didn't really have him pegged as a suspect. Perhaps the search was only cursory. There could be all sorts of hiding places in those big old houses. He could have moved her later.'

'That's true. Although it's not that easy to lug a body around when your wife's in the house. And she would have been there, twenty-four hours a day, for the next few days at least.' Harry scratched his chin, some early-evening stubble starting to emerge. 'He could have done it at night, I suppose, when she was asleep. But the neighbours would have been alert to any unusual activity by then. And although the police were probably watching the Greer house rather than the Mortlakes', it's only down the road and they'd have still noticed if he'd driven off in the early hours.'

'Unless she was never moved.'

'There's that of course.'

'But unlikely. So he's low on the list of suspects,' Jem said. 'Which is a shame. He sounds like a thoroughly unpleasant man. What about the other thing?'

'What thing?'

'You said there were a couple.'

'Oh, yeah.' Harry drank some coffee and looked at her over the rim of his mug. 'I'm not sure I should be telling you all this.'

'Don't stop now. I need the distraction. And don't worry, I won't tell anyone else.' There was no one else *to* tell, she thought.

Her social circle, if it could even be called that, was currently limited to her boss and Harry himself. She had always been careful about what she told Stefan, aware that he liked to gossip and that she had too much to hide to ever be truly open with him. 'I'm the soul of discretion.'

'Good,' he said. 'Okay, well, the other thing's a bit of a random connection. I've learned that Moses lost his wife and child in a hit-and-run a few weeks before Christine disappeared, and I'm wondering . . . God, I'm not sure what I'm wondering. Amy told me that Christine used to know Annie Moss – she was Moses's daughter – from teaching her at Sunday school. St James's. That church near the cemetery. I've been playing with the idea that maybe Moses thought one of the Mortlakes had been responsible for her death and decided to take his revenge.'

'An eye for an eye?'

'I know. It's pretty far-fetched. And I haven't got a shred of evidence. It's just an idea swilling around in my head along with all the other debris.'

'That's sad, about his wife and daughter. It would be enough to push anyone over the edge.'

'It would,' Harry agreed. 'Doesn't mean it's true though. Although he didn't go out to search for Christine on the evening of her disappearance. A group of men went from the Fox, but Moses didn't join them. He said that Arthur Mortlake wouldn't go looking for his kid if she was missing, or something along those lines.'

'Don't they normally *want* to be part of the action? I mean, you hear about it, don't you, killers joining the search party, pretending to be concerned. He did the very opposite. Although I suppose that could have been because he knew it was a waste of time.'

'Yeah, you can look at it both ways. I need to check out this hit-and-run with the *Kellston Gazette*. I've tried the archive on the internet but no joy. I'd like more information if I can get hold of it.'

Jem, remembering when she'd first met Moses, his fingers closing round her wrist, the mania in his eyes, gave a small shiver.

'You're not cold, are you? I can turn the heating up.'

'No, no, I'm fine. I was just ... So Christine would have known Moses if she attended the same church, and if she'd helped with the lessons for his daughter. And if she knew him, she'd have probably trusted him – well, if he wasn't quite as crazy back then as he is now.'

'I don't think he was.'

'So she wouldn't have been worried if he offered her a lift. Did he even have a car?'

'Something else I don't know. But a lift to where?'

Jem shrugged. 'Something to do with the church, maybe? He could have made up some story. She'd have felt sorry for him after losing his wife and daughter like that. She wouldn't have suspected him of planning to harm her in any way.'

'I suppose not.'

Jem wondered if she was encouraging Harry's suspicions purely because the old man had frightened her and felt obliged, in fairness, to temper her suggestions. 'Mind you, it's easy to point the finger at people who seem crazy. It's the ones who *don't* seem mad that you really have to worry about.'

Harry glanced at her as if she might be talking from personal experience, which of course she was. 'So, find the most normal-looking suspect and put them right at the top of the list.'

'Do you have a list?'

'Not exactly.'

'But you don't think it was Arthur Mortlake or George Greer?'

'I haven't entirely ruled them out.'

Jem could hear the frustration in his voice even though he was trying not to show it. 'It must be tough trying to solve a case from that long ago. No other leads, then?'

'No comment. Are you hungry? I was thinking about throwing a couple of pizzas in the oven. I'm going to need some fuel before I face Danny Street.'

46

It was after seven before the Beamer showed up at the Fox. By then Harry had opened a bottle of red wine and was sitting with Jem in the living room. He was trying, very carefully, to prise the lid off her personality, and to get to know her better. But she was mistress of the art of deflection and every time he probed into her life, she either shifted the subject on or asked him a question about himself. He understood her caution, her lack of trust, but was starting to feel that her interrogative skills were superior to his own.

'Are you going over?' she asked him when he told her that Danny Street had arrived.

'I'll give him a while to get settled in. Don't want to look too keen.'

Jem shifted on the sofa, crossing her feet at her ankles and then uncrossing them again. The tension was rising from her like steam. 'It's all too weird. Do you think it's true that Aidan could have set up something like that?'

'You'd know that better than me.'

'Then I suppose the answer's yes. It just freaks me out

thinking of him being here in Kellston – last week, a few days ago, whenever. If he knew where I lived, why didn't he just finish what he'd come to do?'

'Perhaps he wanted a bit of fun first, delayed gratification or whatever they call it. What made you think it was him on the phone?'

'Just a feeling. But it couldn't have been him, could it?'

Jem had taken off her glasses – part of a disguise she longer needed – and now he could clearly see her hazel eyes. He tried to avoid staring at her, without much success. His interest wasn't simply because she was attractive, although that was reason enough, but that he hoped to discover more about her. Maybe clues could be found in the paleness of her skin, in the gentle curve of her lips or the way she slightly inclined her head when she was thinking about something. She was cautious when she talked about herself, leaving small pauses before she spoke, as if she was censoring her speech before she allowed the words to escape from her mouth. A habit, he thought, borne of self-protection, of always being afraid of giving too much away.

It was while all these things were going through his mind that a more important one elbowed its way to the front of the queue. Jem was on tenterhooks, desperate to know what Danny Street had to say, and he was sitting here letting her sweat. It was all very well playing it cool, but when she was suffering as a result, mind games had to be laid aside.

'Perhaps I won't wait,' Harry said, rising to his feet. 'It might be better to catch him before he gets too pissed. You'll be all right on your own? I shouldn't be long. Put the bolt on the door if it makes you feel safer.' As soon as he uttered the last sentence he wished he hadn't. It implied she had something to feel unsafe about, which, as yet, had not been fully established.

Jem took a quick sip of wine. 'I wish I could come with you.

311

Why can't I? This is *my* future you'll be talking about. I think I have a right to hear whatever Danny has to say first hand.'

Harry, who preferred to talk to Street alone, pretended to give the request some thought. 'I'm not sure that's a good idea. Firstly, it's better if you're not connected in any way to Ray Dunn, and secondly, it . . . '

But Jem wasn't taking no for an answer. Before he could even broach his second point – that ran, a little iffily, along the lines of getting more out of Street man to man – she had stood up. 'I don't see what difference Ray Dunn makes. You're not going to tell Danny where he is and there's no reason why he should think that I know. I need to find out what Aidan's done, what this contingency plan is. It's better that *I* talk to Danny about that. You've never even met Aidan. How will you know if Danny's telling the truth? There are things I can ask him that you wouldn't even think to ask.'

'Like what?'

'I'm coming with you,' she said.

'Do you not think that maybe you're too close to all this?'

'It's because I'm close to it that I need to be there.'

Harry, seeing that her mind was made up, decided it was best to give in gracefully. There was no point rowing about it. He gave a shrug and said, 'Okay, whatever you want. Just watch your step with Danny, yeah? He likes playing games.'

'Don't worry, I won't say anything stupid.'

Harry put his jacket on. 'I never thought you would.'

'I'll get my coat. Don't go without me.'

It was dark outside. The wind had got up and squalls of rain flew through the chill night air, smattering against their faces as they crossed the still busy road.

'Are you mad at me?' Jem asked when they reached the other side.

'Why would I be mad?'

'Because you'd rather do this on your own.'

'True,' he said, deciding not to lie to her. 'But that's just because I'm used to working solo. I'm not mad at you, though. It's up to you what you do.' He had a sudden hope that she might change her mind and go back to the flat, but that was quickly dashed. She just gave a shrug and kept on walking towards the Fox.

Monday was one of those quieter evenings in the pub. There were enough customers to ensure that the place didn't look empty but not so many that you had to elbow your way to the bar. Harry did a quick sweep of the room and spotted Danny sitting near the back. Usually, the thug positioned himself close to the door – keeping an eye on everyone who came in, everyone who went out – but tonight, perhaps in anticipation of Harry showing up, he had shifted to a more private spot.

Harry ordered some drinks, a pint for himself, and a red wine for Jem. 'You ready?' he said, handing her the glass.

She smiled wanly back at him, took a fast gulp of wine as if to steady her nerves, and nodded. 'Let's do this.'

As they walked through the pub, Harry's eyes were on the man they'd come to see. He thought that Danny had a cartoonish quality to him, like a caricature of a gangster. But it wouldn't do to underestimate him. Danny Street was possessed of a cold brutality, a psychopathic inability to empathise or sympathise. He'd heard stories of his victims – men who'd been stabbed or strangled, women who'd been beaten half to death and scarred with cigarette burns – and knew that he had to tread carefully. To make an enemy of Street would be a mistake, but he wasn't prepared to show weakness either.

When they were approaching the table, Danny Street leaned over to the man beside him – an overlarge goon who looked like he ate steroids for breakfast – and said something. The goon obediently stood up and headed for the bar. When their paths crossed, he shot Harry an evil look.

'What was that about?' Jem asked softly.

'Just some low-level intimidation in case we don't realise how scary he is. Nothing to worry about.'

When they were within spitting distance Danny looked up at them and grinned. 'Ah, the lovely Jemima and her bodyguard. Good to see you again.' He gestured towards the chairs opposite. 'Grab a pew.'

Harry and Jem sat down. There was an odd silence as if no one wanted to start, a portentous silence filled with menace. It was Danny who eventually broke it.

'Okay, let's get down to business.' He kept his gaze on Harry. 'You tell me where that fucker Ray Dunn is, and I'll tell you what Aidan Hague has planned for your girlfriend.'

'I am here,' Jem said crossly. 'And Harry's saying nothing about Ray until I'm sure you know what you're talking about. How can I be certain you've even met Aidan? Tell me something about him, prove to me that the two of you have actually spoken.'

'That's not very trusting.'

'And why the hell should I trust you?'

Harry was faintly surprised by the vehemence of Jem's retort, and by her lack of fear in addressing Street this way. But then this was her life they were apparently negotiating. Anyway, Danny Street didn't seem put out by her attitude. In fact, his grin had grown even wider, as if he wasn't used to women answering back and found the experience both novel and entertaining. How long this amused benevolence would last, however, was another matter altogether.

'Tall, fair-haired geezer.' Danny said. 'Northern accent.'

Jem hissed out a breath of frustration. 'Oh, come on! You could have got that from anywhere. His picture's all over the internet, and of course he's got a northern accent – he comes from the north.'

'Then what are you after?'

'Something that you'd only know if you'd been in his company, if you'd stared into those cold, sly eyes of his and had a proper conversation.'

This seemed to stymie Danny. His brow furrowed. He drank some Scotch while he thought about what she'd said, swilling it round in his mouth like he was treating a toothache. Then his lips widened again. 'I know,' he said. 'He's got a tell when he's lying. And he lied a lot, that old feller of yours.' Danny touched his forehead, indicating a place just on the outer edge of his right eyebrow. 'Here,' he said. 'Just a twitch. You'd hardly notice it unless you were looking.'

Jem was quiet for a moment, not denying it. 'When did you see him?'

'Not that long ago. Ten days maybe, a fortnight.'

'Why did he come to you?'

'To show some respect,' Danny said, his glance shifting from Jem to Harry and back again, as if to remind them that he was a bloke worthy of respect. 'This is my manor, ain't it? No one does nothing here without coming to me first.'

'Okay, say that's all true about you seeing him and everything. It still doesn't mean that he ... that he made any kind of *arrangement*. You could have made that up.'

'You calling me a liar, babe?'

Harry thought this might be a good time to join the conversation. He'd been watching Danny Street carefully, trying to figure out if he was bullshitting or not. It was impossible to tell. Danny's behaviour was always irrational, always erratic, swinging suddenly from one mood to another. 'No one's calling you a liar. But if you're hoping I can tell you where Ray Dunn is, you're going to be disappointed. I haven't found him yet, although I'm pretty sure I know what country he's in.'

'And what country would that be?'

'Spain of course. On the Costa somewhere. Blokes like Ray don't have much imagination. They get a bit of money in their pocket and that's where they head when they can't think of anywhere else to go. Birds of a feather and all that. I've got some contacts out there, but it'll take a little time to track him down. Even Ray wouldn't be stupid enough to be using his real name.'

Danny stared at him for a long while. 'Who said anything about money?'

'Oh, come on, are you really telling me this is all over some crap second-hand car? I wasn't born yesterday. Ray's out in Spain sunning himself at your expense and that makes you look bad. At least it would if people found out about it. I take it he ripped you off in one way or another?'

Danny didn't answer.

'I'll need some time,' Harry said again. 'The Costa's full of bloody Brits.'

'Trouble is, mate, time ain't what you got.'

'Meaning?'

'Let me explain,' Danny said slowly, like he was talking to a five-year-old. 'Aidan Hague got himself in some bother in Blackpool – well, you've probably already gathered that – and had to make himself scarce for a while. So, having got wind that the lovely Jem was in Kellston . . . '

'How? How did he get wind?' Jem interrupted.

'He didn't go into all the ins and outs. He was just looking forward to the two of you being reunited.' Danny smirked. 'Missed you, didn't he, while he was in the slammer. Although now I think of it, he may have employed one of Harry's mates to find out where you were.'

'What?'

Harry felt Jem stiffen beside him. 'He means another private detective,' he said quickly. 'I'm not the only one in the country.'

She frowned at Danny. 'So are you saying I've got a price on my head? Is that what this is all about? Is that Aidan's "contingency plan"? To make sure that even if he died, I'd die too?'

Danny laughed, sat back and folded his arms. 'Come on, love, now you're angling for something for nothing. Why should I help you when you're not helping me?'

Harry stuck his oar in again. 'Who said we weren't going to help? I'll tell you where Ray Dunn is when I manage to locate him.'

'Better shake a leg then, mate. Time's ticking.'

'I can't conjure him out of thin air. And I need to know that Jem's safe while I'm looking.'

Danny drank some more Scotch. 'Very gallant, I'm sure. Well, I can only tell you what I've heard, on the grapevine like, so don't go running to the law and putting me in the frame.'

'No one's going to do that,' Jem said. 'Just tell us what you know. *Please.*'

Danny let them both sweat for a while. Then he said suddenly, 'Twenty grand.' He looked Jem up and down. 'Not sure if that's a compliment or an insult. What do you think, love?'

Jem stared at him. She'd become very still. 'To kill me?'

'No, to buy you dinner at the fucking Ritz.'

'Why don't you just keep the money?' Harry said. 'It's not as if Aidan will be any the wiser.'

'Who said anything about me having the money? Did I say that? Don't start putting words in my mouth or you and me are going to fall out.'

'Okay, okay,' Harry said, trying to be placatory. 'But you can stop it. You have the power to do that, yeah?'

Danny's lips widened into one of his freakish grins. 'If you make it worth my while.'

'I get it,' Harry said. 'You want Ray Dunn. Well, you can have the stupid fucker. I've already told you that, but it'll take a few weeks to find him.'

'One week,' Danny said.

'I can't do it in a week. Give me two.'

Danny considered it. He took his time. He drank some more Scotch and gazed at Jem.

Jem leaned across the table and said softly, 'How do we even know you're telling the truth?'

Danny laughed, a harsh nasty sound. 'You don't, love. That's the fun of it.' He turned to Harry. 'All right, two weeks. Now fuck off before I change my mind.'

47

Nola Dunn wasn't causing Phillip any trouble. This wasn't just because he'd tied her up – strong string binding her ankles and wrists – but because he'd given her a brandy laced with sleeping pills. She'd gulped that brandy down like it was nectar and fifteen minutes later she'd been out for the count. He'd left her on the sofa so he could keep an eye on her.

Now he sat at the table, head in his hands, trying to figure out what to do next. Nobody had come to the flat so that was a good sign. There was no partner looking for her, no nutter on the rampage. It had been a long time since he'd smashed her over the head. Since then, it had got dark, the floor had been hoovered and the crushed hyacinths along with the shattered bowl consigned to the bin.

Of course it wasn't true to say that she wasn't causing him trouble. She was causing that just by being here. And now kidnap could be added to the list of charges along with assault. Perhaps Chapel had a point. It would almost be easier if she *was* dead. Although disposing of a corpse from a high-rise wasn't the easiest job in the world. It wasn't as if he could just take her downstairs and put her out with the rubbish. And she wouldn't fit in the chute – small bags only – unless he cut her into more manageable pieces.

Chapel sniggered. 'That's where she deserves to be, out with the rubbish. Like that Charlene.'

'If you haven't got anything useful to say, why don't you just shut up?'

'No need to be like that, Phil. *You* were the one who hit her, not me. Although to be honest, I'd have made a better job of it.'

An hour ago, Phillip had opened his emergency bottle of brandy and had already made substantial inroads. He knew that he should stay sober, that getting drunk was a big mistake, but he couldn't face the enormity of it all without a drink inside him. 'I need to persuade her to keep her mouth shut. There must be a way. There has to be.'

'That tart won't ever keep her gob shut. You know that, mate. And once she tells the law what you did you can kiss goodbye to any dreams of becoming a success again. You'll be finished and your book will be too. Although you could always write a memoir of your happy days in the Scrubs.'

Phillip's jaw clenched. 'So what am I supposed to do?'

'You should smother her right now.' Chapel nodded towards the cushions on the sofa. 'Go on, do the sensible thing. She wouldn't know anything about it. A few seconds and it would all be over.'

'And you think a dead body in the flat is going to make everything better?'

'She can do you damage. You know she can . . . and will. Just finish her off and dump her in the lift.'

'DNA,' Phillip said. He wasn't writing a crime novel for nothing. 'Her DNA's going to be all over the flat. And there'll be blood on the carpet, maybe even the walls, even if we can't see it.'

'They can't check every flat in the block. Why should they come here? Why would they suspect you? Dump her in the early hours. No one will find her till the morning. They'll just think a punter gave her a clout and then finished her off.'

Phillip wondered how it was that Chapel made murder sound logical, normal, the rational thing to do. He stared at Nola sleeping on the sofa. Thin whispery breaths came from her mouth. He'd removed the gag in case she choked. He didn't want to kill her; he just wanted her out of his life for ever. 'I could give her money, make a deal with her. She'd take money, wouldn't she?'

'Course she'd take your money. And then she'd come back for more ... and more ... until she's bled you bloody dry.'

'I'd be gone by then. I only need her to keep quiet for a while. I'll get out of here. Once I'm gone, she won't be able to find me.'

'You've still got six months left on this place.'

Phillip flapped a frustrated hand. 'So what? I'll find somewhere else to live. It's better than killing her.'

Chapel wrinkled his nose. 'Even if you do a bunk, she can still report you. That cut on her head isn't going to heal in a hurry, and she doesn't strike me as the forgiving sort. She'll be straight down the nick screaming blue murder about nonces and being attacked and whatever else she might feel like making up when she's got an interested audience. They may just find it a touch suspicious that you've been living under an assumed name, pretending to be someone you're not.'

'Shit. But I can explain, about the book and everything ...'

'Yeah, a book about a psychopathic murderer. That's going to go down well. Maybe they'll think you've been getting some practice in. First, Charlene, then Dion. Look, for as long as that slut's alive, she'll be causing trouble for you. I mean, she's brought it on herself, hasn't she? Calling you a paedo, accusing you of all sorts. She's not going to stop until she's ruined your fucking life. You need to do something about it, mate. You need to take control.'

48

When Harry got up on Tuesday morning, he was relieved to find Jem still in the flat. After their meeting with Danny, she'd been seriously thinking about leaving Kellston. He'd tried to talk her round and encourage her not to make any rash decisions. They had two weeks' grace to find out if what Street had said was true and to come up with a solution. 'We've got some time. Don't leave before you have to. You don't want to be looking over your shoulder for the rest of your life.'

Although she'd agreed to stay, he'd wondered if she might change her mind during the night, head over to the Mansfield, pack her bags and get a bus or a cab to one of the mainline stations. He wouldn't have blamed her. She had come to Kellston searching for sanctuary and had instead discovered the very opposite.

Jem was sitting at the kitchen table playing with a piece of toast. She looked tired but that wasn't surprising. Knowing you might be a target for some random hitman didn't do much for a restful night's sleep.

'Call me,' he said, 'if you're worried about anything. I'll be in Kellston all day.'

'Sure. Thanks.'

Harry suspected she was thinking that there wouldn't be much time for a phone call if the killer walked into the florist's and put a bullet between her eyes, but he might have been mistaken. 'We could go to the police, you know.'

'Danny Street would love that.'

'It might make him think twice about setting the wheels in motion – if there are any wheels, that is.'

'Or it could have the completely opposite effect.'

Harry couldn't argue with that. Danny Street was unpredictable. There was no knowing what he'd do from one day to the next. He wanted to say something reassuring but couldn't think of anything that didn't sound crass or cliched. 'Would you like me to pick you up from work?'

Jem shook her head. 'No, I think I can make it across the road but thanks for the offer. Anyway, I'm not supposed to be at risk right now, am I?'

'Right, well I'm going to head downstairs. I've got an appointment with Celia Mortlake at ten, and I need to go through my notes.'

'Okay. I'll see you later.'

Have a good day, Harry almost said, but managed to stop himself. He went down to the office, opened up, put the kettle on and made himself a coffee. Should he have stayed longer with Jem? He had the feeling that she was all talked out, that she preferred to be alone, but when it came to his instincts about women, he didn't always get it right. And that, probably, was the understatement of the year. In truth, he hadn't slept that well himself, the whole Danny Street thing going round and round in his head while he tried to figure out a plan of action.

He sat down at his desk and took the Mortlake file out of the top drawer. He wasn't looking forward to seeing Celia today. Although he'd spoken to Vivienne Bayle and Amy Bolton since last seeing her, the word 'progress' wouldn't be springing to his lips any time soon. There was the Moses angle, of course, but none of that was clear yet. It needed more detail, more investigation and more evidence than he currently possessed. Hurling random accusations into the mix wasn't going to help anybody.

Harry drank his coffee while he went through his notes on the two meetings, carefully sifting through the conversations and pulling out what he perceived to be the pertinent facts. None of it was very impressive, but at least he could prove that he was doing some work. What he dreaded was the look of disappointment in Celia's eyes, the suspicion that he was no nearer to a breakthrough than when he'd started.

At twenty past eight he heard Jem's footsteps on the stairs. After the front door closed, he turned around in his chair and followed her progress along Station Road. She walked quickly to the pedestrian crossing at the traffic lights and waited impatiently. He could see her agitation even from a distance, the way she kept moving from foot to foot, and glancing over her shoulder. Or perhaps she was just afraid of running into Moses again.

When the lights finally changed, she strode across the road and almost jogged to the florist's. Harry watched until she was safely inside and then turned back to his desk. A minute later Lorna came into reception and immediately called out, 'New client?'

'What?'

Lorna came to stand in the doorway of his office. 'The young lady I just saw coming out of here.' She grinned, looking at her watch. 'Bit early in the day to be hiring a private detective, isn't it?'

'She's not a client. She's just a mate. She's staying with me for a few days.'

Lorna almost rubbed her hands together. She was always interested in his love life – or, more usually, the lack of it. 'Pretty girl. So who is she then? What's her name?'

'It's not what you think.'

'I wasn't thinking anything.'

'That would be a first. Her name's Jem, all right? Jem with a J. And like I said, she's a *mate*, nothing else. Don't start getting any ideas. Now I really have to read through these notes. I've got an appointment at ten.'

But Lorna wasn't deterred so easily. 'It's only half eight. You've got plenty of time. So how did you and Jem meet?'

'Lorna!'

'Oh, come on, you know you'll tell me eventually.'

Harry gathered up the notes, put them back in the file, picked up the file and rose to his feet. It was only a matter of time before Lorna shone a bright light in his eyes and forced him to give her all the details, and then there would have to be a long conversation about where it was all going. 'There's nothing else to tell. I'll see you later, yeah?'

'Where are you going? I thought your appointment wasn't until ten.'

'I've got to drop by the *Gazette* first.'

'They won't be open yet.'

'They will be by the time I've had breakfast.'

As Harry walked past her, Lorna said, 'If I had a suspicious mind, I'd think you were hiding something.'

Harry didn't respond other than to wave a hand as he headed towards the stairs. Outside, it was busy as always. A long line of cars, buses and taxis swept by. The rain had stopped but the street was still slick with water. He jaywalked across to the

Station Café and went inside where it was warm and steamy and, best of all, Lorna free.

There was a queue at the counter for take-out coffees and rolls, but he forged a path through and looked around for a table. Most of them were taken but then he saw Moses sitting on his own with a large mug of tea in front of him. The old bloke stocking up on fluids before a hard morning's harassment. Harry went over, put the file on the table and sat down. 'Mind if I join you?'

Moses gazed at him through rheumy eyes. 'Mr Lind. And how are you today?'

'Hungry,' he said. 'Actually, I'm glad I bumped into you. There was something I wanted to ask.' Before Harry could get started the waitress came over to take his order. Aware that eating healthily hadn't been high on his agenda for the past few weeks, he chose scrambled eggs on toast, and a latte. Then he asked Moses, 'Would you like something? It's on me.'

The old man, who never looked a gift horse in the mouth, immediately said, 'I'll have a full English, ta.'

Harry thought that most of his expense sheet for this month – other than the trip to Whitstable – would be taken up with forking out money for Moses. He waited until the waitress had gone and then leaned across the table so he could talk quietly. 'I'm still working on the Mortlake case, trying to figure out what happened. It was a Sunday that Christine disappeared.' He paused, not wanting his next question to sound like an accusation. 'I've been asking everyone, but I don't suppose you saw her at all that day?'

'Course I did,' Moses said surprisingly.

Harry stared at him, wondering for a few insane seconds whether Moses was about to make a confession. 'You did?'

'She was at St James's, wasn't she? In the morning. With those stuck-up parents of hers.'

'Ah, yes,' Harry said. 'Didn't she help out at the Sunday school?'

'She used to teach my Annie. Now the two of them are gone. God had a plan for them both.'

Harry was tempted to ask exactly what that plan was but thought better of it. A long monologue was likely to follow, liberally scattered with biblical quotations. He thought there was something sinister about the notion of a plan, something that set alarm bells off in his head. But he shouldn't jump to conclusions. It could just be a reflection of the man's religious beliefs, a way of dealing with the horror of loss.

'And how did she seem?'

'Seem?'

'That Sunday morning. Happy, sad, upset about anything? Did you notice?'

Moses shrugged. 'She wasn't in church. She went into the Sunday school.'

'And you didn't see her again that day?'

Moses gave him a long look, his expression wary. 'What do you mean?'

'Nothing,' Harry said quickly. 'Nothing at all. I just thought you might have noticed whether she talked to anyone after church.'

'And why would I notice that?'

Harry was aware that at this point it had only been a few weeks after the death of his wife and daughter. Had he reached the anger stage yet? Had he felt the understandable rage and frustration that often came with loss? Asking himself, perhaps, why his loved ones had been taken rather than someone else's. 'People notice all kinds of things.'

The food came and Moses attacked it like he hadn't eaten for a week. The raw, almost animal smell of him floated across the table, stale and sweaty and unwashed. He ate noisily and voraciously, as if the waitress might come back at any moment and snatch his plate away. Harry picked up his knife and fork, trying to eat without breathing too deeply. He consumed his scrambled egg on toast but barely tasted it, too distracted by his thoughts as he wondered how far he could push it with Moses before his questions began to sound more like accusations.

Moses cleared his plate in record time and pushed it to one side. He picked at his teeth with his grubby fingernails. 'She might have made a phone call.'

'What?'

'There was a payphone in the hallway of the Sunday school. The church hall. I left just before the service finished – I didn't want to talk to no one – and I glanced over as I was going down the path. The doors were open, and she was standing there with the phone against her ear. She was speaking to someone, and she didn't look happy. Frowning, you know, like she had the weight of the world on her shoulders.'

'Did you catch any of it, what she was saying?'

'Nah, I wasn't close enough.'

'Did you tell the police?'

Moses shook his head. 'The police never asked.'

'And you didn't think to volunteer the information?'

'I had other things on my mind, Mr Lind. Didn't think it was important.'

Harry growled in frustration. It was too late now, of course, to trace who she'd been ringing. Amy? Vivienne? Or it could have been someone else entirely, someone who wasn't even in the picture yet. If only Moses had mentioned it all those years ago. At the same time, he felt a surge of excitement. The call was interesting because she'd chosen to make it from the Sunday school rather than home, which meant, surely, that either it was a very urgent call or one she hadn't wanted her parents to overhear.

'Are you sure it was that Sunday? It couldn't have been another one, the week before, maybe?'

'I know what Sunday it was,' Moses said firmly.

Harry nodded. But was Moses telling the truth? If he was guilty of murder, he might just be trying to cover his tracks, to scatter some red herrings and put him off the scent.

49

Harry's next port of call was the *Gazette*. There was no one in the small reception area but he could hear the gentle clatter of fingers on keyboards coming from the room beyond. He put his head round the door – one occupant – and eventually caught the attention of the young man who was staring intently at his computer screen as if the meaning of life might be contained within the words he was writing.

'Sorry to disturb you. I'm looking for some information on an accident that happened years ago, a hit-and-run.'

'Have you tried online?' the young man said. 'There's an archive.'

'Yes, I couldn't find anything there. Do you keep copies of your old papers?'

'Ah, you'd need to talk to Maeve about that. If you wait in reception, I'll give her a buzz.'

'Thanks.' Harry retreated, and while he waited he perused the framed front pages on the wall, the coverage of famous events from a local perspective: wartime damage to the area, VE Day, the election of Margaret Thatcher, jubilee street parties and, most recently, the Queen's death.

It was another five minutes before Maeve appeared. She was a small middle-aged woman with cropped brown hair, bright eyes and a pleasant smile. Harry explained what he was after, the year it had happened and that he hadn't been able to find anything about the accident online.

'Ah, yes,' she said, 'it's a bit too long ago. The archive is what we like to call a work in progress. But if you have an exact date, I should be able to dig it out for you. We have all the old editions in the basement.'

'Exact might be tricky,' Harry said. A few weeks before Christine's disappearance was all he knew, and, even then, he was relying on the recollections of Betty and Lionel. 'I'd say it was in July, though. It was probably quite a big story: a mother and daughter, a child, killed by a car on their way home. Eleanor and Annie Moss.'

'That sounds like it would have been prominent. Front page, I expect, unless something even more dramatic happened that week. Maeve faltered, frowned and said, 'I'm sorry, I didn't mean to sound callous. Are you a relative?'

'No, I'm a private investigator. I'm working on another case but there could be a connection.' Then, because he was in a newspaper office, and reporters were always on the lookout for a good story, he quickly added, 'I dare say there isn't, but I'd like to check it out.'

'A private investigator? That sounds like an interesting job.'

'It has its moments.'

'Are you in a hurry? It might take a while to dig it out.'

'No, no hurry. I've got another appointment so I could come back after that. About eleven? Half eleven?'

'That will be fine,' Maeve said. 'We make a small charge for photocopies. Is that all right?'

'No problem,' Harry said. 'Thanks for your help.'

He left the newspaper office, got in his car and drove to Magellan Street. It was still early – only half past nine – so he parked round the corner in Drake Road and thought about what Moses had told him. That phone call could be the clue to everything. If Moses had been telling the truth. Had he? Then, before he'd come to any conclusions, he got sidetracked and started thinking about Jem and Danny Street, about Aidan Hague and the disturbing legacy he might have left behind. He should talk to Mac, get his take on it. His partner was clever, shrewd, and even though Jem wasn't officially a client, Harry would appreciate having the older man's input.

Too restless to stay still, he got out of the Audi, locked it, and began walking up the road. Perhaps the chill December air would help to concentrate his mind. Drake Road was at right angles to Magellan Street, and the Mortlake residence was one away from the corner. What if Christine had turned right instead of left, and then turned right again? There were high hedges on both sides of the road, obscuring the view from the houses. If someone had parked here, there was every chance that they wouldn't have been seen. But had the hedges even been here in 1971? Harry stared at them, but it didn't help; his horticultural knowledge was minimal.

The houses along Drake Road were large and detached, most of them converted into flats. Harry traipsed through a blanket of soggy leaves, killing time until his appointment with Celia was due. If Christine *had* turned right, then she'd clearly had no intention of going to Amy's. And it would only have taken her twenty seconds to round the corner, a period of time so short that she could easily have been unobserved.

Theories. They were all very well, but unless he could prove them, they were meaningless. He kept going back to that phone call, to Christine's agitation, to her need for privacy. Something had been on her mind. He wondered if the Greers had gone to church that Sunday. If they had, then it couldn't have been Amy she was calling. He made a mental note to follow it up.

At five to ten, Harry turned around and made his way back to the Mortlake house. He opened the gate and walked up the path. The front garden was dim and gloomy, full of overgrown shrubs, and he could hear the dripping of gathered rain falling off the branches of the trees. He rang the bell and waited.

As usual, Mrs Feeney answered the door. As usual, her welcome was less than effusive.

'Back again,' she said, standing aside, unsmiling, to let him in. 'You know where she is.'

'Good morning, Mrs Feeney. Nice to see you too. Before you rush off, I was hoping you could help me with something.'

Mrs Feeney looked sceptical. 'And what would that be then?'

'Have you lived here for long? In this house, I mean.'

Her hands went to her plump hips, her expression darkening. 'And what business would that be of yours?'

Harry ignored the question. 'I was just wondering if you knew anything about those high hedges on Drake Road? Have they always been there?'

'Hedges?' she repeated, staring at him like he was mad.

'Yes, the ones just round the corner. Do you know if they were there when Christine went missing?'

'I've no idea,' she said. 'I wasn't in Kellston then.'

'Okay, thanks anyway.'

Harry walked past her along the hallway towards the drawing room. He could feel her eyes on his back. Was it his imagination or had Mrs Feeney been a touch defensive? As if he was about to accuse her of something. Stealing the family silver, perhaps, or pilfering the housekeeping money. Or something more closely connected to Christine? She had been against the investigation from the very start.

Harry knocked on the door and waited for his summons to enter. Celia Mortlake was seated by the fire, her body ramrod straight, her hands in her lap. The smell of freshly ground coffee wafted in the air. Outside, the sky had darkened and the tall lamp was on, casting shadows across the room. She gestured towards the flimsy yellow chair, and he sat down.

'Good morning, Mr Lind,' she said, picking up the pot to pour his coffee. 'Do you have news for me?'

Harry didn't waste any time. Procrastination was high on the list of Celia Mortlake's pet hates. He succinctly ran through his meetings with Christine's two friends, omitting the less savoury titbits. She smiled when he talked about Vivienne, and scowled when he mentioned Amy.

'She's sticking to her story, then?'

'Yes.'

'Well, that's no big surprise. She's hardly going to tell the truth after all this time.'

Harry let this pass. Celia was closed to the possibility that the Greers were innocent, and there was no point in provoking her. Instead, he said, 'Do you recall if the Greers were at church that Sunday morning?'

'At church? Why is that important?'

'Do you remember seeing them at all?'

Celia thought about it, but then shook her head. 'They might have been there, but I didn't notice them. That service was always busy. People used to go to church in those days. Nowadays, they just worship their phones.'

Which led Harry nicely on to his next point. 'I've been told that Christine made a call from the church hall just before the end of the service.'

'A call? Why on earth would she do that when she had a perfectly good phone at home?'

'Why indeed,' Harry said.

'Who said that?'

Harry hesitated, in two minds as to whether to tell her, but decided he had no good reason to withhold the information. 'A man called Michael Moss. Does the name mean anything to you?'

'I can't say it does.'

'He also goes by the name of Moses. You might have come across him; he likes to spread God's word on the street.'

'Oh, that strange little man. Surely you can't believe anything *he* tells you. He's not quite in his right mind, is he?'

'Hard to tell,' Harry said. 'But he says he left the service early, glanced across at the church hall and noticed Christine on the payphone. He thought she seemed upset or agitated.'

'He's making it up. Maybe he's some kind of attention seeker or he's remembering the wrong girl.'

'Or maybe he's right,' Harry said. 'Which could mean that Christine made an arrangement to meet someone that afternoon.'

'She wouldn't have done that without telling us.'

'It could have been a quick call to Amy if the family wasn't at church. Or someone else entirely. Did she seem upset at all when you met up afterwards?'

'No,' Celia said.

'Or at lunch?'

'If she'd been upset, Mr Lind, I'd have talked to her about it and I'd certainly have mentioned it to the police.'

But Harry thought that Christine could have hidden her

worries. She had been a quiet girl by all accounts, probably not prone to outward shows of emotion. 'Going back to Moses for a second. Were you aware that he'd lost his wife and daughter in a hit-and-run a few weeks before Christine went missing?'

'Did he? I don't recall it.'

'The daughter was called Annie. She was about six. I believe Christine knew her from Sunday school.'

Celia, who was never slow on the uptake despite her advanced years, was quick to make the leap. 'You think there might be a connection?'

Harry didn't want to raise any false hopes or point the finger at Moses. 'I don't see why there should be, especially if you didn't know the man. But it's another tragic event around the same time.'

'Maybe I do remember something about it. Vaguely.' Celia frowned, searching back through her memory. 'The little girl. Yes, it rings a bell. A terrible accident.'

Harry watched her carefully but there was no sign that it touched a nerve, that she or her husband had been the one driving the car. 'Christine must have been upset about it.'

'I suppose so,' Celia said, but Harry could tell that it was all too dim and distant for her to focus on. Whatever had happened to Eleanor and Annie Moss, and how it had affected Christine, had been almost wiped from her memory by what had come after.

Harry moved on to other things, like who had gone out to search for her daughter – Celia didn't know – and how long the hedges had been there in Drake Road. The latter question seemed to bemuse her as much as it had Mrs Feeney.

'Hedges?'

'It was just a thought,' Harry said. 'If Christine left the house

337

and met up with someone round the corner, the hedges would have obscured the view from the houses there.'

'Christine went down to Amy's,' Celia said, as if this was a fact set in stone and no talk of high hedges was going to change it.

'Humour me,' Harry said. 'Have they always been there?'

'Yes, I believe so.'

Harry placed a mental tick beside his theory, and then dropped the subject. He didn't want Celia thinking he was going down blind alleys (hedgerowed or not) and wasting time on pointless speculation. As he got up to leave, their business concluded for the day, he casually said, 'Mrs Feeney must be a great help. Has she been with you for long?'

'Over ten years now.'

'Is she local?'

Celia paused before replying. 'What's this sudden interest in my housekeeper, Mr Lind?'

'I was just thinking that she would have been of an age with Christine.'

'And that's relevant because?'

'Because girls talk, Mrs Mortlake. She could have heard something back then, probably only rumour and gossip but occasionally there are clues even in that.'

'She's not from Kellston. Somewhere in south London, I believe. I don't recall exactly where.'

'Never mind,' Harry said. 'Thank you for the coffee.'

'What about the mother?' Celia suddenly barked.

'The mother?'

'Amy's mother. Mrs Freer. Have you checked that she's as incapable as Amy says she is?'

'Yes. She has dementia.'

'Very convenient,' Celia muttered, as if Pauline Freer had

deliberately lost her mind in order to avoid having to answer any awkward questions.

As Harry walked along the hall towards the front door, he was aware of eyes on his back. He didn't turn around, didn't need to. Mrs Feeney, he knew, was watching him from the shadows.

50

Jem had been curiously calm all day. It was not a natural reaction to being told you might only have two weeks to live but the reality of it had settled over her like a shroud, wrapping her in a strange, almost dream-like state. The shock, perhaps. Or just her mind being so overloaded that it couldn't absorb this latest development with any kind of clarity.

The pungent smell of lilies filled the air. There were people who didn't like the scent – a reminder of funerals – but she found it both beguiling and sad. Her mother had carried lilies at her wedding, a smiling bride with no idea of what was coming. Miriam's bouquet had been big blowsy roses, red as blood. Not that Jem had attended her father's second wedding, but she had seen the pictures. 'Six months,' she could hear her gran saying. 'Has the man got no decency?'

If her mum hadn't died, everything would have been different. If Gramps hadn't died, everything would have been different. If she'd never met Aidan, everything would have been different. But would it? Maybe she had always been fated to meet him one way or another, and if it hadn't been in the shop, it would have been somewhere else, some other time. All roads lead to the same place. But she wasn't sure if she believed in fate or destiny. If everything was preordained, then what was the point of free will?

Jem carefully wrapped the Stargazers in cellophane, glancing up every now and again to look across the road. Harry had gone out at eight thirty this morning and come back at eleven twenty carrying a brown A4 envelope. Not that she was keeping track of him or anything. Was she putting too much faith in his ability to circumvent Aidan's plans? He seemed competent enough, ex-police, used to dealing with dire situations, but this might be a bridge too far. Danny Street wasn't your run-of-the-mill lowlife; he was powerful and callous, twisted and cruel. He was the sort of man who'd kill just for the fun of it.

She couldn't stay in Harry's flat. It was too much of an imposition and anyway there wasn't any point. The immediate danger had passed. They'd been given two weeks so she might as well move back to the Mansfield. There she could pack up her things in case she needed to leave in a hurry. Be prepared. Check out the train times, decide where to head for next. Another day, another city.

Jem attached a long pink ribbon to the bouquet, tied it in a bow, and sighed.

Kayleigh was looking out of the classroom window, pretending that she wasn't, sneaking swift yearning glances while Mrs Sayle was writing on the whiteboard. Maths. Multiplication, addition, subtraction, long division. Numbers that danced around but didn't settle. Mrs Sayle claimed she had eyes in the back of her head, but she clearly hadn't, otherwise she'd have caught Kayleigh in the heinous crime of 'not concentrating'.

The memory had come out of the blue, a flashback, shortly after the lesson had started. Kayleigh didn't know what had prompted it. One minute it wasn't in her head, and then it was. That time, three years ago, when Nola had taken them down to Froome's to raise some hell about Dad. She had seen it then, the long coil of red wire sitting in the corner of the office. The same red wire she had seen around Dion's neck. Well, possibly. And Danny Street had a connection to Froome's and people were saying that Danny had killed Dion, so maybe that was where he'd got the wire from.

She was waiting for the bell to ring so she could escape from school, pick up Kit and pay a visit to Harry Lind. He might have some good news for her. He might have found her dad. Should she tell him about the wire? It didn't have anything to do with his search, but she felt she should tell someone. She didn't want Dion's killer to go free. But she didn't want to get on the wrong side of Danny Street either. And nobody liked grasses.

There was a clock on the wall, its minute hand revolving so slowly that Kayleigh was sure there must be something wrong with it. She urged it forward, desperate to be free from the confined space of the classroom, to breathe fresh air, to feel her legs moving again. Being in school was like being in prison, or at least how she imagined prison to be. Locked doors with maths.

Would Nola be back today? She hadn't come home last night, and Tracey hadn't said anything about her showing up at her place. That was a relief. Her mother was embarrassing enough without adding to it. And Kayleigh didn't want another interrogation as to what she'd really been up to on Friday night. If Harry tracked down her dad, would Nola give him a second chance? Everybody made mistakes.

The bell finally rang. Kayleigh bundled her exercise book and pens into her bag, shot out of the door and retrieved her jacket from the peg in the cloakroom. It was only a short walk to the infant school. Kit was sitting on the low wall by the gate when she got there, his head stuck in a book.

'Hey, soldier. You had a good day?'

Kit looked up and gave her a wan smile. She didn't know why she'd asked really. Did he ever have a good day at school? Making friends was tricky when you couldn't talk to other kids. And it wasn't as if Nola showered him with attention; she was hard pressed most days to even remember she had any offspring. Once Dad was home, everything would change. Kit would start speaking again. She was sure of it. In the meantime, she'd do her best to keep him safe and happy.

'Let's go and see Harry Lind,' she said, taking his hand. 'Find out what's going on.'

It wasn't far to Station Road. Kayleigh was trying not to raise her hopes too much as they headed for the office. Would he even be there? He hadn't been around yesterday when she'd called. Some woman had answered the phone and she hadn't dared leave a message because she'd used Nola's mobile and didn't want Harry ringing her back on it.

They had just passed the caff and were now walking towards the crossing on the corner. It was the long way round – the office was directly opposite on the other side of the road – and Kayleigh would have taken her chances with the traffic if she'd been alone, but Kit couldn't move as quickly as she could, and she didn't want him mown down by some moronic driver.

Then, suddenly, Danny Street came out of the door of the Fox and started strolling towards them. Kayleigh felt her heart miss a beat. She stopped dead in her tracks, her hand tightening around Kit's. She thought of the red wire around Dion's neck and her mouth went dry. Her instinct was to turn tail and run, but that would only draw attention to them.

'Come on,' she muttered, moving forward again as if Kit had been the one to stop rather than her. Danny Street was getting closer. Don't look at him, she told herself. Don't make any eye contact. You're just a couple of schoolkids, nothing for him to concern himself with. He probably doesn't even know who you are.

Danny went past and she heaved a sigh of relief. But then, horror of horrors, she heard a voice bellowing, 'Oi! Hang on. You're Kayleigh Dunn, ain't you?'

Kayleigh's stomach took a dive. She wondered if she should just keep walking, pretend she hadn't heard him or that her name was something quite different. But he'd already retraced his steps and was standing right beside her.

'You're Kayleigh Dunn,' he repeated.

'Yeah,' she said cautiously.

Danny grinned, but there wasn't anything friendly about it. 'Thought it was you. I've been looking for your dad. Do you know where he is?'

Kayleigh gave an exaggerated shake of her head. 'No, we ain't seen him for years.'

'Not popped in for a cup of tea recently, then?'

Kayleigh wondered what part of 'ain't seen him for years' Danny didn't understand. She could smell the booze on him even though it was only ten to four. He was as bad as Nola. 'No,' she said again. 'I don't know where he is.' Then she added for good measure, 'Don't care neither.'

Danny, clearly unwilling to take her word for it, leaned down towards Kit and tried again, 'What about you, son? You know where your dad is?'

Kit shook his head.

'When was the last time you saw him?'

'He was just a toddler,' Kayleigh said. 'He can't remember. It was years ago.'

Danny scowled at her. 'Let him answer for himself. Come on, son. When was the last time you saw your dad?'

Kit shrank against Kayleigh, wide-eyed and scared, unable to answer even if he'd wanted to.

'What's the matter? Cat got your tongue?'

'Leave him alone,' Kayleigh said. 'He doesn't know nothing. I've already told you. Dad cleared off years ago and we ain't seen him since.'

'No postcards from Spain, then? No phone calls to your mum?'

'No,' Kayleigh said, wondering what on earth her dad would be doing in Spain. 'We ain't seen him since he left.'

'I want to hear what the lad's got to say,' Danny snapped. He pushed his face into Kit's and grabbed hold of his elbow. 'Come on, son. Tell your uncle Danny where your dad is. Is he in London? Is he with his mum?'

The voice came from behind Kayleigh, a female's, cool but angry. 'What do you think you're doing?'

Danny Street straightened up, let go of Kit's arm, and stared at her. 'Oh, the lovely Jemima. Fancy seeing you again. Me and the kids here were just having a little chat.'

'Oh, is that what you call it? You're scaring them.'

'Nobody's scared.' Danny fixed his gaze on Kayleigh. 'You scared, hon?'

Kayleigh shook her head. It wasn't true but it seemed like the best thing to do in the circumstances. Her neighbour – was she really called Jemima? – looked like she was ready to punch Danny Street in the face. There were two bright spots of pink on her cheeks and her hands were clenched into fists.

'See?' he said. 'Nothing to worry about.'

'So, are you all done here?' Jem said to Danny. 'I'm sure these kids want to get home.'

He smirked back at her. 'For now. Has that boyfriend of yours found Ray yet?'

'How would I know? He's just across the road. Why don't you go and ask him?'

'Tick tock,' he said, and strode off with a swagger.

Now Kayleigh was thoroughly confused. 'What did he mean by that?'

'Nothing.'

'Is Harry Lind your boyfriend?'

'No.'

'So why did Danny say—'

'Because he's an arse, excuse my language.'

Kayleigh had a lot more questions, but grown-ups never seemed to give proper answers. She tried again. 'Why does Danny Street want to know where Dad is?'

'I've no idea,' Jem said.

Kayleigh didn't believe her. Jem was wearing a blue tabard-type thing with 'Blooms of Kellston' embroidered in pink across her left breast. She must have come from the florist. Although she was grateful for the intervention, Kayleigh was still worried about Danny. He hadn't said anything about Dion, but that didn't mean he hadn't seen her there on Friday. What if he came round to the flat? Nothing as mundane as a locked door would stop him getting in. He might tell Nola that she'd nicked the drugs money and about Harry's search for Dad and then it would all kick off.

'You should go home,' Jem said. 'It's starting to get dark. Do you want me to come with you?'

'No, ta, we're fine. He's gone now.' Kayleigh peered along

the street just to make sure that Danny wasn't hanging around. Then when she was certain that the coast was clear she took hold of Kit's hand and started to walk away. She didn't look back. It was never a good idea to look back.

51

Harry was sitting in Mac's office, watching his partner's face as he told him about Jem and Kayleigh and all the business with Danny Street. He could tell it wasn't going down well from the frown that was growing deeper by the minute, but he went on anyway. When he finally paused for breath Mac made a disapproving clicking noise in the back of his throat, leaned forward and fixed his gaze on Harry.

'So, let's get this right. You're working three cases but only being paid for one of them. What are you trying to do, bankrupt the company?'

'I went looking for Ray Dunn in my own time. And Jem did pay me a deposit, but I gave it her back when Aidan Hague was found murdered.' Then, before Mac could raise any more objections or move on to the dubious decision of trying to help a ten-year-old girl without even informing her mother, he quickly added, 'What do you reckon then, about Danny Street? He could be bluffing but it sounds like he did know Hague. Or met him at least. And Hague was more than capable of arranging a hit.'

'Report it,' Mac said. 'Go to the police.'

'Come on, you know that's not a viable option. Danny will deny all knowledge, and he'll make sure that when it does happen, he has a damn good alibi. *And* he'll be so pissed off at us reporting it that he'll go out of his way to make sure that Jem ends up dead. You know what he's like. The guy's got a screw loose, in fact he's missing a whole bloody toolbox.'

'Why doesn't she just get out of here?'

'Because it doesn't solve the problem. If she's got a price on her head, someone's going to track her down eventually.'

'Then you need to give Danny Street something he wants.'

'He wants Ray Dunn's address, but I can't . . . *won't* give it to him. I don't want that idiot's death on my conscience any more than I want Jem's.'

Mac scratched his head and stared at the ceiling for a few seconds. 'Then you need something else to trade. Get some dirt on him, serious dirt, then you can make a deal.'

'A deal with the devil.'

'It'll teach you not to do anything for free.'

Harry was still thinking of a smart retort to this when the intercom buzzer went. The two men glanced at each other. Lorna had already gone home and so one of them had to answer it.

'Don't look at me,' Mac said. 'It's probably one of your waifs and strays.'

In the event, Mac was right. Kayleigh Dunn's thin childish voice carried over the intercom. 'Got to talk to you, Mr Lind. Can we come up?'

Harry buzzed her in, opened the office door and listened as two pairs of light footsteps ascended the stairs. Kayleigh bounced into reception, followed by a less enthusiastic Kit.

'Before you ask,' Harry said. 'I'm sorry, but I haven't been able to track down your dad yet.' He didn't like lying to her but didn't have a choice about it. 'These things can take a while.'

Kayleigh perched on the edge of Lorna's desk and said, 'Danny Street asked if we'd got any postcards from Spain. Does that mean Dad's in Spain?'

'What? When were you talking to Danny Street?'

'Just now. Across the road. He grabbed hold of Kit, but he let go when Jem showed up. I don't think she likes him very much. Danny, I mean. She sounded kind of mad. Are you Jem's boyfriend? Danny said you were, but Jem said he was an arse.'

'Yeah, well, that pretty well sums him up. And I've no idea whether your dad's in Spain. He might be. He might not.'

'It's hot in Spain, ain't it?' Kayleigh looked towards the window and the darkening sky. 'I wouldn't mind living there. There are beaches and that. Sun. Although we'd have to learn Spanish. Why does Danny want to know where Dad is?'

Harry gave a shrug. 'Could be all sorts of reasons.'

'Nothing good, though. Which means that when you *do* track him down, you'll have to make sure Danny doesn't find out.'

'Good point,' Harry said. 'How's your mum doing?'

'She's okay.'

'Have you thought any more about talking to her about this? She's going to find out eventually and I don't much like going behind her back.'

'It'll be a surprise for her.'

'Yeah, but maybe not the good kind.'

Kayleigh fiddled with the buttons on her thin denim jacket. 'You might not find him. We should wait until we know what's what.'

Harry had to stop himself from smiling at some of the things she came out with. Kayleigh was like a mini adult, old before her years. She had an answer for everything and never gave up.

'All right, but you'd better give it a week or two before you come here again. What if someone sees you? They're going to question what you're doing here.'

'What if you find him?'

'Then a few days isn't going to make any difference. You get off now or your mum's going to wonder where you are.'

'Can I just ask you something before we go?'

'Sure,' Harry said.

'Do you think Danny Street murdered Dion?'

It wasn't a question that Harry had been expecting. 'The guy who was killed on the Mansfield?'

'Yeah, that's him. On Friday. People are saying that it was Danny.'

'Probably not the kind of rumour you want to go around repeating.'

'It's just that . . . ' Kayleigh hesitated, glancing down at Kit as if she wasn't sure about speaking in front of him. Then she made up her mind. 'It's just, you know, the red wire around his neck, I saw something like that when Mum took us to Froome's.'

'That was years ago,' Harry said. 'And how do you even know it was similar?'

Kayleigh hesitated again, briefly examining the carpet before raising her eyes again. 'I saw him. Dion. On Friday night. Before the law came on Saturday. The door was open, and I looked in and . . . he was in the hallway lying on the floor. I was on my way back from a mate's. Don't tell anyone, though, because I wasn't supposed to be there.'

Harry wondered if she was telling the truth, or if this was simply a fantasy, something she'd invented out of a desire for attention or whatever psychological impulse compelled ten-year-old girls to make things up. 'That must have been a shock.'

'I guess,' Kayleigh said.

'And upsetting.'

'Yeah, I liked Dion. He was cool. I knew he was dead 'cause his eyes were open. I'd have called an ambulance otherwise. I wouldn't have just left him there.'

'What time was this?'

'About half nine. A bit after. I thought I heard someone inside, so I scarpered pronto. I didn't want to be next, did I?'

'Did you actually see Danny Street anywhere near the flat or even on the Mansfield?'

'Nah, I didn't see him. I didn't see nobody but Mrs Floyd down in the lobby. That was just a few minutes before. There was music playing: Marvin Gaye. From the living room. Not really loud but ... I just pushed the door open with my foot. I mean, it was already open, I just opened it a bit more. I didn't touch nothing. And I only realised about that red wire today. It was in maths, and I was thinking about Dion, and I suddenly remembered. There was a coil of it on one of those round wheel-type things in Carl Froome's office.'

'Lots of businesses use red wire. Lots of people.'

'It's a clue though, isn't it? Danny Street could have got the wire off him.'

'He could have. Or someone else could. Or it might not have come from Froome's at all.' Harry, who'd been inclined to take her story with a pinch of salt, wasn't so sure now. That was an odd detail about the music, about Marvin Gaye. Not the kind of thing a kid would normally make up. But if she was telling the truth then she'd witnessed something truly dreadful, the aftermath of a gruesome murder. 'Are you sure you're all right? You should have told someone what you'd seen. Why didn't you tell your mum?'

Kayleigh's face became tight and pinched. ''Cause I didn't want her to know that I'd looked in the flat. She'd have only got mad because the law would have wanted to speak to me, and she doesn't like the law. You won't tell her, will you?'

Harry's opinion of Nola Dunn wasn't improving. But he wasn't convinced that Kayleigh was telling him the whole truth either. Something was niggling in the back of his mind, but he didn't have time to drag it out and examine it. If the girl had been traumatised by what she'd seen – *if* she'd seen it – then she wasn't showing any signs. But that was hardly a good thing either. As he knew from experience, the horrors of the past could come back to haunt you. 'You should talk to someone about it. It's not good to keep these things bottled up.'

'I'm talking to you, Mr Lind,' she said.

'Yeah, but I mean someone more ... someone closer, like your mum.'

One of Kayleigh's eyebrows twitched, and her lips pursed as if the very idea caused her more consternation than comfort. Harry glanced at Kit, wondering how much of this exchange he was understanding. The kid stared at him through big blue eyes. Harry smiled at him. He didn't smile back.

'So you'll keep looking for Dad?' she said. 'You have to find him before Danny Street does. I don't want him getting hurt. And when you do find him, you can tell him we don't mind moving to Spain.'

'I'll do that,' Harry said.

'Ta.' Kayleigh stood up, took Kit's hand and the two of them left.

As soon as they had exited reception, Mac emerged from his office. 'Jesus, what sort of kid finds a dead body and doesn't tell anyone about it?'

'The sort of kid who's used to keeping her mouth shut. The sort of kid who's used to bad things happening to her.'

'She's a witness. The police should be told.'

'And what kind of danger is that going to put her in? The murderer might think she saw him going into the flat. And it's not going to help the investigation. They'll know by now what time Dion died so she won't be bringing anything new to the party. Maybe better to let sleeping dogs lie.'

Mac pulled a face. 'If it comes out later that she told you about it, you'll be right in the shit.'

'I'll just say I didn't believe her.'

'And if it comes out that you're working for a ten-year-old girl without her mother's permission, that's not going to look good either.'

'I'm not working for her. She hasn't paid me any money.'

'And you think that makes it okay?'

'No,' Harry said.

'So think on. No one needs that kind of grief, or Danny Street breathing down their neck.'

'I know that,' Harry said.

52

Phillip could feel his future slipping away from him. Time was running out. The longer he kept Nola Dunn here, the more chance there was of her being discovered. He had to make a choice – let her go and take the consequences, or make sure that she could never tell anyone what he'd done – but the more he thought about it, the less decisive he became. There were pros and cons on both sides. He had weighed them up, swayed one way and then the other, but there was no clear winner.

He had taken a long sharp knife from the kitchen and placed it threateningly on the coffee table. 'You make a sound,' he'd told her when she came round from the sleeping pills, 'and I'll cut your bloody throat.'

Nola wasn't quite as cocky now. That could have been down to the aftermath of the pills or, just as likely, the dawning reali-sation that she had picked the wrong man to cross. But that still didn't solve his problem. What the hell was he going to do with her? He watched her like a hawk whenever he untied her hands and took the gag off to let her eat or drink, ready to pounce if she even thought about screaming, but her earlier aggression had died away and been replaced by a false and unpleasant wheedling.

'I've got kids,' she pleaded. 'They need me. They ain't got no dad. Who's going to take care of them if . . . ' Her eyes slid towards the knife. 'If you let me go, I won't say nothing. I swear.'

'Don't believe a word the tart says,' Chapel insisted, worried that Phillip was wavering. 'She'll screw you over the moment she gets out of here.'

'I'm well aware of that, thank you.'

'So what are you waiting for? Do you really want your whole life ruined by a two-bit whore? Finish the job, for God's sake. Those kids will be better off without her.'

Although Phillip suspected he was right, he didn't have the stomach to finish her off. Not in cold blood anyway. He wondered how many sleeping pills it would take to make her go to sleep for ever. He could mix them with brandy or at least he could if he went out to buy another bottle. The one he had started yesterday was almost finished now. The whisky was all gone too.

Nola was eating a ham sandwich, taking small bites before returning it to the plate, making it last as long as possible. 'I'm sorry, you know, about the things I said. It was the shock, you see. Getting the bang to my head. But I'm not a grass. You can ask anyone. I won't go running to the law or nothing.'

'Listen to her,' Chapel growled. 'She'll be offering you a blow job next.'

It was dark outside, late afternoon. Well over twenty-four hours since Nola had turned up at his door shouting the odds. Would the kids have been to the police yet? Or gone running to someone else? How long would they wait? If Edna Floyd was right, then it wouldn't be the first time Nola had gone AWOL. The bitch was hardly in line for World's Best Mother.

Exhaustion was settling on Phillip like a dead weight. He'd had little sleep last night, spending the entire time in the arm-chair and dozing off only occasionally before his brief oblivion was interrupted by Nola's noisy breathing or her restless movements on the sofa. A yawn tugged at his jaw, but he resisted it. He longed for his bed.

'Make some coffee,' Chapel said. 'You need caffeine.'

But Phillip didn't dare leave Nola alone while her hands were untied. He'd given her a plastic bottle of water and she took big gulps while she ate the sandwich. He hoped she didn't drink too much. It was a palaver getting her to the bathroom and back: he had to untie her ankles so she could walk and keep her hands free too. He always walked behind her, brandishing the knife in case she got any ideas about making a run for it.

Chapel said, 'You could drown her in the bath. Easy. Twenty seconds and it's done.'

'You and me just got off on the wrong foot,' Nola said. 'I've got a short fuse. I know that. It was all my fault. I shouldn't have had a go at you.'

Chapel was still putting the pressure on. 'And then you bung her body in the lift in the early hours. Her killer could have come from any flat, or not even from the Mansfield at all.'

'So someone drowned her, dropped her off on the estate, dragged her into the lift and left her there?'

'Now you're just being picky. Although you might have a point. Personally, I'd wait until she was asleep and smother her. Nice and clean, no blood, no struggle. By this time tomorrow it could all be over.'

'What?' Nola said, staring at him.

Phillip realised that his lips must have been moving. 'Nothing,' he said.

*

357

Jem went back into the florist's and from there she watched Kayleigh and Kit walk to the traffic lights, cross over and proceed towards Harry's office.

'What's going on?' Stefan asked, joining her at the window. 'Why did you rush out like that?'

'Danny Street was having a go at a couple of kids. You'd think he'd pick on someone his own size.'

'That man's a nutter. You should be careful. What did he want with them?'

'Oh, I don't know. Something about their dad. I mean, how are they supposed to know where he is?' Jem turned away from the window before Stefan could see them going into Harry's. He hadn't seen her coming out of there this morning, thank God, so she'd been spared the trial of an interrogation, but it was only a matter of time. When it happened, she would either have to pretend that something was going on between her and the private detective or tell him the truth. Neither of these options filled her with joy, but she would, of course, choose the former as being the lesser of two evils. The truth was too complicated, too horrible, and she didn't want to see that pitying look in his eyes.

At around five o'clock there was a short burst of activity as people left work and started their journeys home. For Jem it was a welcome distraction. She kept an eye on the door to Harry's office as she wrapped up bunches of flowers, tied ribbons and took the payments. The kids weren't in there for long, less than ten minutes, and it was too dark to read their faces when they came out. Disappointment, she presumed. Still no news on their dad.

It worried her that Danny might find Ray Dunn. If he did, then the game would be up. Bad news for Ray, and bad news for her. They would both end up on a cold slab in the morgue. She shuddered at the thought of it, the impulse to run sweeping over her again. Still, at least she knew he hadn't found Ray yet; if he had, he wouldn't be trying to prise information from Kayleigh and Kit. This thought kept her going until closing time.

Harry was on his own in the office, examining the cuttings from the *Kellston Gazette* and trying to keep his mind on the Mortlake case. The hit-and-run had been front-page news in the weekly and was a story with enough tragic ingredients to stir the hardest of hearts. The incident had taken place on Wednesday 21 July 1971 on a rainy evening at around seven o'clock. The mother and daughter were almost home after a visit to see the child's grand-mother when they had tried to cross Violet Road and the car had run them over. Six-year-old Annie Moss had died instantly from the impact, Eleanor a few hours later in hospital.

Harry knew Violet Road, not far from the Mansfield, a narrow street of neat council houses. There were no witnesses to the accident – the rain had kept most people inside – but a woman claimed she'd seen a small dark-coloured car – blue or black – speeding along the high street shortly before the child and her mother were hit. Due to the heavy rain, the woman hadn't got a look at the driver but thought the car might have been a Mini. The police had followed it up, asking for the driver to come forward but, unsurprisingly, nobody had.

There was a picture of Annie Moss alongside the story, a sweet-faced little girl with a hesitant smile. Brief quotes from neighbours ran along the lines of being 'shocked' and 'upset' by what had happened, and of the Mosses being 'a lovely family'. There was nothing from Michael Moss although he had prob-ably provided the photo, persuaded no doubt by the argument that the picture might help jog people's memories. Times had been different then and there was no emotional unburdening to the press; he had grieved in private behind closed doors.

Michael – Moses – had been a carpenter. Like Jesus, like Joseph. He would have gone to work that morning a content, probably even happy man, and by the evening his life was in tatters. Harry could barely begin to imagine how that must feel. And because of what? Because someone was so eager to get somewhere that even in bad weather conditions they had not been prepared to slow down. Or to stop after they had ploughed into two pedestrians. Drunk, perhaps, or in a panic.

He carried on reading. The following week the *Gazette* still had the story on the front page, only now it had been relegated to the bottom right-hand corner. The police inquiry was ongoing but there had been no new leads. Already the horror of the accident was starting to fade, to be replaced by other news – life moved on. Although not for everyone. Not for Moses, and maybe not for the person who had killed his wife and daughter. There must have been damage to the car – dents and scratches, even blood – and garages were asked to be alert. By the time Christine Mortlake's disappearance made the front page, the story had shrivelled to a paragraph on page ten.

An idea entered Harry's head, a hunch, and with nothing better to focus on he went along with it. First, he rang Celia Mortlake and asked her a number of questions that clearly bemused her. Then he moved on to Vivienne Bayle, a few fast queries about Amy and Christine. His next port of call was Amy Bolton herself. He was expecting her to ignore him but surprisingly she picked up. They talked for five minutes. When the conversation was over, a small smile of triumph was curling the outer edges of his lips. Don't get *too* bloody smug, he admonished himself: you haven't proved a thing yet.

His final call was to Gerry Whitelaw, the hacker with attitude. 'I've got another job for you. This one might not be so easy.'

'The last one wasn't easy. I just made it look that way.'

'Yeah, I know you're a genius, but this one's historical stuff. I'm not even sure if the information is available.'

'I'll find it,' Gerry said. 'Give me the details.'

Harry told him what he needed to know and then hung up. He leaned forward, placed his elbows on the table, accepted that there was nothing more he could do until he heard back. Now it was time to concentrate his efforts on Danny Street and the threat to Jem. He still wasn't sure if it was a bluff, just a way of getting him to reveal Ray's whereabouts, or if she really was in danger.

Harry thought about what Mac had said, about getting something on Danny that he could use as a trade. But what? If Kayleigh was right, it was possible that Danny *had* killed Dion – but proving it was another matter altogether. A coil of red wire, seen years ago, was hardly evidence. And even if he did turn out to be the murderer, Harry could hardly use it as leverage. He couldn't let a killer go free even in exchange for Jem's safety. The best he could hope for was that Danny got charged and was taken off the streets. But that wouldn't necessarily stop him from activating the hit.

No, he had to find another way. He was an experienced detective, a man not entirely devoid of intelligence, a man who'd been around the block a few times. It shouldn't be *that* hard. He thought about it and sighed into the emptiness of the room.

53

It was almost six o'clock when Jem left work and she could see that the light was still on in Harry's office. She had come to a decision and knew that he wasn't going to like it, but now that it was made, she wanted to tell him as soon as possible. She went down to the traffic lights and crossed the road when the little green man flashed up and the beeping started. Then she quickly walked to Mackenzie, Lind, glanced across at the florist's – Stefan was moving around at the rear of the shop – and unlocked the door as fast as she could.

She jogged up the stairs and went into the reception area, a low buzz announcing her arrival. The door to Harry's office was ajar.

'It's only me,' she called out. 'Are you busy?'

'Come on in.'

Jem crossed reception, nudged the door fully open, stood in the entrance and said, 'Kayleigh came to see you. Did she tell you about Danny Street?'

Harry was behind his desk, his smile not completely cancelling out a general air of weariness. 'Trying to find out where Ray is? Yeah. And a good deal more. Sit down, grab a pew.' He gestured towards the other chair. 'I hear you came to their rescue.'

Jem sat down, shaking her head. 'I wouldn't say that exactly. Kayleigh seemed to be coping. I just ... I don't like seeing a grown man having a go at a pair of kids. It's shitty, isn't it? That man's got no boundaries.'

'That's one way of putting it. What did he say to you?'

'Tick tock.'

'Huh?'

'As in, time's ticking, time's running out.' Jem said this in a deliberately matter-of-fact tone, keeping her voice level and taking care to keep the fear from her face. She didn't want Harry to know how scared she was, how the morning's relative calm had evolved into something tight and tense since seeing Danny Street – her nerves jangling, her mind racing, her heart thumping out a drumbeat in her chest.

'Very subtle.'

'What did you tell Kayleigh about Ray?'

'That I had no news for her yet. What was more interesting was what she told me. Did you know she found Dion Dixon's body on Friday night?'

The shock of this catapulted Jem out of her own anxieties. 'What? I thought he wasn't found until Saturday morning.'

'He wasn't, not officially. Kayleigh came across him earlier – his door was open, and she looked inside – but she didn't tell anyone. Reckons she didn't want the hassle from her mum or the police. She knew he was dead and so she scarpered. Something about her story bothers me, though.'

'You think she's lying?'

'I did at first but now I'm inclined to believe her. She said he'd been strangled with red wire. Now she could have just heard that from someone but . . . ' Harry frowned and then his brow suddenly cleared. 'I know what it is. I've been trying to figure it out since she told me. She lives on the eighth floor, right, just along the corridor from you?'

Jem nodded. 'A couple of doors down.'

'And Dion Dixon lived on the sixth floor. Kayleigh said she'd been to see a mate and when she was on her way back to her flat, she ran into a woman called Mrs Floyd in the lobby.'

'Okay. What's wrong with that?'

'Well, her mate might live on the ground floor or in another block or maybe not on the estate at all. That would account for Kayleigh passing through the lobby. But why would she then go up to the sixth floor rather than the eighth?'

'Unless her mate lives on the sixth.'

'In which case why was she anywhere near the lobby?'

Jem thought about this, getting his point. 'Yeah, I see where you're coming from. Maybe she was just messing about, killing time before she went home. Going up and down in the lift. You know what kids are like.'

'Or maybe Dion was the "mate" she went to see. Perhaps there's more to this than Kayleigh Dunn is letting on.'

'Dion was a dealer, according to Mrs Floyd. I don't know if it's true or not. Why would Kayleigh be going to see him? You don't think . . . ? But she's only ten, she can't be using.'

'She could have been buying for someone else.'

'Nola, you mean? Jesus, I hope that's not true.'

'Except that if it *was* Nola, why wouldn't Kayleigh tell her about the murder? She'd have needed a good reason as to why she came home without the gear.'

Jem nodded. 'That's true. It doesn't quite add up, does it?'

'Nothing about Kayleigh's story quite adds up. And then there's the money.'

'What money?'

'On Saturday, Kayleigh turned up here with two hundred quid to find her dad. She claimed her mum had given it to her, but that was clearly nonsense. Then she said that she'd saved it up.'

'Are you thinking she got it from Dion?'

'It could have been lying around in his flat. She said she didn't go in, but maybe she did.'

'What are you going to do?'

'I haven't decided. What would you do in my shoes?'

Jem's gaze strayed towards the window. If she stood up, she'd be able to see the florist's, the pub and the train station. As it was, the only thing in her eyeline was a watery square of evening and some rooftops. 'I don't know. We don't know anything for a fact, do we? How did Kayleigh seem? If she did find Dion's body, it must have been shocking for her.'

'Hard to tell. She doesn't give much away. She seemed okay, though.'

'The Mansfield might be rough, but you don't come across bodies every day. That would be traumatising for anyone, never mind a kid. Perhaps you should talk to Nola.'

'Even though Kayleigh asked me not to?'

'You're the adult here. You can't take instructions from a ten-year-old.'

'If I talk to Nola about Dion, I'll have to tell her about Kayleigh asking me to look for Ray.'

'Well, she's going to find out eventually. It's better coming from you than from Danny Street. If he confronted the kids, it's only a matter of time before he does the same to Nola. She needs to be prepared.'

Harry leaned back in his chair and folded his arms across his chest. 'The voice of reason. Yeah, you're probably right. I should bite the bullet and get it over with.'

Jem shifted in the chair, suddenly uneasy. 'Although you might want to think about it some more. I'm hardly renowned for my smart decision making.'

'Are you backtracking, Ms Byrne?'

'I'm just saying that maybe you shouldn't rush into anything. It's going to get Kayleigh into a heap of trouble, isn't it? And I'm not sure how Nola will react. From all accounts she's not the most understanding of people.' Jem tapped out an erratic rhythm on the desk, fingertips on oak, trying to get her thoughts in order. 'God, I don't know. What do you reckon?'

Harry grinned. 'Welcome to my world. Nothing's ever easy.'

'Maybe you should give it a day or two.'

'Maybe I should.'

Jem smiled back, but her smile quickly faded. It felt like they were in collusion, a partnership, making decisions – or not making them – together. Why did that unnerve her so much? Because she liked to keep people at a distance, to keep her walls up, to plough a solitary furrow. She was drawn to Harry, but she didn't want to be.

'Anyway,' she said, abruptly changing the subject, 'I've decided to go back to the Mansfield. It was good of you to put me up last night, but I can't stay here for the next two weeks.'

Harry looked surprised. 'What? Why not? I'm not that hard to live with, am I?'

'Impossible,' she said, trying to keep it light. 'No, I just like to have my own things around me. And I'm not in any imminent danger, not if Danny sticks to his word.'

'It's not safe,' Harry insisted. 'You're better off here. And since when was Danny's word worth anything? It isn't. You know that.'

'My being here isn't going to keep me safe. If someone decides to . . . it's going to happen no matter where I'm staying.'

'No point in making it easy for them.'

But Jem had made up her mind. 'I'm grateful, I really am, but I'd rather be at home.'

'Are you going to leave Kellston?'

Jem shrugged. 'Not right away. Not tonight if that's what you're asking. I'll stay another week at least.'

'Only Danny will be expecting you to run. He'll have someone watching.'

'Then I'll have to take my chances. If it comes to that.'

'If it comes to that, I can help. I can get you out of Kellston.'

'You've done enough,' she said.

'I haven't done anything,' Harry said. 'Nothing useful, that's for sure.'

'If it wasn't for you, I wouldn't know about the hit.'

'If there even is a hit. We could be worrying over a pile of bullshit.'

We, Jem thought. There it was again. As if they were in this together, joined by chance or fate or whatever it was that governed the random laws of the universe. It was simultaneously disturbing and comforting. She didn't want to feel attached to him, not in any way, but she couldn't deny that it felt good to have someone care. 'I'll go and get my things.'

'I'll give you a lift.'

'You don't need to do that. I haven't got much. I can walk.'

Harry stood up. 'It's no bother.'

54

Kayleigh sat on the sofa staring at Nola's mobile phone. She'd expected to come home and find it gone – picked up while they were at school – so it was a surprise to find it still there. Usually, her mum didn't go to work without it, partly for safety reasons, partly to give her something to do in those lean periods when there weren't any punters. Should she be worried? But Nola wasn't always logical. Once she had a few drinks inside her, she wouldn't care whether she had the phone or not.

Anyway, she had enough to worry about. Already she was regretting telling Harry about finding Dion's body. She wasn't convinced that he'd keep it to himself. If he went to the law, she'd be in serious trouble. Not reporting a crime was an offence; she'd heard that somewhere. But at least Danny Street hadn't said anything about it. He'd only wanted to know where Dad was.

And that was something else to stress about. If Danny had killed Dion, he could easily kill Dad too. She remembered the money he'd sent, all those twenties, tenners and fivers, and wondered if he'd nicked it off Danny. Or Carl Froome. Which was probably the same thing. Would Dad be hard to find in Spain? You could get cheap flights to Europe – she'd seen them advertised on TV – but without an address they could be searching for ever. There was a small matter of passports too. And the slightly bigger matter of getting Nola to agree to leave.

Kayleigh picked up the phone and scrolled down to Nana Margaret's number. Kit watched her out of the corner of his eye. She wanted to call but she didn't want to blow it. If Dad was in Spain, she didn't have to worry about him doing a runner, but if he wasn't . . . Her finger hovered over the call icon, tempted but not convinced. She'd give Harry a few more days before taking matters into her own hands.

Hunger was making her stomach rumble. She stood up, went through to the kitchen and investigated the fridge. They were getting low on supplies again. She thought about Dion, who would never eat another meal. She thought about the red wire embedded in his neck. Here one minute and gone the next. Would she have nightmares about it? When she put her head on the pillow and closed her eyes, his was the face she saw.

Kayleigh's fingers trembled as she pulled out a packet of chicken nuggets from the ice box. She turned on the oven, and while it was heating up she peeled some potatoes and cut them into quarters. Then she opened a tin of beans and put them in a pan. Should she make enough for Nola? No, she wasn't going to waste good food. If history was anything to go by there was every chance she wouldn't come home tonight. Maybe not to-morrow either.

Jesus, why couldn't they have a *normal* mother.

While she organised dinner, she ran through the afternoon's events in her head. It was lucky that Jem had come along when she did. Not that she couldn't take care of herself – and Kit too, come to that – but no one liked being confronted in the street. Jemima, that was her proper name. Very posh. Except that posh people didn't live on the Mansfield. She said she wasn't Harry's girlfriend, but Danny had called her that. And she obviously knew Harry. Would he tell her about Dion? About Kayleigh looking for her dad? She didn't want everyone knowing her business. The more people knew, the more chance there was of it getting back to Nola.

The TV was on while they ate. She was clearing up the plates when the doorbell went. Two long rings. She stopped, gazing in the direction of the hall. The law? The social? Jemima? Danny Street? The living-room door was closed so they probably couldn't hear the TV, but she quickly reached for the remote and turned the volume down. The bell went again.

55

After Harry left, Jem went over to the window and looked down on the estate. He'd done a quick search of the flat just to make sure there were no unwelcome visitors, declared it free of any threat, declined an offer of coffee and reminded her (again) not to leave Kellston without letting him know. She'd had a moment of panic when he was going, fighting the urge to change her mind. Suddenly she'd felt vulnerable, incapable of being in the flat alone, a sitting duck. But the moment had passed. She had pulled herself together, said goodbye and thanked him for his hospitality and the lift.

Jem waited until Harry appeared below her and then swiftly stood back in case he looked up at the window. She always found it hard to accept help, to put her trust in anyone, but she'd felt safe last night, knowing he was close by. How would she sleep tonight? Alert to any sound inside or outside the flat, probably. Jumping whenever the pipes gurgled, or the cooling radiators ticked, or the wind rattled the windows. Two weeks left, she thought. Well, a little less than that now. Tick tock.

Shouldn't she be doing something?

But that something, apart from packing her bags and running, seemed beyond her. Instead, she made herself a coffee and sat down at the table. Opening the drawing pad, she looked at the painting she'd been working on and decided to finish it off before Aidan's legacy caught up with her. She collected water from the kitchen, returned to the table, sat down, dipped in her brush, chose alizarin crimson for the girl's coat, and started to paint. Her hand remained steady as she filled in the outline, a small splash of colour in a scene that was predominantly grey. Did it work? She sat back and studied it. An air of menace emanated from the picture. Little Red Riding Hood walking among the wolves of the Mansfield.

Jem was considering what to do about the boy – colour his coat or leave it dark grey? – when she heard the commotion outside in the corridor, the sound of a fist hammering on a door, a raised voice. She jumped up and went through to the hallway to listen. It didn't take her long to recognise Danny Street's voice.

'Nola! Open this fucking door! I know you're in there.'

But Nola, unsurprisingly, wasn't playing ball.

'Nola! Open the door or I'll fucking kick it in!' This was followed by a couple of loud thwacks and the sound of splintering wood. 'Nola!'

Jem could imagine how Nola and the kids were feeling right now. She had been there herself, under siege from Aidan, too terrified to even move. She only hesitated for a second – one of those self-preservation moments born of too much experience of a psychopathic man – before opening her own door and stepping out into the corridor.

'What are you doing? Nola's not there.'

Danny stopped and turned to face her, his face red and angry. 'You again! What's your problem?'

'I saw her go out about fifteen minutes ago.'

'What, got X-ray eyes, have you? Can see through walls?'

Jem kept her voice calm, not wanting to provoke him. 'I passed her in the lobby when I was coming in.'

'Bullshit!' Danny snarled. 'The bitch is in there. I can fucking smell her!' He hammered on the door again. 'Nola! You've got ten seconds before I kick this door down. Your bloody choice. Ten, nine, eight . . .'

Jem felt her heart sink as there was the sound of a bolt being pulled across. Damn it. Now he'd know she'd been lying. And no doubt would make her pay for it – after he'd finished with his current business. But she stood her ground, anyway, unwilling to leave Nola and the kids to face Danny's wrath alone. Perhaps a witness would make him think twice about how far he went.

It was Kayleigh, however, who opened the door. Her face was white and pinched, and she stared at Danny through small, scared eyes. 'She ain't here. She's gone to work.'

'Don't give me that shit. She's not at work. The bitch hasn't turned up *again*.' Danny pushed roughly past her. 'Nola! Nola, get your arse out here right now.'

'She ain't here,' Kayleigh persisted. 'She ain't, I swear.'

But Danny was already rampaging through the flat, yelling Nola's name over and over. Jem could hear him taking out his frustration on inanimate objects – a boot against a door, a shattered glass, a crash of pans in the kitchen. The search wouldn't take long. This place was probably bigger than hers – two bedrooms rather than one – but there was still nowhere to hide other than under a bed or in a wardrobe.

Quickly Jem moved into the hallway and said softly to Kayleigh, 'Is she here?'

Kayleigh shook her head. 'No.'

Relief flowed through Jem. 'Thank God for that.' They went

into the living room where Kit was curled up on the sofa with his arms wrapped around his knees. Kayleigh rushed over and sat down beside him.

'It's okay, hon. Don't you worry. He'll be gone soon.'

But it wasn't okay. Thwarted, Danny was back and making a beeline for the weakest person in the room. He loomed over Kit, who shrank back, terrified. 'Where's your mother, son? Where's your bleedin' mother?' When Kit didn't respond, he grabbed Kayleigh's elbow, tight enough to make her yelp, and yanked her to her feet. 'Tell me or I'll break her fuckin' arm.'

Horrified, Jem lunged for Danny's hand, trying to prise his fingers off Kayleigh. 'Stop it! What do you think you're doing? Get off her. Let her go. They're just kids for God's sake.' An ungainly struggle followed, with Danny trying to keep hold of Kayleigh with one hand while shoving Jem away with the other. 'He can't tell you anything. He doesn't talk.'

'What, a fuckin' mute, is he?'

'He can't talk,' she said again, still trying to free Kayleigh. 'So you're wasting your time. He can't tell you anything. I'll ring the police if you don't let go of her.'

'I ain't leaving here, love, until someone tells me where Nola is.' With surprising agility, he let go of Kayleigh, sprang behind Jem, swung his right arm around her neck and squeezed it. 'Someone needs to start talking, now!'

'She went out,' Kayleigh said, sticking to Jem's story. 'About fifteen minutes ago.'

'Out where? Where is the bloody tart?'

'You're hurting me,' Jem said.

'What was that?' Danny said, tightening his hold. 'I can't hear you, love.'

This close, Jem could smell the booze on him, the expensive aftershave and his cigarette breath. She could feel her legs

374

shaking, feel the press of his arm against her windpipe. 'Let go of me.'

Kayleigh, her face ashen, made a choking sound as if she was the one being half strangled. 'She might be at Joe Chapel's. I dunno. She might be.'

'And who the fuck is Joe Chapel?'

'He lives here, on the estate. Downstairs on the sixth floor. I don't know what number. I swear I don't.'

Danny growled, abruptly releasing Jem. 'Seeing punters on the side, is she? I might have fucking guessed. Well, it's the last time she'll ever screw me over.'

Kayleigh shrugged her skinny shoulders like she didn't know what he was talking about.

Danny gave a snort, stormed out of the flat and slammed the splintered door behind him.

Jem rubbed her throat, relieved to be free. She was badly shaken by what had just happened but attempting not to show it. She was the grown-up here, the one who had to at least try and keep things calm.

'Are you okay?' she asked the kids.

Kayleigh nodded. 'Are you?'

'Fine,' Jem said, as though there was nothing extraordinary about a drunken gangster having his arm around her throat. 'I'm fine.'

But Jem's mind was racing. It seemed from the exchange that Nola was a working girl, one of Danny's, and that her absence had been noted down the Albert Road. But that probably wasn't the only reason he wanted to talk to her. There was the small matter of Ray as well. She recalled Joe Chapel, the middle-aged man she'd met in the lobby with Mrs Floyd on Saturday. Was he a client? He hadn't looked the type, but then what was the type?

'He's going to come back,' Kayleigh said. 'We have to get out of here.'

'Is your mum at Mr Chapel's?'

'I shouldn't think so,' Kayleigh said. 'She barely knows the bloke. I only said it so he'd let go of you.'

For which Jem was grateful, although she didn't think Chapel would be. The poor guy was about to get a thoroughly unwelcome visit. Hopefully he'd escape from it unscathed once Danny had established that Nola wasn't there. How long did that give them? Five minutes? Ten? Perhaps a bit longer if he had to look for the flat. But Kayleigh was right; they had to make themselves scarce before he came back for round two.

'Take Kit and go to my place,' she said. 'The door's unlocked. I'll leave a note for your mum.'

'Don't tell her where we are. Danny might get hold of it before she does.'

Jem thought of the front door with the cracks running down it and knew that it wouldn't take much to break in. A few well-aimed kicks and that would be it. 'I'll just leave my number and tell her you're safe. Give me your key and I'll lock up here. Go on. Hurry up. I won't be a minute.'

Finding a piece of paper proved to be harder than she'd expected. In the end she used the back of an envelope, an un-opened letter from Kellston council, and scrawled a quick note to Nola which she left on the coffee table beside the phone. Surely, she'd be back soon. The kids had been left on their own, so she had to be nearby. And her phone was still here, which suggested that she hadn't gone far. God knows what she'd think when she saw the state of the door.

Back in her own flat, the first thing Jem did was ring Harry. 'Sorry,' she said, 'but there's been some trouble here.' Her expla-nation was fast, rather garbled, but he must have got the gist.

'Okay, just sit tight. I'll be with you shortly.'

The kids were standing up, watching from the window. Looking out for Nola? For Danny? Still pumped up with adrenaline, she put the phone down and went over to join them. The estate streetlamps lit the path from the gate to the tower, and the area directly in front of the lobby. It was quiet outside with only a few people coming and going.

'Do you know where your mum really is, Kayleigh?'

'I think she's at work.'

'But Danny says not.'

Kayleigh gave her familiar shrug.

'What time does she normally get home?'

'It depends,' Kayleigh said after a short pause.

Jem couldn't imagine the girls on the Albert Road working nine-to-five, which begged the question of who looked after the kids when she wasn't there. 'When was the last time you saw her?'

'This morning,' Kayleigh said, but her gaze didn't meet Jem's.

'This morning?'

'Yeah.'

Kit shifted awkwardly beside his sister, leaning in as if to protect her from the lie she'd just told.

'You swear?'

Kayleigh didn't answer.

'Kayleigh?'

'It might have been yesterday morning.'

'She's been gone since yesterday?' Jem said, astonished. Her first thoughts were of the murders – Charlene's and Dion's – and she had a sick, panicky feeling, wondering if Nola had been another victim. 'We should call the police, report her as missing.'

'You can't do that! They'll tell the social and put us into care. Anyway, she's not *missing* exactly. She must have got held up. She'll be back before long.'

To Jem this seemed an odd reply, considering Kayleigh didn't know where her mother was. Why wasn't she more worried? And then it occurred to her. 'Has this happened before?'

'Hardly ever. Well, sometimes. But it doesn't matter. Me and Kit can look after ourselves. We've got food and leccy and everything. You're not going to call the law, are you? We don't want to be taken away.'

Jem didn't know what to do. She didn't want to be responsible for the kids being dragged off, but what if Nola was in some kind of trouble? Or worse. The kind of trouble that made Danny Street being on the hunt for her seem like a minor inconvenience. It was one of those situations where she couldn't do right for doing wrong.

'Jem?'

'No, I won't call them. Not right now. I'm sure you're right; she'll turn up before long.'

'She will,' Kayleigh said. 'She always does.'

56

Phillip was escorting Nola back from yet another toilet run – he had to stop allowing her so much water – when the doorbell rang. He froze, startled by the sound. Then he placed the knife against Nola's spine and chivvied her back into the living room.

'Not a word or you're dead,' he hissed.

Nola, dropping her recent act of subservience, stared at him through shining eyes. 'What are you going to do now?'

Phillip pushed her down on to the sofa. 'Shut up!' His best chance, his only chance, was to sit tight and hope that whoever it was went away.

But the doorbell went again, followed by loud aggressive knocking. 'Nola! I know you're in there. Open the fucking door!'

Not the police, then, but someone equally threatening. Phillip felt his blood run cold, all hope draining from him. Jesus, God, he was done for. He dithered, looking to Chapel for guidance, but he was nowhere to be seen. What to do? Fear paralysed him. Do nothing. Stay quiet. Pray that the man would go away.

'I told you,' Nola said smugly. 'I told you he'd come looking.'

He shouldn't have taken the gag off her, shouldn't have given in to her wheedling. She could call out and everything would be lost. He waved the knife at her. 'Shut your mouth. You make another sound and you're dead. I've got nothing to lose now, have I?'

Nola smirked, knowing that he had everything to lose.

Phillip was so scared he thought he might piss himself. Or worse. He could hear his own breathing, fast and ragged, as his lungs tried to pump some much-needed oxygen round his body. So Nola would be rescued and he would go to jail. Even if the man went away, he'd come back. It was only a matter of time before the world came crashing down around his ears.

More hammering on the door. 'Nola!'

Phillip looked wildly around the room. Where was Chapel when he needed him? Nowhere. The cocky shit had done a runner. Think, Phillip, think! He should put the gag back on Nola. At least that way he could buy himself some time and stop her from shouting out. But as she saw him put down the knife and reach for the piece of cloth, she spotted her chance, leapt to her feet and launched herself at him. Caught off balance, Phillip took a few unsteady steps backwards, tripped over the rug and fell.

Even as he lay spreadeagled on the floor, he knew it was over. Nola was already sprinting for the front door. As he struggled to his feet, he heard her pull back the bolts and twist the key. He shouldn't have left the damn key in the lock, but it was too late to do anything about that now. She was about to be saved and he was about to face the consequences of what he'd done.

'Help me, God,' he muttered, having no one else to plead to.

And then things took an unexpected turn.

There was a commotion at the door. Phillip heard voices and

then the hard crack of bone against bone, closely followed by a yelp from Nola. She staggered into the living room with blood pouring from her nose. Danny Street, the most feared man on the Mansfield, was right behind her, cursing like a trooper, a string of expletives spilling from his mouth.

'You think you can fuck me over and get away with it, you whore? Who the fuck do you think you're dealing with?'

Phillip, now on his feet, quickly reversed towards the rear wall, hardly able to believe what he was seeing. Every time Nola tried to speak, Danny hit her again. He should do something. Do what? He was a middle-aged writer, no match for this out-of-control thug. If he intervened, he'd end up with his own brains on the carpet.

'Best stay out of it,' Chapel said.

Nola was still trying to reason with a man who couldn't be reasoned with. 'Danny, listen, I weren't—'

'I'm going to kill you, bitch!'

Another blow, this time to the side of her head. Nola was knocked to the ground, rolled over and then scrambled on to her hands and knees, trying to get away from him. Danny kicked her in the calf. She flinched. Danny kicked her again. She didn't cry out – she was too busy trying to stay alive – but scuttled crab-like towards the coffee table.

Phillip realised what Nola was doing before Danny did. He saw it play out almost in slow motion – her hand grasping for the knife, her fingers closing around the handle, her arm rising, the movement as she raised herself up and plunged the blade between Danny's ribs. She pulled out the knife and stabbed him again. He made a weird sound, an exhalation of breath like a tyre deflating, before falling forwards and collapsing on top of her. The two of them tumbled to the floor.

It took Nola a few frantic seconds to extricate herself. She scrambled backwards, eyes wide, a thin moaning escaping from her lips. There was blood down the front of her dress, blood all over her arms and hands. She was in shock. She stared at the knife as if it had nothing to do with her, as if she was surprised to find herself holding it.

'Messy,' said Chapel, never slow to state the obvious.

Phillip was still trying to take it all in. Carnage in the living room.

'Is he dead?' Nola whimpered, slowly getting to her feet. 'Is he dead?'

There didn't seem much doubt about it, but Phillip ventured over anyway. Danny Street's eyes were partly open, the front of his shirt drenched in red. If he wasn't dead, he was doing a damn good impression of it. 'Yeah, you've killed him,' he said bluntly. 'He's not breathing.'

Nola gave a shudder and laid the knife on the coffee table. As if it was only polite to put it back where she'd found it. 'It wasn't my fault. You saw him. He went for me. I was only defending myself.'

'Here's your opportunity,' Chapel said. 'Don't throw it away. She needs you as a witness – and you need her to keep her mouth shut about the other stuff.'

A short while ago Phillip been facing assault charges, kidnapping, and whatever else Nola had decided to throw at him, but now, thanks to Chapel, he saw that there might be a way out. He had to think on his feet. 'I'm not sure it was exactly like that.'

'What?' There was panic in her voice. Her eyes slid from Phillip to Danny's body and back again. 'What are you talking about? You saw him. He punched me in the face, he battered me. He'd have killed me if I hadn't stopped him. You heard him say that. He said he was going to kill me.'

'Did he?' Phillip said, frowning. 'It all happened so quickly . . .'

Nola backed up against the table, her fear palpable. And then a new tone of defiance suddenly came into her voice. 'I'll say *you* did it. I'll say *you* killed him.'

'Oh, I don't think that's going to wash, love. You're the one who's covered in his blood, and it's your prints on the knife.'

Nola rubbed her palms down the sides of her dress, transferring even more blood on to her clothes. Her voice took on a pleading quality. 'You've got to back me up. Please. It wasn't my fault. I've got my kids to think about. If I go to jail, who's going to take care of them?'

'Listen to her,' Chapel said. '*Now* she's interested in her kids.'

Phillip pretended to think about Nola's request. His own palms were damp, leaking sweat, and he knew that his whole future depended on how he played this. 'I suppose I could back you up, say you did it in self-defence ...'

'It *was* self-defence,' she cried. 'What else could I do?'

'Yeah, I could say that, although ...'

'What? Although what?'

Phillip was frantically trying to form the argument in his head, working out how to frame it in such a way that there couldn't be any misunderstandings – or any backtracking.

'Come on, mate,' Chapel said, 'spit it out. We haven't got all day.'

Phillip took a deep breath. 'Well, we'd have to come to an arrangement about that other business – you know, about me keeping you here after you made all those false accusations. I mean, that's not going to look good, is it? I don't see why I should help you when you're only going to make things bad for me.'

'I won't say nothing about that, I swear.'

'The thing is, Nola, I don't know if I can trust you. What's going to happen when you're down Cowan Road? What if it all just tumbles out of that big mouth of yours? I mean, you're hardly the most trustworthy of people.'

Nola was keeping her distance from the body, but her eyes continually darted towards it, as if she was afraid that Danny might suddenly rise from the dead and finish what he'd started. 'We . . . we don't need to tell the law. We could just get rid of him, couldn't we? Dump the body somewhere. No one would know.'

But Phillip wasn't going down *that* road. He'd spent endless hours deliberating on how to dispose of a corpse and none of his ideas had been anywhere near feasible. 'And what if he told someone he was coming here? Or someone saw him come in? The neighbours must have heard him out in the corridor. No, it's too risky. I'm not taking the rap for something you did, Nola. I'll help you front it out with the police but that's as far as it goes. And if you so much as mention my keeping you here, I'll change my story and say he gave you a slap but that was all. You were the one who went into the kitchen and got the knife and came back and stabbed him. It'll be my word against yours.'

Nola was nodding, her head bobbing up and down like it was on a piece of elastic. 'Yeah, yeah, I swear I won't say nothing.'

Phillip didn't trust her. 'I mean it. I can make things bad for you, really bad. And I won't think twice about it. I catch even a whiff of you betraying me and I'll make sure you spend the next twenty years in prison.'

'I get it,' she said.

'Good. Now we just need to get our stories straight.'

57

Harry had decided that the best course of action was for everyone to come back to his flat. With Danny Street on the rampage, it wasn't safe for Jem or the kids to be on the Mansfield. When Nola got home, she'd find the note and so hopefully wouldn't panic. But he still felt on edge, uneasy, as if he was doing something questionable by removing her offspring and covering up her bad parenting. However, like Jem, he didn't want to be the one who condemned Kayleigh and Kit into the murky depths of care.

It felt odd having a flat full of people, like he'd suddenly acquired a family and wasn't quite sure what to do with it. Kit had been following him around since they'd got here, watching his every move, wide-eyed and curious, as if considering him for the currently vacant position of male role model. Kayleigh had made herself at home on the sofa. Harry wondered if he should call Ray but decided, on balance, that it was probably too soon to bring him into the equation. And it wasn't as if *his* parenting skills were any better than his wife's.

The hours were passing and there was still no call from Nola. It was getting on for nine now and he'd already been out twice to check the Fox and Albert Road, but there was no sign of her. Jem had tried some gentle interrogation of Kayleigh as to where else she might be and if she often went AWOL, but the girl wasn't playing ball.

'She should be back soon,' was all she'd say.

Harry admired how Jem had stood up to Danny Street, especially in the current circumstances. It took guts to cross a man like that. And not just once today, but twice. Despite her surface frailty she had reserves of courage that surprised him. Maybe her past had made her strong. Or maybe it took adversity to bring out the best in her.

Because it was getting late, a decision had been made to put the kids to bed in Harry's room. They could share the double while Jem took the spare room again. They'd been kitted out in Harry's T-shirts, which were way too big for them but better than nothing. Kayleigh had made a feeble protest – why couldn't she stay up and wait for Nola? – but knowing that Kit was unlikely to sleep in a strange place without her, she had given in easily enough and was now tucked up alongside her brother.

'What are you thinking?' Jem asked as she came back into the living room.

Harry looked up. 'I was just wondering where else Nola could be.'

'Danny said she wasn't at work. I think that's why he showed up at the flat, although it could have been to do with Ray too. What are we going to do if she isn't back by morning?'

'Send the kids off to school, and then call Ray. It's about time he stepped up. They're his kids too. I'm sure Nola won't be happy about it but she's hardly in a position to complain.'

Jem sat down on the sofa and yawned, covering her mouth. 'Sorry, it's been a long day. Does Ray know what Nola does for a living?'

'I'm not sure, but I think he may have his suspicions.'

'It must be tough for her, bringing up two kids on her own. Not that that's any excuse for leaving them alone, but I suppose she struggles. Everyone's struggling these days, aren't they?' Jem rubbed her eyes. 'Well, not everyone, but it's like the poor just get poorer and there's nothing they can do about it. Ray should be helping out, but will he, knowing that Danny Street is after him? I can't see him putting his head above the parapet anytime soon.'

Harry thought Jem was probably right. Ray's number one priority seemed to be Ray. 'He won't have a choice, not if he wants to keep them out of care. And he's got a mother to help him. They should be able to organise something between them.' He looked at his watch. 'I'll go out and have another look for Nola. She's got to show her face eventually.'

'Good luck. I'll just stay home and take care of the kids.'

'One day you'll make someone a wonderful wife.'

'Thanks. You've got no idea how much that means to me.'

Harry grinned. 'I won't be long. Call me if you hear from Nola.'

'Don't worry, I'll be straight on the phone.'

Harry picked up his mobile and left the flat quietly so as not to wake Kayleigh and Kit. Now he was a family man he had to think about these things. He crossed the road and went into the Fox. This time there were a few working girls at a table near the bar, their drinks lined up in front of them – some much-needed alcohol to take the edge off the night – and their faces made up with heavy eyeliner and bright red lipstick.

'Evening,' he said. 'I'm looking for Nola Dunn. Have any of you seen her tonight?'

The five women all raised their heads simultaneously to stare at him. 'Nola?' one of them repeated. She was a dyed blonde in her thirties with a thin face and a cagey expression.

'Yeah.'

'You the law?'

'Private investigator,' Harry said, taking out his ID to show them. 'She's not in any trouble, I just need to talk to her.'

'You're a bit behind the times, sweetheart. Trouble is exactly what she's in.'

'That doesn't sound good.'

Another of the girls piped up, 'Oh, put the poor guy out of his misery, Shirl. He's going to find out soon enough anyway.'

Shirl took a drink, put her glass down and studied him, as if trying to decide how helpful she felt like being. 'She's down the nick. She was arrested this afternoon.'

'Oh, right,' Harry said. 'She get done for soliciting?'

One of the girls, a redhead, sniggered.

Shirl threw her a look. 'It's no fucking laughing matter.' She focused her attention back on Harry. 'No, worse than that. She could be on a murder charge.' She left a dramatic pause before continuing. 'She killed Danny Street, knifed him by all accounts.'

Harry felt hard shock run through him. 'What? Are you sure?'

'I wouldn't be telling you otherwise. Everyone knows. It's all round Kellston.'

'She did us a favour if you ask me,' the redhead said. 'I won't miss that toerag.'

'Until someone worse comes along,' Shirl said.

Harry was still trying to absorb the news – bad for Nola, and for the kids, but good for Jem. If Danny Street was dead, then she didn't have to worry about the hit. 'Do you know what happened?'

Shirl gave a half shrug. 'He probably just beat on her too many times. He always was a vicious bastard.'

'Where was this?'

'On the Mansfield. Not at her place, at some bloke's flat.'

Harry thanked her for her help and left. Outside in the street he stood for a moment, looking up at his flat where a light shone behind closed curtains. He could imagine Jem there, curled up on the sofa, waiting for him. He would go back shortly, but first he had some calls to make – to Cowan Road to see if Nola had been charged yet, and then to Ray Dunn to tell him about Nola and Danny Street. He was just reaching for his phone when it started ringing. Gerry Whitelaw.

'Hey,' Harry said.

'I've got that information you wanted.'

Harry listened, a small wave of satisfaction rolling over him as he realised that his hunch had been right. But at the same time a stone was slowly forming in his stomach. He was suddenly transported back to a summer's afternoon in 1971 when a young girl had walked out of her house and never come back home again. He was pretty sure now that he knew what had happened, but although solving the mystery of Christine Mortlake's disappearance might bring closure, it was about to bring fresh pain too.

58

It was after ten by the time Phillip Grosvenor was released from Cowan Road, and he strode into the night air with the relief of a man who has narrowly avoided disaster. His interrogation had been long and repetitive with the same questions asked over and over in different ways, until his head was spinning.

'They think you're a fool,' Chapel had said, sitting to his left. 'Don't fall for their tricks. Just stick to your story and keep it simple.'

Phillip had created an account that was only partly based on truth and had made Nola repeat it numerous times before he'd called the police. *She had come to see him this afternoon at about six o'clock, five minutes before Danny Street showed up. He had lent her £20 last week and she'd come to pay him back. He had gone into the kitchen to put the kettle on, the doorbell had gone, and Nola had answered it. Danny had punched her in the face and pursued her into the living room where he'd continued to attack her until she'd managed to escape to the kitchen where she'd picked up a knife to defend herself. He was drunk and threatening to kill her, and she'd had no choice but to stab him.*

Phillip's greatest fear as he'd sat facing the two officers was that Nola was already spilling her guts in another room, telling them about how she'd been assaulted by him, held prisoner in his flat, and that he, too, was planning on killing her. He would have denied it of course, denied it vigorously, but it would have been his word against hers.

The interview had felt eternal, and Phillip had taken the line that everything had happened very quickly, that he'd been terrified, and that there was no doubt in his mind of Danny Street's intention. The man had been out of control and intent on murder. He should have done more, he'd kept on saying, but had frozen when faced with the horror of it all. How was Nola? Had she been taken to the hospital? It had not been her fault. She had only been defending herself.

There had been a relentless barrage of questions, bullets he had done his best to deflect. Chapel had whispered encouragement in his ear. Chapel had been faintly amused by it all, as if the police were idiots and could easily be duped. But he wasn't the one being interrogated. How had Danny Street known where to find Nola? What *exactly* had Danny said? What was Danny doing when Nola went into the kitchen? How had he reacted when she'd come out with the knife? When in doubt, Phillip had played dumb, said he didn't know, couldn't remember, was still in shock from it all.

The police had seemed suspicious, especially about him living on the estate under an assumed name. He'd explained about being a writer and wanting to immerse himself in the life of the Mansfield, to try and fit in, to get people to talk to him, to take on a different persona, but the officers had listened with sceptical faces. He had sensed a certain doubt about the £20 too, as if no one in their right mind would lend Nola Dunn money.

'They think she was there to give you a blow job,' Chapel had sniggered.

They had asked about Nola's earlier injury to her head, and he'd denied all knowledge of it. They had asked how Nola had 'seemed' when she'd first arrived, and he'd said that she seemed fine. They had asked if he knew Danny Street, and he'd said that he'd known of him. They had asked, asked, asked, until they had finally run out of questions and let him go.

'Well, that was quite a grilling,' Chapel said, as they walked away from the station, 'but I think you held your own.'

'I'm not out of the woods yet. We still don't know what Nola's said.'

'Nothing incriminating. She can't have or they wouldn't have let you go.'

'She's not reliable, though. She could change her mind, change her story. If she thinks she's facing a murder charge . . . '

'Manslaughter, at worst. And the law should be giving her a bloody medal, not charging her. That man's been the scourge of Kellston for years. She's done everyone a favour by getting shot of him. Don't start stressing, mate. You're over the worst.'

But Phillip wasn't convinced of that. 'What about the publicity, the press?'

'What about it?'

'For God's sake, I had a known prostitute in my flat, a prostitute who went on to murder a local gangster *in my flat*. I'm not going to come out of it smelling of roses, am I? Think of the gossip.'

Chapel threw back his head and laughed. 'Jesus, you're so middle class, Phil. You're looking at this in all the wrong way. Who cares what your ex-wives think, or your so-called friends? All publicity's good publicity. That book of yours isn't going to sell itself. This could be just the push it needs.'

Phillip thought about that as they tramped towards the B & B on Station Road. His flat was still a crime scene, and he wouldn't be able to get into it tonight. Not that he wanted to. There was blood on the carpet, blood everywhere. He would have to get the place cleaned before he moved out. There was no question of him staying there now.

It was a cold evening. and the chill pierced his bones. Had he got away with what he'd done to Nola? Would she keep that big mouth of hers shut? It was looking promising, but he couldn't afford to take anything for granted.

59

Harry made numerous phone calls from the kitchen through the rest of the evening, some to do with Nola, and others connected to the Mortlake case. Jem sat in the living room, listening to his side of the conversation, or maybe just watching the TV, her expression impossible to read. When he had told her about the murder of Danny Street, she'd visibly flinched, but that had been as much to do with Nola's part in it than anything else. He hoped that this would enable her to draw a line under Aidan's savage intentions, that it would be a new start for her, and that she could, finally, begin to leave the past behind.

'So what's the plan?' she asked, when the calls were eventually finished and he came back into the living room and slumped down in the easy chair.

'I'll drive the kids over to Essex tomorrow morning. Ray and his mother will take care of them. I think they can do without school for a day or two.'

'What are you going to tell them about Nola? The kids, I mean.'

'I don't know. I haven't decided yet. I've told her solicitor that

Kayleigh and Kit are staying with their grandmother and asked him to pass on the information. At least she'll know they're safe and being looked after. Not that her kids' safety has ever bothered her much in the past.'

Jem looked pensive. 'I wonder what her chances are. I mean, if she'll be charged or not. If it was self-defence, then surely she shouldn't be prosecuted?'

'It depends on whether they believe her. The police don't like it when people pick up knives and use them for something more lethal than chopping onions.'

'Even when their lives are in danger?'

'That's the tricky bit, working out if undue force was used.'

Jem wrinkled her nose. 'How did Ray sound when you told him about it all?'

'Shocked, bewildered, relieved. At least with Street gone, he doesn't need to worry about his past catching up with him. Talking of which, how are *you* feeling about everything?'

Jem briefly turned her face away, leaving a pause before meeting his eyes again and answering. 'You shouldn't be glad that someone's dead, should you? It doesn't feel right. Not even when that person was as vile as Danny Street. But I'm relieved, I suppose, although I'm trying not to hope too much that it's all over now. It seems like every time there's a light, something or someone comes along to blow it out.' She paused again, uneasy, as if she might have said too much, and then moved on to safer ground. 'And I'm worried about the kids. It's going to be tough for them however this pans out.'

'Yeah, it's like they're just swapping one crap parent for another; Nola and Ray are hardly up for a gold medal in the mum and dad stakes. Still, Kayleigh's tough. She'll get through it whatever happens, and Kit's young enough to forget most of the bad stuff.'

'Kayleigh *acts* tough. It's not always the same thing.'

Harry nodded. 'You could have a point. But she'll be glad to see her dad despite everything's he's done.'

Perhaps it was the mention of fathers – Jem didn't seem to have a good relationship with hers – but she immediately changed the subject. 'Is something happening with the Mortlake case? Sorry, but I heard you on the phone to Vivienne and Amy. I wasn't eavesdropping ... well, maybe a bit ... but it sounded like you might have made some progress.'

Harry hesitated, wanting to share his news, but wary of jumping the gun. Nothing was for definite yet. The pieces were falling into place but what if he was wrong? Life was full of co-incidences, and this could just be another one. 'I'm not certain, but I may have a lead. Whether it's a good one or not I'll know for sure tomorrow.'

'That must make you nervous. It's such a huge responsibility, isn't it? Celia's waited a long time.'

'It might not be what she wants to hear.'

'Oh,' Jem said. 'That doesn't sound good.'

Harry resisted the temptation to say any more.

60

In the morning Jem took a quick shower, got dressed for work and helped Harry to sort out breakfast for the kids – cereal, boiled eggs, toast and orange juice. Kayleigh stared at it as if she'd never seen food this early before. She threw furtive glances towards Jem too, sensing that something was going on but reluctant to ask in case it was something she didn't want to hear.

'I'm taking you to your grandmother's after breakfast,' Harry said in a voice that was too casual. 'So no school today.'

'Nana Margaret's?' Kayleigh asked.

'Yes.'

'Does Mum know?'

'Yes,' Harry said again.

'Why are we going to Nana's?'

'Because you can't stay in the flat on your own. We'll call by on the way and you can pick up a few things, clothes and stuff.'

'Where does Nana live now?'

'Essex,' Harry said. 'She still lives in Essex. North Weald. It's not that far away.'

'Will Dad be there?'

'I don't know,' Harry said.

'So he might be?'

'Come on, eat up,' Jem interrupted before Kayleigh could back Harry into a corner. She knew he didn't want to raise their expectations in case Ray decided to take off before they got there. Or to get them over-excited at the thought of seeing their dad again. She looked at Harry. 'Are you sure you don't want me to come too? I could call Stefan, take a couple of hours off.'

'No, we'll be fine. Drop by after work and I'll let you know how it went. And that other business too.'

'What other business?' Kayleigh said.

'Private business. Not for your ears.'

Kayleigh rolled her eyes. 'No one ever tells me anything.'

When breakfast was finished, Kayleigh sent Kit off to the bathroom, waited until she heard the door close and then planted her elbows on the table and stared at them. 'What's going on?'

'Nothing,' Harry said.

'You're both acting weird. Is she dead? Mum, Nola? Is that why we're going to Nana's?'

'No, she's not dead.' Jem said, startled. 'Of course she's not.'

'Then what? Something's happened, ain't it?'

'No,' Harry said.

'Yes,' Jem said, almost simultaneously. She looked at Harry and shrugged. 'You may as well tell her. She'll only be imagining all sorts otherwise.'

Kayleigh listened, thinking it was typical of her mother not to do anything by halves. And now she had gone and killed Danny Street. An accident, Harry said, but she didn't see how you could accidentally kill a man like that. She remembered the way he'd yanked her up by her arm – her shoulder still ached – and threatened to do worse if Kit didn't tell him where Nola was. She was glad he was dead, glad he would never come to the flat again. He'd been a monster, and monsters always hurt people.

'Is she going to go to jail?'

'Let's hope not,' Harry said. 'But they might keep her down the station for a while.'

Kayleigh considered this, and then asked, 'Where did she kill him?'

'Some flat in Haslow. I don't know the details.'

So her mother hadn't been that far away. She wondered why she hadn't come back for her phone. 'Do you think we should tell the law about yesterday, about him coming round?'

'I'm not sure that would be useful. Not for your mum or for you. The police would want to know why you were in the flat on your own.'

'We weren't on our own. Jem was there.'

'Not until Danny Street showed up.'

'We don't have to tell them that.'

Harry gave her a look. 'If we lie to them and they catch us out, it'll only cause a pile more trouble. Let's wait and see how it goes. We don't even know if they're going to charge her yet. Let's not muddy the waters until we know what's what.'

Kayleigh nodded. That was the thing about Harry, he knew how the law worked, and how not to put your foot in it. And he didn't mind avoiding the truth if that worked to your advantage. She was glad he was on her side. She wondered if these latest events might sort out Nola's head, might make her realise that she'd been doing things all wrong, but somehow she doubted it.

*

399

Harry's intention was to be in and out of Haslow House in less than fifteen minutes. There was no sign of the law as they entered the lobby; if they were still on the estate, they must be at the murder scene. Harry had been worried that one of the local cops might recognise Nola's kids and start asking awkward questions, but thankfully they avoided that scenario. The problem with Kayleigh was that you never knew what was going to come out of her mouth.

The flat was cold and smelled of fag smoke, dope and the stale air that comes from not opening the windows for months on end. The furniture was old and shabby, the walls unadorned by any pictures. There were no books, no plants, no photographs. A few cushions were scattered on the sofa, but even some of those had their stuffing coming out. It was a place to live but it wasn't a home.

Harry, keeping his voice brisk, passed the holdall he had brought with him to Kayleigh and said, 'Cram what you can into this. Some warm clothes if you have them, and pyjamas, socks, underwear, anything you might need.'

The bedroom was small with a pair of single beds squashed against the wall. There were a few toys in here, battered bits of plastic and fur, but nothing that looked recent. He quickly realised that choosing clothes wouldn't be a problem; the limited garments they possessed, all well-worn, would easily fit into the holdall with space left over.

Kayleigh sent Kit off to the bathroom to get their toothbrushes and then asked Harry to retrieve the carrier bag off the top of the wardrobe. 'Kit's Christmas present,' she whispered. 'Don't let him see it. Do you think we'll still be at Nana's at Christmas?'

'Maybe,' he said, reaching up. 'You've done your shopping early.'

'He didn't have nothing to open last year. Anyway, it's only a couple of weeks away now.'

Harry felt a tug on his heartstrings, saddened by the thought of a child's Christmas without presents, without a tree – he couldn't imagine Nola going to the trouble – and without any of the usual festive magic. Would it be better this year? He hoped so.

'What if Nana doesn't like us?' Kayleigh asked, taking the carrier bag and manoeuvring it into a corner of the holdall. 'It's been forever since we saw her.'

'Of course she'll like you,' Harry said. 'She's your nan.'

Kayleigh looked dubious.

When Kit came back, Harry drifted into the living room. Jem's note was still on the coffee table alongside Nola's now-dead mobile. He picked up the note and put it in his pocket just in case the police dropped by. Dragging Jem into all this wasn't going to help her, or anyone else either.

He was on edge, concerned that Nola might be released from Cowan Road, come home while they were still here and start a tug-of-war over the kids. If it came to a battle, he was prepared to play dirty and threaten her with social services. Kayleigh and Kit needed some stability in their lives, regular meals, and a warm place to live and sleep. He couldn't see any of these things happening while Nola was taking care of them. Or rather *not* taking care of them.

It was a relief when the packing was done and they could leave. They went down in the lift in silence. In the lobby an old woman darted forward, her eyes bright and curious. Her gaze roamed over Harry, taking in everything from his head to his toes, before shifting to Kayleigh.

'I heard about your mum, love. A terrible business. How are you doing?'

'They're both as well as can be expected,' Harry said, propelling the kids towards the door. 'Sorry, we're in a bit of a rush.'

But the old woman wasn't deterred. She pursued them, leaning on her stick. 'They've released Mr Chapel so maybe your mum won't be too far behind.'

Kayleigh stopped dead and turned around. 'Mr Chapel? What's it got to do with Mr Chapel?'

'Didn't you know, dear? She was at his flat. That's where it happened.'

Kayleigh had gone pale. 'Are you sure?'

'Oh yes, the police were there for hours. It's all very odd, isn't it? I'm as surprised as you are. But they let him go last night. He must have stayed somewhere else because the flat's still got that tape across the door. Still, they should be finished soon. I was just saying to—'

'I'm sorry,' Harry repeated, 'but we're in rather a hurry.' He opened the door, took hold of Kayleigh's elbow, and gently pushed her out on to the forecourt. Then he walked quickly to the car, unlocked it and threw the holdall on to the passenger seat. He could see the woman watching through the glass, her beady eyes fixed on the three of them. 'Come on, get in, before she follows us. Who is that?'

'Mrs Floyd,' Kayleigh said. She got in the back with Kit and buried her face in her hands. 'Oh God, it was all my fault. Mum wouldn't be down the nick if it wasn't for me.'

'It's not your fault.' Harry started the engine and eased the car towards the gates. 'How on earth is any of it your fault?'

'It *is*,' she wailed. 'I told Danny Street that she might be at Mr Chapel's. I didn't think she would be. It was just something I said to get rid of him.'

Harry was beginning to wish he'd taken Jem up on her offer. He could cope with sassy Kayleigh, but the distressed version was more of a challenge. 'So what? If he hadn't found her there, he'd have caught up with her someplace else. Perhaps you did her a favour. If this Chapel bloke was a witness, he can corroborate her story. You know, back her up, say it was self-defence.'

'But Danny was drunk, stinking drunk, and mad as hell. If I hadn't told him where to go, he wouldn't have found her.'

'You don't know that.'

'He'd never have thought of looking there.'

'Don't start playing the blame game. There's only one person responsible for what happened and that's Danny Street.'

Kayleigh shrugged and stared out of the window.

'I mean it,' Harry said, watching her in the rear-view mirror. 'What made you think of Chapel anyway?'

Kayleigh didn't answer.

'Kayleigh?'

'He told Mum that he'd seen me going into Dion's on Friday night. I said he must have got me mixed up with someone else. Not sure if she believed me, though.'

'But he didn't tell the police. That's odd, isn't it?'

'No one tells the law nothing on the Mansfield.'

And that was true, Harry thought. People quickly learned to keep their mouths shut. 'You reckon that was why she was at his place, to talk about what he'd seen?'

'Could have been. I dunno.'

'Well, I wouldn't stress about it. I should think they've both got more important things on their mind than whether you did or didn't drop by Dion's. And if either of them had mentioned it to the police, you'd have known about it by now.'

'But what if they ask her why she was at Mr Chapel's?'

'I'm sure she'll think of something,' Harry said. 'She won't want to get you in trouble.' Or herself, he could have added — having your ten-year-old daughter mixing with a drug dealer wouldn't reflect well on her parenting skills – but decided to keep that opinion to himself.

Kayleigh seemed to perk up at this. 'Will Dad be at Nana's?'

'You've already asked me that.'

'But will he?'

61

Harry had feared awkwardness on their arrival at North Weald, almost three years having passed since the kids had last seen their father. In the event he needn't have worried. Kayleigh gave a cry, flung her arms around Ray, squeezed him tightly, and then stood back on the doorstep and said, 'Where have you been? What have you been doing? Swear you won't ever go away again.'

Kit, whose memories of his dad were only distant impressions, initially hung back, but soon got caught up in the general excitement. If Kayleigh was happy then he was happy too. Margaret bundled them all into the house. She was a large, heavily bosomed woman in her sixties with a no-nonsense air about her. Harry got the impression of brisk efficiency and competence, of someone who would be more than a match for Nola.

While Ray showed the kids to their room, Harry talked to Margaret in the kitchen, telling her about Kit's lack of speech and getting her up to speed with the Nola situation. 'They may let her out this afternoon. If they do, I'm sure she'll be straight on the phone to you. If they don't, if they charge her, then she'll probably be placed on remand.'

'Best place for her,' Margaret proclaimed. 'I always said she was no good. Hanging around with a man like Danny Street. What was all that about? I tried to stay in touch with those kids, but she wasn't having any of it. Spiteful she is, rotten to the core.'

'Yeah, well, from what I've gathered I don't think she was overly impressed with Ray's disappearing act. It was tough for her, bringing them up on her own. I'm not defending her, but for Kayleigh and Kit's sake maybe you could try and come to some arrangement. It's better, don't you think, that they have contact with both parents? So long as Nola gets herself sorted out.'

'That'll be the day.'

Harry didn't push it. He didn't tell her anything about Dion either. That was up to Kayleigh when and if she felt safe enough to share. He drank his tea, thanked Margaret for her hospitality, said goodbye to everyone, and left. Job done. Now it was time to focus on Christine Mortlake.

Jem wondered how Harry was getting on in North Weald. Were the kids okay? Would Ray take his new responsibilities seriously? Would he even be there when Harry showed up? While all this was whirling round her head, Stefan wouldn't stop talking about the trouble on the Mansfield, about the murder of Danny Street, about the altercation that had happened yesterday when she'd intervened on behalf of Kayleigh and Kit.

'To think he'd be dead a short while after. God, Jem, you never know what's going to happen. Do you think the police will want to talk to you?'

Jem frowned. 'What for?'

'I don't know, state of mind or whatever. You can testify that he was drunk and aggressive. It might be important.'

'I should think there were a dozen witnesses to that in the Fox. They don't need me to tell them. They'll know from the autopsy too. That he was drunk, I mean. I'd rather stay out of it, to be honest.'

Stefan wasn't the only one with Danny Street on his mind. When Jem had gone into the café earlier that morning, his name had been on everyone's lips. She had heard the gossip rippling through the room, the half-truths, the speculation, the exclamations, and underlying it all the thinly veiled relief that his reign of terror was finally over.

Stefan nodded. 'Yeah, his family's not going to be happy. I wouldn't like to be in that woman's shoes.'

Jem hadn't even thought about that. It was a good thing that Kayleigh and Kit were away from Kellston. If the Streets worked on the premise of an eye for an eye, both of them could be in danger. And Nola too, if the police decided not to charge her.

She was still dwelling on this when a tall blond man walked past the shop, stopped, turned around and retraced his steps. Jem felt that instinctive inhalation of breath, a tightening of her shoulders, as he stood examining the display. She couldn't help it. Every time she saw a fair-haired man she thought of Aidan. As if his ghost still walked the streets, as if she was doomed to be for ever afraid of him.

Then the man raised his gaze and stared at her through the window. It was a hard, hostile stare. She held his gaze for a moment and then looked away, seeking out the reassurance of Stefan's presence. When she glanced back, he was gone. It had been nothing, she told herself. Now that Danny Street was dead, she no longer needed to worry about Aidan's revenge from beyond the grave. All that was over. Wasn't it?

62

It took Harry almost two hours to get from North Weald to Richmond. While he drove, he listened to Mary Chapin Carpenter's *Stones in the Road*, one of his favourite albums from the nineties. He rarely listened to new music these days. He knew what he liked, and he stuck with it. He knew what made him happy, sad, thoughtful or inspired, and her songs did all of these things. His fingertips followed the beat on the steering wheel.

If today went to plan, then tomorrow he would be driving back to Whitstable to talk to Amy. *If.* If his hunch was right, if he'd put the pieces together correctly, if he wasn't barking up the wrong tree entirely. But his gut told him he was on the right track, and he had enough experience to trust in it. He had done his homework, checked and double-checked the dates. It all added up in a highly unpleasant way.

Vivienne had offered to meet him in the West End again, but Harry had preferred to see her at home. What he had to ask was difficult and, for partly selfish reasons, he preferred her to be in familiar surroundings. Death was an upsetting business, murder even more so, and he suspected it would all get emotional.

He found the house on a leafy road not that far from Kew Gardens. It was an impressive white three-storey building, detached, with a double garage, a wraparound garden and a verandah running along the front. It reminded him of one of those American houses in the Deep South, in Mississippi or Georgia. A grand residence and a valuable one. He could see why Vivienne took in lodgers. It was a big place to rattle around in on your own, and the upkeep probably wasn't cheap either.

Harry parked in front of the house. He was barely out of the car when Vivienne opened the front door, came down the steps and greeted him with a wide smile. She was wearing a long pink skirt and scarlet sweater and had strings of multi-coloured beads hanging round her neck. With her red hair, the colours might have been jarring, but she had the exuberance to carry them off.

'Hello, Harry. You found us all right, then?'

'Yes, no problems. Thanks for seeing me again. I'm sorry to intrude on you.'

She folded her arms across her chest, feeble protection against a chill wind. 'Oh, I was intrigued. New information, you said. Have you really found out something?'

'I believe so.'

'Come on in,' she said. 'It's cold out here.'

Vivienne led him through to the conservatory at the back, a large airy room filled with palms and other greenery and with a view over a well-established garden. It was surprisingly warm here, and comfortable.

'You have a lovely home,' Harry said, settling himself in one of the wicker chairs.

'Thank you, although I can't take any credit. It belonged to my grandparents, then my parents, and now me. I'm just the . . .

what do they call it? – the custodian, I suppose, until someone else takes over. I'm hoping one of my girls will move back in when I kick the bucket. It'd be nice to think of it staying in the family.'

'You're very fortunate.'

'I am,' she agreed. 'You're right. Now, I've got some coffee on the go. Or would you prefer tea?'

'Coffee will be good, thanks.'

While Vivienne went off to get the refreshments, Harry sat back and gazed out at the garden. The long green lawn was scattered with leaves. There were fruit trees at the far end, a small orchard, and an abundance of shrubs. A wooden bench sat at the foot of a brick wall. It was the kind of place that a child would like, with twisty paths and lots of places to hide. He thought of Celia Mortlake sitting in a room overlooking a very different garden, one that had been abandoned and where the plants had been strangled by long grasses, nettles and weeds. An old woman waiting for the truth while everything decayed around her.

Vivienne came back with the coffee, and they made small talk for a few minutes. Then she sat forward and said, 'You've got to tell me what you've found out. I'm dying to hear. You've seen Amy, I presume. Where is she now? What's she doing?'

Harry didn't answer either of her questions. He took a moment to gather his thoughts and then began. 'There was an accident in Kellston, a hit-and-run, a few weeks before Christine disappeared. It was on Violet Road. A young mother was killed along with her daughter.'

'How awful,' Vivienne said.

'You don't remember it?'

Vivienne shook her head. 'No. It was a long time ago and I didn't live in Kellston. Is it important?'

'I think so. Are you sure Christine didn't mention it? She knew the little girl – Annie Moss she was called – and I'm certain she'd have been upset. *Very* upset.'

Vivienne frowned, her brow furrowing into lines as she thought about it. 'Oh, maybe I do remember something vaguely. It was the school holidays, so I wasn't seeing so much of her, but now that you mention it, it does ring a bell somewhere in the back of my mind.'

'The Moss family went to the same church as Christine. She taught Annie at Sunday school.'

'Yes, yes, I think I do recall it now. I suppose with everything that happened after, it just slipped my mind. Christine was upset. Of course she was. She was very sensitive. That poor little girl!' Vivienne put some sugar in her coffee and stirred it. 'But what's this got to do with her disappearance? Are you saying there's some sort of connection?'

'I believe so,' Harry said.

Vivienne stared at him, waiting for him to go on. 'How? What? I don't understand.'

'Eleanor Moss and her daughter were run over on the evening of July twenty-first. That date will be familiar to you. It's your birthday, isn't it?'

'Yes, but . . .'

'Do you remember what you were doing that evening?'

Vivienne laughed. 'God, Harry, how am I supposed to do that? It was over fifty years ago. I've got absolutely no idea.'

'Then it's fortunate that Celia Mortlake recalls it exactly. Let me jog your memory. It was a meal in Chinatown, wasn't it? A special meal for your thirteenth birthday. You and your mum and Christine.'

Vivienne shook her head. 'Was it? If that's what Celia says, but I really don't remember.'

'It was the day you became a teenager. And it must have been one of the last times you saw Christine.'

'Maybe, or maybe Celia's memory is playing tricks on her.'

'Your mother had a dark blue Mini, didn't she? A runaround, a little car to drive about town in.'

'Oh, she had lots of cars. She was always changing them.' And then, as if the light was just dawning, Vivienne sucked in a breath, widened her eyes, and said, 'But you can't be suggesting that . . . No, that's just ridiculous!'

Harry realised then that she was a better actress than he'd given her credit for. The first time they'd met he'd been charmed by her vivacity, and what he had taken for honesty. But now he was sure it was all just part of the act. 'It was raining, wasn't it, when your mother drove Christine back to Kellston? Pouring down. A nasty night, even though it was summer. There was a sudden snarl-up on the high street, a tailback of traffic, and she decided to take a short cut through Violet Road. Perhaps it was the weather, or she was driving too fast or not concentrating on the road, but I'm presuming she didn't see the woman and her child until they stepped out in front of her – and then it was too late.'

'What? This is just fiction, a fantasy. It didn't happen, Harry.'

Harry was vague on the finer details, but knew he had a grasp of the wider picture. 'I'm wondering why she didn't stop. Panic? Fear? Or had she had a few drinks in the restaurant? A glass of wine or two. Was that it? Was she over the limit?'

'Why are you saying these things? They're ludicrous.'

'I did a check on that dark blue Mini. It seemed to disappear off the face of the earth.'

Vivienne stared at him, her eyes full of loathing. 'So what? That doesn't mean anything.'

'You must all have been shocked, being in an accident like

that. Christine would have been in the back seat and probably didn't realise how serious it was. It was raining so hard she might not even have seen exactly what happened, only felt the impact. What did your mother say? That she'd hit a dog, another car? Anyway, she must have driven off quickly. Perhaps she asked Christine to keep quiet about it, to not tell anyone else or she'd lose her licence.'

Vivienne was silent.

'Feel free to contribute if I'm getting anything wrong,' Harry said.

Vivienne stood up, put her hands on her hips and said, 'I'd like you to go now. I'm not listening to any more of this nonsense.'

Harry stayed where he was. 'The car must have had damage, dents, maybe some blood too, although the rain may have washed that off. A bit of mess. Not a car you could park outside a house, not in daylight anyway. Someone might have noticed it. I'm presuming she didn't take it home. Did she bring it here to her mother-in-law's place after dropping off Christine? Did she hide it in the garage?'

'Why are you saying all these things? Has Amy put you up to it? Or are you just so desperate to please Celia Mortlake that you'll twist anything and everything to suit your own needs?'

Harry gazed placidly back at her. Her face had become white, almost translucent. She was putting on a good show, but not good enough. 'And that's not the half of it, is it, Vivienne? All that was bad enough, but then it got even worse.'

63

Harry waited, but Vivienne didn't respond. They were at stalemate. He accused, she denied, and nothing changed. 'Okay,' he said, persevering, 'let's move on. I suppose it can't have taken Christine too long to figure out what had really happened down Violet Road. She would have heard about the deaths of Eleanor and Annie, about the hit-and-run, and put two and two together. Did you beg her not to say anything? Of course you did. Your mother would be facing a manslaughter charge, even time in prison. And nothing was going to bring the Mosses back, so why make even more people suffer?'

Vivienne looked away from him, feigning indifference, but not making a great job of it. Her shoulders were starting to droop. Bit by bit he was chipping away at that carapace of confidence, slowly making progress.

'I'm assuming that Christine called you from church that Sunday. Was she threatening to tell the truth about the accident? Her conscience niggling away after seeing Michael Moss? She probably thought that he had a right to some answers. But you couldn't let her come clean so you arranged to meet up that afternoon, hoping you could persuade her to keep her mouth shut. Best she didn't tell her parents about the meeting as they might start to ask questions. After lunch you told her. She could say she was going to Amy's.'

Vivienne rolled her eyes. 'Have you finished?'

Harry couldn't have said exactly when it had all fallen into place, when he'd made the connection between Christine's disappearance and the Bayles. It had been a combination of things: matching Vivienne's birthday to the date of the hit-and-run, looking at everything from a different angle, realising that he'd been blindsided by her version of the past. That comment she had made about her mother giving up her job – 'The things we do for love' – had set him thinking about sacrifice and unhappiness, and what such things could lead to.

'I don't know what happened that afternoon. Well, not the finer details. I suppose your mum, or your dad, drove you over there and parked round the corner where they wouldn't be noticed. I suppose you went somewhere else after Christine joined you. I suppose there was a row, a difference of opinion. I suppose it all ended badly.'

'That's a lot of supposes.'

'Yes, you're right. I can see that to the police this might all seem a bit circumstantial, but it's the only answer that makes any sense.'

Vivienne stiffened. 'The police? They're not going to believe you.'

'Enough to do a thorough search of the garden.' Harry's gaze travelled the length and breadth, searching for likely places. There were plenty of them. 'I'm presuming this is where she was buried. It was the only safe place, wasn't it? Bodies have a habit of turning up if they're just left anywhere. They've got all sorts of equipment these days; it won't take them long to locate her. It's going to be better if you cooperate, tell them what your parents did. You were a child; you weren't responsible. It's time to stop lying.'

Vivienne's mouth opened as if she was about to protest again, but no words came out.

Harry's feelings were ambiguous. On the one hand, he almost felt sorry for her – all the years of living with this awful truth – but on the other, he couldn't forgive her for all the pain she had caused to Celia and the Greers and to Moses. She could have gone to the police after her parents died, but she hadn't. Instead, she had let the agony continue.

There was a long silence during which Vivienne, he guessed, was weighing up the evidence he had. Her hands began an ungainly wrestling motion. Her scared eyes flew over and over to the garden as if Christine's body might suddenly push up through the grass and reveal itself. She shuddered. And then she made the decision.

'Mum *had* been drinking that night. On my birthday. She drank a lot. She was unhappy, you see, unhappy in the marriage, unhappy about not being able to work, depressed about everything. Drinking was how she coped. Christine was sitting in the back reading a magazine when we hit them. They just stepped out from nowhere. It wasn't really Mum's fault, although she would have been blamed because of all the wine she'd drunk. Christine didn't realise what had happened. Mum said she'd hit another car and asked her not to say anything.'

'But then later she heard about Eleanor and Annie being killed on Violet Road.'

'I told her it was an accident, nobody's fault. But she felt guilty keeping quiet even though it wasn't going to change anything if Mum did confess. I thought I'd persuaded her, but then, a few weeks later, she called again, all upset and incoherent and crying down the phone, and we agreed to meet up.'

Harry kept quiet, relieved that the truth was finally coming out of her mouth, unwilling to interrupt in case she suddenly changed her mind.

'I went over with Mum, and we picked her up round the corner from her house. Dad stayed behind to look after Gran. We couldn't go to a café or anything because someone might have overheard us. Not that anywhere much was open on a Sunday. But it was awkward talking in the car, so Mum pulled into the cemetery and drove round until she found an old, quiet part. It looked like no one ever went there.'

Harry knew the place. The overgrown section of the grave-yard where brambles ran riot, and the ancient headstones were shrouded in ivy. There was something odd, fateful, about the choice of destination, as if somewhere in the back of Jackie Bayle's mind was the knowledge of how it was all going to pan out.

'We got out of the car and started to talk. It was fine at first. Mum tried to reason with her, said that she wouldn't cope in prison and that was where she'd end up if it all came out. She said that being locked up would kill her, and that would be an-other needless death. Was that what she wanted? She was very calm and persuasive. She said she understood how hard it was for Christine, and that was because she was a good person and wanted to do the right thing. But you had to balance it out, had to decide what was the best in the end for everyone.'

Harry could imagine Jackie talking softly to Christine, pleading for her liberty, for her future. Had she been drinking that day too? It was Amy who'd told him she was an alcoholic, information she'd gleaned from Christine and which she'd been more than happy to pass on during their recent phone call. It would have saved him some time, he thought, if she'd mentioned it in Whitstable.

'Christine seemed to be taking it all in, seemed to understand, but then she started droning on about Michael Moss and how terrible it was for him not knowing what had happened.' A hint of impatience came into Vivienne's voice. 'She got all holier-than-thou about telling the truth, about not lying to her parents, and then she started crying and getting hysterical. Mum must have been worried about someone hearing her. She only gave her a tiny slap, just enough to bring her to her senses, but Christine stumbled back and tripped over and hit her head on the edge of a grave.' Vivienne had been staring out over the garden until this point, but now she turned her face and looked directly at Harry. 'It was an accident. I swear it was.'

'I believe you,' Harry said, although he thought that it was just as possible that Vivienne had slapped her. Or worse.

Vivienne's hand went to her mouth and stayed there for a few seconds. 'She was dead. Just like that. Instantly. One moment she was there and then . . . It was awful, a nightmare. There was nothing we could do. I'd never seen Mum in such a state. She always knew what to do but not that day. We were both in shock. She told me to get in the car, got in herself, and then got out again.'

'She didn't think about ringing the police, an ambulance?'

'It was too late for an ambulance. And if she'd told the police . . . well, it wouldn't have looked good, would it? How was she going to explain what we were doing in the middle of a graveyard with Christine? A secret meeting that even her parents didn't know about. And if we'd mentioned the hit-and-run, that would have been it. It would have seemed like we'd lured her there deliberately, that we'd always meant to kill her.'

'Did either of you think about Celia and Arthur?'

Vivienne flinched as if the words had physically wounded her. 'Of course we did. But we were panicking. I think Mum's first impulse was just to leave her there, to let her be found by someone else, but then she started thinking about evidence, about how someone might have seen us drive in, noticed the car and the people in it. I mean, there wasn't all that DNA testing back then, but she still decided it was too risky.'

'And so you took the body with you.'

'Mum wrapped her in the picnic rug we kept in the car, and we managed to get her in the boot. It was Dad's car we were using; hers had been hidden away after the accident. It's still here in fact, rusting away in one of the garages. She drove me home – I don't think we spoke the whole way – and told him what had happened. Poor Dad! I thought he was going to have a heart attack. First the hit-and-run and now . . . He didn't really have time to think anything through. With her body already in the car, it was too late to go to the police. So he brought Christine here. Gran was at ours, so the house was empty. He had a spare key for emergencies.' Vivienne gave an odd laugh. 'Well, it was certainly an emergency.' Then her gaze returned to the garden. 'I think he buried her in the orchard.'

'Hard work for a man on his own.'

Vivienne shrugged. 'He must have managed it. Or maybe he came back the next morning. Gran didn't go home until Monday evening.'

'That's why your parents moved here, to make sure the body was never discovered.'

'Yes.' She wrapped her arms around her chest and sighed. 'What happens now?'

'I'll have to go to the police. But first I'll tell Celia. She deserves to know before they come knocking on her door.'

'Tell her I'm . . . ' But then she thought better of it and shook her head. 'It doesn't matter.'

Harry had the feeling she was already fine-tuning the story of that Sunday in her mind, preparing herself for the police, making sure that all the blame lay with her mother and none of it with her. What had really happened that day? He suspected that Vivienne might not have been as innocent as she made out. But she had her actorly skills to fall back on. She would make them believe what she herself had come to believe through the years.

64

It was two o'clock by the time Harry was back in the East End. He was tempted to go to a café and to delay his meeting with Celia Mortlake but knew that he owed it to her to relay the information as soon as possible. He drove to south Kellston, parked the car round the corner from the house and made the call. Mrs Feeney answered. He explained that he had some news, that he'd like to come round straight away if it was convenient.

'What, right now?' the housekeeper said, her tone implying that there was something irregular, even rude, about visits made without a prior appointment.

'Yes,' Harry said.

'You'll have to hold on. I'll go and see if she's available.' As if Celia's social life was so busy, she might not be able to fit him in.

Harry heard the phone being put down, the dull clunk as it hit something wooden, and waited impatiently for her return. She took her time. Celia would know that it was important, that he wouldn't be asking to see her at such short notice if it wasn't. He stared through the windscreen at the high hedge and thought about Christine hurrying away from the house all those years ago, getting in a car with people she trusted, and embarking on the last journey she would ever make.

Mrs Feeney eventually came back on the line. Yes, Mrs Mortlake would see him. Said begrudgingly and probably with a scowl on her face. Harry didn't care. He was concentrating on how he would break the news to Celia, knowing that it would be both welcome and traumatising at the same time. 'Two minutes,' he said, getting out of the car.

Mrs Feeney already had the door open as he walked up the path. She gave him a hostile look. 'Mrs Mortlake's in the drawing room. I hope you're not going to go upsetting her.'

Harry couldn't promise that, and so he simply nodded. He walked along the hall, knocked lightly on the door to the drawing room, waited for her summons and went in. Celia was sitting in her usual chair, upright as always, although he thought he detected more colour in her parchment cheeks than normal. She must have been desperate to hear what he had to say but didn't show it. Self-restraint was so much a part of her character that even now she couldn't break the habit. She simply gestured towards the flimsy yellow chair and watched him as he sat down.

'You have news, Mr Lind.' It was a statement, not a question.

'Yes.' Harry took a deep breath and proceeded to tell her what he'd found out. He resisted the temptation to elaborate, keeping his account simple and succinct: Vivienne's birthday, the hit-and-run, the secret that Christine had kept, the meeting that Sunday afternoon, the accidental killing in the cemetery, the burying of Christine's body in the garden at Richmond. He kept his eyes on her the whole time, afraid that the revelations might be too much, that she would have a heart attack or a seizure or become hysterical. But he should have known better. If Celia was going to fall apart, it wouldn't be in front of him.

She listened carefully, taking it all in. Occasionally her hand fluttered to her face, or a thin sigh escaped from parted lips. Eventually, when everything had been revealed, she slumped back against the chair and briefly closed her eyes.

Harry kept quiet while she processed it all. He regretted the lack of coffee. He could have done with a strong dose of caffeine and something to do with his hands.

The first question she asked surprised him. 'And the garden,' she said softly. 'Is it a pleasant one?'

And then Harry realised that in her worst nightmares she must have imagined Christine's body dumped without dignity in a ditch or a shallow grave, a bag of bones that would never be discovered. 'Yes, it's a lovely garden. Very peaceful.'

Celia's voice grew stronger. 'He came here that night. Richard Bayle came to Kellston to look for Christine.'

'To deflect suspicion, I guess. Or to make it look like he was doing the right thing. Or to hear what the rumours were. Who knows for sure?'

'Vivienne knows.'

'Perhaps.'

'Do you think she's telling the truth, about the graveyard, about what happened there?'

'Mostly.' Harry couldn't see much point in sharing his own doubts. 'I think so.'

'We've only got her word for it.'

Silence fell across the room. There was just the ticking of the clock and the patter of rain against the windows. Celia was the one to speak first. 'So what next?'

'I'm going to Cowan Road station after I leave here. I wanted to see you first. They'll come and speak to you at some point, and they'll send a team down to Richmond to talk to Vivienne and . . . ' Harry could not quite bring himself to say *dig up the body*, and so said instead, 'deal with everything else.'

Celia nodded and looked away from him.

Harry rose to his feet, sensing that it was time to go, that Celia wanted time alone. 'Call me if there's anything you need or if there's anything you want to ask.'

'Thank you, Mr Lind.'

'I'll be in touch.'

As he opened the door she said with a tremor in her voice, 'She can be with Arthur now. She won't be on her own anymore.'

Harry quietly closed the door behind him.

65

Jem hadn't seen Harry since this morning. It was dark now, the shop was closing, and there was no light on in his office or in the flat above. She tried calling, but his phone was turned off. She didn't leave a message, figuring that he was tied up somewhere and might not be back any time soon. He'd said to drop by but there was clearly no point in doing that. She'd go home, get something to eat and try ringing again later. She was looking forward to seeing him but that was only because she wanted to know about Kayleigh and Kit, to make sure they'd settled in okay, and to hear about the Mortlake case. This was what she told herself even though she knew she was lying.

She said good night to Stefan and began the cold walk back to the Mansfield. There were still plenty of people around, huddled up in thick coats and scarves. She put up her hood as the rain began to come down harder, yet another downpour in an afternoon that had been full of them. The water ran across the uneven pavement and pooled in the gutters where the cars and

425

buses swept it up in a wave, soaking any pedestrians unfortunate enough to get too close.

While she walked, she thought about Whitstable and the sea and the tangy taste of salt in the air. She had taken to the place, felt a connection to it. Even Danny Street's unexpected appearance hadn't tainted it for her. London felt alien, too big and grey and anonymous. It was that anonymity that had drawn her here, but now she had choices.

Jem was still considering these choices when she felt that familiar prickling on the back of her neck. Quickly she stopped and turned around, causing a collision with a woman who was right behind her. By the time apologies had been made, her tail – if there was one – had disappeared. She lingered by the shop fronts for a while, peering along the street, watching everyone who passed, until the cold began to creep into her bones and she set off again.

On reaching the estate, Jem came to the conclusion that the feeling of being followed was just a legacy from the past, a long-established fear, something she would have to learn to let go of. There was no more Aidan, no more Danny Street, no one left to harm her. She had to get a grip, and stop being afraid of her own shadow.

There was no one she knew in the lobby. She took the lift and got out on the eighth floor. As she passed Nola's door, she noticed the long crack running down it, a reminder of all the drama of yesterday. Was Nola home? Out of curiosity, she was briefly tempted to ring the bell but decided against it. Even if Nola had been freed, she probably wouldn't be too happy about Jem's part in removing the kids to North Weald.

Jem unlocked her flat, switched on the lights and went straight to the kitchen to put the heat on. The place was freezing. She took off her coat and hung it over the radiator to dry. After a quick rummage through the half-empty cabinets, she found a tin of tomato soup and decided that would do. She wasn't in the mood for cooking anything complicated. Did soup even count as cooking? A couple of stale bread rolls were in a paper bag on the counter, and she took one out, cut it in half and put it under the grill to toast.

Five minutes later, Jem took her bowl through to the living room, turned the TV on to catch the news and sat down at the table. She was barely two mouthfuls into the soup when the doorbell rang. She thought it must be Harry, stopping by from wherever he had been this afternoon. If she'd thought a bit harder, she would have realised that he'd have called first, but by the time this had entered her head she was already opening the door.

A stranger faced her on the other side. Well, not exactly a stranger. Her heart began to pound. She had seen him once before – the tall blond man who had stared at her through the window of the florist's – and while she instinctively moved to block his path forward, one hand on the door, the other on the jamb – he grinned at her.

'Hello, Jemima. How are you doing?'

'Who are you?'

'Damian,' he said. 'Nice to meet you at last.'

Jem could tell from his cold eyes, from the way he looked at her, that this man was serious trouble. His accent was northern, Mancunian. He was in his mid-thirties, over six foot and solidly built. A spider's web tattoo crawled across his throat and disappeared into the neck of his T-shirt. Her stomach was turning over, adrenaline starting to pump. She quickly tried to slam the door, but she was too late. Already he had shifted forward, using his greater size and strength to power his way past her.

'Now that's not much of a welcome, not when I've travelled all this way to see you.'

427

Panic surged through her. 'What do you want? What are you doing here?'

Damian closed the door and leaned against it. 'I suppose it's been a shock to you, Aidan dying and everything. I'll put your rudeness down to grief.'

'Grief? Why would I be grieving for that monster?'

'That's no way to talk about him.' Damian looked her up and down. 'He was right, you are an ungrateful cow.'

Jem tried to reach around him to open the door again, but he was having none of it.

'In the living room,' he said. 'I like to be comfortable when I chat.'

'We've got nothing to chat about.'

'Now, that's where you're wrong, sweetheart. It's a bit of a cliché, but we can do this the hard way or the easy way. After you,' he said.

Jem reluctantly retreated to the living room, hearing the bolt slide across the front door before he joined her. It was an ominous sound, one that told her she wasn't going to get away in a hurry. Keep him talking, she thought, try to make a connection, but she suspected even from such a short acquaintance that you couldn't make connections with a man like him. A man like Aidan.

'So you were a mate of his,' she said, as Damian swaggered in. He was wearing blue jeans, a leather jacket and a white T-shirt that strained across his chest. She could tell he spent too many hours in the gym, and that he enjoyed throwing his weight around. There were scars on his face, around his hollowed-out eyes and down his left cheek.

'Like brothers. We were banged up together, love.' He looked around the room. 'Nice place you've got here.'

Jem's mind was racing. Prison buddies. Great, that was just

what she needed. Her gaze darted towards her phone lying on the sofa. Could she snatch it up and run into the kitchen? No, there was no lock on the door. By the time she'd called 999, if she even got that far, he'd be on her. Don't do anything stupid. Keep him calm, don't provoke him. 'So how did you find me – or how did Aidan find me? He was here, wasn't he, in Kellston?'

'Yeah, we had a little trip down to the Big Smoke.' Damian was keeping his eyes on her, circling the room like a lion stalking its prey. 'Good to have a change of scene every now and again.'

'How did he know where I was?' she prompted.

'Oh, some skinny tart in the Lytham lettings agency. You know, the one that's dealing with your house up there. Said she wasn't supposed to tell.' He tapped the side of his nose, 'Top secret and all that. Client confidentiality. But Aidan soon had her eating out of his hand. He had a way with women, your Aidan.'

Jem flinched, wanting to say he *wasn't* her Aidan, that she had only seen him twice in ten glorious years, but she wisely kept her mouth shut. She was mad at the Lytham agency for employing a girl who could be so easily seduced by Aidan's charm, and even madder at the thought that she had once *been* that girl, innocent and gullible and willing to believe everything he told her.

'Yeah, it didn't take him long to talk her round. You really should have a word with that office. They're not too hot on security. Still, who's complaining? He got what he wanted, and everyone's happy.' Damian grinned at her again. 'Well, not quite everyone.'

'If he knew where I was, why did he wait?'

'I don't get you,' Damian said.

'If he's known my address for months, why didn't he—'

'Who said anything about months? I didn't say months. A couple of weeks, that's all.'

'But he's been following me, or someone has.'

Damian shrugged his heavy shoulders. 'Not Aidan. Maybe that was just your guilty conscience, love. Or have you pissed off someone else as well? Yeah, that could be it. Maybe there's a whole queue of angry blokes wanting to put things straight.'

Jem backed up towards the window. She wondered if he was lying, or if Aidan had kept him in the dark. She couldn't have imagined all those times when she was sure that somebody's eyes were on her. 'Is that why you're here, to *put things straight*?'

'Unfinished business, isn't it? Aidan can't do it and so it's up to me. He used to talk about you a lot. You fucked him over, love, good and proper, sent him down for a long stretch.'

'He killed Georgia, ran her over. How is that my fault?'

'It was an accident. He was only having a laugh, messing about. He didn't mean to hit her. You could have backed him up, but you didn't. Instead, you came out with a pile of garbage to the law about how he'd been threatening you, about how you feared for your sorry little life, about how he was a sadist.'

'All of that was true.'

'Yeah, right. It's girls like you who give women a bad name.'

Jem could see that Aidan had woven his web of lies, and he'd believed every word of it. Or, just as likely, Damian had the same basic loathing of women as his buddy, convinced they were inferior, stupid and treacherous. Two peas in a pod. Better, perhaps, to change the subject. 'It was you who rang me, wasn't it? The silent caller.'

'I just wanted to hear your voice, sweetheart.'

'You just wanted to scare me.'

'Were you scared? Did you think it was Aidan?'

'No.'

Damian took a cigarette out of a pack and lit it. 'You're a lousy liar, Jem. I could smell you sweating from the other end of the line.'

Jem was glad he was smoking. He couldn't kill and smoke at the same time. How long did that give her? Three minutes, four? She was subtly looking around for a possible weapon, something to defend herself with. The trouble was that Al's style of decor was minimalist – less is more – and she couldn't see much salvation in a heap of tasteful scatter cushions.

Damian flicked his ash on to the carpet. 'You ever heard of karma, love?'

'Is that what you're here to deliver?' Despite her fear, Jem refused to give him the satisfaction of cowering. She had been a victim for too long. There were knives in the kitchen, but she had no way of getting there. The only weapon at her disposal was her own voice. 'You do know that Danny Street's dead, right? So if you're expecting him to pay you, you'd better think again.'

'Why would Danny Street pay me?'

'I know that Aidan met up with him while he was down here. Were you with him? I presume you were.'

'You can presume what you like, sweetheart.'

'And that he and Danny cooked up a plan to have me ... what's the right word? ... *eliminated*, shall we say ... Twenty thousand pounds to wipe me out.'

Damian's lips curled into a sneer. 'And why would he pay twenty k for something he could do himself?'

'Because he wanted to make sure he had a cast-iron alibi, that he was miles away when it happened. Or that he was worried that his own enemies would catch up with him before he had the chance to do it.'

'Danny Street's been stringing you a line, love. Aidan never took out a hit. He wouldn't waste good money on a slag like you.'

'So why have *you* wasted good money coming down to London?'

'Like I said, unfinished business.'

Damian grinned, took a last drag on his unfinished cigarette, dropped the butt on the carpet and ground it in with his heel. He was waiting for a reaction, but she didn't give him one. Irrationally, bearing in mind her current circumstances, she thought about how Al would react to a burn in his carpet and could see the deposit she'd paid going down the toilet.

Jem's phone, lying on the arm of the sofa, started ringing. She stared at it. Was it Harry? Would he worry if he couldn't get through to her, or just think she was in the shower? The latter, knowing her luck.

'Don't even think about answering,' he said.

The phone stopped ringing, but almost immediately started up again. 'He'll come round if I don't pick up.'

Damian reached into his jacket, took out a gun and aimed it at her. 'We'd better get on with it then.'

Jem's throat tightened, and fear knotted in her chest. The gun was small and black, nothing flashy, but lethal enough to put a nice, neat hole through her heart. If it was real. *Was* it real? The phone rang out again. She swallowed hard. 'I hope your friendship is worth another stretch in jail. It won't take the police long to work out who did it. There's CCTV all over the estate.'

'None of those cameras are working.'

'Some of them are,' she lied.

'I think you should just stop talking now.'

'What difference does it make if you're going to kill me anyway?'

Damian gave her another of his evil grins. 'I haven't decided yet. But we may as well have some fun first, huh? Why don't you take off that sweater so I can get a better look at those tits of yours. In fact, take everything off. I want to see you stark fuckin' naked.'

Jem didn't move. She couldn't. She was paralysed with fear but angry too. Only her eyes shifted around the room, searching again for any possible weapon. All she came across was the soup in its bowl, a plate, a bread roll and a spoon, none of which came highly recommended as a defence against a gun. Except the soup would still be hot. And she would, if she played it smart, have the element of surprise on her side.

'What are you waiting for?' Damian's finger tightened on the trigger. 'Do it! Do it now or I'm going to blow that pretty little head of yours into a thousand ugly pieces.'

Jem obediently took off her sweater, grateful for the fact she was wearing a T-shirt underneath. She used the movement involved to edge closer to the table. Then she slowly took off her jeans. Now she was only a foot away. She looked at him. His smirking face reminded her of Aidan's. Damian was too late to take away her innocence, but he could still control, demean and humiliate her.

'Faster,' he said. 'I've not got all fuckin' night.'

She could see his eyes greedily roaming over her body, taking in every curve, every bit of naked flesh. Rage burned in her. She knew that whatever she did he would kill her in the end, that she could identify him, that the road she was walking was only leading to an early grave. She had to take a chance. It was worth the risk. She had nothing to lose.

'I feel sick,' she groaned, leaning forward and clutching the edge of the table as if to steady herself.

'Sick or dead?' he said. 'Which would you prefer? Get on with it!'

Jem sucked in a deep breath, preparing herself. One, two, three ... Then, before her courage could fail her, in one fast movement she grabbed the bowl and hurled it up into his face. It hit him on the right temple with a sharp crack, ceramic against bone. Immediately, he dropped the gun and raised his hands to protect himself. But the hot soup had already made an impact. He clawed at his eyes.

'Bitch!' he yelped. 'Fuckin' bitch!'

Jem bent and quickly picked up the gun. She was tempted to shoot him there and then, to put a bullet right through his chest, to serve him the justice he deserved. For a moment she felt like she was aiming at Aidan, seconds away from squeezing the trigger. *This is for what you did to Georgia! This is for everything you did to me!* The blood was pounding in her head, the desire to finish him off almost overwhelming.

And then the doorbell rang, bringing her to her senses. Harry, she thought. Better late than never. But she had made that mistake once before this evening. What if Damian hadn't come alone? She began to quickly move towards the door, keeping the gun fixed on her enemy. 'Stay where you are,' she ordered, 'or I'll shoot you. I bloody will.'

The bell went again, along with a sharp rapping on the door. 'Jem? Jem, are you there?'

'I'm here,' she yelled. 'I'm coming.'

If Harry was surprised to see her wearing a T-shirt and not much else, he didn't say. Although his eyebrows did shoot up when he noticed the gun. 'He's in there,' she said, waving the weapon at the living room. 'Damian. He's an old mate of Aidan's.' Her legs were shaking, her voice trembling with emotion. She felt like crying with relief. Harry hadn't exactly saved the day – she had done that on her own – but he had saved her from herself.

Epilogue

Six months later

Jem didn't recall much of what happened after she'd launched the soup bowl at Damian. Having thwarted his plans for her, the rest had got lost in a haze of Harry's arrival, of cops and questions, of manic activity. She had withdrawn from it all, closed in on herself, simply gone through the motions of doing what she had to do. It was as if she'd slid into her own personal lockdown. Now, looking back, she could see how badly the shock had affected her.

But all that was over now.

She could have returned to Lytham, picked up where she'd left off and settled back into a life that, Aidan-free, should have been relatively comfortable. Except it wouldn't have been. Too many memories waiting to creep up on her. So instead, she had moved here. It had been an impulsive decision to relocate to Whitstable, but one that she didn't regret. After selling her grandparents' house, she had used the money to purchase a one-bedroom flat in a town she had only visited once but in which she felt strangely at home.

Jem couldn't see the sea from her windows, but she could smell it, taste it, and be on the beach in less than three minutes. She had kept the flat simple with whitewashed walls and limited furniture. It was light and airy and came, thank God, with nothing to remind her of the past. There was even a small balcony where she could sit out and watch the world go by. On the living-room wall – her one nod towards her time in London – she had hung a framed watercolour of two children, hand in hand, walking through the Mansfield estate.

She had started painting again, relaunched her website and even sold a few pictures through local galleries. Business was picking up, and the future was looking bright. Although she had not been sorry to leave London behind, she sometimes missed Stefan and the sociability of her old job. Not Harry Lind, though. There was no need to miss Harry. His spare toothbrush was in her bathroom, and he came to see her most weekends. They spent their time driving, walking, talking and seeking out the best pubs. She didn't think too much about where it was going, what it all meant. For now, she was just happy to live in the moment.

Kayleigh liked it at Nana Margaret's. There was always food on the table, and always someone in when she came home. There was electricity, clean clothes and hot water. True, the house was a bit on the squashed side, but now Dad had a job they were looking to move somewhere bigger. Hopes of a reconciliation between her parents, however, had come to nothing.

Nola had managed to escape being charged for the murder of Danny Street, but this close shave hadn't changed her. She was still boozing too much, smoking too much weed, and generally

436

shirking her responsibilities. None of this surprised Kayleigh. She could count on one hand the number of times Nola had turned up when she was supposed to. There was always some excuse, some naff reason why she couldn't make it. Nana said she wasn't fit to be a parent, but then Nana said a lot of things. She was a woman of opinions.

Kit was managing a few words now. She suspected he'd never be the chatty sort, but it was progress. He still used the night light she'd bought him for Christmas, and when it was dark, she'd stare up at the floating planets and think about stuff: London, Harry Lind, Dion, her mum and dad as they used to be.

Kayleigh still had the money she had taken from Dion, squirrelled away for a rainy day. You could never be too careful. One minute everything was fine and the next it had all fallen apart. The one thing she'd learned in her short life was that it made sense to be prepared.

Phillip was relieved to be back in Primrose Hill, surrounded by his own things, and with a view from the window that was easy on the eye. He didn't miss the Mansfield. What was there to miss? He didn't belong with those people, wasn't one of them. Even the air smelled different here, cleaner, as if it had been freshly laundered and delivered to his door.

His novel was finished, and he had found himself a new publisher. He had high hopes for Joe Chapel and his murderous inclinations. And why stop at one book? A series, he was thinking, an opportunity to explore all the darker sides of his protagonist. Not that there were many light ones. Chapel's tastes leaned towards the macabre.

'Do they?' Chapel said, frowning at him from the leather sofa.

'You wanted me to kill Nola, to finish her off.'

'I was just being practical. Sometimes you have to think outside the box.'

And in a box was where Nola would have been right now if Chapel had got his way. It still felt like a miracle that she had kept quiet about the reason for being in his flat. Even after six months he feared that she might change her mind and go squealing to the police. He dreaded the knock on the door, the handcuffs, the slamming of the cell door.

'She got away with murder,' Chapel said. 'Even Nola knows when to call it quits.'

'Manslaughter,' he said.

Chapel shrugged. 'Call it what you like.' His lips curled into a smile. 'At least we'll always have Charlene.'

Phillip sometimes had strange dreams, half dreams, where he was back in Kellston walking in the rain behind a girl in a red coat. Night-time, dark, with the smell of chow mein and diesel fumes floating in the air. She went on to the estate and he followed her. She went to the bins at the rear of Haslow House. He watched her open the lid and drop in an empty bottle of water. With the takeaway hooked over his left wrist, he felt for the knife in his pocket with his right hand. Why did he have a knife? Chapel had told him to take it. 'It's a jungle out there.' And hadn't Chapel told him to stab her too, to plunge the knife into her chest?

'Don't blame me,' Chapel said. 'You were the one who put her on the list. You were the one on the whisky all night.'

But Phillip knew he wasn't a killer. He'd never have done anything like that. He was a middle-aged balding man whom nobody looked at twice. The dreams were just remnants from his writing, confusions, a hazy merging of fiction and reality. He was innocent.

*

438

Harry still thought about Christine's funeral, and the poignancy of it. The church had been packed after all the publicity in the papers, and he'd had to squeeze into a space at the back. Celia Mortlake could have opted for a private service, but then the sum total of mourners would have barely filled the front pew. There was no immediate family left and most of her friends had predeceased her.

Celia had remained upright, dignified in grief, her face obscured by a black veil. Over fifty years of waiting to bury what was left of her daughter. Mrs Feeney had been at her side, guarding her employer like a rottweiler. It had been hard not to wonder how Christine would have turned out, what she'd have done, what she'd have become. A child's life wiped out in the blink of an eye.

Vivienne Bayle had been charged with withholding information. She had, of course, got herself a good solicitor, refined her account and was sticking to the story that she had not been the one to deliver the blow leading to her friend's death. Too many years had passed for the pathologist to be sure of how Christine had met her end. Vivienne had been a minor at the time of the incident and was now claiming trauma, PTSD, depression and everything else she could throw into the mix. Although she couldn't be held responsible for what had happened back then, she had still failed to come forward as an adult to report what she knew.

When Harry had broken the news to Amy, she'd been enraged. They had met in the same café in Whitstable with what felt like the same heavy rain streaming down the windows. Her face, tight and red, had twisted. 'She knew? She knew?' He got the impression that had Vivienne been in the room at that moment, Amy would have resorted to violence. All those years of pain and torment, of false accusation, of living in dread.

439

Nothing could change that or restore what had been lost. It was closure of a sort, but it was all too late.

From time to time Harry still rang Ray Dunn, just to check on how things were going with Kayleigh and Kit. Now that Danny Street was dead, Ray no longer had to fear his retribution, although he was smart enough to steer clear of Kellston and Carl Froome. However, if Kayleigh had been right about the red wire coming from the showroom, and the rumours were true about the money laundering, then Froome wasn't likely to put his head above the parapet any time soon. The police were convinced that Street had murdered Dion, and Harry had no reason to believe otherwise.

Last but not least, never least, was Jem. According to Lorna, spending almost every weekend in Whitstable constituted a serious relationship. Usually, he'd have challenged her wisdom when it came to matters of *his* heart, but right now he wasn't going to tempt providence. If the Christine Mortlake investigation had taught him anything, it was to grab your happiness where and when you could, and to hang on to it tightly.

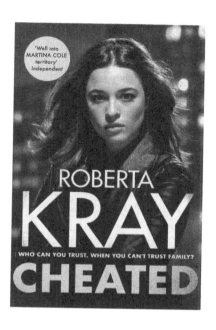

ROBERTA
KRAY

WHO CAN YOU TRUST, WHEN YOU CAN'T TRUST FAMILY?

CHEATED

WHO CAN YOU TRUST, WHEN YOU CAN'T TRUST FAMILY?

Sheltered and naive Carmen Darby has lived under the thumb of her father Rex, a brutal criminal businessman, her whole life. But when Rex announces his retirement and plans to leave his vast wealth to his three daughters, Carmen doesn't thank her father as effusively as he'd like, enraging him. Cast out from her home, Carmen assumes a new identity and starts her life over, but she knows she can't outrun the sins of her family for ever . . .

'A cracking good read'
JESSIE KEANE

Available now . . .

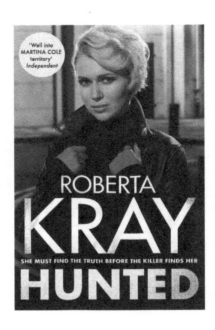

'Well into MARTINA COLE territory'
Independent

ROBERTA KRAY

SHE MUST FIND THE TRUTH BEFORE THE KILLER FINDS HER

HUNTED

Stealing from the rich is what Cara Kendall does for a living. She's twenty-four, bold and fearless, convinced that she'll never get caught. But everyone's luck runs out eventually. When she breaks into a house in Hampstead, she gets more than she bargained for – a body in the study and the law on the doorstep.

As rumours start to circulate about her part in the killing, she finds herself under increasing pressure to give up what she hasn't got and tell a truth she doesn't know. With danger growing by the day, and a killer still on the loose, Cara can't afford to lose any time. She has to find the answers before her enemies catch up with her . . .

Full of the same danger and grit as its London setting, this is bestselling author Roberta Kray at the top of her game. Get ready for a KILLER read . . .

Available now . . .